Dostoevsky to Dorothy Parker . . .
Thomas Hardy to Shirley Jackson . . .
Sholem Aleichem to James T. Farrell . . .

Few anthologies can claim as glittering an array of writers as appear in **75 SHORT MASTERPIECES.** Spanning the centuries from Boccaccio to Bradbury, the selections include works by the finest authors of the Western world.

The best English versions have been used for stories originally written in foreign languages; in many cases new, brilliant translations have been made especially for this anthology.

Horror, comedy, surprise, drama, human interest, pure entertainment, **75 SHORT MASTERPIECES** embraces every kind of short story ever written.

75 SHORT MASTERPIECES

Stories from the World's Literature

Edited By

ROGER B. GOODMAN

75 SHORT MASTERPIECES
STORIES FROM THE WORLD'S LITERATURE
A Bantam Classic / April 1961

2nd printing ... September 1962	*7th printing .. November 1966*
3rd printing ...... August 1963	*8th printing .. September 1967*
4th printing ...... January 1964	*9th printing ... December 1968*
5th printing ...... August 1965	*10th printing .... February 1969*
6th printing ... March 1966	*11th printing .... October 1969*

12th printing ... December 1970
Bantam edition / February 1972

14th printing ... September 1972	*17th printing .... May 1975*
15th printing .... June 1973	*18th printing ... December 1975*
16th printing .... June 1974	*19th printing ... February 1977*

COPYRIGHT NOTICES AND ACKNOWLEDGMENTS

The following selections in this anthology are copyrighted, and they may not be reproduced in any form without the consent of the authors, their publishers or their agents. The copyright notices are listed below and on the pages following (pp. v, vi) which constitute an extension of this copyright page:

"A Wedding Without Musicians" reprinted from Tevye's Daughters by Sholem Aleichem by permission of Crown Publishers, Inc. Copyright 1949 by The Children of Sholem Aleichem and Crown Publishers, Inc.

"He Swung and He Missed" by Nelson Algren reprinted by permission of A. Watkins, Inc. © 1942 Nelson Algren.

"Senor Payroll" by William E. Barrett reprinted from AUTUMN SOUTHWEST REVIEW by permission of the publisher. Copyright 1943 by Southern Methodist University Press.

"Houseparty" by Walter Bernstein originally published in THE NEW YORKER reprinted by permission of the author. Copyright © 1939 THE NEW YORKER MAGAZINE, INC.

"I See You Never" by Ray Bradbury reprinted from THE NEW YORKER by permission of Harold Matson Company Inc. Copyright 1947 by Ray Bradbury.

"The Lottery Ticket" by Ventura Garcia Calderon, translated by Richard Phibbs, reprinted by permission of The Golden Cockerel Press.

"Daughter" reprinted from The Complete Stories of Erskine Caldwell by permission of Little, Brown and Company and the author. Copyright 1935 by Erskine Caldwell.

"The Ghosts" by Lord Dunsany reprinted from The Sword of Welleran by permission of Dowager Lady Dunsany. Copyright 1908.

"The Scoop" reprinted from The Short Stories of James T. Farrell by permission of The Vanguard Press, Inc. Copyright 1937 by The Vanguard Press, Inc.

"The Bedchamber Mystery" by C. S. Forester reprinted from COSMO-POLITAN by permission of Harold Matson Company, Inc. Copyright 1943 by HEARST MAGAZINES, INC.

"Mr. Andrews" reprinted from The Collected Short Stories of E. M. Forster by permission of Sidgwick & Jackson Ltd. and from The Eternal Moment and Other Stories by E. M. Forster by permission of Harcourt, Brace and Company, Inc. and renewed by E. M. Forster.

"The Test" by Angelica Gibbs reprinted from the NEW YORKER by permission. Copyright © 1940 THE NEW YORKER MAGAZINE, INC.

"Truth and Consequences" by Brendan Gill reprinted from THE NEW YORKER by permission of the author. Copyright © 1941 THE NEW YORKER MAGAZINE, INC.

"Virtuoso" by Herbert Goldstone reprinted from FANTASY & SCIENCE FICTION by permission of Mercury Press, Inc. Copyright 1953 by Mercury Press, Inc.

"Her Lover" reprinted from Chelkash and Other Stories by Maxim Gorky by permission of Alfred A. Knopf, Inc. Published 1915 by Alfred A. Knopf, Inc.

"Proof Positive" by Graham Greene reprinted from Nineteen Stories by permission of The Viking Press, Inc., Monica McCall, Inc. and the author. Copyright 1947 by Graham Greene.

"The Butterfly" by James Hanley reprinted from People Are Curious by permission of Harold Ober Associates, Inc. and the author. Copyright 1938, 1941 by James Hanley.

"Moonlight Sonata" by Alexander Woollcott reprinted from White Rome Burns by permission of The Viking Press, Inc. Originally published in THE NEW YORKER. Copyright 1934 by Alexander Woollcott.

"God" by Eugene Ivanovich Zamiatin reprinted from New Russian Stories by permission of New Directions. All Rights Reserved.

"How Grandpa Came Into the Money" by Elsa Zantner reprinted by permission of the author.

"The Three Veterans" by Leane Zugsmith reprinted from THE NEW YORKER by permission of the author. Copyright © 1935 by THE NEW YORKER MAGAZINE, INC.

"Kong at the Seaside" by Arnold Zweig reprinted from Playthings of Time by permission of The Viking Press, Inc. Copyright 1935 by The Viking Press, Inc.

The following translations were originally made for this volume: "The Crime on Calle de la Persequida" by Palacio Valdés, translated by Eugenie Luhn; "A Game of Billiards" by Alphonse Daudet, "The Doctor's Heroism" by Villiers de L'Isle-Adam and "The Jewels of M. Lantin" by Guy de Maupassant, translated by Roger Goodman; "A Wicked Boy" by Anton Chekhov, translated by Helen Reeve.

Contents

INTRODUCTION	xi
A WEDDING WITHOUT MUSICIANS / SHOLEM ALEICHEM	1
HE SWUNG AND HE MISSED / NELSON ALGREN	5
SENOR PAYROLL / WILLIAM E. BARRETT	12
HOUSEPARTY / WALTER BERNSTEIN	16
HOW LIGHT BELIEF BRINGETH DAMAGE / BIDPAI	18
A PSYCHOLOGICAL SHIPWRECK / AMBROSE BIERCE	20
THE FATHER / BJÖRNSTJERNE BJÖRNSON	24
NEIFILE'S STORY / BOCCACCIO	27
I SEE YOU NEVER / RAY BRADBURY	29
THE LOTTERY TICKET / VENTURA GARCIA CALDERÓN	32
DAUGHTER / ERSKINE CALDWELL	35
A WICKED BOY / ANTON CHEKHOV	40
LUCK / SAMUEL CLEMENS	42
THE CHASER / JOHN COLLIER	46
THE UPTURNED FACE / STEPHEN CRANE	49
A GAME OF BILLIARDS / ALPHONSE DAUDET	53
FEAR / RHYS DAVIES	57
THE RIDDLE / WALTER DE LA MARE	61
THE JEWELS OF M. LANTIN / GUY DE MAUPASSANT	65
THE HEAVENLY CHRISTMAS TREE / FYODOR DOSTOEVSKY	71
THE GHOSTS / LORD DUNSANY	75
THE SCOOP / JAMES T. FARRELL	79
THE BEDCHAMBER MYSTERY / C. S. FORESTER	82
MR. ANDREWS / E. M. FORSTER	86
THE TEST / ANGELICA GIBBS	90
TRUTH AND CONSEQUENCES / BRENDAN GILL	93

THE DISABLED SOLDIER / OLIVER GOLDSMITH 97

VIRTUOSO / HERBERT GOLDSTONE 101

HER LOVER / MAXIM GORKY 107

PROOF POSITIVE / GRAHAM GREENE 113

THE BUTTERFLY / JAMES HANLEY 116

ABSENT-MINDEDNESS IN A PARISH CHOIR / THOMAS HARDY 120

THE HOLLOW OF THE THREE HILLS / NATHANIEL HAWTHORNE 123

A QUESTION OF BLOOD / ERNEST HAYCOX 127

THE BOY WHO DREW CATS / LAFCADIO HEARN 131

THE LOST SOUL / BEN HECHT 134

THE EXACT SCIENCE OF MATRIMONY / O. HENRY 138

FARD / ALDOUS HUXLEY 144

THE WIFE / WASHINGTON IRVING 149

CHARLES / SHIRLEY JACKSON 156

THEN CAME THE LEGIONS / MACKINLAY KANTOR 160

IF NOT HIGHER / ISAAC LOEB PEREZ 164

THE WILD DUCK'S NEST / MICHAEL MCLAVERTY 167

A TOAST TO CAPTAIN JERK / RUSSELL MALONEY 171

GERMANS AT MEAT / KATHERINE MANSFIELD 174

BORN OF MAN AND WOMAN / RICHARD MATHESON 177

THE ANT AND THE GRASSHOPPER / SOMERSET MAUGHAM 180

THE GUARDIAN ANGEL / ANDRÉ MAUROIS 184

THE FIDDLER / HERMAN MELVILLE 189

THE PEARL OF TOLEDO / PROSPER MÉRIMÉE 195

THE SNIPER / LIAM O'FLAHERTY 197

THE CRIME ON CALLE DE LA PERSEQUIDA / PALACIO VALDÉS 201

HOW THE DEVIL LOST HIS PONCHO / RICARDO PALMA 206

THE STANDARD OF LIVING / DOROTHY PARKER 209

THE OVAL PORTRAIT / EDGAR ALLAN POE 214

THREE LETTERS . . . AND A FOOTNOTE / HORACIO QUIROGA 218

A DANGEROUS GUY INDEED / DAMON RUNYON 221

REGINALD'S CHOIR TREAT / SAKI 224

THE KISS / WILLIAM SANSOM 227

THE SHEPHERD'S DAUGHTER / WILLIAM SAROYAN 230

THE FOREIGNER / FRANCIS STEEGMULLER 232

TOM VARNISH / RICHARD STEELE   236

OVER THE HILL / JOHN STEINBECK   238

AN ATTEMPT AT REFORM / AUGUST STRINDBERG   240

THE THREE HERMITS / LEO TOLSTOY   243

THE DOCTOR'S HEROISM / VILLIERS DE L'ISLE-ADAM   249

THE BEGGAR-WOMAN OF LOCARNO / HEINRICH VON KLEIST   253

THE PHOENIX / SYLVIA TOWNSEND WARNER   255

SLIPPING BEAUTY / JEROME WEIDMAN   259

THE HOUR OF LETDOWN / E. B. WHITE   263

MOONLIGHT SONATA / ALEXANDER WOOLLCOTT   267

GOD / EUGENE IVANOVICH ZAMIATIN   270

HOW GRANDPA CAME INTO THE MONEY / ELSA ZANTNER   272

THE THREE VETERANS / LEANE ZUGSMITH   275

KONG AT THE SEASIDE / ARNOLD ZWEIG   278

Introduction

📖 📖 📖

The phrase "history repeats itself" is not, these days, accepted without challenge. But even those most critical of the aphorism will acknowledge that certain events and chains of events bear marked resemblance to incidents of earlier history. It is, perhaps, less debatable—especially in contemporary America—to claim that fashions of dress repeat themselves. The sophisticated moderns who screamed with laughter at the women's styles exhibited in films about the twenties are, at the moment of this writing, flaunting the very same short, rhinestone-decorated hair and short skirts as up-to-date fashions.

We can also find this cycle in literary forms. In the heroic age, when time was found for entertainment, for verbal teaching, and for passing down of lore, the epic poem—the *Iliad* and the *Odyssey, Beowulf*—flourished. Later, the stimulation of Oriental models yielded the first European short stories: the brief, moral parable and the brief, immoral anecdote. With the passage of time, the epic gave way to the prose tale until, in the nineteenth century, it became the huge multi-volume novel—*Vanity Fair, War and Peace, Les Misérables*.

The short story also came into its own during the nineteenth century; and, when the rush of the twentieth century began to chop away at the length of the novel— "no time to read. Get the gist of it in a digest!" —the short story became more and more popular and important as a literary form. Thus, the cycle continued and finally we rediscovered the "short-short story"—a tiny, highly polished gem of narration, more fully rounded and developed than the ancient parables and tales, and short enough to be completed in an afternoon or during one of the many short trips that have become an integral part of our lives.

What is presented in these pages is perhaps an ultimate in the refinement of the writer's craft. Notice, among the

authors, men whose greatest fame stems from large novels—
The Brothers Karamazov, Of Human Bondage, Anderson-
ville—but who, attracted by a challenge of a different kind,
ventured into the Lilliputian domain of the short-short story.

ROGER B. GOODMAN
Chairman of the Department of English
Grover Cleveland High School
Ridgewood, New York

75 SHORT MASTERPIECES:
STORIES FROM THE WORLD'S LITERATURE

A Wedding without Musicians

BY SHOLOM ALEICHEM

❑ ❑ ❑

The last time I told you about our Straggler Special, I described the miracle of *Hashono Rabo*. This time I shall tell you about another miracle in which the Straggler Special figured, how thanks to the Straggler Special the town of Heissin was saved from a terrible fate.

This took place during the days of the Constitution when reprisals against the Jews were going on everywhere. Though I must tell you that we Jews of Heissin have never been afraid of pogroms. Why? Simply because there is no one in our town who can carry out a pogrom. Of course you can imagine that if we looked very hard we could find one or two volunteers who wouldn't deny themselves the pleasure of ventilating us a little, that is, breaking our bones or burning down our houses. For example, when reports of pogroms began drifting in, the few squires, who are enemies of our people, wrote confidential letters to the proper authorities, saying it might be a good idea if "something were done" in Heissin also; but since there was no one here to do it, would they be so kind as to send help, in other words, would they dispatch some "people" as quickly as possible.

And before another twenty-four hours had passed a reply came, also confidentially, that "people" were being sent. From where? From Zhmerinko, from Kazatin, Razdilno, Popelno and other such places that had distinguished themselves in beating up Jews. Do you want to know how we learned of this deep secret? We found it out through our regular source of news, Noah Tonkonoy. Noah Tonkonoy is a man whom God has endowed with a pair of extra-long legs and he uses them to good purpose. He never rests and he is seldom to be found at home. He is always busy with a thousand things and most of these things have to do with other

1

people's business rather than his own. By trade he is a printer, and because he is the only printer in Heissin he knows all the squires and the police and has dealings with officialdom and is in on all their secrets.

Noah Tonkonoy spread the good news all over town. He told the secret to one person at a time, in strictest confidence, of course, saying, "I am telling this only to you. I wouldn't tell it to anyone else." And that was how the whole town became aware of the fact that a mob of hooligans was on the way, and that a plan for beating up Jews had been worked out. The plan told exactly when they would start, on which day, at which hour, and from which point, and by what means—everything to the last detail.

You can imagine what terror this struck in our hearts. Panic spread quickly. And among whom do you think it spread first? Among the poor, of course. It's a peculiar thing about poor people. When a rich man is afraid of a pogrom, you can understand why. He is afraid, poor fellow, that he will be turned into a pauper. But those of you who are already paupers, what are you afraid of? What have you got to lose? But you should have seen how they bundled up their children and packed up their belongings and began running hither and yon, looking for a place to hide. Where can a person hide? This one hides in a friendly peasant's cellar, another in the Notary's attic, a third in the Director's office at the factory. Everyone finds a spot for himself.

I was the only one in town who wasn't anxious to hide. I am not boasting about my bravery. But this is the way I see it: what's the sense of being afraid of a pogrom? I don't say that I am a hero. I might have been willing to hide too, when the hour of reckoning came. But I asked myself first, "How can I be sure that during the slaughter the friendly peasant in whose cellar I was hiding, or the Notary, or the Director of the factory himself, wouldn't . . ." You understand. And all that aside, how can you leave a town wide open like that? It's no trick to run away. You have to see about doing something. But, alas, what can a Jew do? He appeals to a friendly official. And that is just what we did.

In every town there is at least one friendly official you can appeal to. We had one too, the Inspector of Police, a jewel of a fellow, willing to listen to us and willing to accept a gift on occasion. We went to the Inspector with the proper gifts and asked for his protection. He reassured us at once. He told us to go home and sleep in peace. Nothing would happen. Sounds good, doesn't it? But we still had our walking newspaper, Noah, who was broadcasting another secret through the length and breadth of the town. The secret was that a telegram had just arrived. He swore by everything holy that he had seen it himself. What was in that telegram? Only one word—*Yediem.* An ugly word. It means simply, "We are coming." We ran back to the Inspector. "Your honor," we told him, "it looks bad." "What looks bad?" he asked, and we told him, "A telegram has just arrived." "From where?" We told him. "And what does it say?" We told him, "*Yediem.*" At this he burst out laughing. "You are big fools," he said. "Only yesterday I ordered a regiment of Cossacks from Tolchin."

When we heard this we breathed more easily. When a Jew hears that a Cossack is coming, he takes courage, he can face the world again. The question remained: who would arrive first, the Cossacks from Tolchin, or the hooligans from Zhmerinko? Common sense told us that the hooligans would arrive first, because they were coming by train, while the Cossacks were coming on horseback. But we pinned all our hopes on the Straggler Special. God is merciful. He would surely perform a miracle and the Straggler would be at least a few hours late. This wasn't too much to hope for, since it happened nearly every day. But this one time it looked as though the miracle wouldn't take place. The Straggler kept going from station to station as regular as a clock. You can imagine how we felt when we learned, confidentially, of course, through Noah Tonkonoy, that a telegram had arrived from the last station, from Krishtopovka. *Yediem,* it said, and not just *yediem*—but *yediem* with a *hurrah!* in front of it.

Naturally we took this last bit of news straight to the Inspector. We begged him not to rely on the Cossacks who might or might not arrive from Tolchin sometime, but to send police to the station, at least for the sake of appearances, so that our enemies wouldn't think that we were completely at their mercy. The Inspector listened to our pleas. He did what we asked, and more. He got himself up in full uniform, with all his orders and medals, and took the whole police force, that is the gendarme and his assistant, to the station with him to meet the train.

But our enemies weren't asleep either. They also put on their full dress uniforms, complete with ribbons and medals, took a couple of priests along, and also came to meet the train. The Inspector asked them sternly, "What are you do-ing here?" And they asked him the same question, "What are you doing here?" They bandied words back and forth, and the Inspector let them know in no uncertain terms that their trouble was for nothing. As long as he was in charge, there would be no pogrom in Heissin. They listened, smiled know-ingly, and answered with insolence, "We shall see."

Just then a train whistle was heard from the distance. The sound struck terror to our hearts. We waited for another whistle to blow and after that for the shouts of "Hurrah!" What would happen after the Hurrah! we knew only too well from hearsay. We waited, but heard nothing more. What had happened? The sort of thing that could only happen to our Straggler Special.

When the Straggler Special drew into the station, the engineer stopped the locomotive, stepped out calmly and made his way toward the buffet. We met him halfway. "Well, my good fellow, and where are the cars?" "Which cars?" "Can't you see that you are here with the locomotive and without cars?"

He stared at us. "What do I care about the cars? They are the business of the crew." "Where is the crew?" "How should I know where the crew is? The conductor blows the whistle when he is ready and I whistle back to let him know that I am starting, and off we go. I don't have an extra pair of eyes in back of my head to see what's going on behind me." That was his story and according to that he was right. But right or wrong, there stood the Straggler Spe-cial without cars and without passengers. In other words, it was a wedding without musicians.

Later we learned that a band of hooligans had been on the way to Heissin, all of them handpicked youths, armed to the teeth with clubs and knives and other weapons. Their spirits were high and liquor flowed freely. At the last sta-tion, Krishtopovka, they invited the crew to join them and treated everybody to drinks—the conductor, the fireman, the gendarmes. But in the midst of this revelry they forgot one little detail, to couple the cars back to the locomotive. And so the locomotive went off at the usual time to Heissin and the rest of the Straggler Special remained standing in Krishtop-ovka.

Neither the hooligans nor the other passengers nor the crew noticed that they were standing still. They continued to empty bottle after bottle and to make merry, until the station master suddenly noticed that the locomotive had gone off and left the cars behind. He spread the alarm, the crew came tumbling out. A hue and cry was raised. The hooligans blamed the crew, the crew blamed the hooligans, but what good did it do? At last they decided that the only thing to do was to set out for Heissin on foot. They took heart and began marching toward Heissin, singing and shouting as they went.

And so they arrived in their usual good form, singing and yelling and brandishing their clubs. But it was already too late. In the streets of Heissin the Cossacks from Tolchin were riding up and down on horseback with whips in their hands. Within half an hour not one of the hooligans remained in town. They ran off like rats in a famine, they melted like ice in summer.

Now, I ask you, didn't the Straggler Special deserve to be showered with gold, or at least written up?

He Swung and He Missed

BY NELSON ALGREN

▱ ▱ ▱

It was Miss Donahue of Public School 24 who finally urged Rocco, in his fifteenth year, out of eighth grade and into the world. She had watched him fighting, at recess times, from his sixth year on. The kindergarten had had no recesses or it would have been from his fifth year. She had nurtured him personally through four trying semesters and so it was with something like enthusiasm that she wrote in his autograph book, the afternoon of graduation day, "Trusting that Rocco will make good."

Ultimately, Rocco did. In his own way. He stepped from the schoolroom into the ring back of the Happy Hour Bar in a catchweight bout with an eight-dollar purse, winner take all. Rocco took it.

Uncle Mike Adler, local promoter, called the boy Young Rocco after that one and the name stuck. He fought through the middleweights and into the light-heavies, while his purses increased to as much as sixty dollars and expenses. In his nineteenth year he stopped growing, his purses stopped growing, and he married a girl called Lili.

He didn't win every one after that, somehow, and by the time he was twenty-two he was losing as often as he won. He fought on. It was all he could do. He never took a dive; he never had a setup or a soft touch. He stayed away from whisky; he never gambled; he went to bed early before every bout and he loved his wife. He fought in a hundred corners of the city, under a half dozen managers, and he fought every man he was asked to, at any hour. He substituted, for better men, on as little as two hours' notice. He never ran out on a fight and he was never put down for a ten-count. He took beatings from the best in the business. But he never stayed down for ten.

He fought a comer from the Coast one night and took the worst beating of his career. But he was on his feet at the end. With a jaw broken in three places.

After that one he was hospitalized for three months and Lili went to work in a factory. She wasn't a strong girl and he didn't like it that she had to work. He fought again before his jaw was ready, and lost.

Yet even when he lost, the crowds liked him. They heckled him when he was introduced as Young Rocco, because he looked like thirty-four before he was twenty-six. Most of his hair had gone during his lay-off, and scar tissue over the eyes made him look less and less like a young anything. Friends came, friends left, money came in, was lost, was saved; he got the break on an occasional decision, and was occasionally robbed of a duke he'd earned. All things changed but his weight, which was 174, and his wife, who was Lili. And his record of never having been put down for ten. That stood, like his name, which was forever Young Rocco.

That stuck to him like nothing else in the world but Lili.

At the end, which came when he was twenty-nine, all he had left was his record and his girl. Being twenty-nine, one of that pair had to go. He went six weeks without earning a dime before he came to that realization. When he found her wearing a pair of his old tennis shoes about the house, to save the heels of her only decent pair of shoes, he made up his mind.

Maybe Young Rocco wasn't the smartest pug in town, but he wasn't the punchiest either. Just because there was a dent in his face and a bigger one in his wallet, it didn't follow that his brain was dented. It wasn't. He knew what the score was. And he loved his girl.

He came into Uncle Mike's office looking for a fight and Mike was good enough not to ask what kind he wanted. He had a twenty-year-old named Solly Classki that he was bringing along under the billing of Kid Class. There was money back of the boy, no chances were to be taken. If Rocco was ready to dive, he had the fight. Uncle Mike put no pressure on Rocco. There were two light-heavies out in the gym ready to jump at the chance to dive for Solly Classki. All Rocco had to say was okay. His word was good enough for Uncle Mike. Rocco said it. And left the gym with the biggest purse of his career, and the first he'd gotten in advance, in his pocket: four twenties and two tens.

He gave Lili every dime of that money, and when he handed it over, he knew he was only doing the right thing for her. He had earned the right to sell out and he had sold. The ring owed him more than a C-note, he reflected soundly, and added loudly, for Lili's benefit, "I'll stop the bum dead in his tracks."

They were both happy that night. Rocco had never been happier since Graduation Day.

He had a headache all the way to the City Garden that night, but it lessened a little in the shadowed dressing room under the stands. The moment he saw the lights of the ring, as he came down the littered aisle alone, the ache sharpened once more.

Slouched unhappily in his corner for the windup, he watched the lights overhead swaying a little, and closed his eyes. When he opened them, a slow dust was rising toward the lights. He saw it sweep suddenly, swift and sidewise, high over the ropes and out across the dark and watchful rows. Below him someone pushed the warning buzzer.

He looked through Kid Class as they touched gloves, and glared sullenly over the boy's head while Ryan, the ref, hurried through the stuff about a clean break in the clinches. He felt the robe being taken from his shoulders, and suddenly, in that one brief moment before the bell, felt more tired than he ever had in a ring before. He went out in a half-crouch and someone called out, "Cut him down, Solly."

He backed to make the boy lead, and then came in long enough to flick his left twice into the teeth and skitter away. The bleachers whooped, sensing blood. He'd give them their money's worth for a couple rounds, anyhow. No use making it look too bad.

In the middle of the second round he began sensing that the boy was telegraphing his right by pulling his left shoulder, and stepped in to trap it. The boy's left came back bloody and Rocco knew he'd been hit by the way the bleachers began again. It didn't occur to him that it was time to dive; he didn't even remember. Instead, he saw the boy telegraphing the right once more and the left protecting the heart slipping loosely down toward the navel, the telltale left shoulder hunching—only it wasn't down, it wasn't a right. It wasn't to the heart. The boy's left snapped like a hurled rock between his eyes and he groped blindly for the other's arms, digging his chin sharply into the shoulder, hating the six-bit bunch out there for thinking he could be hurt so soon. He shoved the boy off, flashed his left twice into the teeth, burned him skillfully against the middle rope, and heeled him sharply as they broke. Then he skittered easily away. And the bell.

Down front, Mike Adler's eyes followed Rocco back to his corner.

Rocco came out for the third, fighting straight up, watching Solly's gloves coming languidly out of the other corner, dangling loosely a moment in the glare, and a flatiron smashed in under his heart so that he remembered, with sagging surprise, that he'd already been paid off. He caught his breath while following the indifferent gloves, thinking vaguely of Lili in oversize tennis shoes. The gloves drifted backward and dangled loosely with little to do but catch light idly four feet away. The right broke again beneath his heart and he grunted in spite of himself; the boy's close-cropped head followed in, cockily, no higher than Rocco's chin but coming neckless straight down to the shoulders. And the gloves were gone again. The boy was faster than he looked. And the pain in his head settled down to a steady beating between the eyes.

The great strength of a fighting man is his pride. That was Young Rocco's strength in the rounds that followed. The boy called Kid Class couldn't keep him down. He was down in the fourth, twice in the fifth, and again in the seventh. In that round he stood with his back against the ropes, standing the boy off with his left in the seconds before the bell. He had the trick of looking impassive when he was hurt, and his face at the bell looked as impassive as a catcher's mitt.

Between that round and the eighth Uncle Mike climbed into the ring beside Young Rocco. He said nothing. Just stood there looking down. He thought Rocco might have forgotten. He'd had four chances to stay down and he hadn't taken one. Rocco looked up. "I'm clear as a bell," he told Uncle Mike. He hadn't forgotten a thing.

Uncle Mike climbed back into his seat, resigned to anything that might happen. He understood better than Young Rocco. Rocco couldn't stay down until his knees would fail to bring him up. Uncle Mike sighed. He decided he liked Young Rocco. Somehow, he didn't feel as sorry for him as he had in the gym.

"I hope he makes it," he found himself hoping. The crowd felt differently. They had seen the lean and scarred Italian drop his man here twenty times before, the way he was trying to keep from being dropped himself now. They felt it was his turn. They were standing up in the rows to see it. The dust came briefly between. A tired moth struggled lamely upward toward the lights. And the bell.

Ryan came over between rounds, hooked Rocco's head back with a crooked forefinger on the chin, after Rocco's Negro handler had stopped the bleeding with collodion, and muttered something about the thing going too far. Rocco spat.

"Awright, Solly, drop it on him," someone called across the ropes.

It sounded, somehow, like money to Rocco. It sounded like somebody was being shortchanged out there.

But Solly stayed away, hands low, until the eighth was half gone. Then he was wide with a right, held and butted as they broke; Rocco felt the blood and got rid of some of it on the boy's left breast. He trapped the boy's left, rapping the kidneys fast before grabbing the arms again, and pressed his nose firmly into the hollow of the other's throat to arrest its bleeding. Felt the blood trickling into the hollow there as into a tiny cup. Rocco put his feet together and a glove on both of Kid Class's shoulders, to shove him sullenly away. And must have looked strong doing it, for he heard the crowd murmur a little. He was in Solly's corner at the bell and moved back to his own corner with his head held high, to control the bleeding. When his handler stopped it again, he knew, at last, that his own pride was double-crossing him. And felt glad for that much. Let them worry out there in the rows. He'd been shortchanged since Graduation Day; let them be on the short end tonight. He had the hundred—he'd get a job in a garage and forget every one of them.

It wasn't until the tenth and final round that Rocco realized he wanted to kayo the boy—because it wasn't until then that he realized he could. Why not do the thing up the right way? He felt his tiredness fall from him like an old cloak at the notion. This was his fight his round. He'd end like he'd started, as a fighting man. And saw Solly Kid Class shuffling his shoulders forward uneasily. The boy would be a full-sized heavy in another six months. He bulled him into the ropes and felt the boy fade sidewise. Rocco caught him off balance with his left hook-fashion, into the short ribs. The boy chopped back with his left uncertainly, as though he might have jammed the knuckles, and held. In a half-rolling clinch along the ropes, he saw Solly's mouthpiece projecting slipping halfway in and halfway out, and then swallowed in again with a single tortured twist of the lips. He got an arm loose and banged the boy back of the ear with an overhand right that must have looked funny because the crowd laughed a little. Solly smeared his glove across his nose, came halfway in and changed his mind, left himself wide and was almost steady until Rocco feinted him into a knot and brought the right looping from the floor with even his toes behind it.

Solly stepped in to let it breeze past, and hooked his right hard to the button. Then the left. Rocco's mouthpiece went spinning in an arc into the lights. Then the right.

Rocco spun halfway around and stood looking sheepishly out at the rows. Kid Class saw only his man's back; Rocco was out on his feet. He walked slowly along the ropes, tapping them idly with his glove and smiling vacantly down at the newspapermen, who smiled back. Solly looked up at Ryan. Ryan nodded toward Rocco. Kid Class came up fast behind his man and threw the left under the armpit flush onto the point of the chin. Rocco went forward on the ropes and hung there, his chin catching the second strand, and hung on and on, like a man decapitated.

He came to in the locker room under the stands, watching the steam swimming about the pipes directly overhead. Uncle Mike was somewhere near, telling him he had done fine, and then he was alone. They were all gone then, all the six-bit hecklers and the iron-throated boys in the sixty-cent seats. He rose heavily and dressed slowly, feeling a long relief that he'd come to the end. He'd done it the hard way, but he'd done it. Let them all go.

He was fixing his tie, taking more time with it than it required, when she knocked. He called to her to come in. She had never seen him fight, but he knew she must have listened on the radio or she wouldn't be down now.

She tested the adhesive over his right eye timidly, fearing to hurt him with her touch, but wanting to be sure it wasn't loose.

"I'm okay," he assured her easily. "We'll celebrate a little 'n forget the whole business." It wasn't until he kissed her that her eyes avoided him; it wasn't till then that he saw she was trying not to cry. He patted her shoulder.

"There's nothin' wrong, Lil'—a couple days' rest 'n I'll be in the pink again."

Then saw it wasn't that after all.

"You told me you'd win," the girl told him. "I got eight to one and put the whole damn bank roll on you. I wanted to surprise you, 'n now we ain't got a cryin' dime."

Rocco didn't blow up. He just felt a little sick. Sicker than he had ever felt in his life. He walked away from the girl and sat on the rubbing table, studying the floor. She had sense enough not to bother him until he'd realized what the score was. Then he looked up, studying her from foot to head. His eyes didn't rest on her face: they went back to her feet. To the scarred toes of the only decent shoes; and a shadow passed over his heart. "You got good odds, honey," he told her thoughtfully. "You done just right. We made 'em sweat all night for their money." Then he looked up and grinned. A wide, white grin.

That was all she needed to know it was okay after all. She went to him so he could tell her how okay it really was.

That was like Young Rocco, from Graduation Day. He always did it the hard way; but he did it.

Miss Donahue would have been proud.

Señor Payroll

BY WILLIAM E. BARRETT

◻ ◻ ◻

Larry and I were Junior Engineers in the gas plant, which means that we were clerks. Anything that could be classified as paper work came to the flat double desk across which we faced each other. The Main Office downtown sent us a bewildering array of orders and rules that were to be put into effect.

Junior Engineers were beneath the notice of everyone except the Mexican laborers at the plant. To them we were the visible form of a distant, unknowable paymaster. We were Señor Payroll.

Those Mexicans were great workmen; the aristocrats among them were the stokers, big men who worked Herculean eight-hour shifts in the fierce heat of the retorts. They scooped coal with huge shovels and hurled it with uncanny aim at tiny doors. The coal streamed out from the shovels like black water from a high-pressure nozzle, and never missed the narrow opening. The stokers worked stripped to the waist, and there was pride and dignity in them. Few men could do such work, and they were the few.

The Company paid its men only twice a month, on the fifth and on the twentieth. To a Mexican, this was absurd. What man with money will make it last fifteen days? If he hoarded money beyond the spending of three days, he was a miser—and when, Señor, did the blood of Spain flow in the veins of misers? Hence, it was the custom for our stokers to appear every third or fourth day to draw the money due to them.

There was a certain elasticity in the Company rules, and Larry and I sent the necessary forms to the Main Office and received an "advance" against a man's pay check. Then, one day, Downtown favored us with a memorandum:

"There have been too many abuses of the advance-

12

against-wages privilege. Hereafter, no advance against wages will be made to any employee except in a case of genuine emergency."

We had no sooner posted the notice when in came stoker Juan Garcia. He asked for an advance. I pointed to the notice. He spelled is through slowly, then said, "What does this mean, this 'genuine emergency'?"

I explained to him patiently that the Company was kind and sympathetic, but that it was a great nuisance to have to pay wages every few days. If someone was ill or if money was urgently needed for some other good reason, then the Company would make an exception to the rule.

Juan Garcia turned his hat over and over slowly in his big hands. "I do not get my money?"

"Next payday, Juan. On the twentieth."

He went out silently and I felt a little ashamed of myself. I looked across the desk at Larry. He avoided my eyes.

In the next hour two other stokers came in, looked at the notice, had it explained and walked solemnly out; then no more came. What we did not know was that Juan Garcia, Pete Mendoza, and Francisco Gonzalez had spread the word, and that every Mexican in the plant was explaining the order to every other Mexican. "To get money now, the wife must be sick. There must be medicine for the baby."

The next morning Juan Garcia's wife was practically dying, Pete Mendoza's mother would hardly last the day, there was a veritable epidemic among children, and, just for variety, there was one sick father. We always suspected that the old man was really sick; no Mexican would otherwise have thought of him. At any rate, nobody paid Larry and me to examine private lives; we made out our forms with an added line describing the "genuine emergency." Our people got paid.

That went on for a week. Then came a new order, curt and to the point: "Hereafter, employees will be paid ONLY on the fifth and the twentieth of the month. No exceptions will be made except in the cases of employees leaving the service of the Company."

The notice went up on the board, and we explained its significance gravely. "No, Juan Garcia, we cannot advance your wages. It is too bad about your wife and your cousins and your aunts, but there is a new rule."

Juan Garcia went out and thought it over. He thought

out loud with Mendoza and Gonzales and Ayala, then, in
the morning, he was back. "I am quitting this company for
different job. You pay me now?"

We argued that it was a good company and that it loved
its employees like children, but in the end we paid off, because Juan Garcia quit. And so did Gonzalez, Mendoza,
Obregon, Ayala and Ortez, the best stokers, men who could
not be replaced.

Larry and I looked at each other; we knew what was coming in about three days. One of our duties was to sit on the
hiring line early each morning, engaging transient workers
for the handy gangs. Any man was accepted who could
walk up and ask for a job without falling down. Never before
had we been called upon to hire such skilled virtuosos as
stokers for handy-gang work, but we were called upon to hire
them now.

The day foreman was wringing his hands and asking the
Almighty if he was personally supposed to shovel this con-
demned coal, while there in a stolid, patient line were
skilled men—Garcia, Mendoza, and others—waiting to be
hired. We hired them, of course. There was nothing else to
do.

Every day we had a line of resigning stokers, and another line of stokers seeking work. Our paper work became very complicated. At the Main Office they were jumping up and down. The procession of forms showing Juan
Garcia's resigning and being hired over and over again was
too much for them. Sometimes Downtown had Garcia on
the payroll twice at the same time when someone down
there was slow in entering a resignation. Our phone rang
early and often.

Tolerantly and patiently we explained: "There's nothing
we can do if a man wants to quit, and if there are stokers
available when the plant needs stokers, we hire them."

Out of chaos, Downtown issued another order. I read
it and whistled. Larry looked at it and said, "It is going to
be very quiet around here."

The order read: "Hereafter, no employee who resigns may
be rehired within a period of 30 days."

Juan Garcia was due for another resignation, and when he
came in we showed him the order and explained that standing in line the next day would do him no good if he resigned
today. "Thirty days is a long time, Juan."

It was a grave matter and he took time to reflect on it.

So did Gonzalez, Mendoza, Ayala and Ortez. Ultimately, however, they were all back—and all resigned.

We did our best to dissuade them and we were sad about the parting. This time it was for keeps and they shook hands with us solemnly. It was very nice knowing us. Larry and I looked at each other when they were gone and we both knew that neither of us had been pulling for Downtown to win this duel. It was a blue day.

In the morning, however, they were all back in line. With the utmost gravity, Juan Garcia informed me that he was a stoker looking for a job.

"No dice, Juan," I said. "Come back in thirty days. I warned you."

His eyes looked straight into mine without a flicker. "There is some mistake, Señor," he said. "I am Manuel Hernandez. I work as the stoker in Pueblo, in Santa Fe, in many places."

I stared back at him, remembering the sick wife and the babies without medicine, the mother-in-law in the hospital, the many resignations and the rehirings. I knew that there was a gas plant in Pueblo, and that there wasn't any in Santa Fe; but who was I to argue with a man about his own name? A stoker is a stoker.

So I hired him. I hired Gonzalez, too, who swore that his name was Carrera, and Ayala, who had shamelessly become Smith.

Three days later the resigning started.

Within a week our payroll read like a history of Latin America. Everyone was on it: Lopez and Obregon, Villa, Diaz, Batista, Gomez, and even San Martín and Bolívar. Finally Larry and I, growing weary of staring at familiar faces and writing unfamiliar names, went to the Superintendent and told him the whole story. He tried not to grin, and said, "Damned nonsense!"

The next day the orders were taken down. We called our most prominent stokers into the office and pointed to the board. No rules any more.

"The next time we hire you hombres," Larry said grimly, "come in under the names you like best, because that's the way you are going to stay on the books."

They looked at us and they looked at the board; then for the first time in the long duel, their teeth flashed white. "Si, Señores," they said.

And so it was.

Houseparty

BY WALTER BERNSTEIN

◻ ◻ ◻

The small room was crowded, but the boy managed to get through without spilling the drink he held in his hand.

"Hello," he said to the girl on the window seat. "You're late," she said. "Last time you were faster."

"I couldn't help it," the boy said. "The place is filling up."

The girl accepted the glass and took a long drink. She looked up at the boy and took another drink. Then she set the glass down. "What do they put this Scotch in with—an eyedropper?" she asked.

"I'll get you some more."

"No, never mind." She turned to look out of the window. "That's the library," the boy said.

"Your friend told me. I guess he wanted me to get the idea. He told me five times. Look," she said, "there's a clock on the other side of that tower, too, isn't there?"

"Sure," said the boy. "Four of them."

"Does it keep the same time as this one?"

"Sure."

The girl looked triumphant. "How do you know?" she asked.

"Well—" the boy said. He was a trifle uneasy. "Well, I guess it does."

"You ought to find out," the girl insisted. "You really ought to find out. That clock on the other side might be slow. If you can see only one clock at a time, how do you know it isn't slow?"

"I guess you don't know," said the boy. "You have to take their word for it."

"I'd find out if I were you," said the girl, shaking her head slowly. She took another drink. "You really ought to know." She looked out of the window, then turned back to the boy. "What do they call this place again?"

"Dartmouth," said the boy.

16

"That's a silly name," said the girl. She finished her drink. "Do you think you could get me another one of these with some Scotch in it?"

"Sure," said the boy. He took the glass and started through the crowd. The girl put her nose against the pane and looked out of the window.

After a while the boy came back, holding the drink above his head so it wouldn't be spilled. He tapped the girl on the shoulder. "Hello," he said. "I'm back."

The girl looked at him. "Go away," she said; "I never heard of you."

"I'm your date," said the boy. "I'm bringing you another drink."

The girl peered at him. "So you are," she said. She took the drink and returned to the window.

"I got a little more Scotch this time," the boy said.

The girl turned around. "You're cute," she said.

The boy blushed. "Look," he said, "are you having a good time?"

"I'm having a wonderful time," the girl said. "I am having a simply wonderful time." Her eyes were very large and bright.

"I'm glad," said the boy. He sat down and took hold of her hand. The girl looked at his hand holding hers and then up at his face. She looked at his hand again and took another drink. The boy held on to her hand and leaned forward. "Do you really dance in a chorus?" he said.

"When I'm working," the girl said. "They call us chorus girls." She put her head next to his. "Who squealed?"

"Oh, no one." The boy was emphatic. "My sister told me. Remember? You know my sister. She introduced us in New York."

The girl nodded. "I know your sister." She hiccuped gently. "Little bitch."

The boy released her hand and sat up straight. Seeing his startled expression, the girl put her fingers to her mouth. "There I go again, always belching in public," she said. She leaned toward the boy. "Pardon me."

"Sure," said the boy. "Sure." He sat up very straight.

The girl was beating out a rhythm on the glass with her fingernails, watching the crowd. "How long do you have to stay in this place?" she asked.

"No special time," said the boy. "We can leave now if you want."

"Not here," said the girl. "I mean in college."

"Oh. Four years. I have one to go."

"That's a long run." She drained her glass and looked at the boy. "You're cute," she said. She put down the glass and took up his hands. "You have nice hands."

The boy gave her hands a slight squeeze. "So have you," he said, but the girl had turned away.

"You touch that glass," she was saying to a girl about to sit down, "and I'll lay you out like a rug." She retrieved the glass and held it out to the boy. "How about another drink?"

"Sure," said the boy. He took the glass and moved into the crowd. As he was pouring the liquor, another boy came over and put an arm around his shoulders.

"How're you doing?" he asked.

The boy spilled a little soda into the glass and started back toward the window.

"Fine," he called back. "Fine." He dodged someone carrying a tray. "She's a cinch," he said.

How Light Belief Bringeth Damage

BY BIDPAI

📖 📖 📖

Two skillful thieves one night entered the house of a wealthy knight, no less wise than worshipped in the community. The gentleman, hearing the noise of their feet in the house, awakened and suspected that they were thieves. They were upon the point of opening the door of the chamber wherein he lay, when he jogged his wife, awakened her, and whispered, "I hear the noise of thieves who have come to rob us. I would have you, therefore, ask me straight, and with great insistence, whence and by what means I came by all I own. Ask me loudly and earnestly, and, as I shall appear reluctant, you must plead and wheedle until, at length, I shall succumb and tell you." The Lady, his wife, being wise and subtle, began in this manner to question her husband—"O, dear sir. Grant me one thing this night that I have for so long desired to know. Tell me how you have come by all these

goods you now possess." He, speaking at random and carelessly, scarce answered. Finally, after she kept pleading, he
said, "I can but wonder, Madam, at what moves you to know
my secrets. Be contented, then, to live well, to dress richly,
and to be waited upon and served. I have heard that all things
have ears, and that many things are spoken which are later
repented. Therefore, I pray you, hold your peace."

But even this did not deter the Lady. Sweetly and lovingly
enticing, she besought him to tell her. Finally, wearying of
her speech, the knight said, "All we have—and I charge you
to say nothing of this to anyone—is stolen. Indeed, of all I
own I got nothing truly." The Lady, unbelieving, so berated
her husband that he answered farther, "You think what I have
already told you is a wonder. Listen then. Even in my cradle
I delighted in stealing and filching. And I lived among thieves
so that my fingers might never be idle. One friend among
them loved me so well that he taught me a rare and singular
trick. He taught me a conjuration which I made to the moonbeams—enabling me to embrace them suddenly. Thus I sometimes came down upon them from a high window—or served
myself with them to go up again to the top of the house. So
I used them as I would. The Moon, hearing my conjuration
seven times, showed me all the money and treasure of the
house and with her beams I flew up and down. And thus,
good wife, I made me rich. Now, no more."

One of the thieves, listening at the door, heard all that was
said and bore it away. Because the knight was known to be a
man of credit and integrity, the thieves believed his story.
The chief thief, desirous to prove in deeds what he had heard
in words, repeated the conjuration seven times, and then, em-
bracing the moonbeams, he cast himself upon them thinking
to go from window to window, and he fell headlong to the
ground. The moon, however, favored him so that he was not
killed, but broke his legs and one arm. He cried aloud in his
pain and at his stupidity in trusting too much to another's
words.

So, lying on the ground expecting death, he was found by
the knight who beat him sorely. The thief begged for mercy,
saying that what hurt him most was that he was such a fool
to believe such words. And he besought him, since he had
hurt him so with words, he would not also hurt him in deeds.

A Psychological Shipwreck

BY AMBROSE BIERCE

In the summer of 1874 I was in Liverpool, whither I had gone on business for the mercantile house of Bronson & Jarrett, New York. I am William Jarrett; my partner was Zenas Bronson. The firm failed last year, and unable to endure the fall from affluence to poverty he died.

Having finished my business, and feeling the lassitude and exhaustion incident to its dispatch, I felt that a protracted sea voyage would be both agreeable and beneficial, so instead of embarking for my return on one of the many fine passenger steamers I booked for New York on the sailing vessel *Morrow*, upon which I had shipped a large and valuable invoice of the goods I had bought. The *Morrow* was an English ship with, of course, but little accommodation for passengers, of whom there were only myself, a young woman and her servant, who was a middle-aged Negress. I thought it singular that a traveling English girl should be so attended, but she afterward explained to me that the woman had been left with her family by a man and his wife from South Carolina, both of whom had died on the same day at the house of the young lady's father in Devonshire—a circumstance in itself sufficiently uncommon to remain rather distinctly in my memory, even had it not afterward transpired in conversation with the young lady that the name of the man was William Jarrett, the same as my own. I knew that a branch of my family had settled in South Carolina, but of them and their history I was ignorant.

The *Morrow* sailed from the mouth of the Mersey on the 15th of June and for several weeks we had fair breezes and unclouded skies. The skipper, an admirable seaman but nothing more, favored us with very little of his society, except at his table; and the young woman, Miss Janette Harford, and I became very well acquainted. We were, in truth, nearly always together, and being of an introspective turn of mind

20

I often endeavored to analyze and define the novel feeling with which she inspired me—a secret, subtle, but powerful attraction which constantly impelled me to seek her; but the attempt was hopeless. I could only be sure that at least it was not love. Having assured myself of this and being certain that she was quite as whole-hearted, I ventured one evening (I remember it was on the 3rd of July) as we sat on deck to ask her, laughingly, if she could assist me to resolve my psychological doubt.

For a moment she was silent, with averted face, and I began to fear I had been extremely rude and indelicate; then she fixed her eyes gravely on my own. In an instant my mind was dominated by as strange a fancy as ever entered human consciousness. It seemed as if she were looking at me, not *with,* but *through,* those eyes—from an immeasurable distance behind them—and that a number of other persons, men, women and children, upon whose faces I caught strangely familiar evanescent expressions, clustered about her, struggling with gentle eagerness to look at me through the same orbs. Ship, ocean, sky—all had vanished. I was conscious of nothing but the figures in this extraordinary and fantastic scene. Then all at once darkness fell upon me, and anon from out of it, as to one who grows accustomed by degrees to a dimmer light, my former surroundings of deck and mast and cordage slowly resolved themselves. Miss Harford had closed her eyes and was leaning back in her chair, apparently asleep, the book she had been reading open in her lap. Impelled by surely I cannot say what motive, I glanced at the top of the page; it was a copy of that rare and curious work, "Denneker's Meditations," and the lady's index finger rested on this passage:

"To sundry it is given to be drawn away, and to be apart from the body for a season; for, as concerning rills which would flow across each other the weaker is borne along by the stronger, so there be certain of kin whose paths intersecting, their souls do bear company, the while their bodies go fore-appointed ways, unknowing."

Miss Harford arose, shuddering; the sun had sunk below the horizon, but it was not cold. There was not a breath of wind; there were no clouds in the sky, yet not a star was visible. A hurried tramping sounded on the deck; the captain, summoned from below, joined the first officer, who stood looking at the barometer. "Good God!" I heard him exclaim.

An hour later the form of Janette Harford, invisible in the darkness and spray, was torn from my grasp by the cruel vortex of the sinking ship, and I fainted in the cordage of the floating mast to which I had lashed myself.

It was by lamplight that I awoke. I lay in a berth amid the familiar surroundings of the stateroom of a steamer. On a couch opposite sat a man, half undressed for bed, reading a book. I recognized the face of my friend Gordon Doyle, whom I had met in Liverpool on the day of my embarkation, when he was himself about to sail on the steamer *City of Prague*, on which he had urged me to accompany him.

After some moments I now spoke his name. He simply said, "Well," and turned a leaf in his book without removing his eyes from the page.

"Doyle," I repeated, "did they save *her?*"

He now deigned to look at me and smiled as if amused. He evidently thought me but half awake.

"Her? Whom do you mean?"

"Janette Harford."

His amusement turned to amazement; he stared at me fixedly, saying nothing.

"You will tell me after a while," I continued; "I suppose you will tell me after a while."

A moment later I asked: "What ship is this?"

Doyle stared again. "The steamer *City of Prague*, bound from Liverpool to New York, three weeks out with a broken shaft. Principal passenger, Mr. Gordon Doyle; ditto lunatic, Mr. William Jarrett. These two distinguished travelers embarked together, but they are about to part, it being the resolute intention of the former to pitch the latter overboard."

I sat bolt upright. "Do you mean to say that I have been for three weeks a passenger on this steamer?"

"Yes, pretty nearly; this is the 3d of July."

"Have I been ill?"

"Right as a trivet all the time, and punctual at your meals."

"My God! Doyle, there is some mystery here; do have the goodness to be serious. Was I not rescued from the wreck of the ship *Morrow?*"

Doyle changed color, and approaching me, laid his fingers on my wrist. A moment later, "What do you know of Janette Harford?" he asked very calmly.

"First tell me what *you* know of her?"

Mr. Doyle gazed at me for some moments as if thinking what to do, then seating himself again on the couch, said:

"Why should I not? I am engaged to marry Janette Harford, whom I met a year ago in London. Her family, one of the wealthiest in Devonshire, cut up rough about it, and we eloped—are eloping rather, for on the day that you and I walked to the landing stage to go aboard this steamer she and her faithful servant, a Negress, passed us, driving to the ship *Morrow*. She would not consent to go in the same vessel with me, and it had been deemed best that she take a sailing vessel in order to avoid observation and lessen the risk of detection. I am now alarmed lest this cursed breaking of our machinery may detain us so long that the *Morrow* will get to New York before us, and the poor girl will not know where to go."

I lay still in my berth—so still I hardly breathed. But the subject was evidently not displeasing to Doyle, and after a short pause he resumed:

"By the way, she is only an adopted daughter of the Harfords. Her mother was killed at their place by being thrown from a horse while hunting, and her father, mad with grief, made away with himself the same day. No one ever claimed the child, and after a reasonable time they adopted her. She has grown up in the belief that she is their daughter."

"Doyle, what book are you reading?"

"Oh, it's called 'Denneker's Meditations.' It's a rum lot, Janette gave it to me; she happened to have two copies. Want to see it?"

He tossed me the volume, which opened as it fell. On one of the exposed pages was a marked passage:

"To sundry it is given to be drawn away, and to be apart from the body for a season; for, as concerning rills which would flow across each other the weaker is borne along by the stronger, so there be certain of kin whose paths intersecting, their souls do bear company, the while their bodies go fore-appointed ways, unknowing."

"She had—she has—a singular taste in reading," I managed to say, mastering my agitation.

"Yes. And now perhaps you will have the kindness to explain how you knew her name and that of the ship she sailed in."

"You talked of her in your sleep," I said.

A week later we were towed into the port of New York. But the *Morrow* was never heard from.

The Father

BY BJÖRNSTJERNE BJÖRNSON

📖 📖 📖

The man whose story is here to be told was the wealthiest and most influential person in his parish; his name was Thord Overaas. He appeared in the priest's study one day, tall and earnest.

"I have gotten a son," said he, "and I wish to present him for baptism."

"What shall his name be?"

"Finn—after my father."

"And the sponsors?"

They were mentioned, and proved to be the best men and women of Thord's relations in the parish.

"Is there anything else?" inquired the priest, and looked up.

The peasant hesitated a little.

"I should like very much to have him baptized by himself," said he, finally.

"That is to say on a week-day?"

"Next Saturday, at twelve o'clock noon."

"Is there anything else?" inquired the priest.

"There is nothing else"; and the peasant twirled his cap, as though he were about to go.

Then the priest rose. "There is yet this, however," said he, and walking toward Thord, he took him by the hand and looked gravely into his eyes: "God grant that the child may become a blessing to you!"

One day sixteen years later, Thord stood once more in the priest's study.

"Really, you carry your age astonishingly well, Thord," said the priest; for he saw no change whatever in the man.

"That is because I have no troubles," replied Thord.

To this the priest said nothing, but after a while he asked: "What is your pleasure this evening?"

"I have come this evening about that son of mine who is going to be confirmed to-morrow."

"He is a bright boy."

"I did not wish to pay the priest until I heard what number the boy would have when he takes his place in church tomorrow."

"He will stand number one."

"So I have heard; and here are ten dollars for the priest."

"Is there anything else I can do for you?" inquired the priest, fixing his eyes on Thord.

"There is nothing else."

Thord went out.

Eight years more rolled by, and then one day a noise was heard outside of the priest's study, for many men were approaching, and at their head was Thord, who entered first.

The priest looked up and recognized him.

"You come well attended this evening, Thord," said he.

"I am here to request that the banns may be published for my son; he is about to marry Karen Storliden, daughter of Gudmund, who stands here beside me."

"Why, that is the richest girl in the parish."

"So they say," replied the peasant, stroking back his hair with one hand.

The priest sat a while as if in deep thought, then entered the names in his book, without making any comments, and the men wrote their signatures underneath. Thord laid three dollars on the table.

"One is all I am to have," said the priest.

"I know that very well; but he is my only child, I want to do it handsomely."

The priest took the money.

"This is now the third time, Thord, that you have come here on your son's account."

"But now I am through with him," said Thord, and folding up his pocket-book he said farewell and walked away.

The men slowly followed him.

A fortnight later, the father and son were rowing across the lake, one calm, still day, to Storliden to make arrangements for the wedding.

"This thwart is not secure," said the son, and stood up to straighten the seat on which he was sitting.

At the same moment the board he was standing on slipped from under him; he threw out his arms, uttered a shriek, and fell overboard.

"Take hold of the oar!" shouted the father, springing to his feet and holding out the oar.

But when the son had made a couple of efforts he grew stiff.

"Wait a moment!" cried the father, and began to row toward his son. Then the son rolled over on his back, gave his father one long look, and sank.

Thord could scarcely believe it; he held the boat still, and stared at the spot where his son had gone down, as though he must surely come to the surface once again. There rose some bubbles, then some more, and finally one large one that burst; and the lake lay there as smooth and bright as a mirror again.

For three days and three nights people saw the father rowing round and round the spot, without taking either food or sleep; he was dragging the lake for the body of his son. And toward morning of the third day he found it, and carried it in his arms up over the hills to his gard.

It might have been about a year from that day, when the priest, late one autumn evening, heard someone in the passage outside of the door, carefully trying to find the latch. The priest opened the door, and in walked a tall, thin man, with bowed form and white hair. The priest looked long at him before he recognized him. It was Thord.

"Are you out walking so late?" said the priest, and stood still in front of him.

"Ah, yes! it is late," said Thord, and took a seat.

The priest sat down also, as though waiting. A long, long silence followed. At last Thord said:

"I have something with me that I should like to give to the poor; I want it to be invested as a legacy in my son's name."

He rose, laid some money on the table, and sat down again. The priest counted it.

"It is a great deal of money," said he.

"It is half the price of my gard. I sold it today."

The priest sat long in silence. At last he asked, but gently:

"What do you propose to do now, Thord?"

"Something better."

They sat there for a while, Thord with downcast eyes, the priest with his eyes fixed on Thord. Presently the priest said, slowly and softly:

"I think your son has at last brought you a true blessing."

"Yes, I think so myself," said Thord, looking up, while two big tears coursed slowly down his cheeks.

Neifile's Story

BY BOCCACCIO

📖 📖 📖

Chichibio, cook to Currado Gianfigliazzi, by a sudden reply which he made to his master, turns his wrath into laughter, and so escapes the punishment with which he had threatened him.

Though ready wit and invention furnish people with words proper to their different occasions, yet sometimes does Fortune, an assistant to the timorous, tip the tongue with a sudden and yet more pertinent reply than the most mature deliberation could ever have suggested, as I shall now briefly relate to you.

Currado Gianfigliazzi, as most of you have both known and seen, was always esteemed a gallant and worthy citizen, delighting much in hounds and hawks, to omit his other excellencies, as no way relating to our present purpose. Now he having taken a crane one day with his hawk, near the village of Peretola, and finding it to be young and fat, sent it home to his cook, who was a Venetian, and called Chichibio, with orders to prepare it delicately for supper. The cook, a poor simple fellow, trussed and spitted it, and when it was nearly roasted, and began to smell pretty well, it chanced that a woman in the neighbourhood called Brunetta, of whom he was much enamoured, came into the kitchen, and, being taken with the high savour, earnestly begged of him to give her a leg. He replied very merrily, singing all the time, "Donna Brunetta, you shall have no leg from me." Upon this she was a good deal nettled, and said, "As I hope to live, if you do not give it me, you need never expect any favour more from me." The dispute, at length, was carried to a great height between them; when, to make her easy, he was forced to give her one of the legs. Accordingly the crane was served up at supper, with only one leg, whereat a friend whom Currado had invited to sup with him expressed surprise. He therefore sent for the fellow, and demanded what was become of the other leg. The Venetian (a liar by nature) answered directly, "Sir, cranes have only one leg." Currado, in great wrath, said, "What the devil does the man talk of? Only one leg! Thou rascal, dost thou think I never saw a crane before?" Chichibio still persisted in his denial, saying, "Believe me, sir, it is as I say, and I will convince you of it whenever you please, by such fowls as are living." Currado was willing to have no more words, out of regard to his friend; only he added, "As thou undertakest to show me a thing which I never saw or heard of before, I am content to make proof thereof to-morrow morning; but I vow and protest, if I find it otherwise, I will make thee remember it the longest day thou hast to live."

Thus there was an end for that night, and the next morning Currado, whose passion would scarcely suffer him to get any rest, arose betimes, and ordered his horses to be brought out, taking Chichibio along with him towards a river where he used early in the morning to see plenty of cranes; and he said, "We shall soon see which of us spoke truth last night." Chichibio, finding his master's wrath not at all abated, and that he was now to make good what he had asserted, nor yet knowing how to do it, rode on first with all the fear imaginable; gladly would he have made his escape, but he saw no possible means, whilst he was continually looking about him, expecting everything that appeared to be a crane with two feet. But being come near to the river, he chanced to see, before anybody else, a dozen or so of cranes, each standing upon one leg, as they use to do when they are sleeping; whereupon, showing them quickly to his master, he said, "Now, sir, you yourself may see that I spoke nothing but truth, when I said that cranes have only one leg: look at those there, if you please." Currado, beholding the cranes, replied, "Yes, sirrah! but stay a while, and I will show thee that they have two." Then riding something nearer to them, he cried out, "Shough! shough!" which made them set down the other foot, and after taking a step or two they all flew away. Then Currado, turning to him, said, "Well, thou lying knave, art thou now convinced that they have two legs?" Chichibio, quite at his wits' end, and knowing scarcely what he said himself, suddenly made answer, "Yes, sir, but you did not shout out to the crane last night, as you have done to these; had you called to it in the same manner, it would have put down the other leg, as these have now done." This pleased Currado so much that, turning all wrath into mirth and laughter, he said, "Chichibio, thou sayest right; I should have done so indeed."

By this sudden and comical answer, Chichibio escaped a sound drubbing, and made peace with his master.

I See You Never

BY RAY BRADBURY

The soft knock came at the kitchen door, and when Mrs. O'Brian opened it, there on the back porch were her best tenant, Mr. Ramirez, and two police officers, one on each side of him. Mr. Ramirez just stood there, walled in and small.

"Why, Mr. Ramirez!" said Mrs. O'Brian.

Mr. Ramirez was overcome. He did not seem to have words to explain.

He had arrived at Mrs. O'Brian's rooming house more than two years earlier and had lived there ever since. He had come by bus from Mexico City to San Diego and had then gone up to Los Angeles. There he had found the clean little room with glossy blue linoleum, and pictures and calendars on the flowered walls, and Mrs. O'Brian as the strict but kindly landlady. During the war he had worked at the airplane factory and made parts for the planes that flew off somewhere, and even now, after the war, he still held his job. From the first he had made big money. He saved some of it, and he got drunk only once a week—a privilege that to Mrs. O'Brian's way of thinking, every good workingman deserved, unquestioned and unreprimanded.

Inside Mrs. O'Brian's kitchen, pies were baking in the oven. Soon the pies would come out with complexions like

Mr. Ramirez'—brown and shiny and crisp, with slits in them for the air almost like the slits of Mr. Ramirez' dark eyes. The kitchen smelled good. The policemen leaned forward, lured by the odor. Mr. Ramirez gazed at his feet, as if they had carried him into all this trouble.

"What happened, Mr. Ramirez?" asked Mrs. O'Brian.

Behind Mrs. O'Brian, as he lifted his eyes, Mr. Ramirez saw the long table laid with clean white linen and set with a platter, cool, shining glasses, and a water pitcher with ice cubes floating inside it, a bowl of fresh potato salad and one of bananas and oranges, cubed and sugared. At this table sat Mrs. O'Brian's children—her three grown sons, eating and conversing, and her two younger daughters, who were staring at the policemen as they ate.

"I have been here thirty months," said Mr. Ramirez quietly, looking at Mrs. O'Brian's plump hands.

"That's six months too long," said one policeman. "He only had a temporary visa. We've just got around to looking for him."

Soon after Mr. Ramirez had arrived he bought a radio for his little room; evenings he turned it up very loud and enjoyed it. And he had bought a wrist watch and enjoyed that too. And on many nights he had walked silent streets and seen the bright clothes in the windows and bought some of them, and he had seen the jewels and bought some of them for his few lady friends. And he had gone to picture shows five nights a week for a while. Then also, he had ridden the streetcars—all night some nights—smelling the electricity, his dark eyes moving over the advertisements, feeling the wheels rumble under him, watching the little sleeping houses and big hotels slip by. Besides that, he had gone to large restaurants, where he had eaten many-course dinners, and to the opera and the theater. And he had bought a car, which later, when he forgot to pay for it, the dealer had driven off angrily from in front of the rooming house.

"So here I am," said Mr. Ramirez now, "to tell you I must give up my room, Mrs. O'Brian. I come to get my luggage and clothes and go with these men."

"Back to Mexico?"

"Yes. To Lagos. That is a little town north of Mexico City."

"I'm sorry, Mr. Ramirez."

"I'm packed," said Mr. Ramirez hoarsely, blinking his dark eyes rapidly and moving his hands helplessly before him. The policemen did not touch him. There was no necessity for that.

"Here is the key, Mrs. O'Brian," Mr. Ramirez said. "I have my bag already."

Mrs. O'Brian, for the first time, noticed a suitcase standing behind him on the porch.

Mr. Ramirez looked in again at the huge kitchen, at the bright silver cutlery and the young people eating and the shining waxed floor. He turned and looked for a long moment at the apartment house next door, rising up three stories, high and beautiful. He looked at the balconies and fire escapes and back-porch stairs, at the lines of laundry snapping in the wind.

"You've been a good tenant," said Mrs. O'Brian.

"Thank you, thank you, Mrs. O'Brian," he said softly. He closed his eyes.

Mrs. O'Brian stood holding the door half open. One of her sons, behind her, said that her dinner was getting cold, but she shook her head at him and turned back to Mr. Ramirez. She remembered a visit she had once made to some Mexican border towns—the hot days, the endless crickets leaping and falling or lying dead and brittle like the small cigars in the shopwindows, and the canals taking river water out to the farms, the dirt roads, the scorched scape. She remembered the silent towns, the warm beer, the hot, thick foods each day. She remembered the slow, dragging horses and the parched jack rabbits on the road. She remembered the iron mountains and the dusty valleys and the ocean beaches that spread hundreds of miles with no sound but the waves—no cars, no buildings, nothing.

"I'm sure sorry, Mr. Ramirez," she said.

"I don't want to go back, Mrs. O'Brian," he said weakly. "I like it here, I want to stay here. I've worked, I've got money. I look all right, don't I? And I don't want to go back!"

"I'm sorry, Mr. Ramirez," she said. "I wish there was something I could do."

"Mrs. O'Brian!" he cried suddenly, tears rolling out under his eyelids. He reached out his hands and took her hand fervently, shaking it, wringing it, holding to it. "Mrs. O'Brian, I see you never, I see you never!"

The policemen smiled at this. But Mr. Ramirez did not notice it, and they stopped smiling very soon.

"Goodby, Mrs. O'Brian. You have been good to me. Oh, goodby, Mrs. O'Brian. I see you never!"

The policemen waited for Mr. Ramirez to turn, pick up
his suitcase, and walk away. Then they followed him, tip-
ping their hats to Mrs. O'Brian. She watched them go down
the porch steps. Then she shut the door quietly and went
slowly back to her chair at the table. She pulled the chair
and sat down. She picked up the shining knife and fork and
started once more upon her steak.

"Hurry up, Mom," said one of the sons. "It'll be cold."

Mrs. O'Brian took one bite and chewed on it for a long,
slow time; then she stared at the closed door. She laid
down her knife and fork.

"What's wrong, Ma?" asked her son.

"I just realized," said Mrs. O'Brian—she put her hand to
her face—"I'll never see Mr. Ramirez again."

The Lottery Ticket

BY VENTURA GARCIA CALDERÓN

You have heard this story before? No matter, I will tell
it again because it points to a moral, and, better than that,
to a state of mind. Also it is not without present-day interest.

The dancer, whom we will call Cielito, was the loveliest
Spanish "bailadora" of about fifteen years ago, though not in
the fashion of Madrid, where the taste in women at that
time was Turkish—for fat all over. She was the Medici
Venus, not the Milo—which measures three feet eleven inches
around the hips.

You remember Cielito's version of the rumba, with a
pink-tipped finger pointing to Heaven; and how the public
used to roar for one more look; and how she allowed it,
just for one second, smiling like an angel fallen in the worst
Gomorrah? If you have not seen Cielito dance the rumba,
you do not know tropical love. In her dancing she played instinctively the cruel game of rousing lust and leaving it. Like
the Persian butterfly, she was always playing with fire without ever getting burnt.

Cielito learned to dance in the West Indies, where this story takes place. The "danse du ventre" is a bourgeois family spectacle beside the swinging of the breasts. Breasts fit to be molded into beautiful cups, or like coupled doves to be caressed. The impish wanton shawl follows the swinging game, and at last, for a too brief unforgettable instant, is thrown aside.

One loses his head when one speaks of Cielito; which would hardly surprise her, for there is not a woman in the world who knows more about men than she does.

Once when she was touring in South America, she drove the men so mad that they had to have a lottery for her. Yes, a singular idea, but not really so strange in Cuba, where we leave everything to chance, even the pretty women. Well, in this distant town of the island of sugar cane and honey, the spectators were able one night to buy with their theater tickets the chance of taking Cielito away with them after the performance. Only one spectator could win, of course, but in the crowds at the booking-office every man was Don Juan looking with hatred at his possible rival, the neighbor who was also buying the right to be the happiest of men.

Even Cielito was a little moved when the evening came, and there was something almost chaste in her languorous glances at the audience who riotously refused any other music-hall items. They only wanted Cielito with her shuffling false-Negro steps and very soft Creole words "arza columpiate." But there were no passionate encores, no one asked Cielito to carry her perversity any further. Everyone was in too great a hurry for the draw, which was very correctly carried out, like a family lottery, on the stage itself.

A top hat was filled with numbered place-slips, and the draw was presided over by the theater manager; rather pale and nervous, for any suspicion of trickery would have been punished on the spot, and there's no knowing what may happen when a lot of violent men are after the same girl. Believe me, it was more than mere lust for a beautiful woman; you have no idea how much magic and romance is attached to any European actress by South Americans dreaming of Montmartre and Andalusia. A Frenchwoman is all Paris to them, a Spaniard is Seville or Granada with the chirrup of grasshoppers in the sunshine. These phantasies are a sort of feverish mental stimulant to our people, and a beautiful body does not help to lessen the fever.

At exactly midnight the winning number, 213, was called by a man in evening dress who had turned his back on the hat and unhesitatingly drawn a slip of paper.

The whole room looked for the winner, some mocking voices called for him to go up on the stage so that everyone could see him before he went into the wings with Cielito.

No one answered, and there was an expectant silence. A spectator who had come very near success jogged the elbow of his neighbor in seat 213, almost forcing him to rise.

He was a fine-looking Negro, "a bit of ebony" the conquistadores would have called him; "black as sin" the old women say even now. He rose slowly with the charming comic solemnity of the colored people, whose vain smile fitly answers the amused glances of the crowd. With deliberate slowness he looked through his note-case for the ticket, found it at last in a greasy envelope, and tore it up into very small pieces which he threw in the air like confetti before the astounded audience.

That ample gesture ought to have made his refusal clear enough. But the people could not believe he was rejecting Cielito, the finest flower of Spain. So he shook his head, looking grave and sulky, but enjoying very much the displeasure he was causing.

All the bitterness of the subject races was in him, all the misery of his ancestors who had died as slaves among the sugar cane. The hot joy of revenge burned on his obstinate coal-black face as he disdained what so many white men had dreamed about with longing. Then with a shrug of his shoulders, very dignified and sure of his importance, he prepared to leave the theater, while from the stage Cielito with her hands on her hips in a truly Spanish fury spat out at him her shame and her disgust.

But there was no need of a word from her. The whole audience rushed on the black man and began to beat him. So he did not want the flower of Spain—he was disgusted with the darling of Andalusia—they would show him—they would finish him.

It was a most unlooked-for lynching, unknown no doubt in the United States where they don't yet punish the abstemious Negro who refuses to "outrage" a white woman.

Half an hour afterwards they sent the dying man to hospital; and as they have given up drawing lots for Cielito, I will not bother you with the address of the theater.

Daughter

BY ERSKINE CALDWELL

At sunrise a Negro on his way to the big house to feed the mules had taken the word to Colonel Henry Maxwell, and Colonel Henry phoned the sheriff. The sheriff had hustled Jim into town and locked him up in the jail, and then he went home and ate breakfast.

Jim walked around the empty cellroom while he was buttoning his shirt, and after that he sat down on the bunk and tied his shoelaces. Everything that morning had taken place so quickly that he had not even had time to get a drink of water. He got up and went to the water bucket near the door, but the sheriff had forgotten to put water into it.

By that time there were several men standing in the jail-yard. Jim went to the window and looked out when he heard them talking. Just then another automobile drove up, and six or seven men got out. Other men were coming towards the jail from both directions of the street.

"What was the trouble out at your place this morning, Jim?" somebody said.

Jim stuck his chin between the bars and looked at the faces in the crowd. He knew everyone there.

While he was trying to figure out how everybody in town had heard about his being there, somebody else spoke to him.

"It must have been an accident, wasn't it, Jim?"

A colored boy hauling a load of cotton to the gin drove up the street. When the wagon got in front of the jail, the boy whipped up the mules with the ends of the reins and made them trot.

"I hate to see the State have a grudge against you, Jim," somebody said.

The sheriff came down the street swinging a tin dinner pail in his hand. He pushed through the crowd, unlocked the door, and set the pail inside.

35

Several men came up behind the sheriff and looked over his shoulder into the jail.

"Here's your breakfast my wife fixed up for you, Jim. You'd better eat a little, Jim boy."

Jim looked at the pail, at the sheriff, at the open jail door, and he shook his head.

"I don't feel hungry," he said. "Daughter's been hungry, though—awful hungry."

The sheriff backed out the door, his hand going to the handle of his pistol. He backed out so quickly that he stepped on the toes of the men behind him.

"Now, don't you get careless, Jim boy," he said. "Just sit and calm yourself."

He shut the door and locked it. After he had gone a few steps towards the street, he stopped and looked into the chamber of his pistol to make sure it had been loaded.

The crowd outside the window pressed in closer. Some of the men rapped on the bars until Jim came and looked out. When he saw them, he stuck his chin between the iron and gripped his hands around it.

"How come it to happen, Jim?" somebody asked. "It must have been an accident, wasn't it?"

Jim's long thin face looked as if it would come through the bars. The sheriff came up to the window to see if everything was all right.

"Now, just take it easy, Jim boy," he said.

The man who had asked Jim to tell what had happened elbowed the sheriff out of the way. The other men crowded closer.

"How come, Jim?" the man said. "Was it an accident?"

"No," Jim said, his fingers twisting about the bars. "I picked up my shotgun and done it."

The sheriff pushed towards the window again.

"Go on, Jim, and tell us what it's all about."

Jim's face squeezed between the bars until it looked as though only his ears kept his head from coming through.

"Daughter said she was hungry, and I just couldn't stand it no longer. I just couldn't stand to hear her say it."

"Don't get all excited now, Jim boy," the sheriff said, pushing forward one moment and being elbowed away the next.

"She waked up in the middle of the night again and said she was hungry. I just couldn't stand to hear her say it."

Somebody pushed all the way through the crowd until he got to the window.

"Why, Jim, you could have come and asked me for something for her to eat, and you know I'd have given you all I got in the world."

The sheriff pushed forward once more.

"That wasn't the right thing to do," Jim said. "I've been working all year and I made enough for all of us to eat."

He stopped and looked down into the faces on the other side of the bars.

"I made enough working on shares, but they came and took it all away from me. I couldn't go around begging after I'd made enough to keep us. They just came and took it all off. Then Daughter woke up again this morning saying she was hungry, and I just couldn't stand it no longer."

"You'd better go and get on the bunk now, Jim boy," the sheriff said.

"It don't seem right that the little girl ought to be shot like that," somebody said.

"Daughter said she was hungry," Jim said. "She'd been saying that for all of the past month. Daughter'd wake up in the middle of the night and say it. I just couldn't stand it no longer."

"You ought to have sent her over to my house, Jim. Me and my wife could have fed her something, somehow. It don't look right to kill a little girl like her."

"I'd made enough for all of us," Jim said. "I just couldn't stand it no longer. Daughter'd been hungry all the past month."

"Take it easy, Jim boy," the sheriff said, trying to push forward.

The crowd swayed from side to side.

"And so you picked up the gun this morning and shot her?" somebody asked.

"When she woke up this morning saying she was hungry, I just couldn't stand it."

The crowd pushed closer. Men were coming towards the jail from all directions, and those who were then arriving pushed forward to hear what Jim had to say.

"The State has got a grudge against you now, Jim," somebody said, "but somehow it don't seem right."

"I can't help it," Jim said. "Daughter woke up again this morning that way."

The jailyard, the street, and the vacant lot on the other side were filled with men and boys. All of them were pushing forward to hear Jim. Word had spread all over town by that time that Jim Carlisle had shot and killed his eight-year-old daughter, Clara.

"Who does Jim share-crop for?" somebody asked.

"Colonel Henry Maxwell," a man in the crowd said. "Colonel Henry has had Jim out there about nine or ten years."

"Henry Maxwell didn't have no business coming and taking all the shares. He's got plenty of his own. It ain't right for Henry Maxwell to come and take Jim's, too."

The sheriff was pushing forward once more.

"The State's got a grudge against Jim now," somebody said. "Somehow it don't seem right, though."

The sheriff pushed his shoulder into the crowd of men and worked his way in closer.

A man shoved the sheriff away.

"Why did Henry Maxwell come and take your share of the crop, Jim?"

"He said I owed it to him because one of his mules died about a month ago."

The sheriff got in front of the barred window.

"You ought to go to the bunk now and rest some, Jim boy," he said. "Take off your shoes and stretch out, Jim boy."

He was elbowed out of the way.

"You didn't kill the mule, did you, Jim?"

"The mule dropped dead in the barn," Jim said. "I wasn't nowhere around it. It just dropped dead."

The crowd was pushing harder. The men in front were jammed against the jail, and the men behind were trying to get within earshot. Those in the middle were squeezed against each other so tightly they could not move in any direction. Everyone was talking louder.

Jim's face pressed between the bars and his fingers gripped the iron until the knuckles were white.

The milling crowd was moving across the street to the vacant lot. Somebody was shouting. He climbed up on an automobile and began swearing at the top of his lungs.

A man in the middle of the crowd pushed his way out and went to his automobile. He got in and drove off alone.

Jim stood holding to the bars and looking through the window. The sheriff had his back to the crowd, and he was saying something to Jim. Jim did not hear what he said.

A man on his way to the gin with a load of cotton stopped to find out what the trouble was. He looked at the crowd in the vacant lot for a moment, and then he turned around and looked at Jim behind the bars. The shouting across the street was growing louder.

"What's the trouble, Jim?"

Somebody on the other side of the street came to the wagon. He put his foot on a spoke in the wagon wheel and looked up at the man on the cotton while he talked.

"Daughter woke up this morning again saying she was hungry," Jim said.

The sheriff was the only person who heard him.

The man on the load of cotton jumped to the ground, tied the reins to the wagon wheel, and pushed through the crowd to the car where all the shouting and swearing was being done. After listening for a while, he came back to the street, called a Negro who was standing with several other Negroes on the corner, and handed him the reins. The Negro drove off with the cotton towards the gin, and the man went back into the crowd.

Just then the man who had driven off alone in his car came back. He sat for a moment behind the steering wheel, and then he jumped to the ground. He opened the rear door and took out a crowbar that was as long as he was tall.

"Pry that jail door open and let Jim out," somebody said. "It ain't right for him to be in there."

The crowd in the vacant lot was moving again. The man who had been standing on top of the automobile jumped to the ground, and the men moved towards the street in the direction of the jail.

The first man to reach it jerked the six-foot crowbar out of the soft earth where it had been jabbed.

The sheriff backed off.

"Now, take it easy, Jim boy," he said.

He turned and started walking rapidly up the street towards his house.

A Wicked Boy

BY ANTON CHEKHOV

▣ ▣ ▣

Ivan Ivanych Lapkin, a young man of nice appearance, and Anna Semionovna Zamblitskaia, a young girl with a little turned-up nose, went down the steep bank and sat down on a small bench. The bench stood right by the water among some thick young osier bushes. What a wonderful little place! Once you'd sat down, you were hidden from the world —only the fish saw you, and the water-tigers, running like lightning over the water. The young people were armed with rods, nets, cans of worms, and other fishing equipment. Having sat down, they started fishing right away.

"I'm glad we're alone at last," Lapkin began, looking around. "I have to tell you a lot of things, Anna Semionovna . . . an awful lot . . . when I saw you the first time. . . . You've got a bite . . . then I understood what I'm living for, understood where my idol was—to whom I must devote my honest, active life . . . that must be a big one that's biting. . . . Seeing you, I feel in love for the first time, feel passionately in love! Wait before you give it a jerk . . . let it bite harder. . . . Tell me, my darling, I adjure you, may I count on—not on reciprocity, no! I'm not worthy of that, I dare not even think of that—may I count on. . . . Pull!"

Anna Semionovna raised her hand with the rod in it, yanked, and cried out. A little silvery-green fish shimmered in the air.

"My Lord, a perch! Ah, ah. . . . Quickly! It's getting free!"

The perch got free of the hook, flopped through the grass toward its native element . . . and plopped into the water!

In pursuit of the fish, Lapkin somehow inadvertently grabbed Anna Semionovna's hand instead of the fish, inadvertently pressed it to his lips. . . . She quickly drew it back, but it was already too late; their mouths inadvertently merged in a kiss. It happened somehow inadvertently. Another kiss followed the first, then vows and protestations . . . What happy minutes! However, in this earthly life there is no absolute happiness. Happiness usually carries a poison in itself, or else is poisoned by something from outside. So this time, too. As the young people were kissing, a laugh suddenly rang out. They glanced at the river and were stupefied: a naked boy was standing in the water up to his waist. This was Kolia, a schoolboy, Anna Semionovna's brother. He was standing in the water, staring at the young people, and laughing maliciously.

"Ah-ah-ah . . . you're kissing?" he said. "That's great! I'll tell Mama."

"I hope that you, as an honest young man, . . ." muttered Lapkin, blushing. "It's low-down to spy, and to tell tales is foul and detestable . . . I assume that you, as an honest and noble young man . . ."

"Give me a ruble and then I won't tell!" said the noble young man. "Or else I will."

Lapkin pulled a ruble out of his pocket and gave it to Kolia. Kolia squeezed the ruble in his wet fist, whistled, and swam off. And the young people didn't kiss any more that time.

The next day Lapkin brought Kolia some paints and a ball from town, and his sister gave him all her empty pill-boxes. After that they had to give him some cuff-links with dogs' heads on them. The wicked boy obviously liked all these things very much and, in order to get still more, he started keeping his eye on them. Wherever Lapkin and Anna Semionovna went, he went, too. He didn't leave them alone for a minute.

"The bastard!" Lapkin gnashed his teeth. "So little, and already such a real bastard! What's he going to be like later?!"

All through June, Kolia made life impossible for the poor lovers. He threatened to tell on them, kept his eye on them, and demanded presents; it all wasn't enough for him, and he finally started talking about a pocket watch. And what then? They had to promise the watch.

One time at dinner, when the waffle cookies were being passed, he suddenly burst out in a guffaw, winked an eye, and asked Lapkin:

"Shall I tell? Huh?"

Lapkin blushed terribly and started eating his napkin instead of the cookie. Anna Semionovna jumped up from the table and ran into the other room.

And the young people found themselves in this position until the end of August, until the very day when, at last, Lapkin proposed to Anna Semionovna. Oh, what a happy day that was! Having talked to the parents of his bride, and having received their consent, Lapkin first of all ran out into the garden and started looking for Kolia. Once he had found him, he almost sobbed from delight and seized the wicked boy by the ear. Anna Semionovna, who had also been looking for Kolia, ran up, and seized him by the other ear. And you really ought to have seen what joy was written all over the lovers' faces as Kolia cried and begged them:

"Dearest, darling, angels, I'll never do it again! Ow, ow! Forgive me!"

And afterwards they both admitted that during the whole time they had been in love with each other they had never once felt such happiness, such breath-taking bliss as during those moments when they were pulling the wicked boy's ears.

Luck

BY SAMUEL CLEMENS

📖 📖 📖

It was at a banquet in London in honor of one of the two or three conspicuously illustrious English military names of this generation. For reasons which will presently appear, I will withhold his real name and titles and call him Lieutenant-General Lord Arthur Scoresby, Y.C., K.C.B., etc, etc, etc. What a fascination there is in a renowned name! There sat the man, in actual flesh, whom I had heard of so many thousands of times since that day, thirty years before, when his name shot suddenly to the zenith from a Crimean battlefield, to remain forever celebrated. It was food and drink to me to look, and look, and look at that demigod; scanning, searching, noting: the quietness, the reserve, the noble gravity of his countenance; the simple honesty that expressed itself all over him; the sweet unconsciousness of his greatness—unconsciousness of the hundreds of admiring eyes fastened upon him, unconsciousness of the deep, loving, sincere worship welling out of the breasts of those people and flowing toward him.

The clergyman at my left was an old acquaintance of mine—clergyman now, but had spent the first half of his life in the camp and field and as an instructor in the military school at Woolwich. Just at the moment I have been talking about a veiled and singular light glimmered in his eyes and he leaned down and muttered confidentially to me—indicating the hero of the banquet with a gesture:

"Privately—he's an absolute fool."

This verdict was a great surprise to me. If its subject had been Napoleon, or Socrates, or Solomon, my astonishment could not have been greater. Two things I was well aware of: that the Reverend was a man of strict veracity and that his judgment of men was good. Therefore I knew, beyond doubt or question, that the world was mistaken about this hero: he *was* a fool. So I meant to find out, at a convenient moment, how the Reverend, all solitary and alone, had discovered the secret.

Some days later the opportunity came, and this is what the Reverend told me:

About forty years ago I was an instructor in the military academy at Woolwich. I was present in one of the sections when young Scoresby underwent his preliminary examination. I was touched to the quick with pity, for the rest of the class answered up brightly and handsomely, while he—why, dear me, he didn't know anything, so to speak. He was evidently good, and sweet, and lovable, and guileless; and so it was exceedingly painful to see him stand there, as serene as a graven image, and deliver himself of answers which were verily miraculous for stupidity and ignorance. All the compassion in me was aroused in his behalf. I said to myself, when he comes to be examined again he will be flung over, of course; so it will be simply a harmless act of charity to ease his fall as much as I can. I took him aside and found that he knew a little of Caesar's history; and as he didn't know anything else, I went to work and drilled him like a galley-slave on a certain line of stock questions concerning Caesar which I knew would be used. If you'll believe me, he went through with flying colors on examination day! He went through on that purely superficial "cram," and got compliments too, while others, who knew a thousand times more than he, got plucked. By some strangely lucky accident—an accident not likely to happen twice in a century —he was asked no question outside of the narrow limits of his drill.

It was stupefying. Well, all through his course I stood by him, with something of the sentiment which a mother feels for a crippled child; and he always saved himself, just by miracle apparently.

Now, of course, the thing that would expose him and kill him at last was mathematics. I resolved to make his death as easy as I could; so I drilled him and crammed him, and crammed him and drilled him, just on the line of questions which the examiners would be most likely to use, and then launched him on his fate. Well, sir, try to conceive of the result: to my consternation, he took the first prize! And with it he got a perfect ovation in the way of compliments.

Sleep? There was no more sleep for me for a week. My conscience tortured me day and night. What I had done I had done purely through charity, and only to ease the poor youth's fall. I never had dreamed of any such preposterous results as the thing that had happened. I felt as guilty and miserable as Frankenstein. Here was a wooden-head whom I had put in the way of glittering promotions and prodigious responsibilities, and but one thing could happen: he and his responsibilities would all go to ruin together at the first opportunity.

The Crimean War had just broken out. Of course there had to be a war, I say to myself. We could have peace and give this donkey a chance to die before he is found out. I waited for the earthquake. It came. And it made me reel when it did come. He was actually gazetted to a captaincy in a marching regiment! Better men grow old and gray in the service before they climb to a sublimity like that. And who could ever have foreseen that they would go and put such a load of responsibility on such green and inadequate shoulders? I could just barely have stood it if they had made him a cornet; but a captain—think of it! I thought my hair would turn white.

Consider what I did—I who so loved repose and inaction. I said to myself, I am responsible to the country for this, and I must go along with him and protect the country against him as far as I can. So I took my poor little capital and went with a sigh and bought a cornetcy in his regiment, and away we went to the field.

And there—oh, dear, it was awful. Blunders?—why, he never did anything *but* blunder. But, you see, nobody was in the fellow's secret. Everybody had him focused wrong, and necessarily misinterpreted his performance every time. Consequently they took his idiotic blunders for inspirations of genius. They did, honestly! His mildest blunders were enough to make a man in his right mind cry; and they did make me cry—and rage and rave, too, privately. And the thing that kept me always in a sweat of apprehension was the fact that every fresh blunder he made always increased the luster of his reputation! I kept saying to myself, he'll get so high that when discovery does finally come it will be like the sun falling out of the sky.

He went right along up, from grade to grade, over the dead bodies of his superiors, until at last, in the hottest moment of the battle of — down went our colonel, and my heart jumped into my mouth, for Scoresby was next in rank! Now for it, said I; we'll all land in Sheol in ten minutes, sure.

The battle was awfully hot; the allies were steadily giving way all over the field. Our regiment occupied a position that was vital; a blunder now must be destruction. At this crucial moment, what does this immortal fool do but detach the regiment from its place and order a charge over a neighboring hill where there wasn't a suggestion of an enemy! "There you go!" I said to myself; "this *is* the end at last."

And away we did go, and were over the shoulder of the hill before the insane movement could be discovered and stopped. And what did we find? An entire and unsuspected Russian army in reserve! And what happened? We were eaten up? That is necessarily what would have happened in ninety-nine cases out of a hundred. But no; those Russians argued that no single regiment would come browsing around there at such a time. It must be the entire English army, and that the sly Russian game was detected and blocked; so they turned tail, and away they went, pell-mell, over the hill and down into the field, in wild confusion, and we after them; they themselves broke the solid Russian center in the field, and tore through, and in no time there was the most tremendous rout you ever saw, and the defeat of the allies was turned into a sweeping and splendid victory! Marshal Canrobert looked on, dizzy with astonishment, admiration, and delight; and sent right off for Scoresby and hugged him, and decorated him on the field in presence of all the armies!

And what was Scoresby's blunder that time? Merely the mistaking his right hand for his left—that was all. An order had come to him to fall back and support our right; and instead, he fell *forward* and went over the hill to the left. But the name he won that day as a marvelous military genius filled the world with his glory, and that glory will never fade while history books last.

He is just as good and sweet and lovable and unpretending as a man can be, but he doesn't know enough to come in when it rains. Now that is absolutely true. He is the supremest ass in the universe; and until half an hour ago nobody knew it but himself and me. He has been pursued, day by day and year by year, by a most phenomenal and astonishing luckiness. He has been a shining soldier in all our wars for a generation; he has littered his whole military life with blunders, and yet has never committed one that didn't make him a knight or a baronet or a lord or something. Look at his breast; why, he is just clothed in domestic and foreign decorations. Well, sir, every one of them is the record of some shouting stupidity or other; and, taken together, they are proof that the very best thing in all this world that can befall a man is to be born lucky. I say again, as I said at the banquet, Scoresby's an absolute fool.

The Chaser

BY JOHN COLLIER

Alan Austen, as nervous as a kitten, went up certain dark and creaky stairs in the neighborhood of Pell Street, and peered about for a long time on the dim landing before he found the name he wanted written obscurely on one of the doors.

He pushed open this door, as he had been told to do, and found himself in a tiny room, which contained no furniture but a plain kitchen table, a rocking-chair, and an ordinary chair. On one of the dirty buff-coloured walls were a couple of shelves, containing in all perhaps a dozen bottles and jars.

An old man sat in the rocking-chair, reading a newspaper. Alan, without a word, handed him the card he had been given. "Sit down, Mr. Austen," said the old man very politely. "I am glad to make your acquaintance."

"Is it true," asked Alan, "that you have a certain mixture that has—er—quite extraordinary effects?"

"My dear sir," replied the old man, "my stock in trade is not very large—I don't deal in laxatives and teething mixtures—but such as it is, it is varied. I think nothing I sell has effects which could be precisely described as ordinary."

"Well, the fact is . . . " began Alan.

"Here, for example," interrupted the old man, reaching for a bottle from the shelf. "Here is a liquid as colourless as water, almost tasteless, quite imperceptible in coffee, wine, or any other beverage. It is also quite imperceptible to any known method of autopsy."

"Do you mean it is a poison?" cried Alan, very much horrified.

"Call it a glove-cleaner if you like," said the old man indifferently. "Maybe it will clean gloves. I have never tried. One might call it a life-cleaner. Lives need cleaning sometimes."

"I want nothing of that sort," said Alan.

"Probably it is just as well," said the old man. "Do you know the price of this? For one teaspoonful, which is sufficient, I ask five thousand dollars. Never less. Not a penny less."

"I hope all your mixtures are not as expensive," said Alan apprehensively.

"Oh dear, no," said the old man. "It would be no good charging that sort of price for a love potion, for example. Young people who need a love potion very seldom have five thousand dollars. Otherwise they would not need a love potion."

"I am glad to hear that," said Alan.

"I look at it like this," said the old man. "Please a customer with one article, and he will come back when he needs another. Even if it *is* more costly. He will save up for it, if necessary."

"So," said Alan, "you really do sell love potions?"

"If I did not sell love potions," said the old man, reaching for another bottle, "I should not have mentioned the other matter to you. It is only when one is in a position to oblige that one can afford to be so confidential."

"And these potions," said Alan. "They are not just—just—er—"

"Oh, no," said the old man. "Their effects are permanent, and extend far beyond the mere casual impulse. But they include it. Oh, yes, they include it. Bountifully, insistently. Everlastingly."

"Dear me!" said Alan, attempting a look of scientific detachment. "How very interesting!"

"But consider the spiritual side," said the old man.

"I do, indeed," said Alan.

"For indifference," said the old man, "they substitute

devotion. For scorn, adoration. Give one tiny measure of this to the young lady—its flavour is imperceptible in orange juice, soup, or cocktails—and however gay and giddy she is, she will change altogether. She will want nothing but solitude and you."

"I can hardly believe it," said Alan. "She is so fond of parties."

"She will not like them any more," said the old man. "She will be afraid of the pretty girls you may meet."

"She will actually be jealous?" cried Alan in a rapture. "Of me?"

"Yes, she will want to be everything to you."

"She is, already. Only she doesn't care about it."

"She will, when she has taken this. She will care intensely. You will be her sole interest in life."

"Wonderful!" cried Alan.

"She will want to know all you do," said the old man. "All that has happened to you during the day. Every word of it. She will want to know what you are thinking about, why you smile suddenly, why you are looking sad."

"That is love!" cried Alan.

"Yes," said the old man. "How carefully she will look after you! She will never allow you to be tired, to sit in a draught, to neglect your food. If you are an hour late, she will be terrified. She will think you are killed, or that some siren has caught you."

"I can hardly imagine Diana like that!" cried Alan, overwhelmed with joy.

"You will not have to use your imagination," said the old man. "And, by the way, since there are always sirens, if by any chance you *should*, later on, slip a little, you need not worry. She will forgive you, in the end. She will be terribly hurt, of course, but she will forgive you—in the end."

"That will not happen," said Alan fervently.

"Of course not," said the old man. "But, if it did, you need not worry. She would never divorce you. Oh, no! And, of course, she will never give you the least, the very least, grounds for—uneasiness."

"And how much," said Alan, "is this wonderful mixture?"

"It is not as dear," said the old man, "as the glove-cleaner, or life-cleaner, as I sometimes call it. No. That is five thousand dollars, never a penny less. One has to be older than you are, to indulge in that sort of thing. One has to save up for it."

"But the love potion?" said Alan.

"Oh, that," said the old man, opening the drawer in the kitchen table, and taking out a tiny, rather dirty-looking phial. "That is just a dollar."

"I can't tell you how grateful I am," said Alan, watching him fill it.

"I like to oblige," said the old man. "Then customers come back, later in life, when they are better off, and want more expensive things. Here you are. You will find it very effective."

"Thank you again," said Alan. "Good-bye."

"Au revoir," said the old man.

The Upturned Face

BY STEPHEN CRANE

 ▨ ▨ ▨

"What will we do now?" said the adjutant, troubled and excited.

"Bury him," said Timothy Lean.

The two officers looked down close to their toes where lay the body of their comrade. The face was chalk-blue; gleaming eyes stared at the sky. Over the two upright figures was a windy sound of bullets, and on top of the hill Lean's prostrate company of Spitzbergen infantry was firing measured volleys.

"Don't you think it would be better—" began the adjutant. "We might leave him until tomorrow."

"No," said Lean. "I can't hold that post an hour longer. I've got to fall back, and we've got to bury old Bill."

"Of course," said the adjutant, at once. "Your men got entrenching tools?"

Lean shouted back to his little line, and two men came slowly, one with a pick, one with a shovel. They started in the direction of the Rostina sharpshooters. Bullets cracked near their ears. "Dig here," said Lean gruffly. The men, thus caused to lower their glances to the turf, became hurried and frightened, merely because they could not look to see whence the bullets came. The dull beat of the pick striking the earth sounded amid the swift snap of close bullets. Presently the other private began to shovel.

"I suppose," said the adjutant slowly, "we'd better search his clothes for—things."

Lean nodded. Together in curious abstraction they looked at the body. Then Lean stirred his shoulders suddenly, arousing himself.

"Yes," he said, "we'd better see what he's got." He dropped to his knee, and his hands approached the body of the dead officer. But his hands wavered over the buttons of the tunic. The first button was brick-red with drying blood, and he did not seem to dare to touch it.

"Go on," said the adjutant, hoarsely.

Lean stretched his wooden hand, and his fingers fumbled the bloodstained buttons. At last he rose with ghastly face. He had gathered a watch, a whistle, a pipe, a tobacco-pouch, a handkerchief, a little case of cards and papers. He looked at the adjutant. There was a silence. The adjutant was feeling that he had been a coward to make Lean do all the grisly business.

"Well," said Lean, "that's all, I think. You have his sword and revolver?"

"Yes," said the adjutant, his face working, and then he burst out in a sudden strange fury at the two privates. "Why don't you hurry up with that grave? What are you doing, anyhow? Hurry, do you hear? I never saw such stupid—"

Even as he cried out in his passion, the two men were labouring for their lives. Ever overhead the bullets were spitting.

The grave was finished. It was not a masterpiece—a poor little shallow thing. Lean and the adjutant again looked at each other in a curious silent communication.

Suddenly the adjutant croaked out a weird laugh. It was a terrible laugh which had its origin in that part of the mind which is first moved by the singing of the nerves. "Well," he said humorously to Lean, "I suppose we had best tumble him in."

"Yes," said Lean. The two privates stood waiting, bent over their implements. "I suppose," said Lean, "it would be better if we laid him in ourselves."

"Yes," said the adjutant. Then, apparently remembering

that he had made Lean search the body, he stooped with great fortitude and took hold of the dead officer's clothing. Lean joined him. Both were particular that their fingers should not feel the corpse. They tugged away; the corpse lifted, heaved, toppled, flopped into the grave, and the two officers, straightening, looked again at each other—they were always looking at each other. They sighed with relief.

The adjutant said, "I suppose we should—we should say something. Do you know the service, Tim?"

"They don't read the service until the grave is filled in," said Lean, pressing his lips to an academic expression.

"Don't they?" said the adjutant, shocked that he had made the mistake. "Oh, well," he cried, suddenly, "let us—let us say something—while he can hear us."

"All right," said Lean. "Do you know the service?"

"I can't remember a line of it," said the adjutant.

Lean was extremely dubious. "I can repeat two lines, but—"

"Well, do it," said the adjutant. "Go as far as you can. That's better than nothing. And the beasts have got our range exactly."

Lean looked at his two men. "Attention," he barked. The privates came to attention with a click, looking much aggrieved. The adjutant lowered his helmet to his knee. Lean, bareheaded, stood over the grave. The Rostina sharpshooters fired briskly.

"O Father, our friend has sunk in the deep waters of death, but his spirit has leaped toward Thee as the bubble arises from the lips of the drowning. Perceive, we beseech, O Father, the little flying bubble, and—"

Lean, although husky and ashamed, had suffered no hesitation up to this point, but he stopped with a hopeless feeling and looked at the corpse.

The adjutant moved uneasily. "And from Thy superb heights," he began, and then he too came to an end.

"And from Thy superb heights," said Lean.

The adjutant suddenly remembered a phrase in the back of the Spitzbergen burial service, and he exploited it with the triumphant manner of a man who has recalled everything, and can go on.

"O God, have mercy—"

"O God, have mercy—" said Lean.

"Mercy," repeated the adjutant, in quick failure.

"Mercy," said Lean. And then he was moved by some

violence of feeling, for he turned upon his two men and tigerishly said, "Throw the dirt in."

The fire of the Rostina sharpshooters was accurate and continuous.

One of the aggrieved privates came forward with his shovel. He lifted his first shovel-load of earth, and for a moment of inexplicable hesitation it was held poised above this corpse which from its chalk-blue face looked keenly out from the grave. Then the soldier emptied his shovel on—on the feet.

Timothy Lean felt as if tons had been swiftly lifted from off his forehead. He had felt that perhaps the private might empty the shovel on—on the face. It had been emptied on the feet. There was a great point gained there—ha, ha!—the first shovelful had been emptied on the feet. How satisfactory!

The adjutant began to babble. "Well, of course—a man we've messed with all these years—impossible—you can't, you know, leave your intimate friends rotting on the field. Go on, for God's sake, and shovel, you."

The man with the shovel suddenly ducked, grabbed his left arm with his right hand, and looked at his officer for orders. Lean picked the shovel from the ground. "Go to the rear," he said to the wounded man. He also addressed the other private. "You get under cover, too; I'll finish this business."

The wounded man scrambled hard for the top of the ridge without devoting any glances to the direction from whence the bullets came, and the other man followed at an equal pace; but he was different, in that he looked back anxiously three times.

This is merely the way—often—of the hit and unhit.

Timothy Lean filled the shovel, hesitated, and then, in a movement which was like a gesture of abhorrence, he flung the dirt into the grave, and as it landed it made a sound—plop. Lean suddenly stopped and mopped his brow—a tired labourer.

"Perhaps we have been wrong," said the adjutant. His glance wavered stupidly. "It might have been better if we hadn't buried him just at this time. Of course, if we advance tomorrow the body would have been—"

"Damn you," said Lean, "shut your mouth." He was not the senior officer.

He again filled the shovel and flung the earth. Always

the earth made that sound—plop. For a space, Lean worked frantically, like a man digging himself out of danger.

Soon there was nothing to be seen but the chalk-blue face. Lean filled the shovel. "Good God," he cried to the adjutant. "Why didn't you turn him somehow when you put him in? This—" Then Lean began to stutter.

The adjutant understood. He was pale to the lips. "Go on, man," he cried, beseechingly, almost in a shout.

Lean swung back the shovel. It went forward in a pendulum curve. When the earth landed it made a sound—plop.

A Game of Billiards

BY ALPHONSE DAUDET

Even veterans are exhausted after two days' fighting, especially if they have passed the night, knapsacks on their backs, standing in torrents of rain. Yet for three mortal hours they had been left to wait in puddles along the highway; in the mire of rain-soaked fields.

Heavy with fatigue, weakened by the effects of previous nights, their uniforms drenched, they press together for warmth and support. Here and there, leaning upon a comrade's knapsack, a man falls asleep—standing; and upon the relaxed faces of these men, overcome by sleep, may be read more plainly than before the traces which weariness and privation have made. In the mud and rain, without fire, without food; overhead the sky heavy and lowering—around them, on every side, the enemy.

Their cannon, mouths turned towards the woods, seem to be lying in wait. The machine guns, from their hiding places, stare fixedly at the horizon. All is ready for an attack. Why is none made? What are they waiting for?

They await orders from headquarters, but none come.

And yet it is only a short distance to headquarters, to that beautiful Louis XIII chateau whose red brick walls, washed by the rain, are seen half way up the hill, glistening through the thickets. Truly a princely dwelling, well worthy of bearing the banner of a Marshal of France. Upon an artificial pond which sparkles like a mirror, swans are swimming, and under the pagoda-shaped roof of a large aviary, peacocks and golden pheasants strut about, spreading their wings and sending their shrill cries through the foliage. Though the owners of the house have departed, nowhere is there a perceptible sign of that ruin and desolation which war brings in its train; not the smallest flower dotting the lawn has been destroyed and it is indescribably charming to observe. Such evenly trimmed shrubbery, such silent avenues of shade; yet so near the battlefield! The scene is peaceful. Were it not for the flag floating from the top of the roof, and the sight of two sentinels before the gate, one would never believe headquarters were here.

In the dining room, whose windows front the entrance of the chateau, is seen a partly cleared table—bottles uncorked, tarnished empty glasses resting upon the wrinkled cloth—in short, every indication that a repast is ended. The guests have departed; but in a side room loud voices are heard, peals of laughter, the rolling of billiard balls, and the clinking of glasses. The Marshal has just started upon his game, and that is why the army is waiting for orders. Once the Marshal has begun, the heavens might fall, but nothing on earth will hinder him from finishing his game.

For if the mighty soldier has a single weakness, it is his fondness for billiards. There he stands, as grave as though a battle had begun, in full uniform, his breast covered with decorations; his repast, the grog he has drunk, and the excitement of the game animate him. His eyes sparkle, and his cheek-bones are flushed. About him gather his aides-de-camp, most assiduous in their attentions, deferential and overcome with admiration at each of his shots. When the Marshal makes a point, they lunge towards the mark. When the Marshal desires a drink, each one rushes to prepare his grog. Such a rustling of epaulettes and panaches; such a rattling of crosses and aiguillettes. How these flunkies bow and smile. What elegance and charm of manner. And such embroideries; so many new uniforms in this lofty chamber carved in oak, opening upon parks and courts of honor. It reminds one of these autumns of Compiègne, and makes him forget, for a moment, those figures in muddied cloaks, gathered yonder in the roads, making such somber groups as they wait in the rain.

The Marshal's adversary is a staff officer, a little captain with curls, laces and light gloves; he is an excellent shot at billiards, and could beat all the marshals on earth, but he understands his chief, and exercises all his skill in playing so that he shall neither win nor seem to lose, too readily. Evidently an officer with a future.

Beware, Captain. The Marshal is five points ahead. If you can complete the game as you have begun it, your promotion is surer than it would be, were you standing outside with the others, beneath those torrents of water. It would be a pity, too, to soil that fine uniform.

The game is fascinating. The balls roll, graze, pass; they rebound. Every moment the play grows more interesting. A flash of light is seen in the sky, and the report of a cannon is heard. A heavy rumbling sound shakes the windows. Everyone starts and casts an uneasy glance about. The Marshal alone remains unmoved. He sees nothing, hears nothing, for, leaning over the table, he is about to make a magnificent draw shot. Draw shots are his forte!

Again that flash! Again! From the cannon, fresh reports, and closer together. The aides-de-camp run to the window. Are the Prussians attacking?

"Let them!" says the Marshal, chalking his cue. "Your turn, Captain."

The staff glows with admiration. Turenne, asleep on the gun-carriage, was nothing compared to this marshal, calmly absorbed in his game at the moment of action. But the tumult increases. The rattling of the machine guns mingles with the blast of the cannon and the rumbling of steady volleys. A reddish cloud, dark at the edges, rises from the further end of the lawn. All the rear of the park is ablaze. Frightened peacocks and pheasants shriek in the aviary. Arabian horses, in their stalls, scent the powder and rear in terror. At headquarters a general commotion begins. Despatch follows despatch. Messengers arrive at a gallop. Everywhere they are asking for the Marshal.

But the Marshal remains unapproachable. Nothing—nothing in the world could hinder him from finishing a game once begun.

"Your play, Captain. . ."

But the captain is distracted. He loses his head; forgets where he is, and he makes two successive runs which almost win the game for him. The Marshal is furious. Surprise and indignation mark his features. At this very moment a horse gallops into the courtyard at full speed. An aide-de-camp, covered with mud, forces the sentry, makes one bound over the stone steps crying, "Marshal, Marshal!" The Marshal, red and swelling with anger, appears at the window, cue in hand.

"Who is there? What is it? Is there no sentry there?"

"But, Marshal . . ."

"Oh, yes, yes—later—let them wait for my orders—in God's name!"

And the window closes with a bang.

Let them wait for his orders. That is exactly what they are doing, those poor fellows. The wind drives rain and grape-shot in their faces. Battalions are slaughtered, while others stand useless, bearing arms, unable to understand why they remain inactive. They wait for orders. But men may die without orders, and these men die in hundreds, falling be-hind bushes, dropping in trenches in front of that great silent chateau. Even after their death, the grapeshot con-tinues to lacerate their bodies; from those gaping wounds flows a silent stream—the generous blood of France. Above, in the billiard room, all is excited as upon the battle-field. The Marshal has regained his advantage, and the little cap-tain is playing like a lion.

Seventeen! eighteen! nineteen! Scarcely time to mark the points. The sound of battle grows nearer and nearer. The Marshal has but on more point to play. Already shells are falling in the park. One has burst in the pond. The glassy sheen reddens, and a terrified swan is seen swimming amid a whirl of bloody plumage. And now the last shot.

And then—deep silence. Only the sound of rain falling; only an indistinct rumbling noise at the foot of the hill, and along the muddy roads a sound like the tramping of hurrying herds. The army is utterly routed. The Marshal has won his game.

Fear

BY RHYS DAVIES

□ □ □

As soon as the boy got into the compartment he felt there was something queer in it. The only other occupant was a slight, dusky man who sat in a corner with that air of propriety and unassertiveness which his race—he looked like an Indian—tend to display in England. There was also a faint sickly scent. For years afterwards, whenever he smelled that musk odour again, the terror of this afternoon came back to him.

He went to the other end of the compartment, sat in the opposite corner. There were no corridors in these local trains. The man looked at him and smiled friendlily. The boy returned the smile briefly, not quite knowing what he was thinking, only aware of a deep, vague unease. But it would look so silly to jump out of the compartment now. The train gave a jerk and began to move.

Then, immediately with the jerk, the man began to utter a low humming chant, slow but with a definite rhythm. His lips did not open or even move, yet the hum penetrated above the noise of the train's wheels. It was in a sort of dreamy rhythm, enticing, lonely and antique; it suggested monotonous deserts, an eternal patience, a soothing wisdom. It went on and on. It was the kind of archaic chant that brings to the mind images of slowly swaying bodies in some endless ceremony in a barbaric temple.

Startled, and very alive to this proof of there being something odd in the compartment, the boy turned from staring out of the window—already the train was deep in the country among lonely fields and dark wooded slopes—and forced himself to glance at the man.

The man was looking at him. They faced each other across the compartment's length. Something coiled up in the boy. It was as if his soul took primitive fear and crouched to hide. The man's brown lips became stretched in a mysterious smile, though that humming chant continued, wordlessly swaying out of his mouth. His eyes, dark and unfathomable, never moved from the boy. The musk scent was stronger.

Yet this was not all. The boy could not imagine what other fearful thing lurked in the compartment. But he seemed to sense a secret power of something evilly antipathetic. Did it come from the man's long pinky-brown hands, the sinewy but fleshless hands of a sun-scorched race? Long tribal hands like claws. Or only from the fact that the man was of a far country whose ways were utterly alien to ours? And he continued to smile. A faint and subtle smile, while his eyes surveyed the boy as if he contemplated action. Something had flickered in and out of those shadowy eyes, like a dancing malice.

The boy sat stiffly. Somehow he could not return to his staring out of the window. But he tried not to look at the man again. The humming did not stop. And suddenly it took a higher note, like an unhurried wail, yet keeping within its strict and narrow compass. A liquid exultance wavered in and out of the wail. The noise of the train, the flying fields and woods, even the walls of the compartment had vanished. There was only this chant, the man who was uttering it, and himself. He did not know that now he could not move his eyes from those of the man.

Abruptly the compartment was plunged into blackness. There was a shrieking rush of air. The train had entered a tunnel. With a sudden jerk the boy crouched down. He coiled into the seat's corner, shuddering, yet with every sense electrically alive now.

Then, above the roar of the air and the hurling grind of the train, that hum rose, dominantly established its insidious power. It called, it unhurriedly exhorted obedience, it soothed. Again it seemed to obliterate the louder, harsher noises. Spent and defeated, helplessly awaiting whatever menace lay in the darkness, the boy crouched. He knew the man's eyes were gazing towards him; he thought he saw their gleam triumphantly piercing the darkness. What was this strange presence of evil in the air, stronger now in the dark?

Suddenly crashing into the compartment, the hard blue and white daylight was like a blow. The train had gained speed in the tunnel, and now hurled on through the light with the same agonising impetus, as if it would rush on for ever. Spent in the dread which had almost cancelled out his senses, the boy stared dully at the man. Still he seemed to hear the humming, though actually it had ceased. He saw the man's lips part in a full enticing smile, he saw teeth dazzlingly white between the dusky lips.

"You not like dark tunnel?" The smile continued seductively; once more the flecks of light danced wickedly in his eyes. "Come!" He beckoned with a long wrinkled finger.

The boy did not move.

"You like pomegranates?" He rose and took from the luggage rack a brown wicker basket. It was the kind of basket in which a large cat would be sent on a journey. "Come!" he smiled friendlily and, as the boy still did not move, he crossed over and sat down beside him, but leaving a polite distance.

The staring boy did not flinch.

"Pomegranates from the East! English boy like, eh?" There seemed a collaboration in his intimate voice; he too was a boy going to share fruit with his friend. "Nice pomegranates," he smiled with good-humour. There was also something stupid in his manner, a fatuous mysteriousness.

The basket lay on his knees. He began to hum again. The boy watched, still without movement, cold and abstract in his nonapprehension of this friendliness. But he was aware of the sickly perfume beside him and, more pronounced than ever, of an insidious presence that was utterly alien. That evil power lay in his immediate vicinity. The man looked at him again and, still humming, drew a rod and lifted the basket's lid.

There was no glow of magically gleaming fruits, no yellow-and-rose-tinted rinds enclosing honeycombs of luscious seeds. But from the basket's depth rose the head of a snake. It rose slowly to the enchantment of the hum. It rose from its sleepy coil, rearing its long brownish-gold throat dreamily, the head swaying out in languor towards the man's lips. Its eyes seemed to look blindly at nothing. It was a cobra.

Something happened to the boy. An old warning of the muscles and the vulnerable flesh. He leapt and flung himself headlong across the compartment. He was not aware that he gave a sharp shriek. He curled against the opposite seat's back, his knees pressing into the cushion. But, half turning, his eyes could not tear themselves from that reared head.

And it was with other senses that he knew most deeply he had evoked rage. The cobra was writhing in disturbed anger, shooting its head in his direction. He saw wakened

pin-point eyes of black malice. More fearful was the
dilation of the throat, its skin swelling evilly into a hood in
which shone two palpitating sparks. In some cell of his
being he knew that the hood was swelling in destructive fury.
He became very still.

The man did not stop humming. But now his narrowed
eyes were focused in glittering concentration on the snake.
And into that hum had crept a new note of tenacious decision. It was a pitting of subtle power against the snake's
wishes and it was also an appeasement. A man was addressing
a snake. He was offering a snake tribute and acknowledgment
of its right to anger; he was honeyed and soothing. At the
same time he did not relax an announcement of being master.
There was courtesy towards one of the supreme powers of
the animal kingdom, but also there was the ancient pride of
man's supremacy.

And the snake was pacified. Its strange reared collar of
skin sank back into its neck; its head ceased to lunge towards the boy. The humming slackened into a dreamy lulla-
by. Narrowly intent now, the man's eyes did not move. The
length of tawny body slowly sank back. Its skin had a
dull glisten, the glisten of an unhealthy torpidity. Now the
snake looked effete, shorn of its venomous power. The
drugged head sank. Unhurriedly the man closed the basket and slipped its rod secure.

He turned angrily to the boy; he made a contemptuous
sound, like a hiss. "I show you cobra and you jump and
shout, heh! Make him angry!" There was more rebuke than
real rage in his exclamations. But also his brown face was
puckered in a kind of childish stupidity; he might have been
another boy of twelve. "I give you free performance with
cobra, and you jump and scream like little girl." The indignation died out of his eyes; they became focused in a more
adult perception. "I sing to keep cobra quiet in train," he
explained. "Cobra not like train."

The boy had not stirred. "You not like cobra?" the man
asked in injured surprise. "Nice snake now, no poison! But
not liking you jump and shout."

There was no reply or movement; centuries and conti-
nents lay between him and the boy's still repudiation. The
man gazed at him in silence and added worriedly: "You
going to fair in Newport? You see me? Ali the Snake
Charmer. You come in free and see me make cobra dance—"

But the train was drawing into the station. It was not the

boy's station. He made a sudden blind leap away from the
man, opened the door, saw it was not on the platform side,
but jumped. There was a shout from someone. He ran up the
track, he dived under some wire railings. He ran with amaz-
ingly quick short leaps up a field—like a hare that knows its
life is precarious among the colossal dangers of the open
world and has suddenly sensed one of them.

The Riddle

BY WALTER DE LA MARE

◪ ◪ ◪

So these seven children, Ann, and Matilda, James, William
and Henry, Harriet and Dorothea, came to live with their
grandmother. The house in which their grandmother had
lived since her childhood was built in the time of the
Georges. It was not a pretty house, but roomy, substantial,
and square; and an elm tree outstretched its branches almost
to the windows.

When the children were come out of the cab (five sitting
inside and two beside the driver), they were shown into their
grandmother's presence. They stood in a little black group
before the old lady, seated in her bow-window. And she
asked them each their names, and repeated each name in
her kind, quavering voice. Then to one she gave a work-box,
to William a jack-knife, to Dorothea a painted ball; to each a
present according to age. And she kissed all her grandchil-
dren to the youngest.

"My dears," she said, "I wish to see all of you bright
and gay in my house. I am an old woman, so that I cannot
romp with you; but Ann must look to you, and Mrs. Fenn
too. And every morning and every evening you must all come
in to see your granny; and bring me smiling faces, that call
back to my mind my own son Harry. But all the rest of the
day, when school is done, you shall do just as you please,
my dears. And there is only one thing, just one, I would have
you remember. In the large spare bedroom that looks out
on the slate roof there stands in the corner an old oak chest;

ay, children, older than I, my dears, a great deal older; older than my grandmother. Play anywhere else in the house, but not there." She spoke kindly to them all, smiling at them; but she was very aged, and her eyes seemed to see nothing of this world.

And the seven children, though at first they were gloomy and strange, soon began to be happy and at home in the great house. There was much to interest and to amuse them there; all was new to them. Twice every day, morning and evening, they came in to see their grandmother, who every day seemed more feeble; and she spoke pleasantly to them of her mother, and her childhood, but never forgetting to visit her store of sugar-plums. And so the weeks passed by.

It was evening twilight when Henry went upstairs from the nursery by himself to look at the oak chest. He pressed his fingers into the carved fruit and flowers, and spoke to the dark smiling heads at the corners; and then, with a glance over his shoulder, he opened the lid and looked in. But the chest concealed no treasure, neither gold nor baubles, nor was there anything to alarm the eye. The chest was empty, except that it was lined with silk of old rose, seeming darker in the dusk, and smelling sweet of pot-pourri. And while Henry was looking in, he heard the softened laughter and the clinking of the cups downstairs in the nursery; and out at the window he saw the day darkening. These things brought strangely to his memory his mother, who in her glimmering white dress used to read to him in the dusk; and he climbed into the chest; and the lid closed gently down over him.

When the other six children were tired with their playing, they filed into their grandmother's room as usual for her good-night and her sugar-plums. She looked out between the candles at them as if she were unsure of something in her thoughts. The next day Ann told her grandmother that Henry was not anywhere to be found.

"Dearie me, child. Then he must be gone away for a time," said the old lady. She paused. "But remember all of you, do not meddle with the oak chest."

But Matilda could not forget her brother Henry, finding no pleasure in playing without him. So she would loiter in the house thinking where he might be. And she carried her wood doll in her bare arms, singing under her breath all she could make up about him. And when in a bright morning she peeped in on the chest, so sweet-scented and secret it seemed that she took her doll with her into it—just as Henry himself had done.

So Ann, and James, and William, Harriet and Dorothea were left at home to play together. "Some day maybe they will come back to you, my dears," said their grandmother, "or maybe you will go to them. Heed my warning as best you may."

Now Harriet and William were friends together, pretending to be sweethearts; while James and Dorothea liked wild games of hunting, and fishing, and battles.

On a silent afternoon in October Harriet and William were talking softly together, looking out over the slate roof at the green fields, and they heard the squeak and frisking of a mouse behind them in the room. They went together and searched for the small, dark hole from whence it had come out. But finding no hole, they began to finger the carving of the chest, and to give names to the dark-smiling heads, just as Henry had done. "I know! Let's pretend you are Sleeping Beauty, Harriet," said William, "and I'll be the Prince that squeezes through the thorns and comes in." Harriet looked gently and strangely at her brother; but she got into the box and lay down, pretending to be fast asleep; and on tiptoe William leaned over, and seeing how big was the chest he stepped in to kiss the Sleeping Beauty and to wake her from her quiet sleep. Slowly the carved lid turned on its noiseless hinges. And only the clatter of James and Dorothea came in sometimes to recall Ann from her book.

But their old grandmother was very feeble, and her sight dim, and her hearing extremely difficult.

Snow was falling through the still air upon the roof; and Dorothea was a fish in the oak chest, and James stood over the hole in the ice, brandishing a walking-stick for a harpoon, pretending to be an Esquimau. Dorothea's face was red, and her wild eyes sparkled through her tousled hair. And James had a crooked scratch upon his cheek. "You must struggle, Dorothea, and then I shall swim back and drag you out. Be quick now!" He shouted with laughter as he was drawn into the open chest. And the lid closed softly and gently down as before.

Ann, left to her self, was too old to care overmuch for sugar-plums, but she would go solitary to bid her grandmother goodnight; and the old lady looked wistfully at her over her spectacles. "Well, my dear," she said with trembling head; and she squeezed Ann's fingers between her own knuckled finger and thumb. "What lonely old people we are, to be sure!" Ann kissed her grandmother's soft, loose cheek. She left the old lady sitting in her easy chair, her hands upon her knees, and her head turned sidelong towards her.

When Ann was gone to bed she used to sit reading her book by candlelight. She drew up her knees under the sheets, resting her book upon them. Her story was about fairies and gnomes; and the gently-flowing moonlight of the narrative seemed to illumine the white pages, and she could hear in fancy fairy voices, so silent was the great many-roomed house, and so mellifluent were the words of the story. Presently she put out her candle, and, with a confused babel of voices close to her ears, and faint swift pictures before her eyes, she fell asleep.

And in the dead of night she arose out of bed in dream, and with eyes wide open yet seeing nothing of reality, moved silently through the vacant house. Past the room where her grandmother was snoring in brief, heavy slumber, she stepped light and surely, and down the wide staircase. And Vega the far-shining stood over against the window above the slate roof. Ann walked in the strange room as if she were being guided by the hand toward the oak chest. There, just as if she was dreaming it was her bed, she laid herself down in the old rose silk, in the fragrant place. But it was so dark in the room that the movement of the lid was indisguishable.

Through the long day, the grandmother sat in her bow-window. Her lips were pursed, and she looked with dim, inquisitive scrutiny upon the street where people passed to and fro, and vehicles rolled by. At evening she climbed the stair and stood in the doorway of the large spare bedroom. The ascent had shortened her breath. Her magnifying spectacles rested upon her nose. Leaning her hand on the doorpost she peered in towards the glimmering square of window in the quiet gloom. But she could not see far, because her sight was dim and the light of day feeble. Nor could she detect the faint fragrance, as of autumnal leaves. But in her mind was a tangled skein of memories—laughter and tears, and little children now old-fashioned, and the advent of friends, and long farewells. And gossiping fitfully, inarticulately, with herself, the old lady went down again to her window-seat.

The Jewels of M. Lantin

BY GUY DE MAUPASSANT

◻ ◻ ◻

M. Lantin, having met this young lady at a party given by his immediate superior, was literally enmeshed by love.

She was the daughter of a provincial tax collector who had died a few years previously. With her mother, she had come to Paris. Her mother became friendly with several middle-class families of the neighborhood in hopes of marrying off the young lady. Mother and daughter were poor, honorable, quiet, and gentle. The girl seemed to be the typical dream woman into whose hands any young man would yearn to entrust his entire life. Her modest beauty had an angelic quality, and the imperceptible smile which constantly graced her lips, seemed a reflection of her heart.

Everyone sang her praises; everyone who knew her repeated incessantly: "It will be a lucky fellow who wins her. You couldn't find a better catch!"

M. Lantin, now chief clerk of the Minister of the Interior, at a salary of 3500 francs, asked and received her hand in marriage.

He was unbelievably happy. She managed the house with such skill that their life was one of luxury. There was no delicacy, no whim of her husband's which she did not secure and satisfy; and her personal charm was such that, six years after their first meeting, he loved her even more than he had initially.

He begrudged her only two traits—her love of the theater and her passion for artificial jewels.

Her friends (she knew the wives of several minor functionaries) were always getting her seats for the fashionable plays, sometimes even for first nights; and she dragged her poor husband, willy-nilly, to these entertainments which completely wore him out, tired as he was after a hard day's work. He begged her to agree to go to the theater with some lady friend of hers who would accompany her home. She took a long time to decide, claiming this a most inconvenient arrangement. At last, however, she agreed, and he was profoundly grateful to her.

Now, this taste for the theater naturally stirred in her the need to primp. Her toilette remained simple, to be sure—always modest but in good taste; and her gentle grace, her irresistible, humble, smiling grace seemed to acquire a new savor from the simplicity of her dress, but she became accustomed to wearing two huge rhinestone earrings, which looked like diamonds; and she had strings of artificial pearls around her neck, and wore bracelets of similar gems.

Her husband, who somewhat scorned this love of garish display, said, "Dearest, when you haven't the means to wear real jewelry, you should show yourself adorned only with your own grace and beauty; these are the true pearls."

But she, smiling quietly, would insist, "Can I help it? I love it so. This is my vice. I know, my dear, how absolutely right you are; but I can't really remake myself, can I? I think I would just idolize real jewelry."

And she would roll the pearls in her fingers. "See how perfect," she'd say. "You'd swear they were real."

Sometimes, during the evening, while they sat before the fire, she would bring out her jewel chest, put it on the tea table, and commence to examine the contents with passionate attention, as though there were some subtle and profound secret delight in this pursuit. She persisted in draping strings of pearls around her husband's neck; then she would laugh merrily, crying, "How silly you look, my darling!" And she would throw herself into his arms and kiss him wildly.

One wintry evening, when she had been at the opera, she came home shivering with cold. The next day she was coughing wretchedly. A week later she died.

Lantin nearly followed her into the tomb. His despair was such that, in a month's time, his hair turned completely white. He wept incessantly, his very soul seared by unbearable suffering, haunted by the memory, the smile, the voice—by the overwhelming beauty of his deceased wife.

Even the passage of time failed to stem his grief. Frequently, at his office, while his colleagues were chatting idly, his cheeks would tremble and his eyes would fill with tears; he would grimace horribly and commence to sob.

He kept his wife's room intact, and sealed himself in every day to meditate. All her furniture and even her dresses remained just where they had been on the fatal day.

Living became difficult for him. His income which, under his wife's management, amply supplied the needs of both, now became insufficient for him alone. Dazed, he wondered how she had been able to purchase the superb wines and delicacies which he could no longer afford.

He fell into debt and began to scurry around for money as does anyone suddenly plunged into poverty. One fine morning, finding himself penniless a full week before payday, he thought about selling something. Suddenly the idea swept over him of taking a look at his wife's treasure trove, because, if the truth be told, he had always harbored some resentment towards this store of brilliants. The mere sight of them slightly tarnished the memory of his beloved.

It was a difficult business, searching through the case of jewels, because, even up to the very last days of her life, his wife had shopped stubbornly, bringing home some new bauble practically every night. He finally chose the magnificent necklace she seemed to have preferred, which, he figured, was worth six or seven francs, because, for artificial gems, it was really a masterpiece of craftsmanship.

With the jewels in his pocket he walked towards the Ministry, looking for a reliable jeweler.

Spotting a store, he entered—somewhat chagrined to be making this public display of his poverty and ashamed at attempting to sell so worthless an object.

He approached the merchant. "Excuse me. I wonder what value you would place on this piece."

The man took the necklace, examined it, turned it over, weighed it, called to his partner, talked to him in low tones, placed the necklace on the counter and scrutinized it carefully from a distance as though judging the effect.

M. Lantin, overwhelmed by this process, opened his mouth to protest: "Oh! I know that piece isn't worth anything," but just at that moment the storekeeper said:

"Monsieur, this piece is worth between twelve and fifteen thousand francs, but I cannot buy it until I learn exactly how you came into possession of it."

Lantin stared, wide-eyed, silent—uncomprehending. He finally stammered, "What? You are absolutely sure?"

The gentleman seemed offended by his attitude, and said wryly, "You may go elsewhere if you think you can do better. To me that is worth fifteen thousand at the very most. If you find no better offer, you may come back here."

M. Lantin, stupified, took the necklace and left, feeling a curious urge to be alone and undisturbed.

But, before he had gone far, he was seized with an impulse to laugh, and he thought, "Imbecile! What a fool! What if I had taken him at his word! What a jeweler—not to know the difference between real gems and fakes!"

And he entered another jewelry store on the Rue de la Paix. As soon as he saw the jewel, the dealer cried, "Of course! I know this necklace well; I sold it!"

Deeply disturbed, M. Lantin asked, "How much is it worth?"

"Sir—I sold it for twenty-five thousand francs. I'm ready to take it back for eighteen thousand, if you will tell me—the law, you know—how you happened to receive it."

This time Lantin sat paralyzed with astonishment. He stuttered, "But—but—examine it very closely, sir. I have always thought it was—artificial."

The jeweler asked, "Would you please tell me your name, sir?"

"Of course. I'm Lantin. I work at the Ministry of the Interior, and I live at 16 Rue des Martyrs."

The merchant opened his ledger, looked through it, and said, "This necklace was sent to Mme. Lantin, 16 Rue des Martyrs, on the twentieth of July, 1876."

And the two men stared at each other, the clerk dumbfounded; the jeweler scenting a robber.

The merchant said, "Would you mind letting me have this for a day? Naturally, I'll give you a receipt."

M. Lantin blurted out, "Of course!" And he left, folding the paper into his pocket.

Then he crossed the street, went back, saw that he had gone out of his way, returned past the Tuileries, saw again he had made a mistake, crossed the Seine, went back to the Champs-Elysées without a single clear notion in his head. He forced himself to think. His wife could not possibly have purchased such valuable jewelry. Absolutely not! Well then? A present? A present! From whom? For what?

He was brought up short, and he stood stock still—there in the middle of the street. A horrible thought flashed across his mind. She? But all those other jewels were also gifts! He felt the earth shiver; a tree just before him seemed to crush him. He threw out his arms and fell, senseless, to the ground.

He regained consciousness in a nearby pharmacy to which

passers-by had carried him. He asked that he be taken home, and he locked himself in.

He wept bitterly until nightfall—stuffing a handkerchief into his mouth to stifle his cries. Then he staggered to bed, wrung out with fatigue and chagrin, and he slept heavily.

A ray of sunshine woke him, and he got up slowly to go to his office. After such a blow, it would be hard to carry on with his work. He felt that he could be excused, and he wrote his superior a note. Then he thought that he ought to go back to the jeweler; and he crimsoned with shame. He could not possibly leave the necklace with that man. He dressed hurriedly and went out.

As he walked along, Lantin said to himself, "How easy it is to be happy when you're rich! With money you can even shake off your sorrows; you can go or stay as you please! You can travel and amuse yourself. If only I were really rich!"

Then he became aware of the fact that he was hungry, not having eaten since the previous evening. But his pockets were empty, and he reminded himself of the necklace. Eighteen thousand francs! Eighteen thousand francs! What a fortune!

He reached the Rue de la Paix, and he began pacing up and down opposite the shop. Eighteen thousand francs! More than twenty times he started to enter; but shame always halted him.

He was still hungry—famished—and without a sou. He finally made up his mind, raced across the street so as not to give himself time to think, and burst into the store.

As soon as he saw him, the merchant greeted him royally, offered him a chair with smiling courtesy. The partners then came in and sat down near Lantin, happiness beaming from their eyes and their lips.

The jeweler declared, "I am satisfied, Monsieur, and if you feel as you did yesterday, I am ready to pay you the sum agreed upon."

"Certainly," stammered Lantin.

The merchant took eighteen large notes from a drawer, counted them, gave them to Lantin, who signed a receipt and, with trembling hand, stuffed the money into his pocket.

Then, just as he was going out, he turned back towards the grinning shopkeeper, and, lowering his eyes, murmured, "I—I have some other gems—which came to me in the same way. Would you be willing to buy those from me?"

The jeweler nodded, "Of course, Monsieur."

One of the partners barely stifled a laugh, while the other was forced to leave the room to hide his mirth.

Lantin, impassive and stern, said, "I'll bring them to you."

When he returned to the store, an hour later, he had still not eaten. They set about examining the jewels piece by piece, assessing each one. Then they all went back to Lantin's house.

Now Lantin entered into the spirit of the business, arguing, insisting that they show him the bills of sale, and getting more and more excited as the values rose.

The magnificent earrings were worth twenty thousand francs; the bracelets, thirty-five thousand. The brooches, pins and medallions, sixteen thousand. The whole collection was valued at one hundred ninety-six thousand francs.

The merchant boomed out in a jolly voice, "That's what happens when you put your money into jewelry."

Lantin said solemnly, "That's one way to invest your money!" Then he left, after having agreed with the purchaser to have a second expert appraisal the following day.

When he was out in the street, he looked up at the Vendôme Column. He felt like leaping up to the top. He felt light enough to play leapfrog with the statue of the Emperor perched up there in the clouds.

He went into an elegant restaurant to eat, and he drank wine at twenty francs a bottle.

Then he took a cab and rode around the Bois de Boulogne. He looked at the gleaming carriages, suppressing a desire to cry out, "I'm rich, too! I have two hundred thousand francs!"

He thought of his office. He drove up, entered his Chief's office solemnly, and announced, "Sir—I'm tendering my resignation! I've just inherited three hundred thousand francs!" He went around shaking hands with his colleagues, and telling them all about his plans for the future. Then he went out to dinner at the Café Anglais.

Finding himself seated alongside a distinguished-looking gentleman, he couldn't resist whispering to him, a little archly, that he had just inherited four hundred thousand francs.

For the first time in his life he enjoyed the theater and he spent the night carousing.

Six months later he remarried. His second wife was a most worthy woman, but rather difficult. She made his life unbearable.

The Heavenly Christmas Tree

BY FYODOR DOSTOYEVSKY

I am a novelist, and I suppose I have made up this story.
I write "I suppose," though I know for a fact that I have
made it up, but yet I keep fancying that it must have happened on Christmas Eve in some great town in a time of
terrible frost.

I have a vision of a boy, a little boy, six years old or
even younger. This boy woke up that morning in a cold
damp cellar. He was dressed in a sort of little dressing-gown
and was shivering with cold. There was a cloud of white
steam from his breath, and sitting on a box in the corner, he
blew the steam out of his mouth and amused himself in his
dullness watching it float away. But he was terribly hungry.
Several times that morning he went up to the plank bed
where his sick mother was lying on a mattress as thin as a
pancake, with some sort of bundle under her head for a pillow. How had she come here? She must have come with
her boy from some other town and suddenly fallen ill. The
landlady who let the "corners" had been taken two days
before to the police station, the lodgers were out and about
as the holiday was so near, and the only one left had been
lying for the last twenty-four hours dead drunk, not having
waited for Christmas. In another corner of the room a
wretched old woman of eighty, who had once been a children's nurse but was now left to die friendless, was moaning
and groaning with rheumatism, scolding and grumbling at
the boy so that he was afraid to go near her corner. He had
got a drink of water in the outer room, but could not find
a crust anywhere, and had been on the point of waking his
mother a dozen times. He felt frightened at last in the darkness: it had long been dusk, but no light was kindled.
Touching his mother's face, he was surprised that she did
not move at all, and that she was as cold as the wall. "It
is very cold here," he thought. He stood a little, uncon-

71

sciously letting his hands rest on the dead woman's shoulders, then he breathed on his fingers to warm them, and then quietly fumbling for his cap on the bed, he went out of the cellar. He would have gone earlier, but was afraid of the big dog which had been howling all day at the neighbour's door at the top of the stairs. But the dog was not there now, and he went out into the street.

Mercy on us, what a town! He had never seen anything like it before. In the town from which he had come, it was always such black darkness at night. There was one lamp for the whole street, the little, low-pitched, wooden houses were closed up with shutters, there was no one to be seen in the street after dusk, all the people shut themselves up in their houses, and there was nothing but the howling of packs of dogs, hundreds and thousands of them barking and howling all night. But there it was so warm and he was given food, while here—oh, dear, if he only had something to eat! And what a noise and rattle here, what light and what people, horses and carriages, and what a frost! The frozen steam hung in clouds over the horses, over their warmly breathing mouths; their hoofs clanged against the stones through the powdery snow, and everyone pushed so, and—oh, dear, how he longed for some morsel to eat, and how wretched he suddenly felt. A policeman walked by and turned away to avoid seeing the boy.

There was another street—oh, what a wide one, here he would be run over for certain; how everyone was shouting, racing and driving along, and the light, the light! And what was this? A huge glass window, and through the window a tree reaching up to the ceiling; it was a fir tree, and on it were ever so many lights, gold papers and apples and little dolls and horses; and there were children clean and dressed in their best running about the room, laughing and playing and eating and drinking something. And then a little girl began dancing with one of the boys, what a pretty little girl! And he could hear the music through the window. The boy looked and wondered and laughed, though his toes were aching with the cold and his fingers were red and stiff so that it hurt him to move them. And all at once the boy remembered how his toes and fingers hurt him, and began crying, and ran on; and again through another window-pane he saw another Christmas tree, and on a table cakes of all sorts —almond cakes, red cakes and yellow cakes, and three grand young ladies were sitting there, and they gave the cakes to any one who went up to them, and the door kept opening, lots of gentlemen and ladies went in from the street. The boy crept up, suddenly opened the door and went in. Oh, how they shouted at him and waved him back! One lady went up to him hurriedly and slipped a kopeck into his hand, and with her own hands opened the door into the street for him! How frightened he was. And the kopeck rolled away and clinked upon the steps; he could not bend his red fingers to hold it right. The boy ran away and went on, where he did not know. He was ready to cry again but he was afraid, and ran on and on and blew his fingers. And he was miserable because he felt suddenly so lonely and terrified, and all at once, mercy on us! What was this again? People were standing in a crowd admiring. Behind a glass window there were three little dolls, dressed in red and green dresses, and exactly, exactly as though they were alive. One was a little old man sitting and playing a big violin, the two others were standing close by and playing little violins, and nodding in time, and looking at one another, and their lips moved, they were speaking, actually speaking, only one couldn't hear through the glass. And at first the boy thought they were alive, and when he grasped that they were dolls he laughed. He had never seen such dolls before, and had no idea there were such dolls! And he wanted to cry, but he felt amused, amused by the dolls. All at once he fancied that some one caught at his smock behind: a wicked big boy was standing beside him and suddenly hit him on the head, snatched off his cap and tripped him up. The boy fell down on the ground, at once there was a shout, he was numb with fright, he jumped up and ran away. He ran, and not knowing where he was going, ran in at the gate of some one's courtyard, and sat down behind a stack of wood: "They won't find me here, besides it's dark!"

He sat huddled up and was breathless from fright, and all at once, quite suddenly, he felt so happy: his hands and feet suddenly left off aching and grew so warm, as warm as though he were on a stove; then he shivered all over, then he gave a start, why, he must have been asleep. How nice to have a sleep here! "I'll sit here a little and go and look at the dolls again," said the boy, and smiled thinking of them. "Just as though they were alive! . . ." And suddenly he heard his mother singing over him. "Mammy, I am asleep; how nice it is to sleep here!"

"Come to my Christmas tree, little one," a soft voice suddenly whispered over his head.

He thought that this was still his mother, but no, it was not she. Who it was calling him, he could not see, but someone bent over and embraced him in the darkness; and he stretched out his hands to him, and . . . and all at once—oh, what a bright light! Oh, what a Christmas tree! And yet it was not a fir tree, he had never seen a tree like that! Where was he now? Everything was bright and shining, and all round him were dolls; but no, they were not dolls, they were little boys and girls, only so bright and shining. They all came flying round him, they all kissed him, took him and carried him along with them, and he was flying himself, and he saw that his mother was looking at him and laughing joyfully. "Mammy, Mammy; oh, how nice it is here, Mammy!" And again he kissed the children and wanted to tell them at once of those dolls in the shop window.

"Who are you, boys? Who are you, girls?" he asked, laughing and admiring them.

"This is Christ's Christmas tree," they answered. "Christ always has a Christmas tree on this day, for the little children who have no tree of their own . . ." And he found out that all these little boys and girls were children just like himself; that some had been frozen in the baskets in which they had as babies been laid on the doorsteps of well-to-do Petersburg people, others had been boarded out with Finnish women by the Foundling and had been suffocated, others had died at their starved mother's breasts (in the Samara famine), others had died in third-class railway carriages from the foul air; and yet they were all here, they were all like angels about Christ, and He was in the midst of them and held out His hands to them and blessed them and their sinful mothers. . . . And the mothers of these children stood on one side weeping; each one knew her boy or girl, and the children flew up to them and kissed them and wiped away their tears with their little hands, and begged them not to weep because they were so happy.

And down below in the morning the porter found the little dead body of the frozen child on the woodstack; they sought out his mother too. . . . She had died before him. They met before the Lord God in heaven.

Why have I made up such a story, so out of keeping with an ordinary diary, and a writer's above all? And I promised two stories dealing with real events! But that is just it, I keep fancying that all this may have happened really —that is, what took place in the cellar and on the wood-stack; but as for Christ's Christmas tree, I cannot tell you whether that could have happened or not.

The Ghosts

BY LORD DUNSANY

▭ ▭ ▭

The argument that I had with my brother in his great lonely house will scarcely interest my readers. Not those, at least, whom I hope may be attracted by the experiment that I undertook, and by the strange things that befell me in that hazardous region into which so lightly and so ignorantly I allowed my fancy to enter. It was at Oneleigh that I had visited him.

Now Oneleigh stands in a wide isolation, in the midst of a dark gathering of old whispering cedars. They nod their heads together when the North Wind comes, and nod again and agree, and furtively grow still again, and say no more awhile. The North Wind is to them like a nice problem among wise old men; they nod their heads over it, and mutter it all together. They know much, those cedars, they have been there so long. Their grandsires knew Lebanon, and the grandsires of these were the sevants of the King of Tyre and came to Solomon's court. And amidst these black-haired children of grey-headed Time stood the old house of Oneleigh. I know not how many centuries had lashed against it their evanescent foam of years; but it was still unshattered, and all about it were the things of long ago, as cling strange growths to some sea-defying rock. Here, like the shells of long-dead limpets, was armour that men encased themselves in long ago; here, too, were tapestries of many colours, beautiful as seaweed; no modern flotsam ever drifted hither, no early Victorian furniture, no electric light. The great trade routes that littered the years with empty meat tins and cheap novels were far from here. Well, well, the centuries will shatter it and drive its fragments on to distant shores.

Meanwhile, while it yet stood, I went on a visit there to my brother, and we argued about ghosts. My brother's intelligence on this subject seemed to me to be in need of correction. He mistook things imagined for things having an actual existence; he argued that second-hand evidence of persons having seen ghosts proved ghosts to exist. I said that even if they had seen ghosts, this was no proof at all; nobody believes that there are red rats, though there is plenty of first-hand evidence of men having seen them in delirium. Finally, I said I would see ghosts myself, and continue to argue against their actual existence. So I collected a handful of cigars and drank several cups of very strong tea, and went without my dinner, and retired into a room where there was dark oak and all the chairs were covered with tapestry; and my brother went to bed bored with our argument and trying hard to dissuade me from making myself uncomfortable. All the way up the old stairs as I stood at the bottom of them, and as his candle went winding up and up, I heard him still trying to persuade me to have supper and go to bed.

It was a windy winter, and outside the cedars were muttering I know not what about; but I think they were Tories of a school long dead, and were troubled about something new. Within, a great damp log upon the fireplace began to squeak and sing, and struck up a whining tune, and a tall flame stood up over it and beat time, and all the shadows crowded round and began to dance. In distant corners old masses of darkness sat still like chaperones and never moved. Over there, in the darkest part of the room, stood a door that was always locked. It led into the hall, but no one ever used it; near that door something had happened once of which the family are not proud. We do not speak of it. There in the firelight stood the venerable forms of the old chairs; the hands that had made their tapestries lay far beneath the soil, the needles with which they wrought were many separate flakes of rust. No one wove now in that old room—no one but the assiduous ancient spiders who, watching by the deathbed of the things of yore, worked shrouds to hold their dust. In shrouds about the cornices already lay the heart of the oak wainscot that the worm had eaten out.

Surely at such an hour, in such a room, a fancy already excited by hunger and strong tea might see the ghosts of former occupants. I expected nothing less. The fire flickered and the shadows danced, memories of strange historic things rose vividly in my mind; but midnight chimed solemnly from a seven-foot clock, and nothing happened. My imagination would not be hurried, and the chill that is with the small hours had come upon me, and I had nearly abandoned myself to sleep, when in the hall adjoining there arose the rustling of silk dresses that I had waited for and expected. Then there entered two by two the high-born ladies and their gallants of Jacobean times. They were little more than shadows—very dignified shadows, and almost indistinct; but you have all read ghost stories before, you have all seen in museums the dresses of those times—there is little need to describe them; they entered, several of them, and sat down on the old chairs, perhaps a little carelessly considering the value of the tapestries. Then the rustling of their dresses ceased.

Well—I had seen ghosts, and was neither frightened nor convinced that ghosts existed. I was about to get up out of my chair and go to bed, when there came a sound of pattering in the hall, a sound of bare feet coming over the polished floor, and every now and then a foot would slip and I heard claws scratching along the wood as some four-footed thing lost and regained its balance. I was not frightened, but uneasy. The pattering came straight towards the room that I was in, then I heard the sniffing of expectant nostrils; perhaps "uneasy" was not the most suitable word to describe my feelings then. Suddenly a herd of black creatures larger than bloodhounds came galloping in; they had large pendulous ears, their noses were to the ground sniffing, they went up to the lords and ladies of long ago and fawned about them disgustingly. Their eyes were horribly bright, and ran down to great depths. When I looked into them I knew suddenly what these creatures were, and I was afraid. They were the sins, the filthy, immortal sins of those courtly men and women.

How demure she was, the lady that sat near me on an old-world chair—how demure she was, and how fair, to have beside her with its jowl upon her lap a sin with such cavernous red eyes, a clear case of murder. And you, yonder lady with the golden hair, surely not you—and yet that fearful beast with the yellow eyes slinks from you to yonder courtier there, and whenever one drives it away it slinks back to the other. Over there a lady tries to smile as she strokes the loathsome furry head of another's sin, but one of her own is jealous and intrudes itself under her hand. Here sits an old nobleman with his grandson on his knee, and one of the great black sins of the grandfather is licking the child's face and has made the child it own. Sometimes a ghost would move and seek another chair, but always his pack of sins would move behind him. Poor ghosts, poor ghosts! how many flights they must have attempted for two hundred years from their hated sins, how many excuses they must have given for their presence, and the sins were with them still—and still unexplained. Suddenly one of them seemed to scent my living blood, and bayed horribly, and all the others left their ghosts at once and dashed up to the sin that had given tongue. The brute had picked up my scent near the door by which I had entered, and they moved slowly nearer to me sniffing along the floor, and uttering every now and then their fearful cry. I saw that the whole thing had gone too far. But now they had seen me, now they were all about me, they sprang up trying to reach my throat; and whenever their claws touched me, horrible thoughts came into my mind and unutterable desires dominated my heart. I planned bestial things as these creatures leaped around me, and planned them with a masterly cunning. A great red-eyed murder was among the foremost of those furry things from whom I feebly strove to defend my throat. Suddenly it seemed to me good that I should kill my brother. It seemed important to me that I should not risk being punished. I knew where a revolver was kept; after I shot him, I would dress the body up and put flour on the face like a man that had been acting as a ghost. It would be very simple. I would say that he had frightened me—and the servants had heard us talking about ghosts. There were one or two trivialities that would have to be arranged, but nothing escaped my mind. Yes, it seemed to me very good that I should kill my brother as I looked into the red depths of this creature's eyes. But one last effort as they dragged me down—"If two straight lines cut one another," I said, "the opposite angles are equal. Let AB, CD, cut one another at E, then the angles CEA, CEB equal two right angles (prop. xiii). Also CEA, AED equal two right angles."

I moved toward the door to get the revolver; a hideous exultation arose among the beasts. "But the angle CEA is common, therefore AED equals CEB. In the same way CEA equals DEB. *Q.E.D.*" It was proved. Logic and reason re-established themselves in my mind, there were no dark hounds of sin, the tapestried chairs were empty. It seemed to me an inconceivable thought that a man should murder his brother.

The Scoop

BY JAMES T. FARRELL

A large *Chicago Questioner* delivery truck parted the traffic as it roared northward toward the Clark Street bridge. It shook the street, emitted carbon monoxide gas from its exhaust pipe, punctuated the atmosphere with the shrillness of an open cutout. And thundered onward.

It was the first truck to be used for deliveries. Dennis McDermott, a circulation slugger, stood on the tail gate and hung onto a stout rope. Husky and handsome, he expressed his pride in a characteristic leering frown. He enjoyed the honor of having been assigned to this new truck while the other sluggers remained at work on horse-drawn vehicles.

Bumping, the truck rattled over the Clark Street bridge. Dennis was tearing through the scenes of his boyhood. He had grown up on the Near North Side, been educated on its streets, and he had served as an altar boy at the Holy Name Cathedral. Nuns had even looked at him with masked wonderment, incapable of understanding why such an intelligent-looking boy, who seemed so holy and devout in his acolyte's cassock, should always be fighting the way he was. That had been before he had been ejected from school for the third and final time in his seventh grade. His father had been an Irish immigrant and an unskilled worker. A precinct Captain in Bart Gallivan's organization had gotten him a job as a street cleaner, and that had elevated Dennis' father to one of the most minor positions in the neighborhood political aristocracy. Dennis had always had before him the example of the local hoodlums, and in his small-boy manner he had emulated them, leading his gang in expeditions to roll drunks, and in fights against neighborhood gangs of Jews and wops. Reckless and possessed of volatile courage, he had grown to be a tough guy, hired as a slugger and strike-breaker, employed in the taxicab wars, and then by *The Questioner* in the newspaper circulation war. Twice, he had been arrested in hold-ups. Duke O'Connell, from Dennis' own neighborhood, had become State's Attorney, and he had sprung Dennis both times. He stood on the tail gate of the truck, delivering papers to the old corners, even to corners where he had sold newspapers himself. And just as earlier sluggers had gypped him by subtracting papers from his order and charging him for them, so he was now gypping newsboys who were acquiring an education similar to his own in the same kind of system.

He clutched his supporting ropes more tightly as the truck curved about a corner. It drew up to a newsstand and Dennis flung down a bundle containing forty-five copies of the paper.

"How many?" asked the newsboy, a tired-looking kid of twelve or thirteen with a hole in the knee of his left stocking.

"What you ordered. Fifty!" Dennis said in his habitually bullying voice.

"Last night there was only forty-five. I counted 'em," the kid said with a nervous and uncertain air of defiance.

"I said there was fifty!"

"Well, I counted 'em!" the kid said, a whine creeping into his voice.

Dennis squeezed the boy's left ear between two strong fingers, and asked him how many there had been.

"I counted 'em!" the kid said, his voice cracking.

Dennis gave him a back-handed slap in the mouth and said that there had been fifty copies. He collected for the papers and jumped on the truck as the sniffling newsboy opened the bundle.

"How's it going, Wop?" Dennis asked Rocko Martini, at the next stop.

"All right, Irish," Rocko replied, winking.

While Rocko opened his bundle of papers, Dennis quickly said that he and a pal were pulling an easy house job on Saturday night and they needed somebody for a lookout. He'd been watching Rocko, and he knew he was all right. If Rocko wanted, they'd let him in with a fourth of the take. Rocko agreed, and Dennis made a date to meet him after work to give him the lowdown.

After two uneventful stops, the truck drew up to a stand where two newsboys were jawing each other. Dennis leaped down and stood over them, sneering, his hands on his hips. He noticed that a freckle-faced kid had a bundle of *The Chicago Clarion*.

"What's the idea, huh?"

"This guy's trying to bust into my business," *The Questioner* kid said.

Dennis looked at the freckle-faced boy, and the latter drew back a few paces.

"This is my corner, ain't it, Denny?"

"Well, I can sell my papers where I wanna. It's a free country, ain't it?"

"So that's the story!" Dennis said, grabbing the freckle-faced kid's papers, and shoving him. The kid reached for his papers, Dennis twisted his arm, booted his tail, and warned him not to be seen selling papers on this corner again. He tore the papers and told *The Questioner* kid to let him know if the punk came back.

Dennis delivered papers to Shorty Ellis, the punk he didn't like. Ellis was always giving *The Questioner* inside place on his stand. He told his driver to go around the block, and jumped off the tail gate. He sauntered back to Ellis. He pointed to the copies of *The Questioner* which were placed on the inside.

"Didn't I tell you where to place our papers?"

"Well, Muggs was around and told me to place his in the same spot."

"He did?"

"Yes."

"What did I tell you?"

"I don't see why you guys can't leave a kid alone to sell his papers."

"You don't, huh!" Dennis said, catching a look in Ellis' eyes that he didn't like.

"Change 'em!"

"And then Muggs'll come around and crack my puss."

"Change 'em!"

Ellis did not obey the command. Dennis slapped his face. Touching the red flush on his cheek, Ellis drew back, pulled out a pocketknife and, waving it before him defensively, told Dennis to let him alone. Dennis advanced on the boy. Ellis, still brandishing his knife, scratched Dennis' wrists. Dennis lost his temper and flashed a razor. When the boy

again struck out defensively, Dennis slashed his throat, almost from ear to ear. The boy fell, his head nearly dis-
membered, his blood gushing over the sidewalk. Dennis
looked around. No one had seen the fracas. He knew the
kid would die quickly. He hastened away and leaped onto
his truck. It raced back to *The Questioner* office. He saw
the night editor, Kelly Malloy, who had worked himself up
from a copy boy and was now only in his thirties. Malloy
always talked hard, but he had a soft, womanish face. He
had been given the job in a change that was calculated to
jack up circulation, and Dennis was the best circulation
man on the force. When Dennis assured him for the fourth
time that no one had seen him slash the boy, he breathed
a sigh of relief. Then he slapped his hands together and said
that the story was worth an extra. He became a dynamo of
energy.

Very soon Dennis was back on the truck with an extra
which bore the headline:

NEWSBOY MURDERED;
SLAYER UNAPPREHENDED
North-Side Boy Slashed with Razor in Suspected
Neighborhood Gang Fight.

At that time *The Questioner* was conducting, as a circulation stunt, one of its wars on crime. On the editorial page
there was a flamboyant editorial demanding that the police
enforce the laws and reduce crime.

The Bedchamber Mystery

BY C. S. FORESTER

▭ ▭ ▭

Now that a hundred years have passed, one of the scandals
in my family can be told. It is very doubtful if in 1843 Miss
Forester (she was Eulalie, but being the eldest daughter
unmarried, she, of course, was Miss Forester) and Miss
Emily Forester and Miss Eunice Forester ever foresaw the

world of 1943 to which their story would be told; in fact it is inconceivable that they could have believed that there ever would be a world in which their story could be told blatantly in public print. At that time it was the sort of thing that could only be hinted at in whispers during confidential moments in feminine drawing rooms; but it was whispered about enough to reach, in the end, the ears of my grandfather, who was their nephew, and my grandfather told it to me.

In 1843 Miss Forester and Miss Emily and Miss Eunice Forester were already maiden ladies of a certain age. The old-fashioned Georgian house in which they lived kept itself modestly retired, just like its inhabitants, from what there was of bustle and excitement in the High Street of the market town. The ladies indeed led a retired life; they went to church a little, they visited those of the sick whom it was decent and proper for maiden ladies to visit, they read the more colorless of the novels in the circulating library, and sometimes they entertained other ladies at tea.

And once a week they entertained a man. It might almost be said that they went from week to week looking forward to those evenings. Dr. Acheson was (not one of the old ladies would have been heartless enough to say "fortunately," but each of them felt it) a widower, and several years older even than my great-great-aunt Eulalie. Moreover, he was a keen whist player and a brilliant one, but in no way keener or more brilliant than were Eulalie, Emily, and Eunice. For years now the three nice old ladies had looked forward to their weekly evening of whist—all the ritual of setting out the green table, the two hours of silent cut-and-thrust play, and the final twenty minutes of conversation with Dr. Acheson as he drank a glass of old Madeira before bidding them good night.

The late Mrs. Acheson had passed to her Maker somewhere about 1830, so that it was for thirteen years they had played their weekly game of whist before the terrible thing happened. To this day we do not know whether it happened to Eulalie or Emily or Eunice, but it happened to one of them. The three of them had retired for the night, each to her separate room, and had progressed far toward the final stage of getting into bed. They were not dried-up old spinsters; on the contrary they were women of weight and substance, with the buxom contours even married women might have been proud of. It was her weight which was the undoing of one of them, Eulalie, Emily or Eunice.

Through the quiet house that bedtime there sounded the crash of china and a cry of pain, and two of the sisters—which two we do not know—hurried in their dressing gowns to the bedroom of the third—her identity is uncertain—to find her bleeding profusely from severe cuts in the lower part of the back. The jagged china fragments had inflicted severe wounds, and, most unfortunately, just in those parts where the injured sister could not attend to them herself. Under the urgings of the other two she fought down her modesty sufficiently to let them attempt to deal with them, but the bleeding was profuse, and the blood of the Foresters streamed from the prone figure face downward on the bed in terrifying quantity.

"We shall have to send for the doctor," said one of the ministering sisters; it was a shocking thing to contemplate.

"Oh, but we cannot!" said the other ministering sister.

"We must," said the first.

"How terrible!" said the second.

And with that the injured sister twisted her neck and joined in the conversation. "I will not have the doctor," she said. "I would die of shame."

"Think of the disgrace of it!" said the second sister. "We might even have to explain to him how it happened!"

"But she's bleeding to death," protested the first sister.

"I'd rather die!" said the injured one, and then, as a fresh appalling thought struck her, she twisted her neck even further. "I could never face him again. And what would happen to our whist?"

That was an aspect of the case which until then had occurred to neither of the other sisters, and it was enough to make them blench. But they were of stern stuff. Just as we do not know which was the injured one, we do not know which one thought of a way out of the difficulty, and we shall never know. We know that it was Miss Eulalie, as befitted her rank as eldest sister, who called to Deborah the maid, to go and fetch Dr. Acheson at once, but that does not mean to say that it was not Miss Eulalie who was the injured sister—injured or not, Miss Eulalie was quite capable of calling to Deborah and telling her what to do.

As she was bid, Deborah went and fetched Dr. Acheson and conducted him to Miss Eunice's bedroom, but, of course, the fact that it was Miss Eunice's bedroom is really no indication that it was Miss Eunice who was in there. Dr. Acheson had no means of knowing; all he saw was a re-

cumbent form covered by a sheet. In the center of the sheet
a round hole a foot in diameter had been cut, and through
the hole the seat of the injury was visible.

Dr. Acheson needed no explanations. He took his needles
and his thread from his little black bag and he set to work
and sewed up the worst of the cuts and attended to the
minor ones. Finally he straightened up and eased his aching
back.

"I shall have to take those stitches out," he explained to
the still and silent figure which had borne the stitching
stoically without a murmur. "I shall come next Wednesday
and do that."

Until next Wednesday the three Misses Forester kept to
their rooms. Not one of them was seen in the streets of the
market town, and when on Wednesday Dr. Acheson
knocked at the door Deborah conducted him once more to
Miss Eunice's bedroom. There was the recumbent form, and
there was the sheet with the hole in it. Dr. Acheson took out
the stitches.

"It has healed very nicely," said Dr. Acheson. "I don't
think any further attention from me will be necessary."

The figure under the sheet said nothing, nor did Dr.
Acheson expect it. He gave some concluding advice and
went his way. He was glad later to receive a note penned
in Miss Forester's Italian hand:

> Dear Dr. Acheson,
>   We will all be delighted if you will come to
> whist this week as usual.

When Dr. Acheson arrived he found that the "as usual"
applied only to his coming, for there was a slight but subtle
change in the furnishings of the drawing room. The stiff,
high-backed chairs on which the three Misses Forester sat
bore, each of them, a thick and comfortable cushion upon
the seat. There was no knowing which of the sisters needed
it.

Mr. Andrews

BY E. M. FORSTER

The souls of the dead were ascending towards the Judgment Seat and the Gate of Heaven. The world soul pressed them on every side, just as the atmosphere presses upon rising bubbles, striving to vanquish them, to break their thin envelope of personality, to mingle their virtue with its own. But they resisted, remembering their glorious individual life on earth, and hoping for an individual life to come.

Among them ascended the soul of a Mr. Andrews who, after a beneficent and honourable life, had recently deceased at his house in town. He knew himself to be kind, upright and religious, and though he approached his trial with all humility, he could not be doubtful of its result. God was not now a jealous God. He would not deny salvation merely because it was expected. A righteous soul may reasonably be conscious of its own righteousness and Mr. Andrews was conscious of his.

"The way is long," said a voice, "but by pleasant converse the way becomes shorter. Might I travel in your company?"

"Willingly," said Mr. Andrews. He held out his hand, and the two souls floated upward together.

"I was slain fighting the infidel," said the other exultantly, "and I go straight to those joys of which the Prophet speaks."

"Are you not a Christian?" asked Mr. Andrews gravely.

"No, I am a Believer. But you are a Moslem, surely?"

"I am not," said Mr. Andrews. "I am a Believer."

The two souls floated upward in silence, but did not release each other's hands. "I am broad church," he added gently. The word "broad" quavered strangely amid the interspaces.

"Relate to me your career," said the Turk at last.

"I was born of a decent middle-class family, and had my education at Winchester and Oxford. I thought of becoming

86

a missionary, but was offered a post in the Board of Trade, which I accepted. At thirty-two I married, and had four children, two of whom have died. My wife survives me. If I had lived a little longer I should have been knighted."

"Now I will relate my career. I was never sure of my father, and my mother does not signify. I grew up in the slums of Salonika. Then I joined a band and we plundered the villages of the infidel. I prospered and had three wives, all of whom survive me. Had I lived a little longer I should have had a band of my own."

"A son of mine was killed travelling in Macedonia. Perhaps you killed him."

"It is very possible."

The two souls floated upward, hand in hand. Mr. Andrews did not speak again, for he was filled with horror at the approaching tragedy. This man, so godless, so lawless, so cruel, so lustful, believed that he would be admitted into Heaven. And into what a heaven—a place full of the crude pleasures of a ruffian's life on earth! But Mr. Andrews felt neither disgust nor moral indignation. He was only conscious of an immense pity, and his own virtues confronted him not at all. He longed to save the man whose hand he held more tightly, who, he thought, was now holding more tightly on to him. And when he reached the Gate of Heaven, instead of saying, "Can I enter?" as he had intended, he cried out, "Cannot *he* enter?"

And at the same moment the Turk uttered the same cry. For the same spirit was working in each of them.

From the gateway a voice replied, "Both can enter." They were filled with joy and pressed forward together.

Then the voice said, "In what clothes will you enter?"

"In my best clothes," shouted the Turk, "the ones I stole." And he clad himself in a splendid turban and a waistcoat embroidered with silver, and baggy trousers, and a great belt in which were stuck pipes and pistols and knives.

"And in what clothes will you enter?" said the voice to Mr. Andrews.

Mr. Andrews thought of his best clothes, but he had no wish to wear them again. At last he remembered and said, "Robes."

"Of what colour and fashion?" asked the voice.

Mr. Andrews had never thought about the matter much. He replied, in hesitating tones, "White, I suppose, of some flowing material," and he was immediately given a garment such as he had described. "Do I wear it rightly?" he asked.

"Wear it as it pleases you," replied the voice. "What else do you desire?"

"A harp," suggested Mr. Andrews. "A small one."

A small gold harp was placed in his hand.

"And a palm—no, I cannot have a palm, for it is the reward of martyrdom; my life has been tranquil and happy."

"You can have a palm if you desire it."

But Mr. Andrews refused the palm, and hurried in his white robes after the Turk, who had already entered Heaven. As he passed in at the open gate, a man, dressed like himself, passed out with gestures of despair.

"Why is he not happy?" he asked.

The voice did not reply.

"And who are all those figures, seated inside on thrones and mountains? Why are some of them terrible, and sad, and ugly?"

There was no answer. Mr. Andrews entered, and then he saw that those seated figures were all the gods who were then being worshipped on the earth. A group of souls stood around each, singing his praises. But the gods paid no heed, for they were listening to the prayers of living men, which alone brought them nourishment. Sometimes a faith would grow weak, and then the god of that faith also drooped and dwindled and fainted for his daily portion of incense. And sometimes, owing to a revivalist movement, or to a great commemoration, or to some other cause, a faith would grow strong, and the god of that faith grow strong also. And, more frequently still, a faith would alter, so that the features of its god altered and became contradictory, and passed from ecstasy to respectability, or from mildness and universal love to the ferocity of battle. And at times a god would divide into two gods, or three, or more, each with his own ritual and precarious supply of prayer.

Mr. Andrews saw Buddha, and Vishnu, and Allah, and Jehovah, and the Elohim. He saw little ugly determined gods who were worshipped by a few savages in the same way. He saw the vast shadowy outlines of the neo-pagan Zeus. There were cruel gods, and coarse gods, and tortured gods, and, worse still, there were gods who were peevish, or deceitful, or vulgar. No aspiration of humanity was unfulfilled. There was even an intermediate state for those who wished it, and for the Christian Scientists a place where they could demonstrate that they had not died.

He did not play his harp for long, but hunted vainly for one of his dead friends. And though souls were continually entering Heaven, it still seemed curiously empty. Though he had all that he expected, he was conscious of no great happiness, no mystic contemplation of beauty, no mystic union with good. There was nothing to compare with that moment outside the gate, when he prayed that the Turk might enter and heard the Turk uttering the same prayer for him. And when at last he saw his companion, he hailed him with a cry of human joy.

The Turk was seated in thought, and round him, by sevens, sat the virgins who are promised in the Koran.

"Oh, my dear friend!" he called out. "Come here, and we will never be parted, and such as my pleasures are, they shall be yours also. Where are my other friends? Where are the men whom I love, or whom I have killed?"

"I, too, have only found you," said Mr. Andrews. He sat down by the Turk, and the virgins, who were all exactly alike, ogled them with coal black eyes.

"Though I have all that I expected," said the Turk, "I am conscious of no great happiness. There is nothing to compare with that moment outside the gate when I prayed that you might enter, and heard you uttering the same prayer for me. These virgins are as beautiful and good as I had fashioned, yet I could wish that they were better."

As he wished, the forms of the virgins became more rounded, and their eyes grew larger and blacker than before. And Mr. Andrews, by a wish similar in kind, increased the purity and softness of his garment and the glitter of his harp. For in that place their expectations were fulfilled, but not their hopes.

"I am going," said Mr. Andrews at last. "We desire infinity and we cannot imagine it. How can we expect it to be granted? I have never imagined anything infinitely good or beautiful excepting in my dreams."

"I am going with you," said the other.

Together they sought the entrance gate, and the Turk parted with his virgins and his best clothes, and Mr. Andrews cast away his robes and his harp.

"Can we depart?" they asked.

"You can both depart if you wish," said the voice, "but remember what lies outside."

As soon as they passed the gate, they felt again the pressure of the world soul. For a moment they stood hand in hand resisting it. Then they suffered it to break in upon them, and they, and all the experience they had gained, and all the love and wisdom they had generated, passed into it, and made it better.

The Test

BY ANGELICA GIBBS

◫ ◫ ◫

On the afternoon Marian took her second driver's test, Mrs. Ericson went with her. "It's probably better to have someone a little older with you," Mrs. Ericson said as Marian slipped into the driver's seat beside her. "Perhaps the last time your Cousin Bill made you nervous, talking too much on the way."

"Yes, Ma'am," Marian said in her soft unaccented voice. "They probably do like it better if a white person shows up with you."

"Oh, I don't think it's *that*," Mrs. Ericson began, and subsided after a glance at the girl's set profile. Marian drove the car slowly through the shady suburban streets. It was one of the first hot days in June, and when they reached the boulevard they found it crowded with cars headed for the beaches.

"Do you want me to drive?" Mrs. Ericson asked. "I'll be glad to if you're feeling jumpy." Marian shook her head. Mrs. Ericson watched her dark, competent hands and wondered for the thousandth time how the house had ever managed to get along without her, or how she had lived through those earlier years when her household had been presided over by a series of slatternly white girls who had considered housework demeaning and the care of children an added insult. "You drive beautifully, Marian," she said. "Now, don't think of the last time. Anybody would slide on a steep hill on a wet day like that."

"It takes four mistakes to flunk you," Marian said. "I don't remember doing all the things the inspector marked down on my blank."

"People say that they only want you to slip them a little something," Mrs. Ericson said doubtfully.

"*No*," Marian said. "That would only make it worse, Mrs. Ericson, I know."

The car turned right, at a traffic signal, into a side road and slid up to the curb at the rear of a short line of parked cars. The inspectors had not arrived yet,

"You have the papers." Mrs. Ericson asked. Marian took them out of her bag: her learner's permit, the car registration, and her birth certificate. They settled down to the dreary business of waiting.

"It will be marvellous to have someone dependable to drive the children to school every day," Mrs. Ericson said.

Marian looked up from the list of driving requirements she had been studying. "It'll make things simpler at the house, won't it?" she said.

"Oh, Marian," Mrs. Ericson exclaimed, "if I could only pay you half of what you're worth!"

"Now, Mrs. Ericson," Marian said firmly. They looked at each other and smiled with affection.

Two cars with official insignia on their doors stopped across the street. The inspectors leaped out, very brisk and military in their neat uniforms. Marian's hands tightened on the wheel. "There's the one who flunked me last time," she whispered, pointing to a stocky, self-important man who had begun to shout directions at the driver at the head of the line. "Oh, Mrs. Ericson."

"Now, Marian," Mrs. Ericson said. They smiled at each other again, rather weakly.

The inspector who finally reached their car was not the stocky one but a genial, middle-aged man who grinned broadly as he thumbed over their papers. Mrs. Ericson started to get out of the car. "Don't you want to come along?" the inspector asked. "Mandy and I don't mind company."

Mrs. Ericson was bewildered for a moment. "No," she said, and stepped to the curb. "I might make Marian self-conscious. She's a fine driver, Inspector."

"Sure thing," the inspector said, winking at Mrs. Ericson. He slid into the seat beside Marian. "Turn right at the corner, Mandy-Lou."

From the curb, Mrs. Ericson watched the car move smoothly up the street.

The inspector made notations in a small black book. "Age?" he inquired presently, as they drove along.

"Twenty-seven."

He looked at Marian out of the corner of his eye. "Old enough to have quite a flock of pickaninnies, eh?"

Marian did not answer.

"Left at this corner," the inspector said, "and park between that truck and the green Buick."

The two cars were very close together, but Marian squeezed in between them without too much maneuvering. "Driven before, Mandy-Lou?" the inspector asked.

"Yes, sir. I had a license for three years in Pennsylvania."

"Why do you want to drive a car?"

"My employer needs me to take her children to and from school."

"Sure you don't really want to sneak out nights to meet some young blood?" the inspector asked. He laughed as Marian shook her head.

"Let's see you take a left at the corner and then turn around in the middle of the next block," the inspector said. He began to whistle "Swanee River." "Make you homesick?" he asked.

Marian put out her hand, swung around neatly in the street, and headed back in the direction from which they had come. "No," she said. "I was born in Scranton, Pennsylvania."

The inspector feigned astonishment. "You-all ain't Southern?" he said. "Well, dog my cats if I didn't think you-all came from down yondah."

"No, sir," Marian said.

"Turn onto Main Street and let's see how you-all does in heavier traffic."

They followed a line of cars along Main Street for several blocks until they came in sight of a concrete bridge which arched high over the railroad tracks.

"Read that sign at the end of the bridge," the inspector said.

"'Proceed with caution. Dangerous in slippery weather,'" Marian said.

"You-all sho can read fine," the inspector exclaimed. "Where d'you learn to do that, Mandy?"

"I got my college degree last year," Marian said. Her voice was not quite steady.

As the car crept up the slope of the bridge the inspector burst out laughing. He laughed so hard he could scarcely give his next direction. "Stop here," he said, wiping his eyes, "then start 'er up again. Mandy got her degree, did she? Dog my cats!"

Marian pulled up beside the curb. She put the car in neutral, pulled on the emergency, waited a moment, and then put the car into gear again. Her face was set. As she released the brake her foot slipped off the clutch pedal and the engine stalled.

"Now, Mistress Mandy," the inspector said, "remember your degree."

"*Damn* you!" Marian cried. She started the car with a jerk.

The inspector lost his joviality in an instant. "Return to the starting place, please," he said, and made four very black crosses at random in the squares on Marian's application blank.

Mrs. Ericson was waiting at the curb where they had left her. As Marian stopped the car, the inspector jumped out and brushed past her, his face purple. "What happened?" Mrs. Ericson asked, looked after him with alarm.

Marian stared down at the wheel and her lip trembled.

"Oh, Marian, *again?*" Mrs. Ericson said.

Marian nodded. "In a sort of different way," she said, and slid over to the right-hand side of the car.

Truth and Consequences

BY BRENDAN GILL

▭ ▭ ▭

She had straight blond hair and a red mouth, and she was lame. Every day she played golf and went swimming in the center of a crowd of boys. Charles, sitting with his mother on the hotel porch, watched her and nodded while his mother repeated, "Isn't it extraordinary, a girl like that? I wonder what in the world they see in her." Charles took to walking past the pool during the morning as the girl and boys lay there side by side, laughing. He listened carefully to her voice. It was low, unhurried, forceful. So, he thought, was her language. Every other word seemed to him to be "damn," "hell," and worse. She spoke of God, to whom Charles was preparing to dedicate his life, as if He were a friend in the next block. "I swear to God," the girl said. "I must have told you this one, for God's sake." Charles walked out of range of the jokes that followed. He was eighteen and he was spending this last vacation with his mother before entering a seminary. In eight more summers he would be a priest. The girl's language sent sharp lightnings through him. He had never seen or heard anyone like her before in his life.

One night after dinner, while his mother was upstairs swallowing a pill, the girl sat down beside him on the hotel porch. Her lips were smiling, her eyes the color of her blue, open blouse. "We ought to know each other," she said. "You ought to join the rest of us at the pool."

"I'm with Mother."

The girl covered his hand with hers. "Well, for God's sake, you're old enough to swim by yourself, aren't you?"

Charles felt that he ought to explain before it was too late, before she said something he could never forget. "I'm going to be a priest," he said.

The girl kept smiling. "A priest? With a turn-around collar and everything?"

He nodded.

"So you can't come swimming with the gang?"

"That has nothing to do with it. I just thought I ought to tell you. I always do tell people."

"You can still come dancing with us if you want to?"

"Certainly."

"Could you take me to a movie if you wanted to?"

"Yes."

"I never met a boy who was going to be a priest. Could you take me out for a ride tonight if you wanted to?"

He said in relief, "We didn't bring our car."

"Oh, hell. I mean in my car. I mean just for example. I didn't say I'd go with you." She stared at him slowly from head to foot. "It would be funny, with a boy who was going to be a priest."

Fortunately, Charles thought, his mother would be coming downstairs at any moment now. She would make short shrift of the girl. "You oughtn't to keep swearing like that," he said.

He expected her to laugh, but she didn't. She ran her hand up and down the bare brown leg that was shorter than the other. "Like what?" she said.

"Like 'for God's sake.' That's taking the name of the Lord in vain. That's one of the Ten Commandments."

"I'm an awful damn fool," the girl said. "I talk like that to keep people from thinking about my leg. But I didn't know you were going to be a priest."

Charles wanted to get rid of her, but he didn't know how. He stood up and said, "I don't think you ought to worry about things like that. I hadn't even noticed."

She stood up beside him. Her eyes shone in the mountain light. "Oh, damn you, please don't lie to me," she said. "Of course you've noticed. But does it bother you? Does it make you want to stay away from me?"

"No," he said. "Oh, no."

She slipped her hand under his arm. "Thanks for saying that so nice and hard. I haven't asked anybody that in a long time."

Without having willed it, stupidly, Charles found himself walking the length of the porch beside the girl. Her blond hair touched the shoulder of his coat. It was difficult to tell, looking down at her, that she was lame. He bent his head to smell her perfume. "Tell me what you do," he said.

"You mean, bang, just like that, what do I do?"

"Not that you have to tell me."

"But I do. It's just that there aren't any surprises in me. I'm not beautiful or tormented—or not much tormented. I don't do anything. I got out of Walker's and I had a party and now I guess I'll be on the loose like this for a couple of years. Finally somebody may ask me to marry him, and quick like a fish I will. I hope I'll have sense enough for that. And I'll be terribly glad when I've done it. I'll try to let him win most of the arguments we'll have. I'll try to be good about satisfying him, the way all those awful books say, and about having good kids for him, and all that."

Charles felt himself stumbling. She had told him everything about herself. She had told him the truth, which he hadn't wanted. They reached the end of the porch and stood facing the valley between the mountains. Two old men were playing croquet in the gathering darkness, the wooden mallets and balls knocking softly together, the white trousers moving like disembodied spirits across the lawn. Charles and the girl could hear, below them in the kitchen, the clatter of dishes being washed and stacked and the high, tired voices of the waitresses.

"Now talk about you," the girl said. "You think you want to be a priest?"

"Why—yes."

"It isn't just a vow your mother made while she was carrying you?"

Charles laughed, and was surprised at how easily he laughed. "Well," he said, "I guess Mother's always wanted me to be a priest, especially after Dad died. We went abroad then, Mother and I. We spent the summer in Rome. We had an audience with the Pope—the old one, a little man with thick glasses and a big ring. We got so we were going to Mass and even to Communion every day. When we came back to this country I started in at a Catholic school. I liked it. I graduated this year. I'm going down to the seminary in the fall. I guess I'll like that, too."

"But isn't there more to it than that?" the girl said. "I'm not a Catholic—I'm not anything—but don't you have to have some kind of a call, bells ringing, something like that?"

"You mean a vocation. Yes. Well, I guess I have a vocation all right."

"But what is it? How can you be sure?"

Charles gripped the railing of the porch. He had never been able to answer that question. He remembered kneeling beside his mother's bed, month after month, year after year. "Don't you feel it, darling?" his mother had whispered. "Don't you feel how wonderful it will be? Don't you feel how God wants you?" Charles had told himself finally that he was able to answer that question. The next day his mother, dabbing her eyes, had said, "Here's my boy, Father Duffy. I'm giving him to you." And Father Duffy had said, "Ah, you're an example to Irish mothers everywhere. Are you sure you want to come with us, boy?" "Yes, Father, I do," Charles had said, watching his mother. He had spoken an answer, written an answer, lived an answer, but he had never believed it. He had been waiting to believe it. Now he heard himself saying, for the first time, "No, I can't be sure."

The girl said, "Then you're not going to be a priest. You mustn't be. Why are you so damned afraid to face the truth?"

Charles saw his mother walking heavily along the porch. He studied her as if she were a stranger. What an enormous old woman she was, and how strong she was, and how she had driven him! He took the girl's hand. It was cool and unmoving. He felt the porch floor trembling under his mother's approach.

The Disabled Soldier

BY OLIVER GOLDSMITH

No observation is more common, and at the same time more true, than that one half of the world are ignorant how the other half lives. The misfortunes of the great are held up to engage our attention; are enlarged upon in tones of declamation; and the world is called upon to gaze at the noble sufferers: the great, under the pressure of calamity, are conscious of several others sympathising with their distress; and have, at once, the comfort of admiration and pity.

There is nothing magnanimous in bearing misfortunes with fortitude, when the whole world is looking on: men in such circumstances will act bravely even from motives of vanity: but he who, in the vale of obscurity, can brave adversity; who without friends to encourage, acquaintances to pity, or even without hope to alleviate his misfortunes, can behave with tranquillity and indifference, is truly great: whether peasant or courtier, he deserves admiration, and should be held up for our imitation and respect.

While the slightest inconveniences of the great are magnified into calamities; while tragedy mouths out their sufferings in all the strains of eloquence, the miseries of the poor are entirely disregarded; and yet some of the lower ranks of people undergo more real hardships in one day, than those of a more exalted station suffer in their whole lives. It is inconceivable what difficulties the meanest of our common sailors and soldiers endure without murmuring or regret; without passionately declaiming against providence, or calling their fellows to be gazers of their intrepidity. Every day is to them a day of misery, and yet they entertain their hard fate without repining.

With what indignation do I hear an Ovid, a Cicero, or a Rabutin complain of their misfortunes and hardships, whose greatest calamity was that of being unable to visit a certain spot of earth, to which they had foolishly attached an idea

of happiness. Their distresses were pleasures, compared to
what many of the adventuring poor every day endure without murmuring. They ate, drank, and slept; they had slaves
to attend them, and were sure of subsistence for life; while
many of their fellow creatures are obliged to wander without
a friend to comfort or assist them, and even without shelter
from the severity of the season.

I have been led into these reflections from accidentally
meeting, some days ago, a poor fellow, whom I knew when a
boy, dressed in a sailor's jacket, and begging at one of the
outlets of the town, with a wooden leg. I knew him to have
been honest and industrious when in the country, and was
curious to learn what had reduced him to his present situation. Wherefore, after giving him what I thought proper, I
desired to know the history of his life and misfortunes, and
the manner in which he was reduced to his present distress.
The disabled soldier, for such he was, though dressed in a
sailor's habit, scratching his head, and leaning on his crutch,
put himself into an attitude to comply with my request, and
gave me his history as follows:

"As for my misfortunes, master, I can't pretend to have
gone through any more than other folks; for, except for the
loss of my limb, and my being obliged to beg, I don't know
any reason, thank Heaven, that I have to complain. There
is Bill Tibbs, of our regiment, he has lost both his legs, and
an eye to boot; but, thank Heaven, it is not so bad with me
yet.

"I was born in Shropshire; my father was a labourer, and
died when I was five years old, so I was put upon the parish.
As he had been a wandering sort of man, the parishioners
were not able to tell to what parish I belonged, or where I
was born, so they sent me to another parish, and that parish
sent me to a third. I thought in my heart, they kept sending
me about so long, that they would not let me be born in any
parish at all; but at last, however, they fixed me. I had some
disposition to be a scholar, and was resolved at least to know
my letters: but the master of the workhouse put me to
business as soon as I was able to handle a mallet; and here
I lived an easy kind of life for five years. I only wrought
ten hours in the day and had my meat and drink provided
for my labour. It was true, I was not suffered to stir out of
the house, for fear, as they said, I should run away; but what
of that? I had the liberty of the whole house, and the yard
before the door, and that was enough for me. I was then

bound out to a farmer, where I was up both early and late; but I ate and drank well; and liked my business well enough, till he died, when I was obliged to provide for myself; so I was resolved to go seek my fortune.

"In this manner I went from town to town, worked when I could get employment, and starved when I could get none; when, happening one day to go through a field belonging to a justice of the peace, I spied a hare crossing the path just before me; and I believe the devil put it into my head to fling my stick at it. Well, what will you have on't? I killed the hare, and was bringing it away, when the justice himself met me; he called me a poacher and a villain, and collaring me, desired I would give an account of myself. I fell upon my knees, begged his worship's pardon, and began to give a full account of all that I knew of my breed, seed, and generation; but though I gave a very true account, the justice said I could give no account; so I was indicted at the sessions, found guilty of being poor, and sent up to London to Newgate, in order to be transported as a vagabond.

"People may say this and that of being in jail, but for my part, I found Newgate as agreeable a place as ever I was in all my life. I had my belly full to eat and drink, and did no work at all. This kind of life was too good to last forever; so I was taken out of prison, after five months, put on board of ship, and sent off, with two hundred more, to the plantations. We had but an indifferent passage, for being all confined to the hold, more than a hundred of our people died for want of sweet air; and those that remained were sickly enough, God knows. When we came ashore we were sold to the planters, and I was bound for seven years more. As I was no scholar, for I did not know my letters, I was obliged to work among the negroes; and I served out my time, as in duty bound to do.

"When my time was expired, I worked my passage home, and glad I was to see old England again, because I loved my country. I was afraid, however, that I should be indicted for a vagabond once more, so did not much care to go down into the country, but kept about the town, and did little jobs when I could get them.

"I was very happy in this manner for some time till one evening, coming home from work, two men knocked me down, and then desired me to stand. They belonged to a press-gang. I was carried before the justice, and as I could give no account of myself, I had my choice left, whether to go on board a man-of-war, or list for a soldier. I chose the latter, and in this post of a gentleman, I served two campaigns in Flanders, was at the battles of Val and Fontenoy, and received but one wound through the breast here; but the doctor of our regiment soon made me well again.

"When the peace came on I was discharged; and as I could not work, because my wound was sometimes troublesome, I listed for a landman in the East India Company's service. I have fought the French in six pitched battles; and I verily believe that if I could read or write, our captain would have made me a corporal. But it was not my good fortune to have any promotion, for I soon fell sick, and so got leave to return home again with forty pounds in my pocket. This was at the beginning of the present war, and I hoped to be set on shore, and to have the pleasure of spending my money; but the Government wanted men, and so I was pressed for a sailor, before ever I could set foot on shore.

"The boatswain found me, as he said, an obstinate fellow: he swore he knew that I understood my business well, but that I shammed Abraham to be idle; but God knows, I knew nothing of sea-business, and he beat me without considering what he was about. I had still, however, my forty pounds, and that was some comfort to me under every beating; and the money I might have had to this day, but that our ship was taken by the French, and so I lost all.

"Our crew was carried into Brest, and many of them died, because they were not used to life in a jail; but, for my part, it was nothing to me, for I was seasoned. One night, as I was asleep on the bed of boards, with a warm blanket about me, for I always loved to lie well, I was awakened by the boatswain, who had a dark lantern in his hand. 'Jack,' says he to me, 'will you knock out the French sentry's brains?' 'I don't care,' says I, striving to keep myself awake, 'if I lend a hand.' 'Then follow me,' says he, 'and I hope we shall do business.' So up I got, and tied my blanket, which was all the clothes I had, about my middle, and went with him to fight the Frenchman. I hate the French, because they are all slaves, and wear wooden shoes.

"Though we had no arms, one Englishman is able to beat five French at any time; so we went down to the door where both sentries were posted, and rushing upon them, seized their arms in a moment, and knocked them down. From thence nine of us ran together to the quay, and seizing the first boat we met, got out of the harbour and put to sea. We had not been here three days before we were taken up by the *Dorset* privateer, who were glad of so many good hands; and we consented to run our chance. However, we had not as much luck as we expected. In three days we fell in with the *Pompadour* privateer of forty guns, while we had but twenty-three, so to it we went, yard-arm and yard-arm. The fight lasted three hours, and I verily believe we should have taken the Frenchman, had we but some more men left behind; but unfortunately we lost all our men just as we were going to get the victory.

"I was once more in the power of the French, and I believe it would have gone hard with me had I been brought back to Brest; but by good fortune we were retaken by the *Viper*. I had almost forgotten to tell you, that in that engagement, I was wounded in two places: I lost four fingers off the left hand, and my leg was shot off. If I had had the good fortune to have lost my leg and the use of my hand on board a king's ship, and not aboard a privateer, I should have been entitled to clothing and maintenance during the rest of my life; but that was not my chance: one man is born with a silver spoon in his mouth, and another with a wooden ladle. However, Blessed be God, I enjoy good health, and will for ever love liberty and old England. Liberty, property, and Old England, for ever, huzza!"

Thus saying, he limped off, leaving me in admiration at his intrepidity and content; nor could I avoid acknowledging that an habitual acquaintance with misery serves better than philosophy to teach us to despise it.

Virtuoso

BY HERBERT GOLDSTONE

🀰 🀰 🀰

"Sir?"

The Maestro continued to play, not looking up from the keys.

"Yes, Rollo?"

"Sir, I was wondering if you would explain this apparatus to me."

The Maestro stopped playing, his thin body stiffly re-laxed on the bench. His long supple fingers floated off the keyboard.

"Apparatus?" He turned and smiled at the robot. "Do you mean the piano, Rollo?"

"This machine that produces varying sounds. I would like some information about it, its operation and purpose. It is not included in my reference data."

The Maestro lit a cigarette. He preferred to do it himself. One of his first orders to Rollo when the robot was delivered two days before had been to disregard his built-in instructions on the subject.

"I'd hardly call a piano a machine, Rollo," he smiled, "although technically you are correct. It is actually, I suppose, a machine designed to produce sounds of graduated pitch and tone, singly or in groups."

"I assimilated that much by observation," Rollo replied in a brassy baritone which no longer sent tiny tremors up the Maestro's spine. "Wires of different thickness and tautness struck by felt-covered hammers activated by manually operated levers arranged in a horizontal panel."

"A very cold-blooded description of one of man's nobler works," the Maestro remarked dryly. "You make Mozart and Chopin mere laboratory technicians."

"Mozart? Chopin?" The duralloy sphere that was Rollo's head shone stark and featureless, its immediate surface unbroken but for twin vision lenses. "The terms are not included in my memory banks."

"No, not yours, Rollo," the Maestro said softly. "Mozart and Chopin are not for vacuum tubes and fuses and copper wire. They are for flesh and blood and human tears."

"I do not understand," Rollo droned.

"Well," the Maestro said, smoke curling lazily from his nostrils, "they are two of the humans who compose, or design successions of notes—varying sounds, that is, produced by the piano or by other instruments, machines that produce other types of sounds of fixed pitch and tone.

"Sometimes these instruments, as we call them, are played, or operated, individually: sometimes in groups—orchestras, as we refer to them—and the sounds blend together, they harmonize. That is, they have an orderly, mathematical relationship to each other which results in . . ."

The Maestro threw up his hands.

"I never imagined," he chuckled, "that I would some day struggle so mightily, and so futilely, to explain music to a robot!"

"Music?"

"Yes, Rollo. The sounds produced by this machine and others of the same category are called music."

"What is the purpose of music, sir?"

"Purpose?"

The Maestro crushed the cigarette in an ash tray. He turned to the keyboard of the concert grand and flexed his fingers briefly.

"Listen, Rollo."

The wraithlike fingers glided and wove the opening bars of "Clair de Lune," slender and delicate as spider silk. Rollo stood rigid, the fluorescent light over the music rack casting a bluish jeweled sheen over his towering bulk, shimmering in the amber vision lenses.

The Maestro drew his hands back from the keys and the subtle thread of melody melted reluctantly into silence.

"Claude Debussy," the Maestro said. "One of our mechanics of an era long past. He designed that succession of tones many years ago. What do you think of it?"

Rollo did not answer at once.

"The sounds were well formed," he replied finally. "They did not jar my auditory senses as some do."

The Maestro laughed. "Rollo, you may not realize it, but you're a wonderful critic."

"This music, then," Rollo droned. "Its purpose is to give pleasure to humans?"

"Exactly," the Maestro said. "Sounds well formed, that do not jar the auditory senses as some do. Marvelous! It should be carved in marble over the entrance of New Carnegie Hall."

"I do not understand. Why should my definition—?"

The Maestro waved a hand. "No matter, Rollo. No matter."

"Sir?"

"Yes, Rollo?"

"Those sheets of paper you sometimes place before you on the piano. They are the plans of the composer indicating which sounds are to be produced by the piano and in what order?"

"Just so. We call each sound a note; combinations of notes we call chords."

"Each dot, then, indicates a sound to be made?"

"Perfectly correct, my man of metal."

Rollo stared straight ahead. The Maestro felt a peculiar sense of wheels turning within that impregnable sphere.

"Sir, I have scanned my memory banks and find no specific or implied instructions against it. I should like to be taught how to produce these notes on the piano. I request that you feed the correlation between those dots and the levers of the panel into my memory banks."

The Maestro peered at him, amazed. A slow grin traveled across his face.

"Done!" he exclaimed. "It's been many years since pupils helped gray these ancient locks, but I have the feeling that you, Rollo, will prove a most fascinating student. To instill the Muse into metal and machinery . . . I accept the challenge gladly!"

He rose, touched the cool latent power of Rollo's arm.

"Sit down here, my Rolleindex Personal Robot, Model M-e. We shall start Beethoven spinning in his grave—or make musical history."

More than an hour later the Maestro yawned and looked at his watch.

"It's late," he spoke into the end of the yawn. "These old eyes are not tireless like yours, my friend." He touched Rollo's shoulder. "You have the complete fundamentals of musical notation in your memory banks, Rollo. That's a good night's lesson, particularly when I recall how long it took me to acquire the same amount of information. Tomorrow we'll attempt to put those awesome fingers of yours to work."

He stretched. "I'm going to bed," he said. "Will you lock up and put out the lights?"

Rollo rose from the bench. "Yes, sir," he droned. "I have a request."

"What can I do for my star pupil?"

"May I attempt to create some sounds with the keyboard tonight? I will do so very softly so as not to disturb you."

"Tonight? Aren't you—?" Then the Maestro smiled. "You must pardon me, Rollo. It's still a bit difficult for me to realize that sleep has no meaning for you."

He hesitated, rubbing his chin. "Well, I suppose a good teacher should not discourage impatience to learn. All right, Rollo, but please be careful." He patted the polished mahogany. "This piano and I have been together for many years. I'd hate to see its teeth knocked out by those sledge-hammer digits of yours. Lightly, my friend, very lightly."

"Yes, sir."

The Maestro fell asleep with a faint smile on his lips, dimly aware of the shy, tentative notes that Rollo was coaxing forth.

Then gray fog closed in and he was in that half-world where reality is dreamlike and dreams are real. It was soft and feathery and lavender clouds and sounds were rolling and washing across his mind in flowing waves.

Where? The mist drew back a bit and he was in red velvet and deep and the music swelled and broke over him.

He smiled.

My recording. Thank you, thank you, thank—

The Maestro snapped erect, threw the covers aside.

He sat on the edge of the bed, listening.

He groped for his robe in the darkness, shoved bony feet into his slippers.

He crept, trembling uncontrollably, to the door of his studio and stood there, thin and brittle in the robe.

The light over the music rack was an eerie island in the brown shadows of the studio. Rollo sat at the keyboard, prim, inhuman, rigid, twin lenses focused somewhere off into the shadows.

The massive feet working the pedals, arms and hands flashing and glinting—they were living entities, separate, somehow, from the machined perfection of his body.

The music rack was empty.

A copy of Beethoven's "Appassionata" lay closed on the bench. It had been, the Maestro remembered, in a pile of sheet music on the piano.

Rollo was playing it.

He was creating it, breathing it, drawing it through silver flame.

Time became meaningless, suspended in midair.

The Maestro didn't realize he was weeping until Rollo finished the sonata.

The robot turned to look at the Maestro. "The sounds," he droned. "They pleased you?"

The Maestro's lips quivered. "Yes, Rollo," he replied at last. "They pleased me." He fought the lump in his throat.

He picked up the music in fingers that shook.

"This," he murmured. "Already?"

"It has been added to my store of data," Rollo replied. "I applied the principles you explained to me to these plans. It was not very difficult."

The Maestro swallowed as he tried to speak. "It was not very difficult . . ." he repeated softly.

The old man sank down slowly onto the bench next to Rollo, stared silently at the robot as though seeing him for the first time.

Rollo got to his feet.

The Maestro let his fingers rest on the keys, strangely foreign now.

"Music!" he breathed. "I may have heard it that way in my soul. I know Beethoven did!"

He looked up at the robot, a growing excitement in his face.

"Rollo," he said, his voice straining to remain calm. "You and I have some work to do tomorrow on your memory banks."

Sleep did not come again that night.

He strode briskly into the studio the next morning. Rollo was vacuuming the carpet. The Maestro preferred carpets to the new dust-free plastics, which felt somehow profane to his feet.

The Maestro's house was, in fact, an oasis of anachronisms in a desert of contemporary antiseptic efficiency.

"Well, are you ready for work, Rollo?" he asked. "We have a lot to do, you and I. I have such plans for you, Rollo —great plans!"

Rollo, for once, did not reply.

"I have asked them all to come here this afternoon," the Maestro went on. "Conductors, concert pianists, composers, my manager. All the giants of music, Rollo. Wait until they hear you play."

Rollo switched off the vacuum and stood quietly.

"You'll play for them right here this afternoon." The Maestro's voice was high-pitched, breathless. "The 'Appassionata' again, I think. Yes, that's it. I must see their faces!

"Then we'll arrange a recital to introduce you to the public and the critics and then a major concerto with one of the big orchestras. We'll have it telecast around the world, Rollo. It can be arranged.

"Think of it, Rollo, just think of it! The greatest piano virtuoso of all time . . . a robot! It's completely fantastic and completely wonderful. I feel like an explorer at the edge of a new world."

He walked feverishly back and forth.

"Then recordings, of course. My entire repertoire, Rollo, and more. So much more!"

"Sir?"

The Maestro's face shone as he looked up at him. "Yes, Rollo?"

"In my built-in instructions, I have the option of rejecting any action which I consider harmful to my owner," the robot's words were precise, carefully selected. "Last night you wept. That is one of the indications I am instructed to consider in making my decisions."

The Maestro gripped Rollo's thick, superbly molded arm.

"Rollo, you don't understand. That was for the moment. It was petty of me, childish!"

"I beg your pardon, sir, but I must refuse to approach the piano again."

The Maestro stared at him, unbelieving, pleading.

"Rollo, you can't! The world must hear you!"

"No, sir." The amber lenses almost seemed to soften.

"The piano is not a machine," that powerful inhuman voice droned. "To me, yes. I can translate the notes into sounds at a glance. From only a few I am able to grasp at once the composer's conception. It is easy for me."

Rollo towered magnificently over the Maestro's bent form.

"I can also grasp," the brassy monotone rolled through the studio, "that this . . . music is not for robots. It is for man. To me it is easy, yes. . . . It was not meant to be easy."

Her Lover

BY MAXIN GORKY

An acquaintance of mine once told me the following story. When I was a student at Moscow I happened to live alongside one of those ladies who—you know what I mean. She was a Pole, and they called her Teresa. She was a tallish, powerfully-built brunette, with black, bushy eyebrows and a large coarse face as if carved out by a hatchet—the bestial gleam of her dark eyes, her thick bass voice, her cab-man-like gait and her immense muscular vigour, worthy of a fishwife, inspired me with horror. I lived on the top flight and her garret was opposite to mine. I never left my door open when I knew her to be at home. But this, after all, was a very rare occurrence. Sometimes I chanced to meet her on the staircase or in the yard, and she would smile upon me with a smile which seemed to me to be sly and cynical. Occasionally, I saw her drunk, with bleary eyes, touzled hair, and a particularly hideous smile. On such occasions she would speak to me:

"How d'ye do, Mr. Student!" and her stupid laugh would still further intensify my loathing of her. I should have liked to have changed my quarters in order to have avoided such encounters and greetings; but my little chamber was a nice one, and there was such a wide view from the window, and it was always so quiet in the street below—so I endured.

And one morning I was sprawling on my couch, trying to find some sort of excuse for not attending my class, when the door opened, and the bass voice of Teresa the loathsome, resounded from my threshold:

"Good health to you, Mr. Student!"

"What do you want?" I said. I saw that her face was confused and supplicatory . . . It was a very unusual sort of face for her.

"Look ye, sir! I want to beg a favour of you. Will you grant it me?"

I lay there silent, and thought to myself:

"Gracious! An assault upon my virtue, neither more nor less.—Courage, my boy!"

"I want to send a letter home, that's what it is," she said, her voice was beseeching, soft, timid.

"Deuce take you!" I thought; but up I jumped, sat down at my table, took a sheet of paper, and said:

"Come here, sit down, and dictate!"

She came, sat down very gingerly on a chair, and looked at me with a guilty look.

"Well, to whom do you want to write?"

"To Boleslav Kashput, at the town of Svyeptsyana, on the Warsaw Road. . . ."

"Well, fire away!"

"My dear Boles ... my darling ... my faithful lover. May the Mother of God protect thee! Thou heart of gold, why hast thou not written for such a long time to thy sorrowing little dove, Teresa?"

I very nearly burst out laughing. "A sorrowing little dove!" more than five feet high, with fists a stone and more in weight, and as black a face as if the little dove had lived all its life in a chimney, and had never once washed itself! Restraining myself somehow, I asked:

"Who is this Bolest?"

"Bolés, Mr. Student," she said, as if offended with me for blundering over the name, "he is Bolés—my young man."

"Young man!"

"Why are you so surprised, sir? Cannot I, a girl, have a young man?"

She? A girl? Well!

"Oh, why not?" I said, "all things are possible. And has he been your young man long?"

"Six years."

"Oh, ho!" I thought. "Well, let us write your letter. ..."

And I tell you plainly that I would willingly have changed places with this Bolés if his fair correspondent had been not Teresa, but something less than she.

"I thank you most heartily, sir, for your kind services," said Teresa to me, with a curtsey. "Perhaps *I* can show *you* some service, eh?"

"No, I most humbly thank you all the same."

"Perhaps, sir, your shirts or your trousers may want a little mending?"

I felt that this mastodon in petticoats had made me grow quite red with shame, and I told her pretty sharply that I had no need whatever of her services.

She departed.

A week or two passed away. It was evening. I was sitting at my window whistling and thinking of some expedient for enabling me to get away from myself. I was bored, the weather was dirty. I didn't want to go out, and out of sheer ennui I began a course of self-analysis and reflection. This also was dull enough work, but I didn't care about doing anything else. Then the door opened. Heaven be praised, someone came in.

"Oh, Mr. Student, you have no pressing business, I hope?"

It was Teresa. Humph!

"No. What is it?"

"I was going to ask you, sir, to write me another letter."

"Very well! To Bolés, eh?"

"No, this time it is from him."

"What?"

"Stupid that I am! It is not for me, Mr. Student, I beg your pardon. It is for a friend of mine, that is to say, not a friend but an acquaintance—a man acquaintance. He has a sweetheart just like me here, Teresa. That's how it is. Will you, sir, write a letter to this Teresa?"

I looked at her—her face was troubled, her fingers were trembling. I was a bit fogged at first—and then I guessed how it was.

"Look here, my lady," I said, "there are no Boleses or Teresas at all, and you've been telling me a pack of lies. Don't you come sneaking about me any longer. I have no wish whatever to cultivate your acquaintance. Do you understand?"

And suddenly she grew strangely terrified and distaught; she began to shift from foot to foot without moving from the place, and spluttered comically, as if she wanted to say something and couldn't. I waited to see what would come of all this, and I saw and felt that, apparently, I had made a great mistake in suspecting her of wishing to draw me from the path of righteousness. It was evidently something very different.

"Mr. Student!" she began, and suddenly, waving her hand, she turned abruptly towards the door and went out. I remained with a very unpleasant feeling in my mind. I listened. Her door was flung violently to—plainly the poor wench was very angry. . . . I thought it over, and resolved to go to her, and, inviting her to come in here, write everything she wanted.

I entered her apartment. I looked round. She was sitting at the table, leaning on her elbows, with her head in her hands.

"Listen to me," I said.

Now, whenever I come to this point in my story, I always feel horribly awkward and idiotic. Well, well!

"Listen to me," I said.

She leaped from her seat, came towards me with flashing eyes, and laying her hands on my shoulders, began to whisper, or rather to hum in her peculiar bass voice:

"Look you, now! It's like this. There's no Bolés at all, and there's no Teresa either. But what's that to you? Is it a hard thing for you to draw your pen over paper? Eh? Ah, and *you,* too! Still such a little fair-haired boy! There's nobody at all, neither Bolés, nor Teresa, only me. There you have it, and much good may it do you!"

"Pardon me!" said I, altogether flabbergasted by such a reception, "what is it all about? There's no Bolés, you say?"

"No. So it is."

"And no Teresa either?"

"And no Teresa. I'm Teresa."

I didn't understand it at all. I fixed my eyes upon her, and tried to make out which of us was taking leave of his or her senses. But she went again to the table, searching about for something, came back to me, and said in an offended tone:

"If it was so hard for you to write to Bolés, look, there's your letter, take it! Others will write for me."

I looked. In her hand was my letter to Bolés. Phew!

"Listen, Teresa! What is the meaning of all this? Why must you get others to write for you when I have already written it, and you haven't sent it?"

"Sent it where?"

"Why, to this—Bolés."

"There's no such person."

I absolutely did not understand it. There was nothing for me but to spit and go. Then she explained.

"What is it?" she said, still offended. "There's no such person, I tell you," and she extended her arms as if she herself did not understand why there should be no such person. "But I wanted him to be . . . Am I then not a human creature like the rest of them? Yes, yes, I know, I know, of course. . . . Yet no harm was done to anyone by my writing to him that I can see. . . ."

"Pardon me—to whom?"

"To Bolés, of course."

"But he doesn't exist."

"Alas! alas! But what if he doesn't? He doesn't exist, but he *might!* I write to him, and it looks as if he did exist. And Teresa—that's me, and he replies to me, and then I write to him again. . . ."

I understood at last. And I felt so sick, so miserable, so ashamed, somehow. Alongside of me, not three yards away, lived a human creature who had nobody in the world to treat her kindly, affectionately, and this human being had invented a friend for herself!

"Look, now! you wrote me a letter to Bolés, and I gave it to someone else to read it to me; and when they read it to me I listened and fancied that Bolés was there. And I asked you to write me a letter from Bolés to Teresa—that is to me. When they write such a letter for me, and read it to me, I feel quite sure that Bolés is there. And life grows easier for me in consequence."

"Deuce take thee for a blockhead!" said I to myself when I heard this.

And from thenceforth, regularly, twice a week, I wrote a letter to Bolés, and an answer from Bolés to Teresa. I wrote those answers well. . . . She, of course, listened to them, and wept like anything, roared, I should say, with her bass voice. And in return for my thus moving her to tears by real letters from the imaginary Bolés, she began to mend the holes I had in my socks, shirts, and other articles of clothing. Subsequently, about three months after this history began, they put her in prison for something or other. No doubt by this time she is dead.

My acquaintance shook the ash from his cigarette, looked pensively at the sky, and thus concluded:

Well, well, the more a human creature has tasted of better things the more it hungers after the sweet things of life. And we, wrapped round in the rags of our virtues, and regarding others through the mist of our self-sufficiency, and persuaded of our universal impeccability, do not understand this.

And the whole thing turns out pretty stupidly—and very cruelly. The fallen classes, we say. And who are the fallen classes, I should like to know? They are, first of all, people with the same bones, flesh, and blood and nerves as ourselves. We have been told this day after day for ages. And we actually listen—and the Devil only knows how hideous the whole thing is. Or are we completely depraved by the loud sermonizing of humanism? In reality, we also are fallen folks, and so far as I can see, very deeply fallen into the abyss of self-sufficiency and the conviction of our own superiority. But enough of this. It is all as old as the hills—so old that it is a shame to speak of it. Very old indeed—yes, that's where it is!

Proof Positive

BY GRAHAM GREENE

📖 📖 📖

The tired voice went on. It seemed to surmount enormous obstacles to speech. The man's sick, Colonel Crashaw thought with pity and irritation. When a young man he had climbed in the Himalayas, and he remembered how at great heights several breaths had to be taken for every step advanced. The five-foot-high platform in the Music Rooms of The Spa seemed to entail for the speaker some of the same effort. He should never have come out on such a raw afternoon, thought Colonel Crashaw, pouring out a glass of water and pushing it across the lecturer's table. The rooms were badly heated, and yellow fingers of winter fog felt for cracks in the many windows. There was little doubt that the speaker had lost all touch with his audience. It was scattered in patches about the hall—elderly ladies who made no attempt to hide their cruel boredom, and a few men, with the appearance of retired officers, who put up a show of attention.

Colonel Crashaw, as president of the local Psychical Society, had received a note from the speaker a little more than a week before. Written by a hand which trembled with sickness, age or drunkenness, it asked urgently for a special meeting of the society. An extraordinary, a really impressive, experience was to be described while still fresh in the mind, though what the experience had been was left vague. Colonel Crashaw would have hesitated to comply if the note had not been signed by a Major Philip Weaver, Indian Army, retired. One had to do what one could for a brother officer; the trembling of the hand must be either age or sickness.

It proved principally to be the latter when the two men met for the first time on the platform. Major Weaver was not more than sixty, tall, thin, and dark, with an ugly obstinate nose and satire in his eye, the most unlikely person to experience anything unexplainable. What antagonized Crashaw most was that Weaver used scent; a white handker-

113

chief which drooped from his breast pocket exhaled as rich
and sweet an odour as a whole altar of lilies. Several ladies
prinked their noses, and General Leadbitter asked loudly
whether he might smoke.

It was quite obvious that Weaver understood. He smiled
provocatively and asked very slowly, "Would you mind not
smoking? My throat has been bad for some time." Crashaw
murmured that it was terrible weather; influenza throats
were common. The satirical eye came round to him and
considered him thoughtfully, while Weaver said in a voice
which carried half-way across the hall, "It's cancer in my
case."

In the shocked vexed silence that followed the unneces-
sary intimacy he began to speak without waiting for any
introduction from Crashaw. He seemed at first to be in a
hurry. It was only later that the terrible impediments were
placed in the way of his speech. He had a high voice, which
sometimes broke into a squeal, and must have been peculiarly
disagreeable on the parade ground. He paid a few compliments to the local society; his remarks were just sufficiently
exaggerated to be irritating. He was glad, he said, to give
them the chance of hearing him; what he had to say might
alter whole view of the relative values of matter and spirit.

Mystic stuff, thought Crashaw.

Weaver's high voice began to shoot out hurried platitudes.
The spirit, he said, was stronger than anyone realized; the
physiological action of heart and brain and nerves were
subordinate to the spirit. The spirit was everything. He said
again, his voice squeaking up like bats into the ceiling. "The
spirit is so much stronger than you think." He put his hand
across his throat and squinted sideways at the window-panes
and the nuzzling fog, and upwards at the bare electric globe
sizzling with heat and poor light in the dim afternoon. "It's
immortal," he told them very seriously, and they shifted,
restless, uncomfortable, and weary, in their chairs.

It was then that his voice grew tired and his speech im-
peded. The knowledge that he had entirely lost touch with
his audience may have been the cause. An elderly lady at
the back had taken her knitting from a bag, and her needles
flashed along the walls when the light caught them, like a
bright ironic spirit. Satire for a moment deserted Weaver's
eyes, and Crashaw saw the vacancy it left, as though the
ball had turned to glass.

"This is important," the lecturer cried to them. "I can

tell you a story—" His audience's attention was momentarily caught by this promise of something definite, but the stillness of the lady's needles did not soothe him. He sneered at them all. "Signs and wonders," he said.

Then he lost the thread of his speech altogether.

His hand passed to and fro across his throat and he quoted Shakespeare, and then St. Paul's Epistle to the Galatians. His speech, as it grew slower, seemed to lose all logical order, though now and then Crashaw was surprised by the shrewdness in the juxtaposition of two irrelevant ideas. It was like the conversation of an old man which flits from subject to subject, the thread a subconscious one. "When I was at Simla," he said, bending his brows as though to avoid the sun flash on the barrack square, but perhaps the frost, the fog, the tarnished room, broke his memories. He began to assure the wearied faces all over again that the spirit did not die when the body died, but that the body only moved at the spirit's will. One had to be obstinate, to grapple . . .

Pathetic, Crashaw thought, the sick man's clinging to his belief. It was as if life were an only son who was dying and with whom he wished to preserve some form of communication. . . .

A note was passed to Crashaw from the audience. It came from a Dr. Brown, a small alert man in the third row; the society cherished him as a kind of pet sceptic. The note read: "Can't you make him stop? The man's obviously very ill. And what good is his talk, anyway?"

Crashaw turned his eyes sideways and upwards and felt his pity vanish at the sight of the roving satirical eyes that gave the lie to the tongue, and at the smell, overpoweringly sweet, of the scent in which Weaver had steeped his handkerchief. The man was an "outsider"; he would look up his record in the old Army Lists when he got home.

"Proof positive," Weaver was saying, sighing a shrill breath of exhaustion between the words. Crashaw laid his watch upon the table, but Weaver paid him no attention. He was supporting himself on the rim of the table with one hand. "I'll give you," he said, speaking with increasing difficulty, "proof pos . . ." His voice scraped into stillness, like a needle at a record's end, but the quiet did not last. From an expressionless face, a sound which was more like a high mew than anything else jerked the audience into attention. He followed it up, still without a trace of any emotion or understanding, with a succession of incomprehensible sounds, a low labial whispering, an odd jangling note, while his fingers tapped on the table. The sounds brought to mind innumerable séances, the bound medium, the tambourine shaken in mid-air, the whispered trivialities of loved ghosts in the darkness, the dinginess, the airless rooms.

Weaver sat down slowly in his chair and let his head fall backwards. An old lady began to cry nervously, and Dr. Brown scrambled on to the platform and bent over him. Colonel Crashaw saw the doctor's hand tremble as he picked the handkerchief from the pocket and flung it away from him. Crashaw, aware of another and more unpleasant smell, heard Dr. Brown whisper: "Send them all away. He's dead."

He spoke with a distress unusual in a doctor accustomed to every kind of death. Crashaw, before he complied, glanced over Dr. Brown's shoulder at the dead man. Major Weaver's appearance disquieted him. In a long life he had seen many forms of death, men shot by their own hand, and men killed in the field, but never such a suggestion of mortality. The body might have been one fished from the sea a long while after death; the flesh of the face seemed as ready to fall as an overripe fruit. So it was with no great shock of surprise that he heard Dr. Brown's whispered statement, "The man must have been dead a week."

What the Colonel thought of most was Weaver's claim—"Proof positive"—proof, he had probably meant, that the spirit outlived the body, that it tasted eternity. But all he had certainly revealed was how, without the body's aid, the spirit in seven days decayed into whispered nonsense.

The Butterfly

BY JAMES HANLEY

📖 📖 📖

Brother Timothy's cassock made a peculiar swishing noise as he strode up and down the passage. His face was red, his mouth twitched, whilst his fingers pulled nervously at the buttons upon the cassock. There was something wild, even a little aimless, about this pacing up and down, a kind of clue as to the chaos of his thoughts. One could see at a glance that he was angry. From time to time he muttered to himself, and when he did this he always cast a quick and furtive glance at a stout wooden door that opened onto the middle of the dark and musty corridor. His thoughts had neither shape nor order. He was a bewildered man. He simply could not understand the boy. Every time the name Cassidy came into his mind the blood mounted to his forehead. It was the boy's silence that was the enraging thing, his infernal silence; and what was even worse was the something serene that this silence betokened. Curse him for his silence, his serenity, and his content. The boy must have no conscience at all.

Suddenly he stopped and stared at the stout door. He knew it would be getting dark in there. He listened. Not a sound. Perhaps the fellow had fallen asleep, but perhaps he had not. He might indeed be standing behind it now, listening, yes, even thinking that he would be let out. Ambitious and fancy thought indeed. Brother Timothy laughed then. What a hope. That boy would stay there until he explained himself. It wasn't the flouting of authority, though that itself manifested a danger looming black upon the horizon of all order and obedience. No; it was this silence, this calm indifference. It wasn't innocence; no, not that. Such a thing was already confounded by his action. Silence was like ignorance, a stout wall, but this boy Cassidy, his was a steel wall, impenetrable. How to break it down then? Yes, one must try to think.

He continued his wild pacing up and down the passage for about five minutes; then he stopped again at the door. He knocked loudly upon it and called out, "Cassidy! You there, Cassidy?" There was no answer. A muttered exclamation came from Brother Timothy. Confound it! He really believed the boy was asleep. What right had he to be asleep? He drew a key from his pocket, opened the door and went inside. The door shut silently behind him. The boy was sitting on the bed. He looked up at the Brother, but something in the other's glance made him hurriedly drop his eyes again.

"Well, Cassidy," said Brother Timothy, "have you come to your senses yet?" The veins in his neck stood out. The silence galled him. "Answer me, I tell you," he shouted. "Answer me, you insolent, you villanious, you. . ." But words failed him.

He stood looking down at the culprit. After a while he drew
a chair and sat down opposite the boy.

"I repeat," he began, "I repeat that you have not yet
offered any explanation of your outrageous conduct. Listen to
me. Look at me, you young. . . Yesterday you missed the mass,
you and this other wretch Byrne; you went off together, but
where? And why did you do it? Did I say you could go?
Answer me, will you? Did you ask permission, even supposing
that I should ever think of granting your request? Why did
you play truant? Why were you so unlike the others, you
and this other wretch? I repeat that you will be kept here
until you offer an explanation. And now, listen further: This
silence, d'you hear me, this silence I will not stand. You've
the devil in you; it's he who has trapped your tongue. But
I'll break you. Do you hear me? I ask you for the last time,
why did you miss the mass?"

Cassidy, a boy of fifteen, looked up at the Brother. His
lips moved, but he made no sound. When the Brother struck
him across the face he said slowly, "Brother Timothy, I told
you yesterday."

"You are determined then. Very well. You will remain
here, you will have your meals sent up, but out of this room
you won't go until you open that mouth of yours." Suddenly
he gripped the boy by the shoulders and shook him. "You
have no right to do it. You have no right. And when you have
explained to me you will go to confession, and you will there
make an act of contrition. Do you understand me? You have
no right to be silent." Then he got up and strode out of the
room.

Cassidy smiled. The door banged, the key turned. He undressed and got into bed. In the morning when he woke the
sun was streaming through the window. It filled him with an
intense longing for the open air, to be free of this room, free
of the sound of those well-known footsteps, from the sight of
that face, which mirrored rage and defeat. He reflected that
he meant no harm. He had simply gone into the lanes with
Byrne, they had become absorbed in the strange life that
abounded in the hedges and ditches, they had not heard the
bell. And here he was stuck in this musty room for two days
because he would not explain. "But I have explained," he
kept saying to himself. "I have explained."

From his pocket he took a cardboard box pinned with air-
holes. He removed the lid. Slowly a green caterpillar crept
out and along his finger. Cassidy watched its slow graceful

movements down his hand. He lowered his head and stared hard at it. What a lovely green it was. And one day it would turn into a beautiful butterfly. How marvellous. He stroked it gently with his finger. The sun came out, it poured through the window, filled the room, the long green caterpillar was bathed in the light.

"I think I'll call you Xavier," he said to the insect, and smiled. For two whole days he had had it in the cardboard box. It made him happy knowing it was there, in the room with him. It made him forget Brother Timothy, forget many things. He knew he would be happy whilst he had the green caterpillar. If it could speak he would explain to it why he was kept in the stuffy room by Brother Timothy. Perhaps this long smooth green thing did know, perhaps it looked at him.

"Oh!" he exclaimed, and the box dropped to the floor. He had heard footsteps in the corridor. A moment later the door was opened and Brother Timothy stepped into the room.

"Well, Cassidy," he said. "Have you come to your senses?" But the boy appeared not to hear him. He was standing with his back to the brother, the sunlight on his face, and he was gently laying the caterpillar on a bit of moss in the cardboard box. He gave the green insect a final stroke and put the lid on.

"Cassidy!" roared the man behind him, and the boy turned round. "What have you there?"

"Nothing—I mean—Brother Timothy, it's a—"

"What! And this is how you spend your time. Aren't you sorry for your sin?"

"Sin? Brother Timothy, I—I mean it's only a little caterpillar."

If silence had been poisonous, this was worse. He pulled the boy's ear.

"Is this how you think upon you conscience? Is this how you think out your explanation? Outrageous, boy! Give me that at once."

"But it's only a caterpillar, Brother Timothy, a little green one. Soon it'll be a butterfly. It's so green and soft, and it crawls up my finger as though it knew me. Please, Brother —I—while I was sitting here all by myself it made me happy, I liked having it, I—"

"How dare you!" Brother Timothy grabbed the box and turned out the caterpillar. It fell to the floor and slowly began to crawl.

"You have no right to miss the mass and you have no right

to be happy or anything else. D'you hear me?" and with a quick movement of his broad foot he trod on the insect and crushed out its life. Cassidy looked up at the Brother. Then he burst into tears.

Absent-Mindedness in a Parish Choir

BY THOMAS HARDY

"It happened on Sunday after Christmas—the last Sunday they ever played in Longpuddle church gallery, as it turned out, though they didn't know it then. As you may know, sir, the players formed a very good band—almost as good as the Mellstock parish players that were led by the Dewys; and that's saying a great deal. There was Nicholas Puddingcome, the leader, with the first fiddle; there was Timothy Thomas, the bass-viol man; John Biles, the tenor fiddler; Dan'l Horn-head, with the serpent; Robert Dowdle, with the clarionet; and Mr. Nicks, with the oboe—all sound and powerful musicians, and strongwinded men—they that blowed. For that reason they were very much in demand Christmas week for little reels and dancing-parties; for they could turn a jig or a hornpipe out of hand as well as ever they could turn out a psalm, and perhaps better, not to speak irreverent. In short, one half-hour they could be playing a Christmas carol in the squire's hall to the ladies and gentlemen, and drinking tay and coffee with 'em as modest as saints; and the next, at the Tinker's Arms, blazing away like wild horses with the 'Dashing White Sergeant' to nine couple of dancers and more, and swallowing rum-and-cider hot as flame.

"Well, this Christmas they'd been out to one rattling randy after another every night, and had got next to no sleep at all. Then came Sunday after Christmas, their fatal day. 'Twas so mortal cold that year that they could hardly sit in the gallery; for though the congregation down in the body of the church had a stove to keep off the frost, the players in the gallery had nothing at all. So Nicholas said at morning service, when 'twas freezing an inch an hour, 'Please the Lord I won't stand this numbing weather no longer; this afternoon we'll have something in our insides to make us warm if it cost a king's ramsom.'

"So he brought a gallon of hot brandy and beer, ready mixed, to church with him in the afternoon, and by keeping the jar well wrapped up in Timothy Thomas' bass-viol bag it kept drinkably warm till they wanted it, which was just a thimbleful in the Absolution, and another after the Creed, and the remainder at the beginning o' the sermon. When they'd had the last pull they felt quite comfortable and warm, and as the sermon went on—most unfortunately for 'em it was a long one that afternoon—they fell asleep, every man jack of 'em; and there they slept on as sound as rocks.

" 'Twas a very dark afternoon, and by the end of the sermon all you could see of the inside of the church were the pa'son's two candles alongside of him in the pulpit, and his soaking face behind 'em. The sermon being ended at last, the pa'son gied out the Evening Hymn. But no choir set about sounding up the tune, and the people began to turn their heads to learn the reason why, and then Levi Limpet, a boy who sat in the gallery nudged Timothy and Nicholas, and said, 'Begin! begin!'

" 'Hey, what?' says Nicholas, starting up; and the church being so dark and his head so muddled he thought he was at the party they had played at all the night before, and away he went, bow and fiddle, at 'The Devil among the Tailors', the favorite jig of our neighborhood at that time. The rest of the band, being in the same state of mind and nothing doubting, followed their leader with all their strength, according to custom. They poured out that there tune till the lower bass notes of 'The Devil among the Tailors' made the cobwebs in the roof shiver like ghosts; then Nicholas, seeing nobody moved, shouted out as he scraped (in his usual commanding way at dances when folks didn't know the figures), 'Top couples cross hands! And when I make the fiddle squeak at the end, every man kiss his pardner under the mistletoe!'

"The boy Levi was so frightened that he bolted down the gallery stairs and out homeward like lightning. The pa'son's hair fairly stood on end when he heard the evil tune raging through the church; and thinking the choir had gone crazy, he held up his hand and said: 'Stop, stop, stop! Stop, stop! What's this?' But they didn't hear 'n for the noise of their own playing, and the more he called the louder they played.

"Then the folks came out of their pews, wondering down

to the ground, and saying: 'What do they mean by such wickedness? We shall be consumed like Sodom and Gomorrah!'

"Then the squire came out of his pew lined wi' green baize, where lots of lords and ladies visiting at the house were worshipping along with him, and went and stood in front of the gallery, and shook his fist in the musicians' faces, saying, 'What! In this reverent edifice! What!'

"And at last they heard 'n through their playing, and stopped.

" 'Never such an insulting, disgraceful thing—never!' says the squire, who couldn't rule his passion.

" 'Never!' says the pa'son, who had come down and stood beside him.

" 'Not if the angels of Heaven,' says the squire, (he was a wickedish man, the squire was, though now for once he happened to be on the Lord's side)—'not if the angels of Heaven come down,' he says, 'shall one of you villainous players ever sound a note in this church again, for the insult to me, and my family, and my visitors, and God Almighty, that you've a-perpetrated this afternoon!'

"Then the unfortunate church band came to their senses, and remembered where they were; and 'twas a sight to see Nicholas Puddingcome and Timothy Thomas and John Biles creep down the gallery stairs with their fiddles under their arms, and poor Dan'l Hornhead with his serpent, and Robert Dowdle with his clarionet, all looking as little as ninepins; and out they went. The pa'son might have forgi'ed 'em when he learned the truth o't, but the squire would not. That very week he sent for a barrel-organ that would play two-and-twenty new psalm tunes, so exact and particular that, however sinful inclined you was, you could play nothing but psalm tunes whatsomever. He had a really respectable man to turn the winch, as I said, and the old players played no more."

The Hollow of the Three Hills

BY NATHANIEL HAWTHORNE

In those strange old times, when fantastic dreams and
madmen's reveries were realised among the actual circumstances of life, two persons met together at an appointed
hour and place. One was a lady, graceful in form and fair
of feature, though pale and troubled, and smitten with an
untimely blight in what should have been the fullest bloom
of her years; the other was an ancient and meanly-dressed
woman, of ill-favoured aspect, and so withered, shrunken
and decrepit, that even the space since she began to decay
must have exceeded the ordinary term of human existence.
In the spot where they encountered, no mortal could observe
them. Three little hills stood by each other, and down in the
midst of them sunk a hollow basin, almost mathematically
circular, two or three hundred feet in breadth, and of such
depth that a stately cedar might but just be visible above
the sides. Dwarf pines were numerous upon the hills, and
partly fringed the outer verge of the intermediate hollow;
within which there was nothing but the brown grass of October, and here and there a tree-trunk, that had fallen long ago,
and lay mouldering with no green successor from its roots.
One of these masses of decaying wood, formerly a majestic
oak, rested close beside a pool of green and sluggish water
at the bottom of the basin. Such scenes as this (so grey tradi-
tion tells) were once the resort of a power of evil and his
plighted subjects; and here, at midnight or on the dim verge
of evening, they were said to stand round the mantling
pool, disturbing its putrid waters in the performance of an
impious baptismal rite. The chill beauty of an autumnal
sunset was now gilding the three hill-tops, whence a paler
tint stole down their sides into the hollow.

"Here is our pleasant meeting come to pass," said the aged
crone, "according as thou hast desired. Say quickly what

123

thou wouldest have of me, for there is but a short hour
that we may tarry here."

As the old, withered woman spoke, a smile glimmered on
her countenance, like lamplight on the wall of a sepulchre.
The lady trembled, and cast her eyes upward to the verge
of the basin, as if meditating to return with her purpose un-
accomplished. But it was not so ordained.

"I am a stranger in this land, as you know," said she, at
length. "Whence I come it matters not; but I have left those
behind me with whom my fate was intimately bound, and
from whom I am cut off for ever. There is a weight in my
bosom that I cannot away with, and I have come hither to
inquire of their welfare."

"And who is there by this green pool that can bring thee
news from the ends of the earth?" cried the old woman,
peering into the lady's face. "Not from my lips mayest thou
hear these tidings; yet, be thou bold, and the daylight
shall not pass away from yonder hill-top before thy wish be
granted."

"I will do your bidding though I die," replied the lady,
desperately.

The old woman seated herself on the trunk of the fallen
tree, threw aside the hood that shrouded her grey locks, and
beckoned her companion to draw near.

"Kneel down," she said, "and lay your forehead on my
knees."

She hesitated a moment, but the anxiety that had long
been kindling burned fiercely up within her. As she knelt
down, the border of her garment was dipped into the pool;
she laid her forehead on the old woman's knees, and the
latter drew a cloak about the lady's face, so that she was in
darkness. Then she heard the muttered words of prayer, in
the midst of which she started, and would have arisen.

"Let me flee—let me flee and hide myself, that they may
not look upon me!" she cried. But, with returning recollec-
tion, she hushed herself, and was still as death.

For it seemed as if other voices—familiar in infancy, and
unforgotten through many wanderings, and in all the vicis-
situdes of her heart and fortune—were mingling with the
accents of the prayer. At first the words were faint and indistinct, not rendered so by distance, but rather resem-
bling the dim pages of a book which we strive to read by
an imperfect and gradually brightening light. In such a
manner, as the prayer proceeded, did those voices strengthen

upon the ear; till at length the petition ended, and the conversation of an aged man, and of a woman broken and decayed like himself, became distinctly audible to the lady as she knelt. But those strangers appeared not to stand in the hollow depth between the three hills. Their voices were encompassed and re-echoed by the walls of a chamber, the windows of which were rattling in the breeze; the regular vibration of a clock, the crackling of a fire, and the tinkling of the embers as they fell among the ashes, rendered the scene almost as vivid as if painted to the eye. By a melancholy hearth sat these two old people, the man calmly despondent, the woman querulous and tearful, and their words were all of sorrow. They spoke of a daughter, a wanderer they knew not where, bearing dishonour along with her, and leaving shame and affliction to bring their grey heads to the grave. They alluded also to other and more recent woe, but in the midst of their talk their voices seemed to melt into the sound of the wind sweeping mournful among the autumn leaves; and when the lady lifted her eyes, there was she kneeling in the hollow between three hills.

"A weary and lonesome time yonder old couple have of it," remarked the old woman, smiling in the lady's face.

"And did you also hear them?" exclaimed she, a sense of intolerable humiliation triumphing over her agony and fear.

"Yea; and we have yet more to hear," replied the old woman. "Wherefore cover thy face quickly."

Again the withered hag poured forth the monotonous words of a prayer that was not meant to be acceptable in heaven; and soon in the pauses of her breath strange murmurings began to thicken, gradually increasing, so as to drown and overpower the charm by which they grew. Shrieks pierced through the obscurity of sound, and were succeeded by the singing of sweet female voices, which in their turn gave way to a wild roar of laughter, broken suddenly by groanings and sobs, forming altogether a ghastly confusion of terror and mourning and mirth. Chains were rattling, fierce and stern voices uttered threats, and the scourge resounded at their command. All these noises deepened and became substantial to the listener's ear, till she could distinguish every soft and dreamy accent of the love songs, that died causelessly into funeral hymns. She shuddered at the unprovoked wrath which blazed up like the spontaneous kindling of flame, and she grew faint at the fearful merriment raging miserably around her. In the midst of this wild scene, where unbound passions jostled each other in a drunken career, there was one solemn voice of a man, and a manly and melodious voice it might once have been. He went to and fro continually, and his feet sounded upon the floor. In each member of that frenzied company, whose own burning thoughts had become their exclusive world, he sought an auditor for the story of his individual wrong, and interrupted their laughter and tears as his reward of scorn or pity. He spoke of women's perfidy, of a wife who had broken her holiest vows, of a home and heart made desolate. Even as he went on, the shout, the laugh, the shriek, the sob, rose up in unision, till they changed into the hollow, fitful, and uneven sound of the wind, as it fought among the pine-trees on those three lonely hills. The lady looked up, and there was the withered woman smiling in her face.

"Couldest thou have thought there were such merry times in a madhouse?" inquired the latter.

"True, true," said the lady to herself, "there is mirth within its walls, but misery, misery without."

"Wouldest thou hear more?" demanded the old woman.

"There is one other voice I would fain listen to again," replied the lady faintly.

"Then lay down thy head speedily upon my knees, that thou mayest get thee hence before the hour be past."

The golden skirts of day were yet lingering upon the hills, but deep shades obscured the hollow and the pool, as if sombre night were rising thence to overspread the world. Again that evil woman began to weave her spell. Long did it proceed unanswered, till the knolling of a bell stole in among the intervals of her words, like a clang that had travelled far over valley and rising ground, and was just ready to die in the air. The lady shook upon her companion's knees as she heard that boding sound. Stronger it grew and sadder, and deepened into the tone of a death-bell knolling dolefully from some ivy-mantled tower, and bearing tidings of mortality and woe to the cottage, to the hall and to the solitary wayfarer, that all might weep for the doom appointed in turn to them. Then came a measured tread, passing slowly, slowly on, as of mourners with a coffin, their garments trailing on the ground, so that the ear could measure the length of their melancholy array. Before them went the priest reading the burial service, while the leaves of his book were rustling in the breeze. And though

no voice but his was heard to speak aloud, still there were
revilings and anathemas whispered, but distinct, from women
and from men, breathed against the daughter who had wrung
the aged hearts of her parents, the wife who had betrayed
the trusting fondness of her husband, the mother who had
sinned against natural affection and left her child to die.
The sweeping sound of the funeral train faded away like
a thin vapour, and the wind, that just before had seemed to
shake the coffin-pall, moaned sadly round the verge of the
hollow between three hills. But when the old woman stirred
the kneeling lady she lifted not her head.

"Here has been a sweet hour's sport," said the withered
crone, chuckling to herself.

A Question of Blood

BY ERNEST HAYCOX

ꊸ ꊸ ꊸ

That fall of 1869 when Frank Isabel settled in the Yellow Hills the nearest town was a four-day ride to the north
and his closest white neighbor lived at the newly established Hat ranch, seventy miles over in Two Dance Valley.
The Indians were on reservation but it was still risky for a
man to be alone in the country.

It made no difference to Isabel. He was young and self-
willed and raised in that impoverished and faction-torn
part of Missouri where manhood came to a male child almost as soon as he could lift a gun. He had a backwood-
man's lank loose height, his eyes were almost black and
though he kept a smooth-shaven face there was always a
clay-blue cast to the long sides of his jaw. The land was
free, well grassed and watered and ideal for a poor man
who had ambition. This is why he had come.

Yet self-sufficient as he was he had made no calculation
for the imperious hungers that soon or late come to a lonely
man. And presently. seeing no hope of a white woman in
the land for many years, he went down to the reservation
and took unto himself a Crow girl, the bargain being sealed

by payment to her father of one horse and a quart of whisky.

She was quick and small and neat, with enormous eyes looking out of a round smooth face. The price paid was small and that hurt her pride for a little while, yet it was a white man who wanted her and the hurt died down and she moved quietly into Frank Isabel's log house and settled down to the long, lonesome days without murmur.

She was more than he had expected in an Indian woman: quick to perceive the way his mind ran, showing him sudden streaks of mischief-making gaiety, and sometimes a flash of affection. Before the boy baby was born he drove her three hundred miles to Cheyenne and married her in the white way.

It was a sense of justice that impelled him to do this rather than any need in her eyes. For he was learning that the horse and bottle of whisky were as binding as any ceremony on earth; and he was also learning that though an Indian woman was a dutiful woman, immemorial custom guided her in a way he could not hope to touch or change. A man's work was a man's; a woman's work was hers and the line was hard and clear. In the beginning he had shocked her by cutting the firewood and by dressing down the game he brought in. It had shamed her for a while that he should descend to those things; and only by angry command had he established the habit of eating at table instead of crosslegged on a floor blanket. She was faithful to the discharge of the duty she owed him, but behind that girlish face was an adamant will. The ways of a thousand generations were ingrained in her.

Often at night, smoking before the fire and watching his boy crawl so awkwardly across the floor, he felt a strangeness at seeing her darkly crouched in a corner, lost in thoughts he could never reach. Sometimes the color and the sound of his early days in Missouri came strongly to him and he wished that she might know what was in his head. But he talked her tongue poorly and she would speak no English; and so silence lay between them.

Meanwhile Two Dance town was born on the empty prairie sixty miles away and the valley below him began to fill up with cattlemen long before he had thought they would come. Looking down from the ramparts of the Yellows he could see houses far off under the sun and dust spiral up along the Two Dance road, signals of a vanishing wilder-

ness. His own people had finally caught up with him. And
then he knew he had become a squaw man.

One by one the few trappers who had pioneered the
Yellows began to send their squaws and their half-breed
children back to the reservation as a shamefaced gesture of
a mistake that had to be righted. He said nothing of this to
the Crow woman, yet when fear showed its luminous shadow
in her eyes he knew she had heard. He said then: "Those
men are fools. I am not ashamed of you." And was happy to
see the fear die.

This was why he took her to Two Dance. It pleased him
to have her be seen in that lively little cattle town for she
was a pretty woman with her black hair braided and her
clothes neat and colorful under the sun. But he had forgotten her customs and when they walked up the street she
followed behind him as a squaw always did, obediently and
with her head faintly lowered. He knew how Two Dance
would see that and anger colored his talk to her on the way
home. "A white man's wife walks beside him, not behind."

He saw that dark fear in her eyes again, and had no way
of softening it. Never afterwards did she come to town.

He knew then how it was to be. At hay time when he
went down to help out on Hat he could feel that faint line
drawn between him and the others; at the roundup fire he sat
apart, with the strangeness there—a white man who was yet
not quite white. One fall night at town he stepped in to
watch the weekly dance and felt all the loose bitterness of
his position rise and grow to be a hard lump in his chest.
Once he would have had a part in this, but the odor of the
blanket was upon him now and those fair, pleasant girls
went wheeling by and he saw their eyes touch him and
pass on. Over the whisky bottle in Faro Charley's saloon
later he understood how fatal his mistake had been; and
how everlastingly long its penalty would be.

He went home late that night quite drunk. In the morning
the Crow girl was gone with her boy.

He didn't follow, for he knew that either she would return or she wouldn't, and that nothing he did could change
her mind. Late in the third day she came back without a
word. When he went in to supper that night he sat down to
a single plate on the table. Her own plate and the boy's were
on a floor blanket in a corner of the room.

It was, he saw, her decision. He had told her nothing of

the misery in his mind, but she knew it without need of speech and so had answered him. He was white and might eat at his table. But she was Indian and so was the boy, and the table was not for them.

There was a kindness in Frank Isabel that governed the strongest of his emotions and this was what held him still as the days went on. He was remembering back to the horse and bottle of whisky and to the time when her lips had been warm with humor. In those days the Yellows had been wild and his world had not caught up with him, but he could see the depth and the length of his mistake now. He had committed it and could stand it. Yet it had passed beyond him and touched the Crow girl and the boy who was neither Crow nor white. For himself, Frank Isabel thought, there was no help. For the girl, none. It was the boy he kept weighing in his mind, so slowly and so painfully.

One winter night at meal time Jim Benbow of Hat dropped in for a cup of coffee. There was a little talk of cattle snowed into the timber and afterwards Benbow put on his hat and went to the door. As he left his glance crossed to the Crow woman and to the boy crouched in the corner and he said briefly: "Your youngster's growin' up, Frank," and left.

There was the rush of wind along the cabin eaves and deep silence inside. Isabel sat with his arms idle on the table remembering Benbow's words, which had contained a note of judgment. Presently he rose and brought another chair to the table and went over to where the Crow girl crouched mutely in the corner. He lifted the boy and put him in the chair at the table and stood there a moment, a long man throwing a thin shadow across the room. He said: "Hereafter he eats at the table."

She drew farther and farther back into the corner, like a shadow vanishing. And then, with his face turned suddenly away, he heard her stifled and terrible crying tremble the room's silence.

The Boy Who Drew Cats

BY LAFCADIO HEARN

▱ ▱ ▱

A long, long time ago, in a small country village in Japan, there lived a poor farmer and his wife, who were very good people. They had a number of children, and found it very hard to feed them all. The elder son was strong enough when only fourteen years old to help his father; and the little girls learned to help their mother almost as soon as they could walk.

But the youngest, a little boy, did not seem to be fit for hard work. He was very clever—cleverer than all his brothers and sisters; but he was quite weak and small, and people said he could never grow very big. So his parents thought it would be better for him to become a priest than to become a farmer. They took him with them to the village-temple one day, and asked the good old priest who lived there if he would have their little boy for his acolyte, and teach him all that a priest ought to know.

The old man spoke kindly to the lad, and asked him some hard questions. So clever were the answers that the priest agreed to take the little fellow into the temple as an acolyte, and to educate him for the priesthood.

The boy learned quickly what the old priest taught him, and was very obedient in most things. But he had one fault. He liked to draw cats during study-hours, and to draw cats even where cats ought not to have been drawn at all.

Whenever he found himself alone, he drew cats. He drew them on the margins of the priest's books, and on all the screens of the temple, and on the walls, and on the pillars. Several times the priest told him this was not right; but he did not stop drawing cats. He drew them because he could not really help it. He had what is called "the genius of an artist," and just for that reason he was not quite fit to be an acolyte;—a good acolyte should study books.

One day after he had drawn some very clever pictures of

cats upon a paper screen, the old priest said to him severely: "My boy, you must go away from this temple at once. You will never make a good priest, but perhaps you will become a great artist. Now let me give you a last piece of advice, and be sure you never forget it. *Avoid large places at night; —keep to small!*"

The boy did not know what the priest meant by saying, "*Avoid large places;—keep to small.*" He thought and thought, while he was tying up his little bundle of clothes to go away; but he could not understand those words, and he was afraid to speak to the priest any more, except to say goodbye.

He left the temple very sorrowfully, and began to wonder what he should do. If he went straight home he felt sure his father would punish him for having been disobedient to the priest; so he was afraid to go home. All at once he remembered that at the next village, twelve miles away, there was a very big temple. He had heard there were several priests at that temple; and he made up his mind to go to them and ask them to take him for their acolyte.

Now that big temple was closed up but the boy did not know this fact. The reason it had been closed up was that a goblin had frightened the priests away, and had taken possession of the place. Some brave warriors had afterward gone to the temple at night to kill the goblin; but they had never been seen alive again. Nobody had ever told these things to the boy;—so he walked all the way to the village hoping to be kindly treated by the priests.

When he got to the village, it was already dark, and all the people were in bed; but he saw the big temple on a hill at the other end of the principal street, and he saw there was a light in the temple. People who tell the story say the goblin used to make that light, in order to tempt lonely travelers to ask for shelter. The boy went at once to the temple, and knocked. There was no sound inside. He knocked and knocked again; but still nobody came. At last he pushed gently at the door, and was quite glad to find that it had not been fastened. So he went in, and saw a lamp burning— but no priest.

He thought some priest would be sure to come very soon, and he sat down and waited. Then he noticed that everything in the temple was gray with dust, and thickly spun over with cobwebs. So he thought to himself that the priests would certainly like to have an acolyte, to keep the place clean. He wondered why they had allowed everything to get so dusty. What most pleased him, however, were some big white screens, good to paint cats upon. Though he was tired, he looked at once for a writing pad, and found one and ground some ink, and began to paint cats.

He painted a great many cats upon the screens; and then he began to feel very, very sleepy. He was just on the point of lying down to sleep beside one of the screens, when he suddenly remembered the words, "*Avoid large places;—keep to small!*"

The temple was very large; he was all alone; and as he thought of these words—though he could not quite understand them—he began to feel for the first time a little afraid; and he resolved to look for a *small place* in which to sleep. He found a little cabinet, with a sliding door, and went into it, and shut himself up. Then he lay down and fell fast asleep.

Very late in the night he was awakened by a most terrible noise—a noise of fighting and screaming. It was so dreadful that he was afraid even to look through a chink in the little cabinet; he lay very still, holding his breath for fright.

The light that had been in the temple went out; but the awful sounds continued, and became more awful, and all the temple shook. After a long time silence came; but the boy was still afraid to move. He did not move until the light of the morning sun shone into the cabinet through the chinks of the little door.

Then he got out of his hiding place vary cautiously, and looked about. The first thing he saw was that all the floor of the temple was covered with blood. And then he saw, lying dead in the middle of it, an enormous, monstrous rat—a goblin-rat—bigger than a cow!

But who or what could have killed it? There was no man or other creature to be seen. Suddenly the boy observed that the mouths of all the cats he had drawn the night before, were red and wet with blood. Then he knew that the goblin had been killed by the cats which he had drawn. And then also, for the first time, he understood why the wise old priest had said to him, "*Avoid large places at night;— keep to small.*"

Afterward that boy became a very famous artist. Some of the cats which he drew are still shown to travelers in Japan.

The Lost Soul

BY BEN HECHT

It would be dawn soon.

The man in the cell was unable to sleep. He had dressed himself. He stood looking out of a small barred window at the waning night and the winter stars going away.

Two heavy-set men with tired puffy unshaven faces were also in this cell. They stared at the cell walls with a remarkable ox-like persistency.

Then, as if overcome by a secret curiosity, they turned their eyes on the man at the barred window and looked shyly over his shoulder at the first colours of dawn.

Yet a fourth man appeared.

The two heavy-set men greeted him with unexpected dignity in their voices.

"Hello, Doc," said one.

"What time is it?" said the other.

The cell door was unlocked. The doctor came in. He took a small silver pencil out of his vest pocket and began rolling it back and forth between his thumb and fingers. Then he cocked his eye at the unshaded electric light burning high up in the cell. He was very nervous.

"Hello," he said.

The one at the window turned. He was smiling.

"How do you feel?" the doctor asked, continuing with the silver pencil.

The one at the window shook his head with a rather queer good-humoured politeness.

"I didn't sleep well," he answered. "I suppose it doesn't help any to worry. But . . . well . . . I was just talking to these two men here who have been good enough to keep me company. You see, I'm in a very awkward predicament . . . I don't know who I am."

The doctor blinked. Then he turned and stared at the two heavy-set men. They looked remarkably inscrutable—

134

even for oxen. The doctor put the silver pencil away and removed a black leather case from his coat pocket. He opened it and took out a stethoscope.

"Just a formality," he muttered. "Open your shirt, please."

He put the instrument on the man's chest and listened.

"Very remarkable," he spoke after a long pause of listening. "Normal. Absolutely normal heart action."

The two heavy-set men nodded mechanically but correctly. There is a certain etiquette of nodding and staring which the laity proudly observe in their relation with the professions.

"I don't know who I am," the man at the window resumed in a slightly high-pitched tone, rebuttoning his shirt. "I feel all right, doctor. But I haven't the faintest idea"— the queer, good-natured smile played apologetically behind his words—"I haven't the slightest idea what my name is. I presume the officials are working hard and doing all they can . . . to determine. But it's getting a little on my nerves. It's lucky I have a sense of humour. Otherwise. Well. Imagine finding yourself in jail. And just not knowing who the deuce you are or where you come from. I suppose I was picked up roaming around. Nevertheless it doesn't seem right to me to put a man in jail. They might have been decent enough to think of a hospital. Or a hotel. I unquestionably have a family who are worrying. You know, I've been trying to figure out what sort of man I am. It's very interesting. For instance, I'm obviously educated and unused to jails."

The doctor turned to the two heavy-set men. They shrugged their shoulders. The doctor looked at his wrist-watch hurriedly.

"What time is it?" one of the heavy-set men asked in a shy voice.

The one at the window sighed and went on talking as the doctor, with a secretive gesture, held his wrist-watch for the two heavy-set men to look at. They looked and nodded.

"I've searched through my pockets," he was saying from the window, "and not a shred of identification. No pocketbook or handkerchief or any marks. Of course—my hands. Not those of a working man, I should say. And—a—"

He stopped and began rubbing the back of his head.

"Don't you remember coming here?" the doctor asked, looking intently at the man.

"No, I can't say I do," he answered. "I feel quite aware

of everything in the present. But the past. Well! the past—"

He closed his eyes and frowned. A slightly bewildered and contemptuous chuckle started his words again.

"Of course, efficiency is more than one has a right to expect from the police. Or they would have had me photographed. As I was telling these two men. And my picture put in the newspapers so that my family would see it and sort of claim me. Obviously"— he stared at the doctor with some anger—"obviously I'm somebody of importance."

"The doctor drew a deep breath.

"Don't you remember," he began.

"Nothing," the man at the window interrupted irritably. "Pardon me. I don't mean to get angry. But it's damned awkward. You know, I might be somebody very important—with all sorts of people dependent and worried. There's some medical term for this condition, isn't there, doctor? I forget at the moment. The sensation is decidedly queer. And amusing."

He was staring at the beginning of morning light beyond the barred window.

"I don't know why I should feel amused," he chuckled. "In reality what it amounts to, I suppose, is that I have lost my soul. Or, that is, misplaced it for the time being. A most serious matter, it seems to me. But, damn it, I must be a humorist or something. Because the situation makes me want to laugh. I'm sure most men would be wailing and tearing their hair if they suddenly lost their soul. But really, I—"

His face spread in a grin and he began laughing softly.

"By God, what a beautiful morning," he murmured, his eyes again on the world outside. "Doctor,"—he crossed to where the doctor stood regarding him, the silver pencil again working between his thumb and fingers. "Doctor, if I could only get hold of my name," he whispered, "who am I . . . who . . ."

The doctor cleared his throat.

"Your name is," he began, "is—"

He stopped. There were footsteps in the corridor. People were coming.

A group of six men came walking toward the cell. The two heavy-set men stood up and shook their legs. The doctor grew excited. He stepped into the group and began talking hurriedly and in a lowered voice.

"Don't read it," he repeated, "it'll just give us a lot of

trouble, sheriff. He's amnesic. It'd just be borrowing trouble
to wake him up. Let him go this way."

"Well, he'll find out pretty soon," said the sheriff.

"I doubt it," the doctor whispered. "Anyway, by the time
he does you'll have him strapped and—"

"All right"—the sheriff thrust a sheet of typewritten paper
in his pocket—"let's go."

"Come on." The doctor returned to the cell.

The man at the window nodded good-naturedly. The doctor took his arm and led him into the group.

They fell into place around him—two on each side, two in
front, the two heavy-set men behind and the doctor still
holding his arm and watching his face.

"You see," the man in the centre began talking at once,
eagerly, quickly, as if a dizziness swayed the edges of his
words, "I haven't the least idea who I am, gentlemen. But if
you'll be patient with me, I'm sure my family or some other
clue . . . I dislike being such a bother. Is that a clergyman?
Where, by the way, are you taking me? Please . . . I insist!
I must know! Where are you taking me? Good God!"

Silently, without answer to this amazing question, the
marchers escorting James Hartley to the gallows continued
on their way.

And in the tall, gloomy death chamber a hundred or more
spectators sat waiting for the hanging of the creature known
as the Axe Fiend who a few months ago had murdered his
wife and two children in their sleep.

The group of marchers stepped through an opened
door on to the gallows platform.

A confusion ensued. Figures moved about on the platform. Then, out of the bustle on the high platform, an
amazed face looked down on the spectators. The mouth of
this face was opened as if it were about to scream. Its eyes
moved wildly as if they had become uncentred. Gasps
came from it.

A shiny yellow rope was being tightened around its
neck.

A man was adjusting a voluminous white wrapper about
the figure under the rope.

Another man was stepping forward with a white hood in
his hands. Suddenly the face screamed.

Three words filled the smoke-laden air—three words
uttered in a sob so pitiful, so agonized, so startled that the
sheriff paused with the white hood.

"This ain't me!" screamed the face. "This ain't ME!"
The spectators held their breaths, and stared.
A white bundle was swaying and twisting on the end of
a long thin yellow rope.

The Exact Science of Matrimony

BY O. HENRY

□□ □□ □□

"As I have told you before," said Jeff Peters, "I never
had much confidence in the perfidiousness of woman. As
partners or coeducators in the most innocent line of graft
they are not trustworthy."

"They deserve the compliment," said I. "I think they are
entitled to be called the honest sex."

"Why shouldn't they be?" said Jeff. "They've got the
other sex either grafting or working overtime for 'em.
They're all right in business until they get their emotions or
their hair touched up too much. Then you want to have a
flat-footed, heavy-breathing man with sandy whiskers, five
kids and a building and loan mortgage ready as an under-
study to take her desk. Now there was that widow lady that
me and Andy Tucker engaged to help us in that little matrimonial agency scheme we floated out in Cairo.

"When you've got enough advertising capital—say a roll
as big as the little end of a wagon tongue—there's money in
matrimonial agencies. We had about $6,000 and we ex-
pected to double it in two months, which is about as long as
a scheme like ours can be carried on without taking out a
New Jersey charter.

"We fixed up an advertisement that read about like this:

'Charming widow, beautiful, home loving, 32
years, possessing $3,000 cash and owning valuable
country property, would remarry. Would prefer a
poor man with affectionate disposition to one with
means, as she realizes that the solid virtues are

oftenest to be found in the humble walks of life.
No objection to elderly man or one of homely
appearance if faithful and true and competent to
manage property and invest money with judgment.
Address, with particulars,

Lonely,
Care of Peters & Tucker, agents, Cairo, Ill.'

" 'So far, so pernicious,' says I, when we had finished the
literary concoction. 'And now,' says I, 'where is the lady?'

"Andy gives me one of his looks of calm irritation.

" 'Jeff,' says he, 'I thought you had lost them ideas of
realism in your art. Why should there be a lady? When they
sell a lot of watered stock on Wall Street would you expect
to find a mermaid in it? What has a matrimonial ad got to
do with a lady?'

" 'Now listen,' says I. 'You know my rule, Andy, that in
all my illegitimate inroads against the legal letter of the
law the article sold must be existent, visible, producible.
In that way and by a careful study of city ordinances and
train schedules I have kept out of all trouble with the police
that a five-dollar bill and a cigar could not square. Now, to
work this scheme we've got to be able to produce bodily a
charming widow or its equivalent with or without the beauty,
hereditaments and appurtenances set forth in the catalogue
and writ of errors, or hereafter be held by a justice of the
peace."

" 'Well,' says Andy, reconstructing his mind, 'maybe it
would be safer in case the post office or the peace commission should try to investigate our agency. But where,' he
says, 'could you hope to find a widow who would waste
time on a matrimonial scheme that had no matrimony in it?'

"I told Andy that I thought I knew of the exact party. An
old friend of mine, Zeke Trotter, who used to draw soda
water and teeth in a tent show, had made his wife a widow
a year before by drinking some dyspepsia cure of the old
doctor's instead of the liniment that he always got boozed
up on. I used to stop at their house often, and I thought we
could get her to work with us.

" 'Twas only sixty miles to the little town where she lived,
so I jumped out on the I.C. and finds her in the same cottage with the same sunflowers and roosters standing on the
washtubs. Mrs. Trotter fitted our ad first rate except, may-

be, for beauty and age and property valuation. But she looked feasible and praiseworthy to the eye, and it was a kindness to Zeke's money to give her the job.

" 'Is this an honest deal you are putting on, Mr. Peters?' she asks me when I tell her what we want.

" 'Mrs. Trotter,' says I, 'Andy Trotter and me have computed the calculation that 3,000 men in this broad and fair country will endeavor to secure your fair hand and ostensible money and property through our advertisement. Out of that number something like thirty hundred will expect to give you in exchange, if they should win you, the carcass of a lazy and mercenary loafer, a failure in life, a swindler and contemptible fortune seeker.

" 'Me and Andy,' says I, 'propose to teach these preyers upon society a lesson. It was with difficulty,' says I, 'that me and Andy could refrain from forming a corporation under the title of the Great Moral and Millenial Malevolent Matrimonial Agency. Does that satisfy you?'

" 'It does, Mr. Peters,' says she. 'I might have known you wouldn't have gone into anything that wasn't opprobrious. But what will my duties be? Do I have to reject personally these 3,000 ramscallions you speak of, or can I throw them out in bunches?'

" 'Your job, Mrs. Trotter,' says I, 'will be practically a cynosure. You will live at a quiet hotel and will have no work to do. Andy and I will attend to all the correspondence and business end of it.

" 'Of course,' says I, 'some of the more ardent and impetuous suitors who can raise the railroad fare may come to Cairo to personally press their suit or whatever fraction of a suit they may be wearing. In that case you will be probably put to the inconvenience of kicking them out face to face. We will pay you $25 per week and hotel expenses.'

" 'Give me five minutes,' says Mrs. Trotter, 'to get my powder rag and leave the front door key with a neighbor and you can let my salary begin.'

"So I conveys Mrs. Trotter to Cairo and establishes her in a family hotel far enough away from mine and Andy's quarters to be unsuspicious and available, and I tell Andy.

" 'Great,' says Andy. 'And now that your conscience is appeased as to the tangibility and proximity of the bait, and leaving mutton aside, suppose we revenoo a noo fish.'

"So, we began to insert our advertisement in newspapers covering the country far and wide. One ad was all we used.

We couldn't have used more without hiring so many clerks and marcelled paraphernalia that the sound of the gum chewing would have disturbed the Postmaster-General.

"We placed $2,000 in a bank to Mrs. Trotter's credit and gave her the book to show in case anybody might question the honesty and good faith of the agency. I knew Mrs. Trotter was square and reliable and it was safe to leave it in her name.

"With that one ad Andy and me put in twelve hours a day answering letters.

"About one hundred a day was what came in. I never knew there was so many large hearted but indigent men in the country who were willing to acquire a charming widow and assume the burden of investing her money.

"Most of them admitted that they ran principally to whiskers and lost jobs and were misunderstood by the world, but all of 'em were sure that they were so chock full of affection and manly qualities that the widow would be making the bargain of her life to get 'em.

"Every applicant got a reply from Peters & Tucker informing him that the widow had been deeply impressed by his straightforward and interesting letter and requesting them to write again stating more particulars; and enclosing photograph if convenient. Peters & Tucker also informed the applicant that their fee for handing over the second letter to their fair client would be $2, enclosed therewith.

"There you see the simple beauty of the scheme. About 90 percent of them domestic foreign noblemen raised the price somehow and sent it in. That was all there was to it. Except that me and Andy complained an amount about being put to the trouble of slicing open them envelopes, and taking the money out.

"Some few clients called in person. We sent 'em to Mrs. Trotter and she did the rest; except for three or four who came back to strike us for carfare. After the letters began to get in from the r.f.d. districts Andy and me were taking in about $200 a day.

"One afternoon when we were busiest and I was stuffing the two and ones into cigar boxes and Andy was whistling 'No Wedding Bells for Her' a small, slick man drops in and runs his eye over the walls like he was on the trail of a lost Gainesborough painting or two. As soon as I saw him I felt a glow of pride, because we were running our business on the level.

" 'I see you have quite a large mail today,' says the man.
"I reached and got my hat.

" 'Come on,' says I. 'We've been expecting you. I'll show you the goods. How was Teddy when you left Washington?'"

"I took him down to the Riverview Hotel and had him shake hands with Mrs. Trotter. Then I showed him her bank book with the $2,000 to her credit.

" 'It seems to be all right,' says the Secret Service.

" 'It is,' says I. 'And if you're not a married man I'll leave you to talk a while with the lady. We won't mention the two dollars.'

" 'Thanks,' says he. 'If I wasn't, I might. Good day, Mr. Peters.'

"Toward the end of three months we had taken in something over $5,000, and we saw it was time to quit. We had a good many complaints made to us; and Mrs. Trotter seemed to be tired of the job. A good many suitors had been calling to see her, and she didn't seem to like that.

"So we decides to pull out, and I goes down to Mrs. Trotter's hotel to pay her last week's salary and say farewell and get her check for $2,000.

"When I get there I found her crying like a kid that don't want to go to school.

" 'Now, now,' says I, 'what's it all about? Somebody sassed you or you getting homesick?'

" 'No, Mr. Peters,' says she. 'I'll tell you. You was always a friend of Zeke's, and I don't mind. Mr. Peters, I'm in love. I just love a man so hard I can't bear not to get him. He's just the ideal I've always had in mind.'

" 'Then take him,' says I. 'That is, if it's a mutual case. Does he return the sentiment according to the specifications and painfulness you have described?'

" 'He does,' says she. 'But he's one of the gentlemen that's been coming to see me about the advertisement and he won't marry me unless I give him the $2,000. His name is William Wilkinson.' And then she goes off again in the agitations and hysterics of romance.

" 'Mrs. Trotter,' says I, 'there's no man more sympathizing with a woman's affections than I am. Besides, you was once a life partner of one of my best friends. If it was left to me I'd say take this $2,000 and the man of your choice and be happy.

" 'We could afford to do that, because we have cleaned up

over $5,000 from these suckers that wanted to marry you. But,' says I, 'Andy Tucker is to be consulted.'

"I goes back to our hotel and lays the case before Andy.

" 'I was expecting something like this all the time,' says Andy. 'You can't trust a woman to stick by you in any scheme that involves her emotions and preferences.'

" 'It's a sad thing, Andy,' says I, 'to think that we've been the cause of the breaking of a woman's heart.'

" 'It is,' says Andy, 'and I tell you what I'm willing to do, Jeff. You've always been a man of a soft and generous disposition. Perhaps I've been too hard and worldly and suspicious. For once I'll meet you half way. Go to Mrs. Trotter and tell her to draw the $2,000 from the bank and give it to this man she's infatuated with and be happy.'

"I jumps and shakes Andy's hand for five minutes, and then I goes back to Mrs. Trotter and tells her, and she cries as hard for joy as she did for sorrow.

"Two days afterward me and Andy packed to go.

" 'Wouldn't you like to go down and meet Mrs. Trotter once before we leave?' I asks him. 'She'd like mightily to know you and express her encomiums and gratitude.'

" 'Why, I guess not,' says Andy. 'I guess we'd better hurry and catch that train.'

"I was strapping our capital around me in a memory belt like we always carried it, when Andy pulls a roll of large bills out of his pocket and asks me to put 'em with the rest.

" 'What's this?' says I.

" 'It's Mrs. Trotter's two thousand,' says Andy.

" 'How do you come to have it?' I asks.

" 'She gave it to me,' says Andy. 'I've been calling on her three evenings a week for more than a month.'

" 'Then you are William Wilkinson?' says I.

" 'I was,' says Andy."

Fard

BY ALDOUS HUXLEY

🕮 🕮 🕮

They had been quarrelling now for nearly three-quarters of an hour. Muted and inarticulate, the voices floated down the corridor, from the other end of the flat. Stooping over her sewing, Sophie wondered, without much curiosity, what it was all about this time. It was Madame's voice that she heard most often. Shrill with anger and indignant with tears, it burst out in gusts, in gushes. Monsieur was more self-controlled, and his deeper voice was too softly pitched to penetrate easily the closed doors and to carry along the passage. To Sophie, in her cold little room, the quarrel sounded, most of the time, like a series of monologues by Madame, interrupted by strange and ominous silences. But every now and then Monsieur seemed to lose his temper outright, and then there was no silence between the gusts, but a harsh, deep, angry shout. Madame kept up her loud shrillness continuously and without flagging; her voice had, even in anger, a curious, level monotony. But Monsieur spoke now loudly, now softly, with emphases and modulations and sudden outbursts, so that his contributions to the squabble, when they were audible, sounded like a series of separate explosions. Bow, wow, wow-wow-wow, wow—a dog barking rather slowly.

After a time Sophie paid no more heed to the noise of quarrelling. She was mending one of Madame's camisoles, and the work required all her attention. She felt very tired; her body ached all over. It had been a hard day; so had yesterday, so had the day before. Every day was a hard day, and she wasn't so young as she had been. Two years more and she'd be fifty. Every day had been a hard day since she could remember. She thought of the sacks of potatoes she used to carry when she was a little girl in the country. Slowly, slowly she was walking along the dusty road with the sack over her shoulder. Ten steps more; she could manage that. Only it never was the end; one always had to begin again.

144

She looked up from her sewing, moved her head from side to side, blinked. She had begun to see lights and spots of color dancing before her eyes; it often happened to her now. A sort of yellowish bright worm was wriggling up towards the right-hand corner of her field of vision; and though it was always moving upwards, upwards, it was always there in the same place. And there were stars of red and green that snapped and brightened and faded all round the worm. They moved between her and her sewing; they were there when she shut her eyes. After a moment she went on with her work; Madame wanted her camisole most particularly tomorrow morning. But it was difficult to see round the worm.

There was suddenly a great increase of noise from the other end of the corridor. A door had opened; words articulated themselves.

". . . bien tort, mon ami, si tu crois que je suis ton esclave. Je ferai ce que je voudrai."

"Moi aussi." Monsieur uttered a harsh, dangerous laugh. There was the sound of heavy footsteps in the passage, a rattling in the umbrella stand; then the front door banged.

Sophie looked down again at her work. Oh, the worm, the coloured stars, the aching fatigue in all her limbs! If one could only spend a whole day in bed—in a huge bed, feathery, warm and soft, all the day long. . . .

The ringing of the bell startled her. It always made her jump, that furious wasplike buzzer. She got up, put her work down on the table, smoothed her apron, set straight her cap, and stepped out into the corridor. Once more the bell buzzed furiously. Madame was impatient.

"At last, Sophie. I thought you were never coming."

Sophie said nothing; there was nothing to say. Madame was standing in front of the open wardrobe. A bundle of dresses hung over her arm, and there were more of them lying in a heap on the bed.

"Une beauté à la Rubens," her husband used to call her when he was in an amorous mood. He liked these massive, splendid, great women. None of your flexible drainpipes for him. "Helene Fourmont" was his pet name for her.

"Some day," Madame used to tell her friends, "some day I really must go to the Louvre and see my portrait. By Rubens, you know. It's extraordinary that one should have lived all one's life in Paris and never have seen the Louvre. Don't you think so?"

She was superb tonight. Her cheeks were flushed; her blue

eyes shone with an unusual brilliance between their long lashes; her short, red-brown hair had broken wildly loose.

"Tomorrow, Sophie," she said dramatically, "we start for Rome. Tomorrow morning." She unhooked another dress from the wardrobe as she spoke, and threw it on to the bed. With the movement her dressing-gown flew open, and there was a vision of ornate underclothing and white exuberant flesh. "We must pack at once."

"For how long, Madame?"

"A fortnight, three months—how should I know?"

"It makes a difference, Madame."

"The important thing is to get away. I shall not return to this house, after what has been said to me tonight, till I am humbly asked to."

"We had better take the large trunk, then, Madame; I will go and fetch it."

The air in the box-room was sickly with the smell of dust and leather. The big trunk was jammed in a far corner. She had to bend and strain at it in order to pull it out. The worm and the coloured stars flickered before her eyes; she felt dizzy when she straightened herself. "I'll help you to pack, Sophie," said Madame, when the servant returned, dragging the heavy trunk after her. What a death's-head the old woman looked nowadays! She hated having old, ugly people near her. But Sophie was so efficient; it would be madness to get rid of her.

"Madame need not trouble." There would be no end to it, Sophie knew, if Madame started opening drawers and throwing things about. "Madame had much better go to bed. It's late."

No, no. She wouldn't be able to sleep. She was to such a degree enervated. These men . . . What an embeastment! One was not their slave. One would not be treated in this way.

Sophie was packing. A whole day in bed, in a huge, soft bed, like Madame's. One would doze, one would wake up for a moment, one would doze again.

"His latest game," Madame was saying indignantly, "is to tell me he hasn't got any money. I'm not to buy any clothes, he says. Too grotesque. I can't go about naked, can I?" She threw out her hands. "And as for saying he can't afford it, that's simply nonsense. He can, perfectly well. Only he's mean, mean, horribly mean. And if he'd only do a little honest work, for a change, instead of writing silly verses and publishing them at his own expense, he'd have plenty and to spare." She walked up and down the room. "Besides," she went on, "there's his old father. What's he for, I should like to know? 'You must be proud of having a poet for a husband,' he says." She made her voice quaver like an old man's. "It's all I can do not to laugh in his face. 'And what beautiful verses Hegesippe writes about you! What passion, what fire!'" Thinking of the old man, she grimaced, wobbled her head, shook her finger, doddered on her legs. "And when one reflects that poor Hegesippe is bald and dyes the few hairs he has left." She laughed. "As for the passion he talks so much about in his beastly verses," she laughed—"that's all pure invention. But, my good Sophie, what are you thinking of? Why are you packing that hideous old green dress?"

Sophie pulled out the dress without saying anything. Why did the woman choose this night to look so terribly ill? She had a yellow face and blue teeth. Madame shuddered; it was too horrible. She ought to send her to bed. But, after all, the work had to be done. What could one do about it? She felt more than ever aggrieved.

"Life is terrible." Sighing, she sat down heavily on the edge of the bed. The buoyant springs rocked her gently once or twice before they settled to rest. "To be married to a man like this. I shall soon be getting old and fat. And never once unfaithful. But look how he treats me." She got up again and began to wander aimlessly about the room. "I won't stand it though," she burst out. She had halted in front of the long mirror, and was admiring her own splendid tragic figure. No one would believe, to look at her, that she was over thirty. Behind the beautiful tragedian she could see in the glass a thin, miserable, old creature, with a yellow face and blue teeth, crouching over the trunk. Really, it was too disagreeable. Sophie looked like one of those beggar women one sees on a cold morning, standing in the gutter. Does one hurry past, trying not to look at them? Or does one stop, open one's purse, and give them one's copper and nickel—even as much as a two-franc note, if one has no change? But whatever one did, one always felt uncomfortable, one always felt apologetic for one's furs. That was what came of walking. If one had a car—but that was another of Hegesippe's meannesses—one wouldn't, rolling along behind closed windows, have to be conscious of them at all. She turned away from the glass.

"I won't stand it," she said, trying not to think of the

beggar women, of blue teeth in a yellow face; "I won't stand it." She dropped into a chair.

But think of a lover with a yellow face and blue uneven teeth! She closed her eyes, shuddered at the thought. It would be enough to make one sick. She felt impelled to take another look: Sophie's eyes were the color of greenish lead, quite without life. What was one to do about it? The woman's face was a reproach, an accusation. And besides, the sight of it was making her feel positively ill. She had never been so profoundly enervated.

Sophie rose slowly and with difficulty from her knees; an expression of pain crossed her face. Slowly she walked to the chest of drawers, slowly counted out six pairs of silk stockings. She turned back towards the trunk. The woman was a walking corpse.

"Life is terrible," Madame repeated with conviction. "terrible, terrible, terrible."

She ought to send the woman to bed. But she would never be able to get her packing done by herself. And it was so important to get off tomorrow morning. She had told Hegesippe she would go, and he had simply laughed; he hadn't believed it. She must give him a lesson this time. In Rome she would see Luigino. Such a charming boy, and a marquis, too. Perhaps . . . But she could think of nothing but Sophie's face; the leaden eyes, the bluish teeth, the yellow, wrinkled skin.

"Sophie," she said suddenly; it was with difficulty that she could prevent herself screaming, "look on my dressing table. You'll see a box of rouge, the Dorin number twenty-four. Put a little on your cheeks. And there's a stick of lip salve in the right-hand drawer."

She kept her eyes resolutely shut while Sophie got up—with what a horrible creaking of the joints!—walked over to the dressing table, and stood there, rustling faintly through what seemed an eternity. What a life, my God, what a life! Slow footsteps trailed back again. She opened her eyes. Oh, that was far better, far better.

"Thank you, Sophie. You look much less tired now." She got up briskly. "And now we must hurry." Full of energy she ran to the wardrobe. "Goodness me," she exclaimed, throwing up her hands, "you've forgotten to put in my blue evening dress. How could you be so stupid, Sophie?"

The Wife

BY WASHINGTON IRVING

The treasures of the deep are not so precious
As are the conceal'd comforts of a man
Locked up in woman's love. I scent the air
Of blessings, when I come but near the house.
What a delicious breath marriage sends forth . . .
The violet bed's not sweeter.

MIDDLETON

I have often had the occasion to remark the fortitude with which women sustain the most overwhelming reverses of fortune. Those disasters which break down the spirit of a man, and prostrate him in the dust, seem to call forth all energies of the softer sex, and give such intrepidity and elevation to their character, that at times it approaches to sublimity. Nothing can be more touching than to behold a soft and tender female, who had been all weakness and dependence, and alive to every trivial roughness, while treading the prosperous paths of life, suddenly rising in mental force to be the comforter and support of her husband under misfortune, and abiding, with unshrinking firmness, the bitterest blasts of adversity.

As the vine, which has long twined its graceful foliage about the oak, and been lifted by it into sunshine, will, when the hardy plant is rifted by the thunderbolt, cling round it with its caressing tendrils and bind up its shattered boughs, so is it beautifully ordered by Providence, that woman, who is the mere dependent and ornament of man in his happier hours, should be his stay and solace when smitten with sudden calamity; winding herself into the rugged recesses of his nature, tenderly supporting the drooping head, and binding up the broken heart.

I was once congratulating a friend, who had around him

a blooming family, knit together in the strongest affection. "I can wish you no better lot," said he with enthusiasm, "than to have a wife and children. If you are prosperous, there they are to share your prosperity; if otherwise, there they are to comfort you." And indeed, I have observed that a married man falling into misfortune is more apt to retrieve his situation in the world than a single one; partly because he is more stimulated to exertion by the necessities of the helpless and beloved beings who depend upon him for subsistence; but chiefly because his spirits are soothed and relieved by domestic endearments, and his self-respect kept alive by finding that, though all abroad is darkness and humiliation, yet there is still a little world of love at home, of which he is the monarch. Whereas a single man is apt to run to waste and self-neglect; to fancy himself lonely and abandoned, and his heart to fall to ruin like some deserted mansion, for want of an inhabitant.

These observations call to mind a little domestic story, of which I was once a witness. My intimate friend, Leslie, had married a beautiful and accomplished girl, who had been brought up in the midst of fashionable life. She had, it is true, no fortune, but that of my friend was ample; and he delighted in the anticipation of indulging her in every elegant pursuit, and administering to those delicate tastes and fancies that spread a kind of witchery about the sex.—"Her life," said he, "shall be like a fairy tale."

The very difference in their characters produced a harmonious combination: he was of a romantic and somewhat serious cast; she was all life and gladness. I have often noticed the mute rapture with which he would gaze upon her in company, of which her sprightly powers made her the delight; and how, in the midst of applause, her eyes would still turn to him, as if there alone she sought favor and acceptance. When leaning on his arm, her slender form contrasted finely with his tall manly person. The fond confiding air with which she looked up at him seemed to call forth a flush of triumphant pride and cherishing tenderness, as if he doted on his lovely burden for its very helplessness. Never did a couple set forward on the flowery path of early and well-suited marriage with a fairer prospect of felicity.

It was the misfortune of my friend, however, to have embarked his property in large speculations; and he had not been married many months when, by a succession of sudden disasters, it was swept from him, and he found himself reduced almost to penury. For a time he kept his situation to himself, and went about with a haggard countenance and a breaking heart. His life was but a protracted agony; and what rendered it more insupportable was the necessity of keeping up a smile in the presence of his wife; for he could not bring himself to overwhelm her with the news. She saw, however, with the quick eye of affection, that all was not well with him. She marked his altered looks and stifled sighs, and was not to be deceived by his sickly and vapid attempts at cheerfulness. She tasked all her sprightly powers and tender blandishments to win him back to happiness; but she only drove the arrow deeper into his soul. The more he saw cause to love her, the more torturing was the thought that he was soon to make her wretched. A little while, thought he, and the smile will vanish from that cheek—the song will die away from those lips—the lustre of those eyes will be quenched with sorrow; and the happy heart, which now beats lightly in that bosom, will be weighed down like mine by the cares and miseries of the world.

At length he came to me one day, and related his whole situation in a tone of the deepest despair. When I heard him through I inquired, "Does your wife know all this?"—At the question he burst into an agony of tears. "For God's sake!" cried he, "if you have any pity on me, don't mention my wife; it is the thought of her that drives me almost to madness!"

"And why not?" said I. "She must know it sooner or later: you cannot keep it long from her, and the intelligence may break upon her in a more startling manner, than if imparted by yourself; for the accents of those we love soften the harshest tidings. Besides, you are depriving yourself of the comforts of her sympathy; and not merely that, but also endangering the only bond that can keep hearts together—an unreserved community of thought and feeling. She will soon perceive that something is secretly preying upon your mind; and true love will not brook reserve; it feels under-valued and outraged, when even the sorrows of those it loves are concealed from it."

"Oh, but my friend! to think what a blow I am to give to all her future prospects—how I am to strike her very soul to the earth by telling her that her husband is a beggar; that she is to forego all the elegancies of life—all the pleasures of society—to shrink with me into indigence and obscurity! To tell her that I have dragged her down from the sphere in

which she might have continued to move in constant bright-
ness—the light of every eye—the admiration of every heart!—
How can she bear poverty? she has been brought up in all the
refinements of opulence. How can she bear neglect? she
has been the idol of society. Oh! it will break her heart—it
will break her heart!—"

I saw his grief was eloquent, and I let it have its flow; for
sorrow relieves itself by words. When his paroxysm had
subsided, and he had relapsed into moody silence, I resumed
the subject gently, and urged him to break his situation at
once to his wife. He shook his head mournfully, but positively.

"But how are you going to keep it from her? It is necessary she should know it, that you may take the steps proper
to the alteration of your circumstances. You must change your
style of living—nay," observing a pang to pass across his
countenance, "don't let that afflict you. I am sure you have
never placed your happiness in outward show—you have yet
friends, warm friends, who will not think the worse of you
for being less splendidly lodged; and surely it does not
require a palace to be happy with Mary—"

"I could be happy with her," cried he, convulsively, "in a
hovel!—I could go down with her into poverty and the dust!
—I could—I could—God bless her!—God bless her!" cried he,
bursting into a transport of grief and tenderness.

"And believe me, my friend," I said, stepping up and
grasping him warmly by the hand, "believe me she can be
the same with you. Ay, more: it will be a source of pride
and triumph to her—it will call forth all the latent energies
and fervent sympathies of her nature; for she will rejoice to
prove that she loves you for yourself. There is in every true
woman's heart a spark of heavenly fire, which lies dormant
in the broad daylight of prosperity; but which kindles up and
beams and blazes in the dark hour of adversity. No man
knows what the wife of his bosom is—no man knows what a
ministering angel she is—unless he has gone with her through
the fiery trials of this world."

There was something in the earnestness of my manner,
and the figurative style of my language, that caught the
excited imagination of Leslie. I knew the auditor I had to
deal with; and following up the impression I had made, I
finished by persuading him to go home and unburden his
sad heart to his wife.

I must confess, notwithstanding all I had said, I felt some

little solicitude for the result. Who can calculate on the fortitude of one whose life has been a round of pleasures? Her gay spirits might revolt at the dark downward path of low humility suddenly pointed out before her, and might cling to the sunny regions in which they had hitherto revelled. Besides, ruin in fashionable life is accompanied by so many galling mortifications, to which in other ranks it is a stranger.—In short, I could not meet Leslie the next morning without trepidation. He had made the disclosure.

"And how did she bear it?"

"Like an angel! It seemed rather to be a relief to her mind, for she threw her arms round my neck, and asked if this was all that had lately made me unhappy.—But, poor girl," added he, "she cannot realize the change we must undergo. She has no idea of poverty but in the abstract; she has only read of it in poetry, where it is allied to love. She feels as yet no privation; she suffers no loss of accustomed conveniences nor elegancies. When we come practically to experience its sordid cares, its paltry wants, its petty humiliations—then will be the real trial."

"But," said I, "now that you have got over the severest task, that of breaking it to her, the sooner you let the world into the secret the better. The disclosure may be mortifying; but then it is a single misery and soon over: whereas you otherwise suffer it in anticipation, every hour of the day. It is not poverty so much as pretence, that harasses a ruined man—the struggle between a proud mind and an empty purse—the keeping up a hollow show that must soon come to an end. Have the courage to appear poor and you disarm poverty of its sharpest sting." On this point I found Leslie perfectly prepared. He had no false pride himself, and as to his wife, she was only anxious to conform to their altered fortunes.

Some days afterwards he called upon me in the evening. He had disposed of his dwelling house and taken a small cottage in the country, a few miles from town. He had been busied all day in sending out furniture. The new establishment required few articles, and those of the simplest kind. All the splendid furniture of his late residence had been sold, excepting his wife's harp. That, he said, was too closely associated with the idea of herself; it belonged to the little story of their loves; for some of the sweetest moments of their courtship were those when he had leaned over that instrument and listened to the melting tones of her voice. I could not but smile at this instance of romantic gallantry in a doting husband.

He was now going out to the cottage, where his wife had been all day superintending its arrangements. My feelings had become strongly interested in the progress of this family story, and, as it was a fine evening, I offered to accompany him.

He was wearied with the fatigues of the day, and as he walked out, fell into a fit of gloomy musing.

"Poor Mary!" at length broke, with a heavy sigh, from his lips.

"And what of her?" asked I: "has anything happened to her?"

"What," said he, darting an impatient glance, "is it nothing to be reduced to this paltry situation—to be caged in a miserable cottage—to be obliged to toil almost in the menial concerns of her wretched habitation?"

"Has she then repined at the change?"

"Repined! she has been nothing but sweetness and good humor. Indeed, she seems in better spirits than I have ever known her; she has been to me all love, and tenderness, and comfort!"

"Admirable girl!" exclaimed I. "You call yourself poor, my friend; you never were so rich—you never knew the boundless treasures of excellence you possess in that woman."

"Oh! but, my friend, if this first meeting at the cottage were over, I think I could then be comfortable. But this is her first day of real experience; she has been introduced into a humble dwelling—she has been employed all day in arranging its miserable equipments—she has, for the first time, known the fatigues of domestic employment—she has, for the first time, looked round her on a home destitute of everything elegant,—almost of everything convenient; and may now be sitting down, exhausted and spiritless, brooding over a prospect of future poverty."

There was a degree of probability in this picture that I could not gainsay, so we walked on in silence.

After turning from the main road up a narrow lane, so thickly shaded with forest trees as to give it a complete air of seclusion, we came in sight of the cottage. It was humble enough in its appearance, for the most pastoral poet; and yet it had a pleasing rural look. A wild vine had overrun one end in a profusion of foliage; a few trees threw their branches gracefully over it; and I observed several pots of flowers tastefully disposed about the door and on the grassplot in front. A small wicket gate opened upon a footpath that wound through some shrubbery to the door. Just as we approached, we heard the sound of music—Leslie grasped my arm; we paused and listened. It was Mary's voice singing, in a style of the most touching simplicity, a little air of which her husband was peculiarly fond.

I felt Leslie's hand tremble on my arm. He stepped forward to hear more distinctly. His step made a noise on the gravel walk. A bright beautiful face glanced out at the window and vanished—a light footstep was heard—and Mary came tripping forth to meet us: she was in a pretty rural dress of white; a few wild flowers were twisted in her fine hair; a fresh bloom was on her cheek; her whole countenance beamed with smiles—I had never seen her look so lovely.

"My dear George," cried she, "I am so glad you are come! I have been watching and watching for you; and running down the lane, and looking out for you. I've set out a table under a beautiful tree behind the cottage; and I've been gathering some of the most delicious strawberries for I know you are fond of them—and we have such excellent cream—and everything is so sweet and still here—Oh!" said she, putting her arm within his, and looking up brightly in his face, "Oh, we shall be so happy!"

Poor Leslie was overcome. He caught her to his bosom—he folded his arms round her—he kissed her again and again—he could not speak, but the tears gushed into his eyes; and he has often assured me, that though the world has since gone prosperously with him, and his life has, indeed, been a happy one, yet never has he experienced a moment of more exquisite felicity.

Charles

BY SHIRLEY JACKSON

📖 📖 📖

The day my son Laurie started kindergarten he renounced corduroy overalls with bibs and began wearing blue jeans with a belt. I watched him go off the first morning with the older girl next door, seeing clearly that an era of my life was ended, my sweet-voiced nursery-school tot replaced by a long-trousered, swaggering character who forgot to stop at the corner and wave good-bye to me.

He came home the same way, the front door slamming open, his hat on the floor, and the voice suddenly become raucous shouting, "Isn't anybody *here*?"

At lunch he spoke insolently to his father, spilled his baby sister's milk, and remarked that his teacher said we were not to take the name of the Lord in vain.

"How *was* school today?" I asked, elaborately casual.

"All right," he said.

"Did you learn anything?" his father asked.

Laurie regarded his father coldly. "I didn't learn nothing," he said.

"Anything," I said. "Didn't learn anything."

"The teacher spanked a boy, though," Laurie said, addressing his bread and butter. "For being fresh," he added, with his mouth full.

"What did he do?" I asked. "Who was it?"

Laurie thought. "It was Charles," he said. "He was fresh. The teacher spanked him and made him stand in a corner. He was awfully fresh."

"What did he do?" I asked again, but Laurie slid off his chair, took a cookie, and left, while his father was still saying, "See here, young man."

The next day Laurie remarked at lunch, as soon as he sat down, "Well, Charles was bad again today." He grinned enormously and said, "Today Charles hit the teacher."

"Good heavens," I said, mindful of the Lord's name. "I suppose he got spanked again?"

"He sure did," Laurie said. "Look up," he said to his father.

"What?" his father said, looking up.

"Look down," Laurie said. "Look at my thumb. Gee, you're dumb." He began to laugh insanely.

"Why did Charles hit the teacher?" I asked quickly.

"Because she tried to make him color with red crayons," Laurie said. "Charles wanted to color with green crayons so he hit the teacher and she spanked him and said nobody play with Charles but everybody did."

The third day—it was Wednesday of the first week—Charles bounced a see-saw on the head of a little girl and made her bleed, and the teacher made him stay inside all during recess. Thursday Charles had to stand in a corner during story-time because he kept pounding his feet on the floor. Friday Charles was deprived of blackboard privileges because he threw chalk.

On Saturday I remarked to my husband, "Do you think kindergarten is too unsettling for Laurie? All this toughness and bad grammar, and this Charles boy sounds like such a bad influence."

"It'll be all right," my husband said reassuringly. "Bound to be people like Charles in the world. Might as well meet them now as later."

On Monday Laurie came home late, full of news. "Charles," he shouted as he came up the hill; I was waiting anxiously on the front steps. "Charles," Laurie yelled all the way up the hill, "Charles was bad again."

"Come right in," I said, as soon as he came close enough. "Lunch is waiting."

"You know what Charles did?" he demanded, following me through the door. "Charles yelled so in school they sent a boy in from first grade to tell the teacher she had to make Charles keep quiet, and so Charles had to stay after school. And so all the children stayed to watch him."

"What did he do?" I asked.

"He just sat there," Laurie said, climbing into his chair at the table. "Hi, Pop, y'old dust mop."

"Charles had to stay after school today," I told my husband. "Everyone stayed with him."

"What does this Charles look like?" my husband asked Laurie. "What's his other name?"

"He's bigger than me," Laurie said. "And he doesn't have any rubbers and he doesn't ever wear a jacket."

Monday night was the first Parent-Teachers meeting, and only the fact that the baby had a cold kept me from going; I wanted passionately to meet Charles' mother. On Tuesday Laurie remarked suddenly, "Our teacher had a friend come to see her in school today."

"Charles's mother?" my husband and I asked simultaneously.

"Naaah," Laurie said scornfully. "It was a man who came and made us do exercises, we had to touch our toes. Look." He climbed down from his chair and squatted down and touched his toes. "Like this," he said. He got solemnly back into his chair and said, picking up his fork, "Charles didn't even *do* exercises."

"That's fine," I said heartily. "Didn't Charles want to do the exercises?"

"Naaah," Laurie said. "Charles was so fresh to the teacher's friend he wasn't *let* do exercises."

"Fresh again," I said.

"He kicked the teacher's friend," Laurie said. "The teacher's friend told Charles to touch his toes like I just did and Charles kicked him."

"What are they going to do about Charles, do you suppose?" Laurie's father asked him.

Laurie shrugged elaborately. "Throw him out of school, I guess," he said.

Wednesday and Thursday were routine; Charles yelled during story hour and hit a boy in the stomach and made him cry. On Friday Charles stayed after school again and so did all the other children.

With the third week of kindergarten Charles was an institution in our family; the baby was being a Charles when he filled his wagon full of mud and pulled it through the kitchen; even my husband, when he caught his elbow in the telephone cord and pulled telephone, ashtray, and a bowl of flowers off the table, said, after the first minute, "Looks like Charles."

During the third and fourth weeks it looked like a reformation in Charles; Laurie reported grimly at lunch on Thursday of the third week, "Charles was so good today the teacher gave him an apple."

"What?" I said, and my husband added warily, "You mean Charles?"

"Charles," Laurie said. "He gave the crayons around and

he picked up the books afterward and the teacher said he
was her helper."

"What happened?" I asked incredulously.

"He was her helper, that's all," Laurie said, and shrugged.

"Can this be true, about Charles?" I asked my husband
that night. "Can something like this happen?"

"Wait and see," my husband said cynically. "When
you've got a Charles to deal with, this may mean he's only
plotting."

He seemed to be wrong. For over a week Charles was the
teacher's helper; each day he handed things out and he picked
things up; no one had to stay after school.

"The PTA meeting's next week again," I told my husband
one evening. "I'm going to find Charles's mother there."

"Ask her what happened to Charles," my husband said.
"I'd like to know."

"I'd like to know myself," I said.

On Friday of that week things were back to normal. "You
know what Charles did today?" Laurie demanded at the lunch
table, in a voice slightly awed. "He told a little girl to say a
word and she said it and the teacher washed her mouth out
with soap and Charles laughed."

"What word?" his father asked unwisely, and Laurie said,
"I'll have to whisper it to you, it's so bad." He got down
off his chair and went around to his father. His father bent
his head down and Laurie whispered joyfully. His father's
eyes widened.

"Did Charles tell the little girl to say *that?*" he asked respectfully.

"She said it *twice*," Laurie said. "Charles told her to say it
twice."

"What happened to Charles?" my husband asked.

"Nothing," Laurie said. "He was passing out the crayons."

Monday morning Charles abandoned the little girl and
said the evil word himself three or four times, getting his
mouth washed out with soap each time. He also threw chalk.

My husband came to the door with me that evening as I
set out for the PTA meeting. "Invite her over for a cup of tea
after the meeting," he said. "I want to get a look at her."

"If only she's there," I said prayerfully.

"She'll be there," My husband said. "I don't see how they
could hold a PTA meeting without Charles's mother."

At the meeting I sat restlessly, scanning each comfortable

matronly face, trying to determine which one hid the secret of Charles. None of them looked to me haggard enough. No one stood up in the meeting and apologized for the way her son had been acting. No one mentioned Charles.

After the meeting I identified and sought out Laurie's kindergarten teacher. She had a plate with a cup of tea and a piece of chocolate cake; I had a plate with a cup of tea and a piece of marshmallow cake. We maneuvered up to one another cautiously, and smiled.

"I've been so anxious to meet you," I said. "I'm Laurie's mother."

"We're all so interested in Laurie," she said.

"Well, he certainly likes kindergarten," I said. "He talks about it all the time."

"We had a little trouble adjusting, the first week or so," she said primly, "but now he's a fine little helper. With occasional lapses, of course."

"Laurie usually adjusts very quickly," I said. "I suppose this time it's Charles's influence."

"Charles?"

"Yes," I said, laughing, "you must have your hands full in that kindergarten, with Charles."

"Charles?" she said. "We don't have any Charles in the kindergarten."

Then Came the Legions

BY MACKINLAY KANTOR

⚏ ⚏ ⚏

The Guards were drilling, but Cap had not gone up the crooked street to watch them.

In the first place, he had seen a great many soldiers drilled, before this. In the second place, a substantial farmer has just entered the leather-store, and Cap surmised that he had come to buy that double-harness which Orvil had been trying to sell him since the autumn before.

Cap was quite aware that he was incapable of managing

this sale or any other sale. If he tried, and bungled the job, he would be subjected to the wrath and sarcasm of Orvil and Simpson. Cap planned to stay out of their way until the harness sale was consummated.

The Guards were at drill. . . . Along brick façades sounded their trampling. The young officer who shepherded them seemed almost fearful of the boyish rabble who trooped behind.

From his seat on the empty barrel in a walled nook beside his brothers' store, Cap squinted into the late afternoon sunshine. The approaching column was awkward enough. They didn't keep their lines dressed or their files closed. All the boys talked in ranks; they waved their guns and hooted pleasantries to citizens who lined the sidewalk.

At Crary's grocery-store, Ephraim Crary and Lawyer Hollingsworth stood in the open doorway. "There comes the company," announced Crary.

The lawyer played with the snuff under his lip. "Look at Cap, over there on that barrel. Been drinking again."

"Anyway," said the grocer more charitably, "whether he's been drinking or not, he's playing hooky from the store, certain. I don't see how Orvil and Simpson put up with him."

"I don't see *how*, but I certainly see *why*." Hollingsworth felt the quid of snuff bite into his tongue. "It's because their old man in Covington pays the bills. He really set the boys up in that business, Crary. And when Cap got down-and-out, his old father had him and his wife and children all shipped up here to live off the family. I hear his folks pay him seventy dollars a month. Seventy dollars a month more'n he's worth!"

Crary said, against the hubbub of the approaching Guards: "I hear he had quite a record in the regular army."

"Record for drinking!" snapped the lawyer. "That was what cooked his goose for him."

The militia reached the half-turn in front of the store, parading directly toward the cubstone. His face scarlet, the young lieutenant ran backward ahead of them, waving his sword. He opened his mouth; he tried to howl a command, but no words came. Steadily, gleefully, the column mounted the curbstone.

"Stop, fellows—hang it—*Stop!*"

Snickers exploded along the ranks. But even so, the Guards did not falter. At least they had been taught to march in a straight line, and march in a straight line they would, for all the vagaries of their village street.

With a muffled thud the foremost squad halted with its noses against the window of Crary's store. The Guards marked time. They counted in humorous chorus: "*One*, two; *one*, two; *one* ..."

The boy officer slammed his sword into its scabbard. He stood with eyes blazing, fists clenched.

"Think you're smart, don't you? Well, I'll lick you for this, one at a time! Just because I didn't know the proper ..."

Lawyer Hollingsworth recovered from his laughter enough to thrust his face past the door-jamb. "Harry, why'n't you ask Cap to help you?"

The youth's eye followed his indication: that squat figure on the upended barrel by the leather-store.

"I guess I will," he said decisively. "Cap ought to know, anyway.—Column—*halt*," he told his army, and crossed the street.

Cap climbed down from his perch.

The lieutenant prayed: "Cap, will you help me out?"

Whisky breathed in a faint perfume. "Certainly, Harry," said Cap. "What seems to be the trouble?" His voice was calm, level; and again the young militiaman felt a queer respect rising in his mind—the respect which was so aborted when applied to a ne'er-do-well like Cap.

"You see, the street bends a little. It isn't a right-angular turn. I couldn't wheel 'em completely to the right or left—"

The bearded face moved in a nod of understanding.

"Take this sword," offered Harry. "I want to see how you'd do it. Like—when you were in the army." And then he held his tongue; every person in town knew the story of this man's disgrace.

Cap accepted the sword and buckled the sword-belt over his shabby coat. He walked out into the street.

"Fall out!" he ordered. And then: "The company will form, in column, ten paces in front of me."

They got into line, still snickering. This was odd, being ordered about by such a man as Cap. But there was something—

"The order for a half-turn is 'Left oblique,' or 'Right oblique.' It is followed by a command of execution. The company will observe the officer."

He pivoted, drew Harry's sword, and held it to his shoulder. "Forward," he chanted. *"Ha!"* His left foot lifted. He paced steadily away from them. *"Left oblique"*—his voice seemed more crusty and alert than ever they had heard it—*"Ha!"*

He returned to the staring militia.

"You see how it goes. Now we'll try to back up the street."

He strode to the rear of the column, eyes fixed on nothingness.

"Company—right-shoulder—Ha!" And they did that as their young officer had learned it from his Primary Manual.

"Company—Right about—Ha!"

Now their eyes were staring into his blue ones, where little pink flames of whisky still danced. . . . They marched. It was a right oblique, this time, and they followed him very well.

Harry came up, full of admiration.

"You're a trump, Cap," he said.

"Glad to be of service, Harry."

The officer accepted the sword-belt as the older man relinquished it, but he seemed unwilling to buckle it on.

"Cap," he said, "it's hard lines, drilling, when you don't know how. Our own captain is—Cap, I wish they'd elect you captain of the Guards. Anyway, will you come to drill tonight and help me some more with the company?"

A small boy in a ragged shirt scampered forward to grasp Cap's hand.

"Hello, Buck," Cap greeted him. But he kept looking at the youthful lieutenant.

Buck chirped: "Pa, Ma says she's tired, and wants to have supper early. Says for you to hustle up."

"Very well, sonny." The bearded man was glad, even after this military triumph, that he didn't have to go back and face his brothers, Simpson and Orvil.

He told the officer: "You can count on me. I'll be glad to help in any way I can. You see, I was trained at the expense of the National Government. And in this emergency which faces—"

"You'll be a lot of help!" The young militiaman raced to take care of his hungry squads.

Trudging behind Buck as they climbed steep steps toward their little brick house on the north hill, Cap played with the idea. He imagined himself fashioning the Jo Daviess Guards into a veritable Old Guard. Yes, he should write to the War Department. It was human decency for him to do so. And he need not mention Fort Humboldt, the whisky-barrel, and the resigned commission.

He began to build a letter in his mind: *"I have the honor to tender my services. . . . In view of my present age and length of service, I feel myself competent to command a regiment, if the President in his judgment should see fit to intrust one to me. . . . I am very respectfully, your obedient servant, U.S. Grant."*

If Not Higher

BY ISAAC LOEB PEREZ

    📖   📖   📖

And the Rebbe of Nemirov, every Friday morning early at Sliches-time, disappeared, melted into thin air! He was not to be found anywhere, either in the synagogue or in the two houses-of-study, or worshipping in some minyan, and most certainly not at home. His door stood open, people went in and out as they pleased—no one ever stole anything from the Rebbe—but there was not a soul in the house.

Where can the Rebbe be?

Where should he be, if not in heaven?

It is likely a Rebbe should have no affairs on hand with the Solemn Days so near?

Jews (no evil eye!) need a livelihood, peace, health, successful matchmakings; they wish to be good and pious and their sins are great, and Satan with his thousand eyes spies out the world from one end to the other, and he sees, and accuses, and tells tales—and who shall help if not the Rebbe? So thought the people.

Once, however, there came a Lithuanian—and he laughed! You know the Lithuanian Jews—they rather despise books of devotion, but stuff themselves with the Talmud and the codes. Well, the Lithuanian points out a special bit of the Gemara—and hopes it is plain enough: even Moses our Teacher could not ascend into heaven, but remained suspended thirty inches below it—and who, I ask you, is going to argue with a Lithuanian?

What becomes of the Rebbe?

"I don't know, and I don't care," says he, shrugging his shoulders, and all the while (what it is to be a Lithuanian!) determined to find out.

The very same evening, soon after prayers, the Lithuanian steals into the Rebbe's room, lays himself down under the Rebbe's bed and lies low.

He intends to stay there all night to find out where the Rebbe goes, and what he does at Sliches-time.

Another in his place would have dozed and slept the time away. Not so a Lithuanian—he learned a whole treatise of the Talmud by heart!

Day has not broken when he hears the call to prayer.

The Rebbe has been awake some time. The Lithuanian has heard him sighing and groaning for a whole hour. Whoever has heard the groaning of the Nemirover Rebbe knows what sorrow for All-Israel, what distress of mind, found voice in every groan. The soul that heard was dissolved in grief. But the heart of a Lithuanian is of cast-iron. The Lithuanian hears and lies still. The Rebbe lies still, too—the Rebbe, long life to him, *upon* the bed and the Lithuanian *under* the bed.

After that the Lithuanian hears the beds in the house squeak—the people jump out of them—a Jewish word is spoken now and again—water is poured on the fingers—a door is opened here and there. Then the people leave the house; once more it is quiet and dark, only a very little moonlight comes in through the shutter.

He confessed afterwards, did the Lithuanian, that when he found himself alone with the Rebbe terror took hold of him. He grew cold all over, and the roots of his ear-locks pricked his temples like needles. An excellent joke, to be left alone with the Rebbe at Sliches-time before dawn!

But a Lithuanian is dogged. He quivers and shakes like a fish—but he does not budge.

At last the Rebbe, long life to him, rises in his turn.

First he does what beseems a Jew. Then he goes to the wardrobe and takes out a packet—which proves to be the dress of a peasant: linen trousers, high boots, a pelisse, a wide felt hat, and a long and broad leather belt studded with brass nails. The Rebbe put them on.

Out of the pockets of the pelisse dangles the end of a thick cord, a peasant's cord.

On his way out the Rebbe steps aside into the kitchen, stoops, takes a hatchet from under a bed, puts it into his belt, and leaves the house. The Lithuanian trembles but he persists.

A fearful, Solemn-Day hush broods over the dark streets, broken not unfrequently by a cry of supplication from some little minyan, or the moan of some sick person behind a window.

The Rebbe keeps to the street side, and walks in the shadow of the houses.

He glides from one to the other, the Lithuanian after him. And the Lithuanian hears the sound of his own heartbeats mingle with the heavy footfall of the Rebbe; but he follows on, and together they emerge from the town.

Behind the town stands a little wood. The Rebbe, long life to him, enters it. He walks on thirty or forty paces, and then he stops beside a small tree. And the Lithuanian, with amaze, sees the Rebbe take his hatchet and strike the tree. He sees the Rebbe strike blow after blow, he hears the tree creak and snap. And the little tree falls, and the Rebbe splits it up into logs, and the logs into splinters. Then he makes a bundle, binds it round with the cord, throws it on his shoulder, replaces the hatchet in his belt, leaves the wood, and goes back into the town.

In one of the back streets he stops beside a poor, tumble-down little house, and taps at the window.

"Who is there?" cries a frightened voice within. The Lithuanian knows it to be the voice of a Jewess, a sick Jewess.

"I," answers the Rebbe in the peasant tongue.

"Who is I?" inquires the voice further. And the Rebbe answers again in the Little-Russian speech:

"Vassil."

"Which Vassil? and what do you want, Vassil?"

"I have wood to sell," says the sham peasant, "very cheap, for next to nothing."

And without further ado he goes in. The Lithuanian steals in behind him, and sees, in the gray light of dawn, a poor room with poor, broken furniture.

In the bed lies a sick Jewess huddled up in rags, who says bitterly:

"Wood to sell—and where am I, a poor widow, to get the money from to buy it?"

"I will give you a six-groschen worth on credit."

"And how am I ever to repay you?" groans the poor woman.

"Foolish creature!" the Rebbe upbraids her. "See here: you are a poor sick Jewess, and I am willing to trust you with the little bundle of wood; I believe that in time you will repay me. And you, you have such a great mighty God, and you do not trust Him! not even to the amount of a miserable six-groschen for a little bundle of wood!"

"And who is to light the stove?" groans the widow. "Do I look like getting up to do it? and my son away at work!"

"I will also light the stove for you," said the Rebbe.

And the Rebbe, while he laid the wood in the stove, repeated groaning the first part of Sliches.

Then, when the stove was alight, and the wood crackled cheerily, he repeated, more gaily, the second part of Sliches.

He repeated the third part when the fire had burnt itself out, and he shut the stove doors. . . .

The Lithuanian who saw all this remained with the Rebbe, as one of his followers.

And later, when anyone told how the Rebbe early every morning at Sliches-time raised himself and flew up into heaven, the Lithuanian, instead of laughing, added quietly:

"If not higher."

The Wild Duck's Nest

BY MICHAEL MCLAVERTY

📖 📖 📖

The sun was setting, spilling gold light on the low western hills of Rathlin Island. A small boy walked jauntily along a hoof-printed path that wriggled between the folds of these hills and opened out into a crater-like valley on the cliff-top. Presently he stopped as if remembering something, then suddenly he left the path and began running up one of

the hills. When he reached the top he was out of breath and
stood watching streaks of light radiating from golden-edged
clouds, the scene reminding him of a picture he had seen of
the Transfiguration. A short distance below him was the cow
standing at the edge of a reedy lake. Colm ran down to meet
her waving his stick in the air, and the wind rumbling in
his ears made him give an exultant whoop which splashed
upon the hills in a shower of echoed sound. A flock of gulls
lying on the short grass near the lake rose up languidly, drifting like blown snowflakes over the rim of the cliff.

The lake faced west and was fed by a stream, the drainings
of the semi-circling hills. One side was open to the winds from
the sea and in winter a little outlet trickled over the cliffs
making a black vein in their gray sides. The boy lifted stones
and began throwing them into the lake, weaving web after
web on its calm surface. Then he skimmed the water with
flat stones, some of them jumping the surface and coming to
rest on the other side. He was delighted with himself and
after listening to his echoing shouts of delight he ran to
fetch his cow. Gently he tapped her on the side and reluctantly she went towards the brown-mudded path that led
out of the valley. The boy was about to throw a final stone
into the lake when a bird flew low over his head, its neck
astrain, and its orange-colored legs clear in the soft light. It
was a wild duck. It circled the lake twice, thrice, coming
lower each time and then with a nervous flapping of wings it
skidded along the surface, its legs breaking the water into a
series of silvery arcs. Its wings closed, it lit silently, gave a
slight shiver, and began pecking indifferently at the water.

Colm, with dilated eyes, eagerly watched it making for the
farther end of the lake. It meandered between tall bulrushes,
its body black and solid as stone against the graying water.
Then as if it had sunk it was gone. The boy ran stealthily
along the bank looking away from the lake, pretending indifference. When he came opposite to where he had last seen
the bird he stopped and peered through the sighing reeds
whose shadows streaked the water in a maze of black strokes.
In front of him was a soddy islet guarded by the spears of
sedge and separated from the bank by a narrow channel of
water. The water wasn't too deep—he could wade across with
care.

Rolling up his short trousers he began to wade, his arms
outstretched, and his legs brown in the mountain water. As
he drew near the islet, his feet sank in the cold mud and

bubbles winked up at him. He went more carefully and nervously. Then one trouser leg fell and dipped into the water; the boy dropped his hands to roll it up, he unbalanced, made a splashing sound, and the bird arose with a squawk and whirred away over the cliffs. For a moment the boy stood frightened. Then he clambered on to the wet-soaked sod of land, which was spattered with sea gulls' feathers and bits of wind-blown rushes.

Into each hummock he looked, pulling back the long grass. At last he came on the nest, facing seawards. Two flat rocks dimpled the face of the water and between them was a neck of land matted with coarse grass containing the nest. It was untidily built of dried rushes, straw and feathers, and in it lay one solitary egg. Colm was delighted. He looked around and saw no one. The nest was his. He lifted the egg, smooth and green as the sky, with a faint tinge of yellow like the reflected light from a buttercup; and then he felt he had done wrong. He put it back. He knew he shouldn't have touched it and he wondered would the bird forsake the nest. A vague sadness stole over him and he felt in his heart he had sinned. Carefully smoothing out his footprints he hurriedly left the islet and ran after his cow. The sun had now set and the cold shiver of evening enveloped him, chilling his body and saddening his mind.

In the morning he was up and away to school. He took the grass rut that edged the road for it was softer on the bare feet. His house was the last on the western headland and after a mile or so he was joined by Paddy McFall; both boys, dressed in similar hand-knitted blue jerseys and gray trousers, carried home-made school bags. Colm was full of the nest and as soon as he joined his companion he said eagerly: "Paddy, I've a nest—a wild duck's with one egg."

"And how do you know it's a wild duck's?" asked Paddy, slightly jealous.

"Sure I saw her with my own two eyes, her brown speckled back with a crow's patch on it, and her yellow legs—"

"Where is it?" interrupted Paddy in a challenging tone.

"I'm not going to tell you, for you'd rob it!"

"Aach! I suppose it's a tame duck's you have or maybe an old gull's."

Colm put out his tongue at him. "A lot you know!" he said, "for a gull's egg has spots and this one is greenish-white, for I had it in my hand."

And then the words he didn't want to hear rushed from

Paddy in a mocking chant, "You had it in your hand! . . . She'll forsake it! She'll forsake it! She'll forsake it!" he said, skipping along the road before him.

Colm felt as if he would choke or cry with vexation.

His mind told him that Paddy was right, but somehow he couldn't give in to it and he replied: "She'll not forsake it! She'll not. I know she'll not!"

But in school his faith wavered. Through the windows he could see moving sheets of rain—rain that dribbled down the panes filling his mind with thoughts of the lake creased and chilled by wind; the nest sodden and black with wetness; and the egg cold as a cave stone. He shivered from the thoughts and fidgeted with the inkwell cover, sliding it backwards and forwards mechanically. The mischievous look had gone from his eyes and the school day dragged on interminably. But at last they were out in the rain, Colm rushing home as fast as he could.

He was no time at all at his dinner of potatoes and salted fish until he was out in the valley now smoky with drifts of slanting rain. Opposite the islet he entered the water. The wind was blowing into his face, rustling noisily the rushes heavy with the dust of rain. A moss-cheeper, swaying on a reed like a mouse, filled the air with light cries of loneliness.

The boy reached the islet, his heart thumping with excitement, wondering did the bird forsake. He went slowly, quietly, on to the strip of land that led to the nest. He rose on his toes, looking over the ledge to see if he could see her. And then every muscle tautend. She was on, her shoulders hunched up, and her bill lying on her breast as if she were asleep. Colm's heart hammered wildly in his ears. She hadn't forsaken. He was about to turn stealthily away. Something happened. The bird moved, her neck straightened, twitching nervously from side to side. The boy's head swam with lightness. He stood transfixed. The wild duck with a panicky flapping, rose heavily, and flew off towards the sea. . . . A guilty silence enveloped the boy. . . . He turned to go away, hesitated, and glanced back at the bare nest; it'd be no harm to have a look. Timidly he approached it; standing straight, and gazing over the edge. There in the nest lay two eggs. He drew in his breath with delight, splashed quickly from the island, and ran off whistling in the rain.

A Toast to Captain Jerk

BY RUSSELL MALONEY

📖 📖 📖

Saturday night is the night the little actors sit up late, getting drunk and boasting. Oreste's, the Italian restaurant near Eighth Avenue which is the semi-official clearing house for forty-dollar Equity minimum salary checks, was almost filled by eleven-thirty. There was a surge of words in the little smoky room, properly sustained on a column of breath, pushed forward by well-exercised, perfectly controlled diaphragms, sharply audible: *Orson definitely told me but no casting till week after next from hunger what does he think Skowhegan who else could they get for that money little bitch left my pictures three months on the Coast fake the dancing but they cut half my lines Chamberlain Brown Sardi's out of town but his secretary said they say Crosby Gaige but I can't see Zelda in one of those grass skirts from hunger.*

Only one girl in Oreste's was eating alone. She was a slender, long-boned girl, attractive in a manner that represented a definite choice. The candid wideness of her eyes was the result of spaced eyebrows and eyeshadow on the outer corners of the lids. Her hair was brushed away from her brow to make her face naked and without guile. Girls of this candid type can be becomingly greedy, and this one was eating a plate of spaghetti, winding up neat forkfuls with precise motions of her narrow brown hands, stopping now and then to drink from a tumbler of red wine. She glanced at the doorway every few minutes, raising her chin and turning her head with unconscious theatrical emphasis.

The man she was waiting for arrived a little before midnight, running lithely down the three steps that led from the street and striding straight to her table. He wore a homburg, a blue serge suit, white shirt, starched collar, plain tie, and black shoes with only a dull polish. "Mona, my dear. I'm late," he said, sitting down. He had a lean, brownish head and wide shoulders.

"That's all right," the girl said. "It must have taken you three hours to dress. You eaten?"

"Yes, yes, hours ago." The man looked over his shoulder, caught the waiter's eye, and called, "Whiskey soda."

The waiter crossed the room and stood at the man's shoulder. "Rye whiskey or Scotch?" he said.

"Oh, for God's sake," the man said. "*Scotch.*"

"The idea, Joe! Only Americans drink rye," Mona said to the waiter. "Filthy stuff, rye," she added to the man, speaking in an approximation of his own clipped accent.

"Now, Mona," the man said, "let's not—"

"Now, Tracy," she said. "Let's." Looking at him calmly, she searched her patent-leather handbag for cigarettes and matches. "Very interesting," she said, taking out a cigarette and tapping it on a scarlet thumbnail. "The clothes, I mean." She tapped the cigarette once more, and put the wrong end in her mouth. "The last time I saw you in those particular clothes, Tracy, my dear, was two summers ago, when we did 'The End of the Story.' Detective Inspector Harrod of Scotland Yard." She lit the cigarette and flicked the match across the room. "Veddy stiff, veddy British. 'I'm afraid this is murder. No one must leave the house.' So on and so on . . . . Joe!" she called suddenly to the waiter. "Joe, I'd like another glass of this lovely red ink. Ink-and-soda, eh, Tracy?"

"I hoped we wouldn't get tight," Tracy said. "Tonight."

"Well, I decided we would, so shut up," she said. "As I was saying, I note with interest that we have combed our wardrobe. I know your wardrobe as well as you do, darling—do you mind? We decided against the brown tweeds, and gray jacket with flannels, and the double-breasted pin stripe and the single-breasted herring-bone. And, of course, the dinner jacket, and the tails. No, we wanted something solid and respectable, because we were mousing around in banks and steamship offices, and maybe even in the British Ambassador's office."

"The Consulate," Tracy said. "For God's sake."

"And all because we've decided that our wardrobe isn't quite complete. We want a nice little uniform, too. 'Journey's End.' Captain Stanhope."

"That's not the way to take it," Tracy said. "I'm going to do it, and you might as well make up your mind."

"My mind's made up, all right," she said. "And you're not going to do it."

"Yes."

"No. For one thing, they won't let you. With your first papers and all."

"It'll be a little irregular, perhaps," he said. "But don't tell me you don't think people are getting over. And there's Canada."

"Listen," the girl said, a note of urgency in her voice. "We won't be in it. Stay here, and you won't be in it. Why do you think you have to be in it? I bet they can have a dandy war without you."

"It's no use, Mona."

"Well, aren't actors supposed to keep on being actors in a war? In canteens and so on? They did before."

"My God, the war's *real*," the man said. "It's got nothing to do with all this we've had over here."

"And *I'm* not real. And it isn't real that we were both getting screen tests this fall, or that Gordon talked to you about that thing he's doing."

"No, not a bit real," Tracy said, "Everything I've done here is perfectly silly make-believe. You're a nice bit of make-believe, and the rest of it isn't so nice—all the cheap hotel rooms and the bit parts, and making believe that I or you or Brooks Atkinson or anybody else on earth cares whether I'm any good at pretending to be Detective Inspector Harrod. Over there, it'll be real, at least."

The girl settled back in her chair. "I've lent you money for some damn silly things, but you won't get it for this," she said.

"I won't have to. I borrowed some tonight from some friends of Mother's uptown, and besides, I haven't paid my room rent for the past month, I've kept that."

"So that's what's really real, is it?" she said. "All that over there."

"It is now, for me."

"Captain Stanhope," the girl said. "Captain Jerk, the unknown fall guy. You know what I'm going to do, when this is all over? I'm going to find where they've buried you, and put a special little epitaph over you. I'll say 'He skipped his bill at the Trafton Hotel. He was in arrears with his Equity dues. He owed Oreste twelve dollars for drinks. He behaved just as badly as everybody else in the world today.' " She sat up straight in her chair, in the smoke and the noise of the laughter around her. "And if you think I'm going to apologize tomorrow for saying this, you're wrong. Because it's what I think. You're just skipping your hotel bill."

"It'll be real, at least," he said again, but there was no certainty in his face. He looked as if he might never know what was real, even if he died trying to find out.

Germans at Meat

BY KATHERINE MANSFIELD

▢ ▢ ▢

Bread soup was placed upon the table. "Ah," said the Herr Rat, leaning upon the table as he peered into the tureen, "that is what I need. My 'magen' has not been in order for several days. Bread soup, and just the right consistency. I am a good cook myself"— He turned to me.

"How interesting," I said, attempting to infuse just the right amount of enthusiasm into my voice.

"Oh yes—when one is not married it is necessary. As for me, I have had all I wanted from women without marriage." He tucked his napkin into his collar and blew upon his soup as he spoke. "Now at nine o'clock I make myself an English breakfast, but not much. Four slices of bread, two eggs, two slices of cold ham, one plate of soup, two cups of tea—that is nothing to you."

He asserted the fact so vehemently that I had not the courage to refute it.

All eyes were suddenly turned upon me. I felt I was bearing the burden of the nation's preposterous breakfast—I who drank a cup of coffee while buttoning my blouse in the morning.

"Nothing at all,'" cried Herr Hoffman from Berlin. "Ach, when I was in England in the morning I used to eat."

He turned up his eyes and his moustache, wiping the soup drippings from his coat and waistcoat.

"Do they really eat so much?" asked Fraulein Stiegelauer. "Soup and baker's bread and pig's flesh, and tea and coffee and stewed fruit, and honey and eggs, and cold fish and kidneys, and hot fish and liver. All the ladies eat, too, especially the ladies?"

"Certainly. I myself have noticed it, when I was living in

a hotel in Leicester Square," cried the Herr Rat. "It was a good hotel, but they could not make tea—now—"

"Ah, that's one thing I *can* do," said I, laughing brightly. "I can make very good tea. The great secret is to warm the teapot."

"Warm the teapot," interrupted the Herr Rat, pushing away his soup plate. "What do you warm the teapot for? Ha! ha! that's very good! One does not eat the teapot, I suppose?"

He fixed his cold blue eyes upon me with an expression which suggested a thousand premeditated invasions.

"So that is the great secret of your English tea? All you do is to warm the teapot."

I wanted to say that was only the preliminary canter, but could not translate it, and so was silent.

The servant brought in veal, with sauerkraut and potatoes.

"I eat sauerkraut with great pleasure," said the Traveller from North Germany, "but now I have eaten so much of it that I cannot retain it. I am immediately forced to—"

"A beautiful day," I cried, turning to Fraulein Stiegelauer. "Did you get up early?"

"At five o'clock I walked for ten minutes in the wet grass. Again in bed. At half-past five I fell asleep, and woke at seven, when I made an 'overbody' washing! Again in bed. At eight o'clock I had a cold-water poultice, and at half-past eight I drank a cup of mint tea. At nine I drank some malt coffee, and began my 'cure.' Pass me the sauerkraut, please. You do not eat it?"

"No, thank you. I still find it a little strong."

"Is it true," asked the Widow, picking her teeth with a hairpin as she spoke, "that you are a vegetarian?"

"Why, yes; I have not eaten meat for three years."

"Im-possible! Have you any family?"

"No."

"There now, you see, that's what you're coming to! Who ever heard of having children upon vegetables? It is not possible. But you never have large families in England now; I suppose you are too busy with your suffragetting. Now I have nine children, and they are all alive, thank God. Fine, healthy babies—though after the first one was born I had to—"

"How *wonderful!*" I cried.

"Wonderful," said the Widow contemptuously, replacing the hairpin in the knob which was balanced on the top of her head. "Not at all! A friend of mine had four at the same time. Her husband was so pleased he gave a supper-party and had them placed on the table. Of course she was very proud."

"Germany," boomed the Traveller, biting round a potato which he had speared with his knife, "is the home of the Family."

Followed an appreciative silence.

The dishes were changed for beef, red currants and spinach. They wiped their forks upon black bread and started again.

"How long are you remaining here?" asked the Herr Rat.

"I do not know exactly. I must be back in London in September."

"Of course you will visit München?"

"I am afraid I shall not have time. You see, it is important not to break in my 'cure.'"

"But you *must* go to München. You have not seen Germany if you have not been to München. All the Exhibitions, all the Art and Soul life of Germany are in München. There is the Wagner Festival in August, and Mozart and a Japanese collection of pictures—and there is the beer! You do not know what good beer is until you have been to München. Why, I see fine ladies every afternoon, but fine ladies, I tell you, drinking glasses so high." He measured a good washstand pitcher in height, and I smiled.

"If I drink a great deal of München beer I sweat so," said Herr Hoffman. "When I am here, in the fields or before my bath, I sweat, but I enjoy it; but in the town it is not at all the same thing."

Prompted by the thought, he wiped his neck and face with his dinner napkin and carefully cleaned his ears.

A glass dish of stewed apricots was placed upon the table.

"Ah, fruit!" said Fraulein Stiegelauer, "that is so necessary to health. The doctor told me this morning that the more fruit I could eat the better."

She very obviously followed the advice.

Said the Traveller: "I suppose you are frightened of an invasion, too, eh? Oh, that's good. I've been reading all about your English play in a newspaper. Did you see it?"

"Yes." I sat upright. "I assure you we are not afraid."

"Well, then, you ought to be," said the Herr Rat. "You have got no army at all—a few little boys with their veins full of nicotine poisoning."

"Don't be afraid," Herr Hoffman said. "We don't want

England. If we did we would have had her long ago. We really do not want you."

He waved his spoon airily, looking across at me as though I were a little child whom he would keep or dismiss as he pleased.

"We certainly do not want Germany," I said.

"This morning I took a half bath. Then this afternoon I must take a knee bath and an arm bath," volunteered the Herr Rat; "then I do my exercises for an hour, and my work is over. A glass of wine and a couple of rolls with some sardines—"

They were handed cherry cake with whipped cream.

"What is your husband's favorite meat?" asked the Widow.

"I really do not know," I answered.

"You really do not know? How long have you been married?"

"Three years."

"But you cannot be in earnest! You would not have kept house as his wife for a week without knowing that fact."

"I really never asked him; he is not at all particular about his food."

A pause. They all looked at me, shaking their heads, their mouths full of cherry stones.

"No wonder there is a repetition in England of that dreadful state of things in Paris," said the Widow, folding her dinner napkin. "How can a woman expect to keep her husband if she does not know his favorite food after three years?"

"Mahlzeit!"

"Mahlzeit!"

I closed the door after me.

Born of Man and Woman

BY RICHARD MATHESON

▯ ▯ ▯

X—This day when it had light mother called me a retch. You retch she said. I saw in her eyes the anger. I wonder what it is a retch.

This day it had water falling from upstairs. It fell all around. I saw that. The ground of the back I watched from the little window. The ground it sucked up the water like thirsty lips. It drank too much and it got sick and runny brown. I didn't like it.

Mother is a pretty thing I know. In my bed place with cold walls around I have a paper things that was behind the furnace. It says on it SCREENSTARS. I see in the pictures faces like of mother and father. Father says they are pretty. Once he said it.

And also mother he said. Mother so pretty and me decent enough. Look at you he said and didn't have the nice face. I touched his arm and said it is alright father. He shook and pulled away where I couldn't reach.

Today mother let me off the chain a little so I could look out the little window. That's how I saw the water falling from upstairs.

XX—This day it had goldness in the upstairs. As I know when I looked at it my eyes hurt. After I looked at it the cellar is red.

I think this was church. They leave the upstairs. The big machine swallows them and rolls out past and is gone. In the back part is the *little* mother. She is much small than me. I am big. It is a secret but I have pulled the chain out of the wall. I can see out the little window all I like.

In this day when it got dark I had eat my food and some bugs. I hear laughs upstairs. I like to know why there are laughs for. I took the chain from the wall and wrapped it around me. I walked squish to the stairs. They creak when I walk on them. My legs slip on them because I don't want on stairs. My feet stick to the wood.

I went up and opened a door. It was a white place. White as white jewels that come from upstairs sometime. I went in and stood quiet. I hear the laughing some more. I walk to the sound and look through to the people. More people than I thought was. I thought I should laugh with them.

Mother came out and pushed the door in. It hit me and hurt. I fell back on the smooth floor and the chain made noise. I cried. She made a hissing noise into her and put her hand on her mouth. Her eyes got big.

She looked at me. I heard father call. What fell he called. She said a iron board. Come help pick it up she said. He came and said now is *that* so heavy you need me. He saw me and grew big. The anger came in his eyes. He hit me. I spilled some of the drip on the floor from one arm. It was not nice. It made ugly green on the floor.

Father told me to go to the cellar. I had to go. The light it hurt now in my eyes. It is not like that in the cellar.

Father tied my legs and arms up. He put me on my bed. Upstairs I heard laughing while I was quiet there looking on a black spider that was swinging down to me. I thought what father said. Ohgod he said. And only eight.

XXX—This day father hit in the chain again before it had light. I have to try to pull it out again. He said I was bad to come upstairs. He said never do that again or he would beat me hard. That hurts.

I hurt. I slept the day and rested my head against the cold wall. I thought of the white place upstairs.

XXXX—I got the chain from the wall out. Mother was upstairs. I heard little laughs very high. I looked out the window. I saw all little people like the little mother and little fathers too. They are pretty.

They were making nice noise and jumping around the ground. Their legs was moving hard. They are like mother and father. Mother says all right people look like they do.

One of the little fathers saw me. He pointed at the window. I let go and slid down the wall in the dark. I curled up as they would not see. I heard their talks by the window and foots running. Upstairs there was a door hitting. I heard the little mother call upstairs. I heard heavy steps and I rushed to my bed place. I hit the chain in the wall and lay down on my front.

I heard mother come down. Have you been at the window she said. I heard the anger. *Stay* away from the window. You have pulled the chain out again.

She took the stick and hit me with it. I didn't cry. I can't do that. But the drip ran all over the bed. She saw it and twisted away and made a noise. Oh mygod mygod she said why have you *done* this to me? I heard the stick go bounce on the stone floor. She ran upstairs. I slept the day.

XXXXX—This day it had water again. When mother was upstairs I heard the little one come slow down the steps. I hidded myself in the coal bin for mother would have anger if the little mother saw me.

She had a little live thing with her. It walked on the arms and had pointy ears. She said things to it.

It was all right except the live thing smelled me. It ran

up the coal and looked down at me. The hairs stood up. In the throat it made an angry noise. I hissed but it jumped on me.

I didn't want to hurt it. I got fear because it bit me harder than the rat does. I hurt and the little mother screamed. I grabbed the live thing tight. It made sounds I never heard. I pushed it all together. It was lumpy and red on the black coal.

I hid there when mother called. I was afraid of the stick. She left. I crept over the coal with the thing. I hid it under my pillow and rested on it. I put the chain in the wall again.

X—This is another times. Father chained me tight. I hurt because he beat me. This time I hit the stick out of his hands and made noise. He went away and his face was white. He ran out of my bed place and locked the door.

I am not so glad. All day it is cold in here. The chain comes slow out of the wall. And I have a bad anger with mother and father. I will show them. I will do what I did that once.

I will screech and laugh loud. I will run on the walls. Last I will hang head down by all my legs and laugh and drip green all over until they are sorry they didn't be nice to me.

If they try to beat me again I'll hurt them. I will.

The Ant and the Grasshopper

BY SOMERSET MAUGHAM

When I was a very small boy I was made to learn by heart certain of the fables of La Fontaine, and the moral of each was carefully explained to me. Among those learned was *The Ant and the Grasshopper*, which is devised to bring home to the young the useful lesson that in an imperfect world industry is rewarded and giddiness punished. In this admirable fable (I apologise for telling something which everyone is politely, but inexactly, supposed to know) the ant spends a laborious summer gathering its winter store, while the grasshopper sits on a blade of grass singing to the sun. Winter comes and the ant is comfortably provided for, but the grasshopper has an empty larder: he goes to the ant and begs for a little food. Then the ant gives him her classic answer:

"What were you doing in the summer time?"

"Saving your presence, I sang. I sang all day, all night."

"You sang. Why, then go and dance."

I do not ascribe it to perversity on my part, but rather to the inconsequence of childhood, which is deficient in moral sense, that I could never quite reconcile myself to the lesson. My sympathies were with the grasshopper and for some time I never saw an ant without putting my foot on it. In this summary (and as I have discovered since, entirely human) fashion I sought to express my disapproval of prudence and common-sense.

I could not help thinking of this fable when the other day I saw George Ramsay lunching by himself in a restaurant. I never saw anyone wear an expression of such deep gloom. He was staring into space. He looked as though the burden of the whole world sat upon his shoulders. I was sorry for him: I suspected at once that his unfortunate brother had been causing trouble again. I went up to him and held out my hand.

"How are you?" I asked.

"I'm not in hilarious spirits," he answered.

"Is it Tom again?"

He sighed.

"Yes, it's Tom again."

"Why don't you chuck him? You've done everything in the world for him. You must know by now that he's quite hopeless."

I suppose every family has a black sheep. Tom had been a sore trial to his for twenty years. He had begun life decently enough: he went into business, married and had two children. The Ramsays were perfectly respectable people and there was every reason to suppose that Tom Ramsay would have a useful and honourable career. But one day, without warning, he announced that he didn't like work and that he wasn't suited for marriage. He wanted to enjoy himself. He would listen to no expostulations. He left his wife and his office. He had a little money and he spent two happy years in various capitals of Europe. Rumours of his doings reached his relations from time to time and they were profoundly shocked. He certainly had a very good time. They shook their heads and asked what would happen when his

money was spent. They soon found out: he borrowed. He was
charming and unscrupulous. I have never met anyone to
whom it was more difficult to refuse a loan. He made a steady
income from his friends and he made friends easily. But he
always said that the money you spent on necessities was
boring; the money that was amusing to spend was the money
you spent on luxuries. For this he depended on his brother
George. He did not waste his charm on him. George was
respectable. Once or twice he fell to Tom's promises of
amendment and gave him considerable sums in order that he
might make a fresh start. On these Tom bought a motorcar
and some very nice jewellery. But when circumstances forced
George to realise that his brother would never settle down
and he washed his hands of him, Tom, without a qualm,
began to blackmail him. It was not very nice for a respectable lawyer to find his brother shaking cocktails behind the
bar of his favourite restaurant or to see him waiting on the
box-seat of a taxi outside his club. Tom said that to serve in
a bar or to drive a taxi was a perfectly decent occupation, but
if George could oblige him with a couple of hundred pounds
he didn't mind for the honour of the family giving it up.
George paid.

Once Tom nearly went to prison. George was terribly upset.
He went into the whole discreditable affair. Really Tom had
gone too far. He had been wild, thoughtless and selfish, but
he had never before done anything dishonest, by which
George meant illegal; and if he were prosecuted he would
assuredly be convicted. But you cannot allow your only brother to go to gaol. The man Tom had cheated, a man called
Cronshaw, was vindictive. He was determined to take the
matter into court; he said Tom was a scoundrel and should be
punished. It cost George an infinite deal of trouble and five
hundred pounds to settle the affair. I have never seen him in
such a rage as when he heard that Tom and Cronshaw had
gone off together to Monte Carlo the moment they cashed the
cheque. They spent a happy month there.

For twenty years Tom raced and gambled, philandered
with the prettiest girls, danced, ate in the most expensive
restaurants, and dressed beautifully. He always looked as if
he had just stepped out of a bandbox. Though he was forty-
six you would never have taken him for more than thirty-five.
He was a most amusing companion and though you knew he
was perfectly worthless you could not but enjoy his society.
He had high spirits, an unfailing gaiety and incredible

charm. I never grudged the contributions he regularly levied
on me for the necessities of his existence. I never lent him
fifty pounds without feeling that I was in his debt. Tom Ramsay knew everyone and everyone knew Tom Ramsay. You
could not approve of him, but you could not help liking him.

Poor George, only a year older than his scapegrace brother,
looked sixty. He had never taken more than a fortnight's
holiday in the year for a quarter of a century. He was in his
office every morning at nine-thirty and never left it till six. He
was honest, industrious and worthy. He had a good wife, to
whom he had never been unfaithful even in thought, and
four daughters to whom he was the best of fathers. He made
a point of saving a third of his income and his plan was to
retire at fifty-five to a little house in the country where he
proposed to cultivate his garden and play golf. His life was
blameless. He was glad that he was growing old because Tom
was growing old too. He rubbed his hands and said:

"It was all very well when Tom was young and good-
looking, but he's only a year younger than I am. In four years
he'll be fifty. He won't find life too easy then. I shall have
thirty thousand pounds by the time I'm fifty. For twenty-five
years I've said that Tom would end in the gutter. And we
shall see how he likes that. We shall see if it really pays
best to work or be idle."

Poor George! I sympathised with him. I wondered now as
I sat down beside him what infamous thing Tom had done.
George was evidently very much upset.

"Do you know what's happened now?" he asked me.

I was prepared for the worst. I wondered if Tom had got
into the hands of the police at last. George could hardly bring
himself to speak.

"You're not going to deny that all my life I've been hard
working, decent, respectable and straightforward. After a life
of industry and thrift I can look forward to retiring on a
small income in gilt-edged securities. I've always done my
duty in that state of life in which it has pleased Providence
to place me."

"True."

"And you can't deny that Tom has been an idle, worthless dissolute and dishonourable rogue. If there were any
justice he'd be in the workhouse."

"True."

George grew red in the face.

"A few weeks ago he became engaged to a woman old

enough to be his mother. And now she's died and left him everything she had. Half a million pounds, a yacht, a house in London and a house in the country."

George Ramsay beat his clenched fist on the table.

"It's not fair, I tell you, it's not fair. Damn it, it's not fair."

I could not help it. I burst into a shout of laughter as I looked at George's wrathful face. I rolled in my chair, I very nearly fell on the floor. George never forgave me. But Tom often asks me to excellent dinners in his charming house in Mayfair, and if he occasionally borrows a trifle from me, that is merely from force of habit. It is never more than a sovereign.

The Guardian Angel

BY ANDRÉ MAUROIS

❧ ❧ ❧

When Jeanne Bertaut died, at thirty, we all thought that Victor Bertaut's career was ended. A determined worker and one of the finest orators of his generations, Victor by all signs seemed destined for political success. But those of us who, like myself, had been through school and in the service with him knew his weaknesses too well to think that he had within him the makings of a statesman. We certainly knew him capable of getting himself elected deputy and of dazzling the Chamber with his verbal fireworks. But we couldn't possibly visualize him heading a ministry, working harmoniously with his colleagues, or winning the respect of the nation. His defeats were no less spectacular than his triumphs. He had too great a fondness for women and had a bland confidence in his powers of seduction. In debate, always convinced of being right, he was completely incapable of considering the merits of his opponents' arguments. In addition, he was subject to such outbursts of rage that he frequently alienated the very men whom he needed.

For these reasons I felt that his success, despite his brilliance, would be limited. That is until the day when, to my great surprise, he married Jeanne. I never learned how he got to know her. What was surprising was not that he had met her, but that he appreciated her. She was as different from him as possible—calm as he was furious; moderate as he was fanatical; indulgent as he was sharp; reticent as he was garrulous. And she seemed to have set herself—and succeeded at—the double task of conquering him and changing him. Much less beautiful than his other women, she had an undeniable fresh charm, blooming health, a frank regard, and a gay smile.

I must admit that I could never have anticipated Bertaut's ability to discover, much less to appreciate such hidden virtues. But I was wrong. From the time she married her great man, Jeanne and he were never apart. She worked with him, went to the Chamber daily, accompanied him on the rounds of his constituency, and, finally, with great tact, advised him in such a manner that he could not take offense.

Bertaut's position in his party was transformed by the marriage. No longer did the political bigwigs say: "Bertaut? Yes—very brilliant—a good talker—but a crackpot!" Now they nodded in approval: "Bertaut? A bit young perhaps, but very promising." Sometimes he'd burst out again—but a word from Jeanne, a handshake—and all would be smoothed over. As for the "great lover"—he was faithful to one woman—his own.

This success and good fortune was cut short by Jeanne's death. I remember returning from the cemetery with Bertrand Schmitt, the novelist, and one of the couple's best friends.

"She made him over from head to toe," he said. "She saved him from himself. Without her he'll go to Hell with himself again. Well, we'll have to wait and see."

For some months, outside of writing to assure Bertaut that I would assist him if and when he desired, I did not disturb his grief. He reappeared at the Palais-Bourbon in October when the Chamber reconvened. His colleagues greeted him with sympathy, but they soon found him as hard to get along with as before. Even more difficult, for an icy bitterness was added to his former rages. I, however, had nothing to complain about. We dined together a couple of times a month; he treated me with a sulky affection which was not unpleasant. But he never mentioned his wife, and developed, in this regard, a cynicism which I interpreted as defense.

When, in December, the Ministry resigned, the newspapers announced that Briand, charged with forming a new cabinet, had offered Victor, Deputy from Drôme, the office of Postmaster General. Shortly after his name appeared in the official list, I went to congratulate Victor. I found him in one of his bad moods.

"Keep your congratulations," he snapped. "I've taken part in only two Council meetings—and I'll probably resign. I've had furious battles with Finance and with Public Works. Anyway, this Ministry is a shambles. Everyone's in charge except me—the Minister."

For a few days after that I expected, daily, to read of Bertaut's resignation. This did not occur. The following week I encountered Bertrand Schmitt, and, of course, we spoke of Victor:

"Have you heard about his amazing experience?" asked Schmitt. "Concerning the letter?"

"What letter?" said I.

"Ah, what a subject for a novel," sighed Schmitt. "I don't know if you know that Bertaut, a fledgling in office, started acting like a bull in a china shop."

"Yes, yes," I said.

"And you know that Briand is patient—but even his patience has its limits. And when Bertaut insulted poor C— before the entire Chamber, the President was about to demand his resignation. Then there was a real coup de theatre. To the surprise of all his colleagues, our intransigent Victor voluntarily apologized to Cheron in such an outspoken, sincere, repentant manner that Cheron himself went to Briand to plead for him. And, of course, everything has been patched up."

"How," I asked, "do you explain this reversal of character?"

"Victor himself explained it to me," Schmitt said. "The day after the run in with Cheron, as he was leaving his house, his secretary gave him a letter marked PERSONAL which had just arrived. With surprise, emotion, and even terror he thought he recognized Jeanne's handwriting. He ripped open the envelope—the letter was, beyond a doubt, from his wife. He read me some passages from it; naturally, I didn't memorize them, but as a novelist it's easy for me to reconstruct such things. In effect, Jeanne had written:

"Dearest—at first you'll be upset at receiving a letter from me. Be reassured—this is not a letter from the tomb, nor from Hades. Before entering the clinic, feeling very weak and not knowing whether or not the operation would succeed, I thought, naturally, of you. I tried to imagine what would become of you if I did not survive. I know you, my dear, better than you know yourself, and I am a little afraid for you. I am certainly not your equal, dear, but I have acted as a brake for you. A brake is essential to a racer.

"There is nothing, I said to myself, to keep me from being with you in spirit, so I wrote this letter for you. I am confiding it to the care of a friend with instructions to deliver it to you only if certain things which I feel may occur really do happen. In that case, if I have not erred, you will find written here the things I would have said were I present. The proof of the correctness of my prophecies rests in the fact that this letter is now in your hands. Stretch out near me, my sweet; hold my hand; rest your head upon my shoulder and listen as you always used to. . . ."

"Are you making this up, Bertrand?"

"Even if all the words are not hers, the thoughts are those of Jeanne Bertaut. She had foreseen both honors and disputes. And she advised generosity, moderation, and frankness."

"And that's why he went to see Cheron?"

"That's why he apologized."

When I saw Bertaut the following week, he confirmed Schmitt's story. His guardian angel, caressing him with her wing, affected him strongly, and I thought I saw his hard shell of cynicism crack and vanish. I was not wrong. Several of Victor's colleagues commented upon the happy effects of this message.

For several months all went well for Bertaut. He straightened things out in the Post Office Department. All France sang his praises. His star was in the ascendant. When the Briand cabinet fell, Bertaut left for a vacation in Morocco. There he fell under the spell of Dora Bergmann, explorer and poet, who had wandered disguised as a Arab scout, through North Africa, and who had aroused considerable talk. Now none of us had ever expected or wanted Victor, a young man, to remain wedded to a memory. His choice,

however, did perturb us. In her strange fashion, Dora Bergmann was beautiful—and talented. But her past and her
reputation were not such as inspire confidence. She had had
several affairs, always with officers or high officials of the
Colonial Service; it was even suspected that she was a
foreign agent. Be that as it may, there was nothing more
certain to ruin a man's prestige and opportunities for ad-
vancement than any intimacy with this adventuress.

When Bertaut returned to Paris, with Dora Bergmann in
tow, some of us tried to advise him. The rule, alas, holds
true without exception—who tries to protect a friend from a
woman he loves, loses friend without touching the woman.
Victor, furious, cast Bertrand Schmitt, and me, among others,
out of his life. Talk of his affair spread through parliamentary
circles, and harmed him grievously.

"There's only one hope," I said to Bertrand one evening.
"And that's that Jeanne anticipated something like this and
that Bertaut will receive a warning from her. I feel that
only she has sufficient authority over him to make him open
his eyes."

"I am certain that such a letter will arrive," said Bertrand.
"After all Jeanne could have assumed that such a woman as
Dora would swoop down upon Victor. She could have left a
letter to handle just such an emergency."

Despite my scoffing at the novelist, the facts proved Schmitt
correct. We were delighted, one fine day, to see Victor
leave hurriedly for his district. He told no one; left no explanation. He buried himself in his small country house near
Montelimar. Dora Bergmann followed him; he refused to
see her. She persisted, raved, pleaded, withdrew. The papers
announced that she was going to explore the Rio de Oro.
Victor was saved. When he returned to Paris, he was
delighted to see me.

And he told me about the second letter from beyond the
grave. He had found it one morning in his mail. Jeanne
advised him that if some imprudent love affair really threatened him, he should flee the very moment he received the
letter. "I know you, my love," she wrote. "If you remain—if
you see the woman again, you will fall victim to your sense
of honor, your desires, and your pride. At a distance your own
intelligence will prevail. You will suddenly perceive clearly
what, at close range, you missed seeing. So don't hesitate;
don't stop to consider. Fold up this letter instantly, put it

in your pocket, pack your bag and leave for Drôme immediately!"— And he had obeyed her.

"That's the extent of the trust I placed in my wife's wisdom," he said.

But I wondered if he would be shielded throughout his life by this dead woman.

All his life? No. But two years later, when he was hesitant about remarrying, Bertaut received a third letter which approved the idea and shaped his decision. Had Jeanne left any others? Or had the first wife, with that curious foreknowledge of her husband's destiny, abdicated before the accession of the second? We will never know.

Bertrand Schmitt says that once, in 1936, when Bertaut, minister, found himself confronted by a delicate matter of conscience, he hopefully awaited the advice of his guardian angel. This time, however, the message did not come. Bertaut made the decision, alone, and was wrong. That was the end of his political career.

But in his country retreat, ruling his small family domain, with his second wife who, annually, presents him with a child, Bertaut does not seem unhappy. And it may be that it is just this sort of good fortune his posthumous counsellor wished for him.

The Fiddler

BY HERMAN MELVILLE

   📖 📖 📖

So my poem is damned, and immortal fame is not for me! I am nobody forever and ever. Intolerable fate!

Snatching my hat, I dashed down the criticism, and rushed out into Broadway, where enthusiastic throngs were crowding to a circus in a side-street near by, very recently started, and famous for a capital clown.

Presently my old friend Standard rather boisterously accosted me.

"Well met, Helmstone, my boy! Ah! what's the matter?

Haven't been committing murder? Ain't flying justice? You look wild!"

"You have seen it, then?" said I, of course referring to the criticism.

"Oh yes; I was there at the morning performance. Great clown, I assure you. But here comes Hautboy. Hautboy—Helmstone."

Without having time or inclination to resent so mortifying a mistake, I was instantly soothed as I gazed on the face of the new acquaintance so unceremoniously introduced. His person was short and full, with a juvenile, animated cast to it. His complexion rurally ruddy; his eye sincere, cheery, and gray. His hair alone betrayed that he was not an overgrown boy. From his hair I set him down as forty or more.

"Come, Standard," he gleefully cried to my friend, "are you not going to the circus? The clown is inimitable, they say. Come; Mr. Helmstone, too—come both; and circus over, we'll take a nice stew and punch at Taylor's."

The sterling content, good humor, and extraordinary ruddy, sincere expression of this most singular new acquaintance acted upon me like magic. It seemed mere loyalty to human nature to accept an invitation from so unmistakably kind and honest a heart.

During the circus performance I kept my eye more on Hautboy than on the celebrated clown. Hautboy was the sight for me. Such genuine enjoyment as his struck me to the soul with a sense of the reality of the thing called happiness. The jokes of the clown he seemed to roll under his tongue as ripe magnum bonums. Now the foot, now the hand, was employed to attest his grateful applause. At any hit more than ordinary, he turned upon Standard and me to see if his rare pleasure was shared. In a man of forty I saw a boy of twelve; and this too without the slightest abatement of my respect. Because all was so honest and natural, every expression and attitude so graceful with genuine good-nature, that the marvelous juvenility of Hautboy assumed a sort of divine and immortal air, like that of some forever youthful god of Greece.

But much as I gazed upon Hautboy, and much as I admired his air, yet that desperate mood in which I had first rushed from the house had not so entirely departed as not to molest me with momentary returns. But from these relapses I would rouse myself, and swiftly glance round the broad amphitheatre of eagerly interested and all-applauding human faces. Hark! claps, thumps, deafening huzzas; the vast assembly seemed frantic with acclamation; and what, mused I, has caused all this? Why, the clown only comically grinned with one of his extra grins.

Then I repeated in my mind that sublime passage in my poem, in which Cleothemes the Argive vindicates the justice of the war. Aye, aye, thought I to myself, did I now leap into the ring there, and repeat that identical passage, nay, enact the whole tragic poem before them, would they applaud the poet as they applaud the clown? No! They would hoot me, and call me doting or mad. Then what does this prove? Your infatuation or their insensibility? Perhaps both; but indubitably the first. But why wail? Do you seek admiration from the admirers of a buffoon? Call to mind the saying of the Athenian, who, when the people vociferously applauded in the forum, asked his friend in a whisper, what foolish thing had he said?

Again my eye swept the circus, and fell on the ruddy radiance of the countenance of Hautboy. But its clear honest cheeriness disdained my disdain. My intolerant pride was rebuked. And yet Hautboy dreamed not what magic reproof to a soul like mine sat on his laughing brow. At the very instant I felt the dart of the censure, his eye twinkled, his hand waved, his voice was lifted in jubilant delight at another joke of the inexhaustible clown.

Circus over, we went to Taylor's. Among crowds of others, we sat down to our stews and punches at one of the small marble tables. Hautboy sat opposite to me. Though greatly subdued from its former hilarity, his face still shone with gladness. But added to this was a quality not so prominent before: a certain serene expression of leisurely, deep good sense. Good sense and good humor in him joined hands. As the conversation proceeded between the brisk Standard and him—for I said little or nothing—I was more and more struck with the excellent judgment he evinced. In most of his remarks upon a variety of topics Hautboy seemed intuitively to hit the exact line between enthusiasm and apathy. It was plain that while Hautboy saw the world pretty much as it was, yet he did not theoretically espouse its bright side nor its dark side. Rejecting all solutions, he but acknowledged facts. What was sad in the world he did not superficially gainsay; what was glad in it he did not cynically slur; and all which was to him personally enjoyable, he gratefully took to his heart. It was plain, then—so it seemed at that moment, at least—that his extraordinary cheerfulness did not arise either from deficiency of feeling or thought.

Suddenly remembering an engagement, he took up his hat, bowed pleasantly, and left us.

"Well, Helmstone," said Standard, inaudibly drumming on the slab, "what do you think of your new acquaintance?"

The two last words tingled with a peculiar and novel significance.

"New acquaintance indeed," echoed I. "Standard, I owe you a thousand thanks for introducing me to one of the most singular men I have ever seen. It needed the optical sight of such a man to believe in the possibility of his existence."

"You rather like him, then," said Standard, with ironical dryness.

"I hugely love and admire him, Standard. I wish I were Hautboy."

"Ah? That's a pity, now. There's only one Hautboy in the world."

This last remark set me to pondering again, and somehow it revived my dark mood.

"His wonderful cheerfulness, I suppose," said I, sneering with spleen, "originates not less in a felicitous fortune than in a felicitous temper. His great good sense is apparent; but great good sense may exist without sublime endowments. Nay, I take it, in certain cases, that good sense is simply owing to the absence of those. Much more, cheerfulness. Unpossessed of genius, Hautboy is eternally blessed."

"Ah? You would not think him an extraordinary genius, then?"

"Genius? What! such a short, fat fellow a genius! Genius, like Cassius, is lank."

"Ah? But could you not fancy that Hautboy might formerly have had genius, but luckily getting rid of it, at last fatted up?"

"For a genius to get rid of his genius is as impossible as for a man in the galloping consumption to get rid of that."

"Ah? You speak very decidedly."

"Yes, Standard," cried I, increasing in spleen, "your cheery Hautboy, after all, is no pattern, no lesson for you and me. With average abilities; opinions clear, because circumscribed; passions docile, because they are feeble; a temper hilarious, because he was born to it—how can your Hautboy be made a reasonable example to a heady fellow like you, or an ambitious dreamer like me? Nothing tempts him beyond common

limit; in himself he has nothing to restrain. By constitution
he is exempted from all moral harm. Could ambition but
prick him; had he but once heard applause, or endured
contempt, a very different man would your Hautboy be.
Acquiescent and calm from the cradle to the grave, he obviously slides through the crowd."

"Ah?"

"Why do you say *Ah* to me so strangely whenever I speak?"

"Did you ever hear of Master Betty?"

"The great English prodigy, who long ago ousted the
Siddons and the Kembles from Drury Lane, and made the
whole town run mad with acclamation?"

"The same," said Standard, once more inaudibly drumming on the slab.

I looked at him perplexed. He seemed to be holding the
master-key of our theme in mysterious reserve; seemed to
be throwing out his Master Betty, too, to puzzle me only the
more.

"What under heaven can Master Betty, the great genius
and prodigy, an English boy twelve years old, have to do with
the poor commonplace plodder, Hautboy, an American of
forty?"

"Oh, nothing in the least. I don't imagine that they ever
saw each other. Besides, Master Betty must be dead and
buried long ere this."

"Then why cross the ocean, and rifle the grave to drag
his remains into this living discussion?"

"Absent-mindedness, I suppose. I humbly beg pardon.
Proceed with your observations on Hautboy. You think he
never had genius, quite too contented, and happy and fat
for that—ah? You think him no pattern for men in general?
affording no lesson of value to neglected merit, genius ignored,
or impotent presumption rebuked?—all of which three amount
to much the same thing. You admire his cheerfulness, while
scorning his commonplace soul. Poor Hautboy, how sad that
your very cheerfulness should, by a by-blow, bring you
despite!"

"I don't say I scorn him; you are unjust. I simply declare
that he is no pattern for me."

A sudden noise at my side attracted my ear. Turning, I
saw Hautboy again, who very blithely reseated himself on
the chair he had left.

"I was behind time with my engagement," said Hautboy,
"so thought I would run back and rejoin you. But come,

you have sat long enough here. Let us go to my rooms. It is only a five minutes' walk."

"If you will promise to fiddle for us, we will," said Standard.

Fiddle! thought I—he's a jiggumbob *fiddler*, then? No wonder genius declines to measure its pace to a fiddler's bow. My spleen was very strong on me now.

"I will gladly fiddle you your fill," replied Hautboy to Standard. "Come on."

In a few minutes we found ourselves in the fifth story of a sort of storehouse, in a lateral street to Broadway. It was curiously furnished with all sorts of odd furniture which seemed to have been obtained, piece by piece, at auctions of old-fashioned household stuff. But all was charmingly clean and cozy.

Pressed by Standard, Hautboy forthwith got out his dented old fiddle and, sitting down on a tall rickety stool, played away right merrily at "Yankee Doodle" and other off-handed, dashing, and disdainfully care-free airs. But common as were the tunes, I was transfixed by something miraculously superior in the style. Sitting there on the old stool, his rusty hat sideways cocked on his head, one foot dangling adrift, he plied the bow of an enchanter. All my moody discontent, every vestige of peevishness, fled. My whole splenetic soul capitulated to the magical fiddle.

"Something of an Orpheus, ah?" said Standard, archly nudging me beneath the left rib.

"And I, the charmed Bruin," murmured I.

The fiddle ceased. Once more, with redoubled curiosity, I gazed upon the easy, indifferent Hautboy. But he entirely baffled inquisition.

When, leaving him, Standard and I were in the street once more, I earnestly conjured him to tell me who, in sober truth, this marvelous Hautboy was.

"Why, haven't you seen him? And didn't you yourself lay his whole anatomy open on the marble slab at Taylor's? What more can you possibly learn? Doubtless, your own masterly insight has already put you in possession of all."

"You mock me, Standard. There is some mystery here. Tell me, I entreat you, who is Hautboy?"

"An extraordinary genius, Helmstone," said Standard, with sudden ardor, "who in boyhood drained the whole flagon of glory; whose going from city to city was a going from triumph to triumph. One who has been an object of wonder

to the wisest, been caressed by the loveliest, received the
open homage of thousands on thousands of the rabble. But
to-day he walks Broadway and no man knows him. With
you and me, the elbow of the hurrying clerk, and the pole
of the remorseless omnibus, shove him. He who has a hundred times been crowned with laurels, now wears, as you see,
a bunged beaver. Once fortune poured showers of gold into
his lap, as showers of laurel leaves upon his brow. To-day,
from house to house he hies, teaching fiddling for a living.
Crammed once with fame, he is now hilarious without
it. *With* genius and *without* fame, he is happier than a king.
More a prodigy now than ever."

"His true name?"

"Let me whisper it in your ear."

"What! Oh, Standard, myself, as a child, have shouted
myself hoarse applauding that very name in the theatre."

"I have heard your poem was not very handsomely
received," said Standard, now suddenly shifting the subject.

"Not a word of that, for Heaven's sake!" cried I. "If Cicero,
traveling in the East, found sympathetic solace for his grief
in beholding the arid overthrow of a once gorgeous city,
shall not my petty affair be as nothing, when I behold in
Hautboy the vine and the rose climbing the shattered shafts
of his tumbled temple of Fame?"

Next day I tore all my manuscripts, bought me a fiddle,
and went to take regular lessons of Hautboy.

The Pearl of Toledo

BY PROSPER MÉRIMÉE

Who can say whether the sun is most beautiful at dawn or
at dusk? Who can tell whether the olive tree or the almond
is the more beautiful? Who can tell whether Andalusia or
Valencia breeds the bravest knight? What man can say who
is the fairest of women? But I will tell you who is the fairest.
She is Aurora de Vargas, the Pearl of Toledo.

Swarthy Suzani calls for his lance; he calls for his buckler.

He grasps his lance in his strong right hand; his buckler hangs from his neck. He goes down to his stable, and, in proper order, he surveys his forty fiery chargers. Then he says:

"Berja is the swiftest and trustiest of them all. On her sure back will I carry away the Pearl of Toledo. As mine I will bear her away, or by Allah, Cordova shall see me no more."

So he sets forth. He rides on till at length he reaches Toledo. Hard by Zucatin he meets an old man.

"Old snowy beard, carry this letter to Don Guttiera de Saldana. If he is a man he will come and meet me in single combat . . . at the fountain of Almami. The Pearl of Toledo must belong to one of us two."

The old man takes the letter and carries it to the Count of Saldana, as he sits playing chess with the Pearl of Toledo. The count reads the letter. Then, with his closed fist he smites the table so mightily that all the chessmen fall to the ground. Then he rises and calls for his lance and his steed. All trembling, the Pearl of Toledo rises, for she perceives that he is going forth to combat.

"My Lord Guttiera de Saldana, do not go hence I pray. Stay and continue this game with me."

"I may play chess no longer. I must play the game of lances at the fountain of Almami."

And the tears of Aurora avail not. Then the Pearl of Toledo takes her mantle, and, mounting upon her mule she goes her way to the fountain of Almami.

All about the fountain the grass is crimson, and the waters of the fountain. But it is not the blood of a Christian that stains the greensward and the waters of the fountain. The dusky Suzani lies there with his face to the sky. The lance of Don Guttiera is splintered in his breasts; all his life blood spends itself drop by drop. His faithful steed, Berja, looks down upon him weeping, for she can not heal her master's wound.

The Pearl of Toledo alights from her mule. "Take heart, good sir, for you will live yet to wed some fair Moorish maiden; my hand has cunning to heal the wound made by my knight."

"O Pearl so white, O Pearl so fair, draw forth from my breast the splinter of the lance which rends it. The cold of the steel chills me and freezes my heart."

Trustingly she approaches him, but he, with a last effort, gathers together his failing strength, and with his saber's sharp blade, gashes the face so fair, so tender.

The Sniper

BY LIAM O'FLAHERTY

💭 💭 💭

The long June twilight faded into night. Dublin lay enveloped in darkness but for the dim light of the moon that shone through fleecy clouds, casting a pale light as of approaching dawn over the streets and the dark waters of the Liffey. Around the beleaguered Four Courts the heavy guns roared. Here and there through the city, machine-guns and rifles broke the silence of the night, spasmodically, like dogs barking on lone farms. Republicans and Free Staters were waging civil war.

On a roof-top near O'Connell Bridge, a Republican sniper lay watching. Beside him lay his rfle and over his shoulders were slung a pair of field glasses. His face was the face of a student, thin and ascetic, but his eyes had the cold gleam of the fanatic. They were deep and thoughtful, the eyes of a man who is used to look at death.

He was eating a sandwich hungrily. He had eaten nothing since morning. He had been too excited to eat. He finished the sandwich, and, taking a flask of whiskey from his pocket, he took a short draught. Then he returned the flask to his pocket. He paused for a moment, considering whether he should risk a smoke. It was dangerous. The flash might be seen in the darkness and there were enemies watching. He decided to take the risk.

Placing a cigarette between his lips, he struck a match. There was a flash and a bullet whizzed over his head. He dropped immediately. He had seen the flash. It came from the opposite side of the street.

He rolled over the roof to a chimney stack in the rear, and slowly drew himself up behind it, until his eyes were level with the top of the parapet. There was nothing to be seen—just the dim outline of the opposite housetop against the blue sky. His enemy was under cover.

Just then an armored car came across the bridge and advanced slowly up the street. It stopped on the opposite of the street, fifty yards ahead. The sniper could hear the dull panting of the motor. His heart beat faster. It was an enemy car. He wanted to fire, but he knew it was useless. His bullets would never pierce the steel that covered the gray monster.

Then round the corner of a side street came an old woman, her head covered by a tattered shawl. She began to talk to the man in the turret of the car. She was pointing to the roof where the sniper lay. An informer.

The turret opened. A man's head and shoulders appeared, looking toward the sniper. The sniper raised his rifle and fired. The head fell heavily on the turret wall. The woman darted toward the side street. The sniper fired again. The woman whirled round and fell with a shriek into the gutter.

Suddenly from the opposite roof a shot rang out and the sniper dropped his rifle with a curse. The rifle clattered to the roof. The sniper thought the noise would wake the dead. He stopped to pick the rifle up. He couldn't lift it. His forearm was dead.

"Christ," he muttered, "I'm hit."

Dropping flat onto the roof, he crawled back to the parapet. With his left hand he felt the injured right forearm. There was no pain—just a deadened sensation, as if the arm had been cut off.

Quickly he drew his knife from his pocket, opened it on the breast-work of the parapet, and ripped open the sleeve. There was a small hole where the bullet had entered. On the other side there was no hole. The bullet had lodged in the bone. It must have fractured it. He bent the arm below the wound. The arm bent back easily. He ground his teeth to overcome the pain.

Then taking out the field dressing, he ripped open the packet with his knife. He broke the neck of the iodine bottle and let the bitter fluid drip into the wound. A paroxysm of pain swept through him. He placed the cotton wadding over the wound and wrapped the dressing over it. He tied the ends with his teeth.

Then he lay against the parapet, and, closing his eyes, he made an effort of will to overcome the pain.

In the street beneath all was still. The armored car had retired speedily over the bridge, with the machine-gunner's head hanging lifelessly over the turret. The woman's corpse lay still in the gutter.

The sniper lay still for a long time nursing his wounded arm and planning escape. Morning must not find him wounded on the roof. The enemy on the opposite roof covered his escape. He must kill that enemy and he could not use his rifle. He had only a revolver to do it. Then he thought of a plan.

Taking off his cap, he placed it over the muzzle of his rifle. Then he pushed the rifle slowly over the parapet, until the cap was visible from the opposite side of the street. Almost immediately there was a report, and a bullet pierced the center of the cap. The sniper slanted the rifle forward. The cap slipped down into the street. Then catching the rifle in the middle, the sniper dropped his left hand over the roof and let it hang, lifelessly. After a few moments he let the rifle drop to the street. Then he sank to the roof, dragging his hand with him.

Crawling quickly to the left, he peered up at the corner of the roof. His ruse had succeeded. The other sniper, seeing the cap and rifle fall, thought he had killed his man. He was now standing before a row of chimney pots, looking across, with his head clearly silhouetted against the western sky.

The Republican sniper smiled and lifted his revolver above the edge of the parapet. The distance was about fifty yards— a hard shot in the dim light, and his right arm was paining him like a thousand devils. He took a steady aim. His hand trembled with eagerness. Pressing his lips together, he took a deep breath through his nostrils and fired. He was almost deafened with the report and his arm shook with the recoil.

Then when the smoke cleared he peered across and uttered a cry of joy. His enemy had been hit. He was reeling over the parapet in his death agony. He struggled to keep his feet, but he was slowly falling forward, as if in a dream. The rifle fell from his grasp, hit the parapet, fell over, bounded off the pole of a barber's shop beneath and then clattered on the pavement.

Then the dying man on the roof crumpled up and fell forward. The body turned over and over in space and hit the ground with a dull thud. Then it lay still.

The sniper looked at his enemy falling and he shuddered. The lust of battle died in him. He became bitten by remorse. The sweat stood out in beads on his forehead. Weakened by his wound and the long summer day of fasting and watching on the roof, he revolted from the sight of the shattered mass of his dead enemy. His teeth chattered, he began to gibber to himself, cursing the war, cursing himself, cursing everybody.

He looked at the smoking revolver in his hand, and with an oath he hurled it to the roof at his feet. The revolver went off with the concussion and the bullet whizzed past the sniper's head. He was frightened back to his senses by the shock. His nerves steadied. The cloud of fear scattered from his mind and he laughed.

Taking the whiskey flask from his pocket, he emptied it at a draught. He felt reckless under the influence of the spirit. He decided to leave the roof now and look for his company commander, to report. Everywhere around was quiet. There was not much danger in going through the streets. He picked up his revolver and put it in his pocket. Then he crawled down through the sky-light to the house underneath.

When the sniper reached the laneway on the street level, he felt a sudden curiosity as to the identity of the enemy sniper whom he had killed. He decided that he was a good shot, whoever he was. He wondered did he know him. Perhaps he had been in his own company before the split in the army. He decided to risk going over to have a look at him. He peered round the corner into O'Connell Street. In the upper part of the street there was heavy firing, but around here all was quiet.

The sniper darted across the street. A machine-gun tore up the ground around him with a hail of bullets, but he escaped. He threw himself face downward beside the corpse. The machine-gun stopped.

Then the sniper turned over the dead body and looked into his brother's face.

The Crime on Calle de la Persequida

BY PALACIO VALDES

▭ ▭ ▭

"Here, as you see me, sits before you a murderer."

"How's that, Don Elias!" I exclaimed, laughing, as I filled his glass with beer.

Don Elias is the kindest individual, the most reserved and disciplined in the Telegraph Corps. He is incapable of going on strike even though his boss should order him to dust off his trousers.

"Yes, sir. There are circumstances in life—there comes a moment when the most peace-loving man . . ."

"Come, come; tell me about this," I said, piqued with curiosity.

It was in the winter of '78. Because of reorganization I was out of a job and had gone to live in O. with a married daughter of mine. My life there was too easy—eat, stroll about, sleep. Sometimes I helped my son-in-law, who is employed by the Municipal Government, copying the secretary's minutes. We dined invariably at eight. After putting my granddaughter to bed—she was then three years old and is today a good-looking blonde, plump, one of those you like (I modestly lowered my eyes and took a gulp of beer)—and after that I used to spend the evening with Doña Nieves, a widow who lives alone on Persequida Street and to whom my son-in-law owes his job. She lives on her property in a huge old one-story house which has a dark entrance gate with a stone stairway. Don Gerardo Piquero also used to drop around; he had been Customs Administrator in Puerto Rico and was retired. The poor fellow died a couple of years ago. He'd get there around nine; I'd never get there until after nine-thirty. However, he'd pull out at ten-thirty sharp, while I'd stay on until eleven or later.

One night I left, as usual, at about this time. Doña Nieves is very economical and puts on a show of being poor

201

when actually she owns enough property to do herself proud and live like a grand lady. She'd never set out any lamp to light the stairs or portal. When Don Gerardo or I departed, the maid would light the way with a lamp from the kitchen. As soon as we'd close the gate, she would put out the light and leave us in almost utter darkness, since there was scarcely any light penetrating from the street.

As I took the first step I felt what is vulgarly called a slap; that is to say with one heavy blow my hat was rammed down to my nose. I was paralyzed with fear and fell against the wall. I thought I heard tittering, and somewhat recovered from my fright I pulled off my hat.

"Who goes there?" I shouted in a loud and threatening voice.

No one replied. Rapidly I imagined various possibilities. Was I about to be robbed? Did some little hoodlums wish to entertain themselves at my expense? Could it be a friend playing a practical joke? I resolved to depart immediately, since the gate was open. When I reached the niddle of the portal, I received a heavy blow on the thighs, delivered by the palm of a hand, and at the same time a group of five or six men blocked the gateway.

"Help!" I screamed in a strangled voice, retreating once again toward the wall. The men began to jump up and down in front of me with wild gesticulations. My terror knew no bounds.

"Where are you going at this hour, thief?" asked one.

"He must be going to steal a corpse. He's the doctor," said another.

It then occurred to me that they were drunk, and pulling myself together, I loudly exclaimed,

"Out, dogs! Let me by, or I'll kill one of you." At the same time I grasped an iron club which had been given me by a foreman in the Arms Factory and which I always carried about with me at night.

The men, paying no attention, continued dancing before me, using the same wild gestures. I could observe by the dim light from the street, that they kept one man in the foreground as the strongest and most determined behind whom the rest took shelter.

"Out of the way!" I shouted again, swinging my club like a windmill.

"Give up, dog!" they replied without ceasing their fantastic dance.

I was no longer in any doubt: they were drunk. Because of this conviction and because no weapons glittered in their hands, I became relatively calm. I lowered the club, and, endeavoring to give my words a note of authority, I said,

"Come on, now. Stop the clowning! Make way."

"Give up, dog! Are you going to suck blood from the dead? Are you going to cut off someone's leg? Tear off his ear! Tear out an eye! Pull his nose!"

These were the replies that came in answer to my request. At the same time they advanced upon me. One of them, not the one in the foreground, but another, reached over the shoulder of the first and, grabbing my nose, gave it such an awful yank that I cried out in pain. I leaped sideways, because my back was against the wall, and I managed to separate myself from them somewhat; I raised the club and, blind with rage, brought it down on the first fellow. He fell heavily to the ground without uttering a cry. The rest fled.

I was alone and waited anxiously for the wounded man to groan or to move. Nothing—not even a whimper; not even the slightest movement. Then it occurred to me that I might have killed him. The club was really heavy, and all my life my hobby has been keeping fit. I hurried, with trembling hands, to get out my match box and light a match. . . .

I can't describe to you what went through my mind at that moment. Stretched on the ground, face up, lay a dead man. Yes, dead! I clearly read death on the pale features. The match fell from my hands and once again I was in darkness. I saw him only for a moment, but the spectre was so vivid that no detail escaped me. He was a heavy fellow with a black and tangled beard, a nose large and beaked; he wore a blue shirt, colored trousers, and sandals. On his head was a black beret. He appeared to be a workman from the arms plant—a gunsmith, as they call him around there.

I can tell you for certain that the things I thought of in one instant there in the darkness, I'd never have time to think of now in an entire day. I clearly foresaw what would happen: the death of that man divulged immediately throughout the city; the police laying hands on me; the consternation of my son-in-law; the dismay of my daughter; the wails of my granddaughter. Then imprisonment, the weary process dragging through months and perhaps years; the difficulty of proving that the deed was done in self-defense; the accusation of the district attorney naming me an assassin as always happens in such cases; my lawyer's defense citing my noble antecedents; then the verdict of the Court absolving me perhaps, perhaps condemning me to prison.

With one leap I landed in the street and ran to the corner, but then I realized I'd come without my hat, and I turned back. Once again I went through the portal with the greatest fear and revulsion. I lit another match and threw a sidewise glance at my victim in the hope of seeing him breathe. Nothing—there he lay in the same spot, rigid and yellowed, without a tinge of color in his face, which made me think that he had died of a cerebral concussion. I found my hat, ran my hand inside it to get it back in shape, and putting it on, got out of there.

But this time I took care not to run. The instinct of self-preservation had taken hold of me completely, and helped me to think up all ways of evading justice. I hugged the wall along the shadows, and as noiselessly as possible soon rounded the corner of Persequida Street to enter San Joaquin and return home. I endeavored to give my gait all the assurance and composure possible. But behold, there on Altavilla Street, just as I had begun to calm down, there unexpectedly appeared a police officer from the City Hall.

"Don Elias, could you kindly tell me. . .?"

I heard no more. I leaped so far that I placed several yards between the constable and myself. Then, without glancing back I took off in a desperate mad race through the streets. I reached the outskirts of the city and halted, panting and perspiring. Then I regained my senses. What madness had I committed! That constable knew me. Most probably he had approached me to ask me something concerning my son-in-law. My outlandish behavior had filled him with amazement. He may have thought I'd gone crazy; but by morning when news of the crime was known, he would surely start conjecturing and make his suspicions known to the judge. Suddenly I felt an icy chill.

Appalled, I walked toward and and soon reached home. As I got in, I suddenly had a happy thought. I went straight to my room, put away the iron club in the closet and took up another cudgel which I had and went out again. My daughter appeared in the doorway, much surprised. I invented the pretext of a date with a friend at the Casino, and did in fact make my way hurriedly to this spot. There were still quite a few men gathered there in the room next to the billiard room who were part of the late conversation group.

I sat down among them, put on a good-natured demeanor and was exceedingly jovial and gay, managing by all manner of devices to have them notice the light stick I carried in my hand. I would bend it into an arc; I'd switch it against my trousers. I'd brandish it like a foil, touch the back of one of the talkers to ask him anything at all. I'd let it fall to the floor. In short, nothing was left undone to call attention to the stick.

When at last the gathering broke up and I separated from my companions on the street, I was somewhat calmed. But once at home and in my room, I was seized with a mortal sorrow. I realized that these wiles would only serve to aggravate my situation should suspicion fall on me. Mechanically I undressed and remained sitting on the edge of my bed for a long while absorbed in dark thoughts. At length the cold forced me into bed.

I couldn't close my eyes. I turned and twisted a thousand times between the sheets, prey to a dreadful anxiety and fear which the silence and solitude rendered more acute. At each instant I expected to hear a pounding on the door and the constabulary's step upon the stair. Nevertheless, at dawn, sleep overcame me; that is to say, it was more like a deep lethargy from which my daughter's voice roused me.

"Father, it's already ten o'clock! Your eyes look terrible! Have you had a bad night?"

"On the contrary, I slept beautifully," I hastened to reply.

I didn't even trust my daughter. Then, affecting nonchalance, "Has the *Echo of Commerce* arrived yet?"

"What a question! I should say so!"

"Bring it to me."

I waited until my daughter had left and unfolded the newspaper with a trembling hand. I skimmed over it with anxious eyes, but could find nothing. Suddenly I read in big headlines, *The Crime on Persequida Street* and froze with fear. Then I looked again more closely. It had been a hallucination. It was an article entitled, "The Criterion of the Padres of the Province." At length, making a supreme effort to control myself, I managed to read the gossip column where I found a section that read:

Mysterious Occurrence

The male nurses at the County Hospital have the dubious practice of using the harmless inmates

of this insane asylum to run various errands, among
them that of transfering corpses to the Autopsy
Room. Last night, four of these demented men,
engaged in such an errand, found the garden gate
which opens onto San Idelfonso Park ajar, and they
escaped through it carrying the corpse with them.
As soon as the Hospital Administrator became
aware of the situation, he sent various emissaries
in search of them, but to no avail. At one o'clock
in the morning these four demented men returned
to the hospital, but without the corpse. The latter
was found by a watchman on Persequida Street
inside the gateway to Dona Nieves Menendez's
home.

We implore the Dean of the County Hospital
to take the necessary measures so that these scandalous goings-on are not repeated.

I let the paper fall from my hands and was stricken with
convulsive laughter which worked itself into hysterics.

"So that, actually, you had really killed a man who was
already dead?"

"Precisely."

How the Devil Lost His Poncho

BY RICARDO PALMA

Once, when Our Lord was traveling about the world
upon His gentle little donkey, restoring sight to the blind
and recovering the use of their limbs to the lame, He came
into a region where there was nothing at all but sand. Here
and there was a rustling, slender palm under whose shade
Gentle Jesus would stop with His disciples, who would fill
their sacks with dates.

As eternal as the Lord Himself seemed that desert, with
neither beginning nor end. The travelers, heavy-hearted,
prepared to spend the night with only a starry sky for

shelter, when, picked out by the last ray of the setting sun, the silhouette of a belfry showed upon the horizon.

Lord Jesus, shading His eyes to see better, said: "I see a town over there. Peter, you know all about geography. Could you tell me what city that is?"

St. Peter grinned at the compliment.

"Master, that is the city of Ica."

"Well, then. Let us move along."

The donkeys jogged along briskly, and they all soon reached town. Jesus, just before they entered, gently reminded Peter that he must not lose his temper. "You're always getting us into trouble with your temper," said Our Lord. "Please try to keep it under control."

The people of the city rolled out the welcome mat for these illustrious visitors. Even though the little party was anxious to be on its way, the townsfolk made everything so pleasant that a week had passed before you could whistle. During that week the city of Ica seemed like the alcove of Paradise. Doctors and dentists sat idly in their offices, and the druggists made up no prescriptions. Not a complaint was registered before the advocates. There was not even a cross word between husband or wife, nor any—miracle of miracles!—nor any malice expressed by mothers and sisters-in-law.

How long this idyllic existence might have gone on nobody knows, for on the eighth day Our Lord received a message calling Him to return to Jerusalem to stand between Mary Magdalene and the unfriendly Samaritan women. Rather than bother the hospitable folk of Ica with long-winded excuses and explanations, the Gentle Traveler decided to leave suddenly, during the night, with His companions.

Early the next morning, then, when the city council called to give a special morning concert, they found their guests gone.

But after He and His party had gone several miles from the city, the Lord turned and blessed the little town of Ica in the name of the Father, the Son, and the Holy Ghost.

Naturally such a succession of events could not remain out of the newspapers. The Devil, therefore, received the news by the earliest mail. He gnashed his teeth with chagrin and swore that no one could steal a march on him. Calling together the chief of his demons he had them disguise themselves as disciples. The art of make-up and disguise is certainly close to the heart of the Horned One. So, putting on high boots and ponchos, he and his party started on their journey.

The citizens of Ica, seeing the travelers in the distance, rushed out to greet them, hoping this time that The Lord and His companions would remain with them forever.

Up to this time, of course, there had been happiness and content in Ica such as existed nowhere else. The citizens paid their taxes without complaint, let the politicians run politics, and regarded helping their neighbors as the most important thing in life.

Needless to say this bliss made the Devil quiver with rage, and he determined to upset the apple cart at the first opportunity.

Just at the time the Devil arrived, a marriage was about to take place between a young man and a young girl made for each other as ewe for ram; here was a perfect match.

Satan waited his time, as he always does, and when the toasts began to go down the thirsty gullets, the liquor produced not the friendly elevation of spirits that banquets should foster, but a coarse, indecent frenzy. Insulting remarks were hurled at the bride, and several women made advances towards the handsome groom.

And things went further than this. For all the doctors and dentists and druggists and advocates began to do a rushing business. Family squabbles flourished; mothers-in-law seemed to make up for time lost; wives remembered it was their duty and prerogative to whine and cry for new dresses and expensive jewelry. To top it all, the city council decided it was time to levy new taxes. It was obvious, wasn't it, that only the Devil could be at the bottom of this?

In the meantime the poor bride, trying desperately to stop the fighting and brawling, kept muttering, "It must be the Devil gotten into them. That's what it must be."

She rushed to the Evil One in disguise and tugged at his poncho.

"Oh, Lord," she cried. "They are all going to kill one another."

"What do I care?" sneered old Cloven Hoof. "It's no concern of mine. The worse it gets, the better I like it."

The poor girl, amazed, berated him.

"What a heart Your Excellency has. It's like a stone. You must be the Devil himself." And she made the sign of the cross with her fingers.

No sooner had the Evil One seen her gesture than he tried to race from the scene. But she had a strong hold on his poncho, and he had to duck his head through the opening, leaving the cape in the girl's hand.

The Devil's party disappeared in a puff, but, since then, every once in a while, old Satan comes back to Ica, searching for his poncho. Whenever this happens the liquor starts flowing, of course, and things get really lively all over again.

The Standard of Living

BY DOROTHY PARKER

Annabel and Midge came out of the tea room with the arrogant slow gait of the leisured, for their Saturday afternoon stretched ahead of them. They had lunched, as was their wont, on sugar, starches, oils, and butter-fats. Usually they ate sandwiches of spongy new white bread greased with butter and mayonnaise; they ate thick wedges of cake lying wet beneath ice cream and whipped cream and melted chocolate gritty with nuts. As alternates, they ate patties, sweating beads of inferior oil, containing bits of bland meat bogged in pale, stiffening sauce; they ate pastries, limber under rigid icing, filled with an indeterminate yellow sweet stuff, not still solid, not yet liquid, like salve that has been left in the sun. They chose no other sort of food, nor did they consider it. And their skin was like the petals of wood anemones, and their bellies were as flat and their flanks as lean as those of young Indian braves.

Annabel and Midge had been best friends almost from the day that Midge had found a job as stenographer with the firm that employed Annabel. By now, Annabel, two years longer in the stenographic department, had worked up to the wages of eighteen dollars and fifty cents a week; Midge was still at sixteen dollars. Each girl lived at home with her family and paid half her salary to its support.

The girls sat side by side at their desks, they lunched together every noon, together they set out for home at the end of the day's work. Many of their evenings and most of their Sundays were passed in each other's company. Often they were joined by two young men, but there was no steadiness to any such quartet; the two young men would give place, unlamented, to two other young men, and lament would have been inappropriate, really, since the newcomers were scarcely distinguishable from their predecessors. Invariably the girls spent the fine idle hours of their hot-weather Saturday afternoons together. Constant use had not worn ragged the fabric of their friendship.

They looked alike, though the resemblance did not lie in their features. It was in the shape of their bodies, their movements, their style, and their adornments. Annabel and Midge did, and completely, all that young office workers are besought not to do. They painted their lips and their nails, they darkened their lashes and lightened their hair, and scent seemed to shimmer from them. They wore thin, bright dresses, tight over their breasts and high on their legs, and tilted slippers, fancifully strapped. They looked conspicuous and cheap and charming.

Now, as they walked across to Fifth Avenue with their skirts swirled by the hot wind, they received audible admiration. Young men grouped lethargically about newsstands awarded them murmurs, exclamations, even—the ultimate tribute—whistles. Annabel and Midge passed without the condescension of hurrying their pace; they held their heads higher and set their feet with exquisite precision, as if they stepped over the necks of peasants.

Always the girls went to walk on Fifth Avenue on their free afternoons, for it was the ideal ground for their favorite game. The game could be played anywhere, and indeed, was, but the great shop windows stimulated the two players to their best form.

Annabel had invented the game; or rather she had evolved it from an old one. Basically, it was no more than the ancient sport of what-would-you-do-if-you-had-a-million-dollars? But Annabel had drawn a new set of rules for it, had narrowed it, pointed it, made it stricter. Like all games, it was the more absorbing for being more difficult.

Annabel's version went like this: You must suppose that somebody dies and leaves you a million dollars, cool. But there is a condition to the bequest. It is stated in the will that you must spend every nickel of the money on yourself.

There lay the hazard of the game. If, when playing it, you

forgot and listed among your expenditures the rental of a
new apartment for your family, for example, you lost your
turn to the other player. It was astonishing how many—and
some of them among the experts, too—would forfeit all their
innings by such slips.

It was essential, of course, that it be played in passionate
seriousness. Each purchase must be carefully considered and,
if necessary, supported by argument. There was no zest to
playing it wildly. Once Annabel had introduced the game to
Sylvia, another girl who worked in the office. She explained
the rules to Sylvia and then offered her the gambit "What
would be the first thing you'd do?" Sylvia had not shown
the decency of even a second of hesitation. "Well," she said,
"the first thing I'd do, I'd go out and hire somebody to shoot
Mrs. Gary Cooper, and then . . ." So it is to be seen that she
was no fun.

But Annabel and Midge were surely born to be comrades,
for Midge played the game like a master from the moment
she learned it. It was she who added the touches that
made the whole thing cozier. According to Midge's innova-
tions, the eccentric who died and left you the money was
not anybody you loved, or, for the matter of that, anybody
you even knew. It was somebody who had seen you somewhere and had thought, "That girl ought to have lots of nice
things. I'm going to leave her a million dollars when I die."
And the death was to be neither untimely nor painful. Your
benefactor, full of years and comfortably ready to depart,
was to slip softly away during sleep and go right to heaven.
These embroideries permitted Annabel and Midge to play
their game in the luxury of peaceful consciences.

Midge played with a seriousness that was not only proper
but extreme. The single strain on the girls' friendship had
followed an announcement once made by Annabel that the
first thing she would buy with her million dollars would be
a silver-fox coat. It was as if she had struck Midge across the
mouth. When Midge recovered her breath, she cried that
she couldn't imagine how Annabel could do such a thing—
silver-fox coats were so common! Annabel defended her taste
with the retort that they were not common, either. Midge then
said that they were so. She added that everybody had a
silver-fox coat. She went on, with perhaps a slight loss of
head, to declare that she herself wouldn't be caught dead
in silver fox.

For the next few days, though the girls saw each other as

constantly, their conversation was careful and infrequent, and they did not once play their game. Then one morning, as soon as Annabel entered the office, she came to Midge and said she had changed her mind. She would not buy a silver-fox coat with any part of her million dollars. Immediately on receiving the legacy, she would select a coat of mink.

Midge smiled and her eyes shone. "I think," she said, "you're doing absolutely the right thing."

Now, as they walked along Fifth Avenue, they played the game anew. It was one of those days with which September is repeatedly cursed; hot and glaring, with slivers of dust in the wind. People drooped and shambled, but the girls carried themselves tall and walked a straight line, as befitted young heiresses on their afternoon promenade. There was no longer need for them to start the game at its formal opening. Annabel went direct to the heart of it.

"All right," she said. "So you've got this million dollars. So what would be the first thing you'd do?"

"Well, the first thing I'd do," Midge said, "I'd get a mink coat." But she said it mechanically, as if she were giving the memorized answer to an expected question.

"Yes," Annabel said. "I think you ought to. The terribly dark kind of mink." But she, too, spoke as if by rote. It was too hot; fur, no matter how dark and sleek and supple, was horrid to the thoughts.

They stepped along in silence for a while. Then Midge's eye was caught by a shop window. Cool, lovely gleamings were there set off by chaste and elegant darkness.

"No," Midge said, "I take it back. I wouldn't get a mink coat the first thing. Know what I'd do? I'd get a string of pearls. Real pearls."

Annabel's eyes turned to follow Midge's.

"Yes," she said, slowly. "I think that's a kind of a good idea. And it would make sense, too. Because you can wear pearls with anything."

Together they went over to the shop window and stood pressed against it. It contained but one object—a double row of great, even pearls clasped by a deep emerald around a little pink velvet throat.

"What do you suppose they cost?" Annabel said.

"Gee, I don't know," Midge said. "Plenty, I guess."

"Like a thousand dollars?" Annabel said.

"Oh, I guess like more," Midge said. "On account of the emerald."

"Well, like ten thousand dollars?" Annabel said.

"Gee, I wouldn't even know," Midge said.

The devil nudged Annabel in the ribs. "Dare you to go in and price them," she said.

"Like fun!" Midge said.

"Dare you," Annabel said.

"Why, a store like this wouldn't even be open this afternoon," Midge said.

"Yes, it is so, too," Annabel said. "People just came out. And there's a doorman on. Dare you."

"Well," Midge said. "But you've got to come too."

They tendered thanks, icily, to the doorman for ushering them into the shop. It was cool and quiet, a broad, gracious room with paneled walls and soft carpet. But the girls wore expressions of bitter disdain, as if they stood in a sty.

A slim, immaculate clerk came to them and bowed. His neat face showed no astonishment at their appearance.

"Good afternoon," he said. He implied that he would never forget it if they would grant him the favor of accepting his soft-spoken greeting.

"Good afternoon," Annabel and Midge said together, and in like freezing accents.

"Is there something—?" the clerk said.

"Oh, we're just looking," Annabel said. It was as if she flung the words down from a dais.

The clerk bowed.

"My friend and myself merely happened to be passing," Midge said, and stopped, seeming to listen to the phrase. "My friend here and myself," she went on, "merely happened to be wondering how much are those pearls you've got in your window."

"Ah, yes," the clerk said. "The double rope. That is two hundred and fifty thousand dollars, Madam."

"I see," Midge said.

The clerk bowed. "An exceptionally beautiful necklace," he said. "Would you care to look at it?"

"No, thank you," Annabel said.

"My friend and myself merely happened to be passing," Midge said.

They turned to go; to go, from their manner, where the tumbrel awaited them. The clerk sprang ahead and opened the door. He bowed as they swept by him.

The girls went on along the Avenue and disdain was still on their faces.

"Honestly!" Annabel said. "Can you imagine a thing like that?"

"Two hundred and fifty thousand dollars!" Midge said. "That's a quarter of a million dollars right there!"

"He's got his nerve!" Annabel said.

They walked on. Slowly the disdain went, slowly and completely as if drained from them, and with it went the regal carriage and tread. Their shoulders dropped and they dragged their feet; they bumped against each other, without notice or apology, and caromed away again. They were silent and their eyes were cloudy.

Suddenly Midge straightened her back, flung her head high, and spoke, clear and strong.

"Listen, Annabel," she said. "Look. Suppose there was this terribly rich person, see? You don't know this person, but this person has seen you somewhere and wants to do something for you. Well, it's a terribly old person, see? And so this person dies, just like going to sleep, and leaves you ten million dollars. Now, what would be the first thing you'd do?"

The Oval Portrait

BY EDGAR ALLEN POE

🔲 🔲 🔲

The chateau in which my valet had ventured to make forcible entrance, rather than permit me, in my desperately wounded condition, to pass a night in the open air, was one of those piles of commingled gloom and grandeur which have so long frowned among the Apennines, not less in fact than in the fancy of Mrs. Radcliffe. To all appearance it had been temporarily and very lately abandoned. We established ourselves in one of the smallest and least sumptuously furnished apartments. It lay in a remote turret of the building. Its decorations were rich, yet tattered and antique. Its walls were hung with tapestry and bedecked with manifold and

multiform armorial trophies, together with an unusually great
number of very spirited modern paintings in frames of rich
golden arabesque. In these paintings, which depended from
the walls not only in their main surfaces, but in very many
nooks which the bizarre architecture of the chateau rendered
necessary—in these paintings my incipient delirium, perhaps,
had caused me to take deep interest; so that I bade Pedro to
close the heavy shutters of the room, since it was already
night, to light the tongues of a tall candelabrum which
stood by the head of the bed, and to throw open far and
wide the fringed curtains of black velvet which enveloped
the bed itself. I wished all this done that I might resign
myself, if not to sleep, at least alternately to the contemplation of these pictures, and the perusal of a small volume
which had been found upon the pillow, and which purported
to criticize and explain them.

Long, long I read—and devoutly, devotedly I gazed. Rapidly and gloriously the hours flew by and the deep midnight
came. The position of the candelabrum displeased me, and
outreaching my hand with difficulty, rather than disturb my
slumbering valet, I placed it so as to throw its rays more
fully upon the book.

But the action produced an effect altogether unanticipated.
The rays of the numerous candles (for there were many)
now fell within a niche of the room which had hitherto been
thrown into deep shade by one of the bed-posts. I thus saw
in vivid light a picture all unnoticed before. It was the
portrait of a young girl just ripening into womanhood. I
glanced at the painting hurriedly, and then closed my eyes.
Why I did this was not at first apparent even to my own
perception. But while my lids remained thus shut, I ran over
in my mind my reason for so shutting them. It was an im-
pulsive movement to gain time for thought, to make sure
that my vision had not deceived me, to calm and subdue
my fancy for a more sober and more certain gaze. In a very
few moments I again looked fixedly at the painting.

That I now saw aright I could not and would not doubt;
for the first flashing of the candles upon that canvas had
seemed to dissipate the dreamy stupor which was stealing
over my senses, and to startle me at once into waking life.

The portrait, as I have already said, was that of a young
girl. It was a mere head and shoulders, done in what is
technically termed a vignette manner, much in the style of
the favorite heads of Sully. The arms, the bosom, and even

the ends of the radiant hair melted imperceptibly into the vague yet deep shadow which formed the background of the whole. The frame was oval, richly gilded and filagreed in Moresque. As a thing of art nothing could be more admirable than the painting itself. But it could have been neither the execution of the work, nor the immortal beauty of the countenance, which had so suddenly and so vehemently moved me. Least of all, could it have been that my fancy, shaken from its half slumber, had mistaken the head for that of a living person. I saw at once that the peculiarities of the design, of the vignetting, and of the frame, must have instantly dispelled such idea—must have prevented even its momentary entertainment. Thinking earnestly upon these points, I remained, for an hour perhaps, half sitting, half reclining, with my vision riveted upon the portrait. At length, satisfied with the true secret of its effect, I fell back within the bed. I had found the spell of the picture in an absolute *life-likeness* of expression, which, at first startling, finally confounded, subdued, and appalled me. With deep and reverent awe I replaced the candelabrum in its former position. The cause of my deep agitation being thus shut from view, I sought eagerly the volume which discussed the paintings and their histories. Turning to the number which designated the oval portrait, I there read the vague and quaint words which follow:

> She was a maiden of rarest beauty, and not more lovely than full of glee. And evil was the hour when she saw, and loved, and wedded the painter. He, passionate, studious, austere, and having already a bride in his Art: she a maiden of rarest beauty, and not more lovely than full of glee; all light and smiles, and frolicsome as the young fawn; loving and cherishing all things; hating only the Art which was her rival; dreading only the palette and brushes and other untoward instruments which deprived her of the countenance of her lover. It was thus a terrible thing for this lady to hear the painter speak of his desire to portray even his young bride. But she was humble and obedient, and sat meekly for many weeks in the dark high turret-chamber where the light dripped upon the pale canvas only from overhead. But he, the painter, took glory in his work, which went on from hour to hour, and from

day to day. And he was a passionate and wild, and
moody man, who became lost in reveries; so that
he *would* not see the light which fell so ghastly in
that lone turret withered the health and the spirits
of his bride, who pined visibly to all but him. Yet
she smiled on and still on, uncomplainingly, because she saw that the painter (who had high
renown) took a fervid and burning pleasure in his
task, and wrought day and night to depict her who
so loved him, yet who grew daily more dispirited
and weak. And in sooth some who beheld the portrait spoke of its resemblance in low words, as of a
mighty marvel, and a proof not less of the power
of the painter than of his deep love for her whom
he depicted so surpassingly well. But at length, as
the labor drew nearer to its conclusion, there were
admitted none into the turret; for the painter had
grown wild with the ardor of his work, and turned
his eyes from the canvas rarely, even to regard
the countenance of his wife. And he *would* not
see that the tints which he spread upon the canvas
were drawn from the cheeks of her who sat beside
him. And when many weeks had passed, and but
little remained to do, save one brush upon the
mouth and one tint upon the eye, the spirit of the
lady again flickered up as the flame within the
socket of the lamp. And then the brush was given,
and then the tint was placed; and for one moment,
the painter stood entranced before the work which
he had wrought; but in the next, while he yet
gazed, he grew tremulous and very pallid, and
aghast, and crying with a loud voice, "This
is indeed *Life* itself!" turned suddenly to regard his
beloved—*She was dead.*

Three Letters . . . and a Footnote

BY HORACIO QUIROGA

▫ ▫ ▫

Sir:

I am taking the liberty of sending you these lines, hoping you will be good enough to publish them under your own name. I make this request of you because I am informed that no newspaper would accept these pages if I sign them myself. If you think it wiser, you may alter my impressions by giving them a few masculine touches, which indeed may improve them.

My work makes it necessary for me to take the streetcar twice a day, and for five years I have been making the same trip. Sometimes, on the return ride, I travel in the company of some of my girl friends, but on the way to work I always go alone. I am twenty years old, tall, not too thin, and not at all dark-complexioned. My mouth is somewhat large but not pale. My impression is that my eyes are not small. These outward features which I've estimated modestly, as you have observed, are nevertheless all I need to help me form an opinion of many men, in fact so many that I'm tempted to say all men.

You know also that you men have the habit before you board a streetcar of looking rapidly at its occupants through the windows. In that way you examine all the faces (of the women, of course, since they are the only ones that have any interest for you). After that little ceremony, you enter and sit down.

Very well then; as soon as a man leaves the sidewalk, walks over to the car and looks inside, I know perfectly what sort of fellow he is, and I never make a mistake. I know if he is serious, or if he merely intends to invest ten cents of his fare in finding an easy pick-up. I quickly distinguish between those who like to ride at their ease, and those who prefer less room at the side of some girl.

When the place beside me is unoccupied, I recognize

accurately, according to the glance through the window, which men are indifferent and will sit down anywhere, which are only half-interested and will turn their heads in order to give us the once-over slowly, after they have sat down; and finally, which are the enterprising fellows who will pass by seven empty places so as to perch uncomfortably at my side, way back in the rear of the vehicle.

Presumably, these fellows are the most interesting. Quite contrary to the regular habit of girls who travel alone, instead of getting up and offering the inside place to the newcomer, I simply move over toward the window to leave plenty of room for the enterprising arrival.

Plenty of room. That's a meaningless phrase. Never will the three quarters of a bench abandoned by a girl to her neighbor be sufficient. After moving and shifting at will, he seems suddenly overcome by a surprising motionlessness, to the point where he seems paralyzed. But that is mere appearance, for if anyone watches with suspicion this lack of movement, he will note that the body of the gentleman, imperceptibly, and with a slyness that does honor to his absent-minded look, is slipping little by little down an imaginary inclined plane toward the window, where the girl happens to be, although he isn't looking at her and apparently has no interest in her at all.

That's the way such men are: one could swear that they're thinking about the moon. However, all this time, the right foot (or the left) continues slipping delicately down the aforementioned plane.

I'll admit that while this is going on, I'm very far from being bored. With a mere glance as I shift toward the window, I have taken the measure of my gallant. I know whether he is a spirited fellow who yields to his first impulse or whether he is really someone brazen enough to give me cause for a little worry. I know whether he is a courteous young man or just a vulgar one, whether a hardened criminal or a tender pickpocket, whether he is really a seductive Beau Brummel (the *seduisant* and not the *seducteur* of the French) or a mere petty masher.

At first view it might seem that only one kind of man would perform the act of letting his foot slip slyly over while his face wears a hypocritical mask, namely the thief. However that is not so, and there isn't a girl that hasn't made this observation. For each different type she must have ready a special defense. But very often, especially if the man is quite young or poorly dressed, he is likely to be a pickpocket.

The tactics followed by the man never vary. First of all the sudden rigidity and the air of thinking about the moon. The next step is a fleeting glimpse at our person which seems to linger slightly over our face, but whose sole purpose is to estimate the distance that intervenes between his foot and ours. This information acquired, now the conquest begins.

I think there are few things funnier than that maneuver you men execute, when you move your foot along in gradual shifts of toe and heel alternately. Obviously you men can't see the joke; but this pretty cat and mouse game played with a size eleven shoe at one end, and at the other, up above, near the roof, a simpering idiotic face (doubtless because of emotion), bears no comparison so far as absurdity is concerned with anything else you men do.

I said before that I was not bored with these performances. And my entertainment is based upon the following fact: from the moment the charmer has calculated with perfect precision the distance he has to cover with his foot, he rarely lets his gaze wander down again. He is certain of his measurement and he has no desire to put us on our guard by repeated glances. You will clearly realize that the attraction for him lies in making contact, and not in merely looking.

Very well then: when this amiable neighbor has gone about halfway, I start the same maneuver that he is executing, and I do it with equal slyness and the same semblance of absent-minded preoccupation with, let us say, my doll. Only, the movement of my foot is away from his. Not much; a few inches are enough.

It's a treat to behold, presently, my neighbor's surprise when, upon arriving finally at the calculated spot, he contacts absolutely nothing. Nothing! His size eleven shoe is entirely alone. This is too much for him; first he takes a look at the floor, and then at my face. My thought is still wandering a thousand leagues away, playing with my doll; but the fellow begins to understand.

Fifteen out of seventeen times (I mention these figures after long experience) the annoying gentleman gives up the enterprise. In the two remaining cases I am forced to resort to a warning look. It isn't necessary for this look to indicate by its expression a feeling of insult, or contempt, or anger: it is enough to make a movement of the head in his direction, toward him but without looking straight at him. In these cases it is better always to avoid crossing glances with a man who by chance has been really and deeply attracted to us. There may be in any pickpocket the makings of a dangerous thief. This fact is well known to the cashiers who guard large amounts of money and also to young women, not thin, not dark, with mouths not little and eyes not small, as is the case with yours truly,

M.R.

Dear Miss:

Deeply grateful for your kindness. I'll sign my name with much pleasure to the article on your impressions, as you request. Nevertheless, it would interest me very much and purely as your collaborator to know your answer to the following questions: Aside from the seventeen concrete cases you mention, haven't you ever felt the slightest attraction toward some neighbor, tall or short, blond or dark, stout or lean? Haven't you ever felt the vaguest temptation to yield, ever so vague, which made the withdrawing of your own foot disagreeable and troublesome?

H.Q.

Sir:

To be frank, yes, once in my life, I felt that temptation to yield to someone, or more accurately, that lack of energy in my foot to which you refer. That person was *you*. But you didn't have the sense to take advantage of it.

M.R.

A Dangerous Guy Indeed

BY DAMON RUNYON

It is maybe a matter of thirty-five years ago that a young fellow by the name of Morgan Johnson comes to my old home town and starts in living there.

In those days back in my old home town it is not considered polite to ask a man where he comes from, and as

Morgan Johnson never mentions the place himself nobody ever knows. Furthermore, he never tells much of anything about himself outside of this, so he is considered something of a mystery.

He is a hard-looking citizen in many respects, what with having a scar across his nose, and a pair of black eyebrows which run right together, and black hair, and black eyes, and a way of looking at people, and the first time he goes down Santa Fe Avenue thirty-five years ago, somebody or other says:

"There is a very dangerous man."

Well, the next time Morgan Johnson goes down Santa Fe Avenue somebody who hears what is said about him the first time, says to somebody else:

"There is certainly a very dangerous man."

By and by everybody who sees Morgan Johnson with the scar across his nose, and his black eyes, and all, says:

"There is a dangerous man."

Finally it is well known to one and all back in my old home town that Morgan Johnson IS a dangerous man, and everybody is most respectful to him when he goes walking up and down and around and about, looking at people in that way of his.

If he happens into a saloon where an argument is going on, the argument cools right off. If he happens to say anything, no matter what it is, everybody says it is right, because naturally nobody wishes any truck with a dangerous man.

This scar on Morgan Johnson's nose shows that he has been in plenty of trouble sometime or other, and the fact that he is alive and walking up and down in my old home town out West shows that he can take care of himself.

He never states how he comes to get this scar, but finally somebody says they hear he gets it in a fight with ten very bad men one night in New York, one of them zipping a bullet across his nose, and that Morgan Johnson finally kills all ten.

Who starts this story nobody knows, but Morgan Johnson never denies it, even when the number of parties he kills gets up to as high as twenty. In fact Morgan Johnson never denies anything that is said about him, being something of a hand for keeping his mouth shut, and minding his own business.

Well, sir, he lives in my old home town out West for many

years, and is often pointed out to visitors to our city by
citizens who say:

"There is a very dangerous man, indeed."

By the time Morgan Johnson is getting along toward fifty
years old, some people start shivering the minute he comes
in sight and never stop shivering until he goes on past.

Then one day what happens but Morgan Johnson is going along the street when a little old guy by the name of
Wheezer Gamble comes staggering out of the Greenlight
saloon, this Wheezer Gamble being nothing but a sheepman
from down on the Huerfano River.

He is called Wheezer because he wheezes more than
somewhat, on account of having the asthma, and he is so
old, and so little that nobody ever thinks of bothering him
even though he is nothing but a sheepman. He comes to
town once a month to get his pots on, and this day he
staggers out of the Greenlight is the first of the month.

The whiskey they sell in the Greenlight saloon is very
powerful whiskey, and often makes people wish to fight who
never think of fighting before in their life, although, of
course, nobody ever figures it is powerful enough to make a
sheepman fight. But what does Wheezer Gamble do when
he sees Morgan Johnson, but grab Morgan by the coat,
to hold himself up, and say to Morgan like this:

"So you are a dangerous man, are you?"

Well, everybody who sees this come off feels very sorry
for poor old Wheezer because they figure Morgan Johnson
will chew him up at once and spit him out, but Morgan only
blinks his eyes and says:

"What?"

"They tell me you are a dangerous man," Wheezer says.
"I am now about to cut you open with my jack-knife and
see what it is that makes you dangerous."

At this he lets go Morgan's coat and outs with a big jack-
knife, which is an article he uses in connection with cooking
and skinning dead sheep and one thing and another, and
opens it up to carve Morgan Johnson.

But Morgan Johnson does not wait to be carved. The
minute he sees this knife he turns around and hauls it, which
is a way of saying he leaves. Furthermore, he leaves on a
dead run, and everybody says that if he is not a fast runner
that day he will do until a fast one comes along.

Of course, Wheezer Gamble cannot chase him very far,
being old, and also drunker than somewhat, and Morgan

Johnson never stops until he is plumb out of town. The last anybody sees of him he is still going in the direction of Denver and the chances are he reaches there, as he is never seen in my old home town again.

Then it comes out that the story about him being dangerous is by no means true, and furthermore that he does not kill ten men back in New York or any men whatever. As for the scar across his nose, somebody says that he gets it from being busted across the nose by a woman with a heavy pocketbook which Morgan Johnson is trying to pick off her arm.

The chances are this story is no truer than the story about him killing the ten men, but that is the story everybody back in my old home town believes to this day.

My Grandpap often speaks of Morgan Johnson, and says it goes to prove something or other about human nature. My Grandpap says you can say a man is a good man or a bad man, and if you say it often enough people will finally believe it, although the chances are when it comes to a showdown he is not a good man or a bad man, as the case may be.

My Grandpap says he always suspects Morgan Johnson is not a dangerous man, but if you ask my Grandpap why he does not prove it the same as Wheezer Gamble, my Grandpap says like this:

"Well," he says. "You know there is always the chance that he may be just what they say. There is always that chance, and I am never any hand for going around trying to bust up traditions if there is a chance they may be true."

Reginald's Choir Treat

BY SAKI

"Never," wrote Reginald to his most darling friend, "be a pioneer. It's the Early Christian that gets the fattest lion."

Reginald, in his way, was a pioneer.

None of the rest of his family had anything approaching

Titian hair or a sense of humour, and they used primroses
as a table decoration.

It follows that they never understood Reginald, who came
down late to breakfast, and nibbled toast, and said disrespect-
ful things about the universe. The family ate porridge, and
believed in everything, even the weather forecast.

Therefore the family was relieved when the vicar's daughter undertook the reformation of Reginald. Her name was
Amabel; it was the vicar's one extravagance. Amabel was
accounted a beauty and intellectually gifted: she never
played tennis, and was reputed to have read Maeterlinck's
Life of the Bee. If you abstain from tennis *and* read Maeterlinck in a small country village, you are of necessity intel-
lectual. Also she had been twice to Fécamp to pick up a
good French accent from the Americans staying there; consequently she had a knowledge of the world which might
be considered useful in dealings with a worldling.

Hence the congratulations in the family when Amabel
undertook the reformation of its wayward member.

Amabel commenced operations by asking her unsuspecting
pupil to tea in the vicarage garden; she believed in the
healthy influence of natural surroundings, never having been
in Sicily, where things are different.

And like every woman who has ever preached repentance
to unregenerate youth, she dwelt on the sin of an empty
life, which always seems so much more scandalous in the
country, where people rise early to see if a new strawberry
has happened during the night.

Reginald recalled the lilies of the field, "which simply sat
and looked beautiful, and defied competition."

"But that is not an example for us to follow," gasped
Amabel.

"Unfortunately, we can't afford to. You don't know what
a world of trouble I take in trying to rival the lilies in their
artistic simplicity."

"You are really indecently vain of your appearance. A
good life is infinitely preferable to good looks."

"You agree with me that the two are incompatible. I
always say beauty is only sin deep."

Amabel began to realize that the battle is not always to
the strong-minded. With the immemorial resource of her sex,
she abandoned the frontal attack and laid stress on her
unassisted labours in parish work, her mental loneliness, her
discouragements—and at the right moment she produced

strawberries and cream. Reginald was obviously affected by
the latter, and when his preceptress suggested that he might
begin the strenuous life by helping her to supervise the
annual outing of the bucolic infants who composed the
local choir, his eyes shone with the dangerous enthusiasm of
a convert.

Reginald entered on the strenuous life alone, as far as
Amabel was concerned. The most virtuous women are not
proof against damp grass, and Amabel kept her bed with a
cold. Reginald called it a dispensation; it had been the
dream of his life to stage-manage a choir outing. With
strategic insight, he led his shy, bullet-headed charges to
the nearest woodland stream and allowed them to bathe; then
he seated himself on the discarded garments and discoursed
on their immediate future, which, he decreed, was to embrace
a Bacchanalian procession through the village. Forethought
had provided the occasion with a supply of tin whistles,
but the introduction of a he-goat from a neighbouring orchard
was a brilliant afterthought. Properly, Reginald explained,
there should have been an outfit of panther skins; as it was,
those who had spotted handkerchiefs were allowed to wear
them, which they did with thankfulness. Reginald recognized
the impossibility in the time at his disposal, of teaching his
shivering neophytes a chant in honour of Bacchus, so he
started them off with a more familiar, if less appropriate,
temperance hymn. After all, he said, it is the spirit of the
thing that counts. Following the etiquette of dramatic authors
on first nights, he remained discreetly in the background
while the procession, with extreme diffidence and the goat,
wound its way lugubriously towards the village. The singing
had died down long before the main street was reached,
but the miserable wailing of pipes brought the inhabitants
to their doors. Reginald said he had seen something like it
in pictures; the villagers had seen nothing like it in their
lives, and remarked as much freely.

Reginald's family never forgave him. They had no sense
of humour.

The Kiss

BY WILLIAM SANSOM

📖 📖 📖

As Rolfe began to lean over her, knowing the moment had come, he understood for the first time the meaning of isolation. On the very brink of it he was separated from her suddenly by a grim and cold distance along whose way could be detected the chill of reality.

She lay back in the cushions, her hair loose on the taffeta, her lips parted in a smile of invitation. The pink tip of her tongue lingered between her teeth. In that hot weather there were night-flies, and away by the lamp one of these hummed through the stillness of an apprehensive room. Only once was this silence, the silence of the dynamo, disturbed—when the girl raised her arms towards his, when the taffeta cushions rustled and the starched crinkle of her silken dress livened the air with whispers that seemed to mould musically the shape of her own delighted motion.

Why should he have felt at that time so separate, more separated from her than ever before, more even than at their first strange meeting? In the wisp of time when his lips approached hers—even then!—he sought wildly for the reason. Perhaps he had flung himself back the better to leap forward, recoiling instinctively for the assault? Perhaps he was afraid of refusal, so that in his wounded pride the hate had already begun to crystallize? Perhaps he was certain of acceptance; and thus with the knowledge of conquest saturating his hope, he was already reaching out for another star, belittling the planet whose illusory brilliance had faded in the shadow of his near approach. All these three emotions had a part in him, then, but the last predominated.

Yet—whatever the mind said, the lips and the instincts were already on the move. Wherever hope had flown, desire was gathering momentum; desire must be consuaged. Now it seemed to freewheel—like the gilded mountain train that had strained so desperately towards the summit, with pis-

227

tons boiling, with each socket shuddering in a cloud of steam
and smoke and noise, only to reach the top, pause and then
run coolly into its descent, freewheeling with relief, sure of
its rails and its effortless glide down to an inevitable des-
tination below. How simple it seemed! Yet that was only
the beginning.

For as his head bent lower the idea of conquest became
an idea of possession. Still from a distance, but nearer, so
much nearer, he saw his love as he wished her to be. He saw
the curve of her bare shoulder shining whitely even in the
pink glow of the shaded gaslight. He saw how the shoulder
was thrust towards him, so that her cheek nestled against it,
her head thrust a little to one side, not coquettish, but
thoughtful, as though she were considering carefully and
with deep satisfaction on the beloved moment and the fulfilment that lay at its end. Her eyes half-closed, so that under
dark brows their blue gleamed cloudily between lids heavy
with the night's honey. And one strand of her hair blew
free across her cheek, touching the corner of her mouth. She
smiled lazily, with teeth so slightly parted, the smile of one
awakening from the warmth of sleep. At the collar of her
dress an ivory locket breathed quickly and lightly. He repeated and repeated to himself: "This is mine! This is all
mine to kiss!" This is the property of that stranger I call
myself, whom I have watched growing, whom I have applauded and despised, whom once I saw as a little boy
breaking his nails on a walnut shell, running to his mother,
carrying a prize off the school platform with violent self-
satisfaction: and as a young man miserable in the first se-
crecies of love, walking cleverly to the office, always seeing
himself as a different person much older; and now as a man
whose ambitions are outlined, who has failed often, but who
has known small successes too, and feels them rising into a
tide of achievement. And now—once more a moment of
success, the greatest yet! The stranger has achieved the ability to kiss this lovely and fabulous creature, so recently held
to be far beyond his feeble reach! The stranger has exerted
his charms and he has won, so that now the treasure lies at
his feet, and he himself stands above that which was once
considered too high for him.

Shall the stranger now brush this treasure aside with his
boots?

Not on his life! For the momentum of desire is piling up
its swift descent, Rolfe's head is bending lower, the lips are

forming themselves into the framework of a kiss. Besides, vanity is not the only emotion that stirs the stranger's heart; he begins as well to appreciate purely and profoundly the loveliness that lies before him.

As Rolfe bends forward, the room around departs, his eyes focus only on the figure in the light beneath, and then softly over this vision creeps a sentimental mist that suffuses the hair, the eyes, the lips, the face with a lustre of even great beauty, as though a halo had been thrown around it and over it, as though it were a face seen through tears. A wishful sob mounts in his throat. Her hands touch his shoulders.

But—even then he is distracted. At one side of the halo a golden tassel shines in the light. Somehow, although he is looking directly down into her face, the corner of his eye manages to digest the fact of this golden tassel. In an instant his mind has travelled all the way to a theatre curtain, a stage, a particular play, and a tired quarrel afterwards in a drawing-room where there was no fire and the sandwiches were bent and stale.

Then his eyes advance, so that the tassel is lost in the gray mists that circle his vision, departing as suddenly as it had arrived, leaving no impression at all.

His eyes are so near to her face that suddenly he can see everything! He can see clearly, as though through an optical glass, the lowered lids with their rim of blue mascara, the pubic tenderness of the hairs at her brow, the mineral lustre of the greasepaint that makes a black beauty spot of the brown mole on her cheek. Her lips are filmed with wetness through which he can see the dry rouge. There is a tiny bubble of saliva between two teeth. He notices that there are larger pores on the sides of her nostrils, and that the powder has caked beneath them. She has a mustache! But how fine, how sweet, a mirage of the softest down!

And now truly love sweeps over him. For he loves all these things, their nearness, their revelation, their innocent nudity offered without care. He loves it that beneath the perfect vision there lie these pathetic and human strugglings. The vision has become a person. He has at last penetrated beneath the cloak of the perfume and smells at last the salt that breathes closest to her skin. This is a magic moment when ambitions are more than realized, even before they are tasted! For now the moment of fulfilment is so very close that the urgency of desire's speed seems to vanish.

There is a second of leisure, a last fondling of the object soon to be grasped—that will never recur. Perhaps the only real moment of possession, the moment just before possession, when desire knows that there is no longer even the necessity to freewheel! Can there be such a pause in the great momentum? It must be so. Just as the mountain train having completed the swift gradient runs for the last lap once more on level rails, slowing without effort its speed, but never doubting that it will glide surely to its final rest at the buffers.

Their eyes closed. With parted lips they kissed. He opened his eyes, so slightly, to look once more at the face he loved. An agony clutched his spine! He saw with terror that her eyes were wide open, wide and blue, staring at the ceiling! Heavens—had they ever closed? Had they opened at the very moment that their lips had touched? Had she remained unkissed? Had she never kissed him? Would he ever know? How could he trust her answer—perhaps that her dress had caught, or that her eyes were open in a dream? Were these eyes blind with the distances of passion, or were they alert with thought? And what thought? How could he ever know? Even as he tried to solve them her eyes turned from above and stared straight into his.

The Shepherd's Daughter

BY WILLIAM SAROYAN

□□ □□ □□

It is the opinion of my grandmother, God bless her, that all men should labour, and at the table, a moment ago, she said to me: You must learn to do some good work, the making of some item useful to man, something out of clay, or out of wood, or metal, or cloth. It is not proper for a young man to be ignorant of an honourable craft. Is there anything you can make? Can you make a simple table, a chair, a plain dish, a rug, a coffee pot? If there anything you can do?

And my grandmother looked at me with anger.

I know, she said, you are supposed to be a writer, and I suppose you are. You certainly smoke enough cigarettes to be anything, and the whole house is full of the smoke, but you must learn to make solid things, things that can be used, that can be seen and touched.

There was a king of the Persians, said my grandmother, and he had a son, and this son fell in love with a shepherd's daughter. He went to his father and he said, My Lord, I love a shepherd's daughter, and I would have her for my wife. And the king said, I am king and you are my son, and when I die you shall be king, how can it be that you would marry the daughter of a shepherd? And the son said, My Lord, I do not know but I know that I love this girl and would have her for my queen.

The king saw that his son's love for the girl was from God, and he said, I will send a message to her. And he called a messenger to him and he said, Go to the shepherd's daughter and say that my son loves her and would have her for his wife. And the messenger went to the girl and he said, The king's son loves you and would have you for his wife. And the girl said, What labour does he do? And the messenger said, Why, he is the son of the king; he does no labour. And the girl said, He must learn to do some labour. And the messenger returned to the king and spoke the words of the shepherd's daughter.

The king said to his son, The shepherd's daughter wishes you to learn some craft. Would you still have her for your wife? And the son said, Yes, I will learn to weave straw rugs. And the boy was taught to weave rugs of straw, in patterns and in colours and with ornamental designs, and at the end of three days he was making very fine straw rugs, and the messenger returned to the shepherd's daughter, and he said, These rugs of straw are the work of the king's son.

And the girl went with the messenger to the king's palace, and she became the wife of the king's son.

One day, said my grandmother, the king's son was walking through the streets of Baghdad, and he came upon an eating place which was so clean and cool that he entered it and sat at a table.

This place, said my grandmother, was a place of thieves and murderers, and they took the king's son and placed him in a large dungeon where many great men of the city were being held, and the thieves and murderers were killing the fattest of the men and feeding them to the leanest of them, and making sport of it. The king's son was of the leanest of the men, and it was not known that he was the son of the king of the Persians, so his life was spared, and he said to the thieves and murderers, I am a weaver of straw rugs and these rugs have great value. And they brought him straw and asked him to weave and in three days he weaved three rugs, and he said, Carry these to the palace of the king of the Persians, and for each rug he will give you a hundred gold pieces of money. And the rugs were carried to the palace of the king, and when the king saw the rugs he saw that they were the work of his son and he took the rugs to the shepherd's daughter and he said, These rugs were brought to the palace and they are the work of my son who is lost. And the shepherd's daughter took each rug and looked at it closely and in the design of each rug she saw in the written language of the Persians a message from her husband, and she related this message to the king.

And the king, said my grandmother, sent many soldiers to the place of the thieves and murderers, and the soldiers rescued all the captives and killed all the thieves and murderers, and the king's son was returned safely to the palace of his father, and to the company of his wife, the little shepherd's daughter. And when the boy went into the palace and saw again his wife, he humbled himself before her and he embraced her feet, and he said, My love, it is because of you that I am alive, and the king was greatly pleased with the shepherd's daughter.

Now, said my grandmother, do you see why every man should learn an honourable craft?

I see very clearly, I said, and as soon as I earn enough money to buy a saw and a hammer and a piece of lumber I shall do my best to make a simple chair or a shelf for books.

The Foreigner

BY FRANCIS STEEGMULLER

📖 📖 📖

If it hadn't been raining as I came out of the cinema, I should have walked home: my apartment was nearby and the route anything but complicated—straight down the boule-

vard, crossing two streets and turning right on the third, the
Rue de Grenelle, for about half a block. As if was, however,
I hailed a taxi, and it was scarcely a moment before I realized that its driver, a ruddy-faced old man, was in the midst
of an attack of perversity and nerves. "No! No!" I cried, as
he started to turn up the *first* street, the Rue St. Dominique.
"Two more blocks!" He muttered something, swung down
the boulevard again, and then in a moment he was turning
up the *second* street, the Rue Las Casses. "No! No!" I cried
again. "The next one, please! The next street is mine! The
Rue de Grenelle!" At this he turned around and gave me a
baleful stare; then he spurted ahead, didn't turn up my street
at all, and continued rapidly down the boulevard, as though
forever. "But now you have passed it!" I cried. "You should
have turned to the right, as I said! Please turn around,
and drive up the Rue de Grenelle to Number 36."

To my horror, the old man made a noise like a snarl. Spinning his car around in a U turn on the slippery pavement,
he speeded back, crossed the boulevard, and stopped at the
corner of my street with a jerk. "Get out!" he almost
screamed, his face crimson with rage. "Get out of my automobile at once! I refuse absolutely to drive you any further!
Three times you have treated me like an idiot! Three times
you have grossly insulted me! My automobile is not for
foreigners, I tell you! Get out at once!"

"In this rain?" I cried, indignantly. "I shall do nothing of
the kind. I did not insult you even once, Monsieur, let alone
three times. You know quite well I did nothing but urge you,
in vain, to drive me home. Now kindly do so. I shall give you
a good *pourboire*," I added, more amiably, "and we shall take
leave of each other in a friendly fashion."

He barely waited for me to finish. "Get out!" he cried.
"Get out, I tell you! You have insulted me too often, and
you will get out!"

I glanced at the rain. "Indeed I will not," I said.

His manner calmed ominously. "Either you will leave
my taxi," he said in an even, hoarse tone, "or I shall drive
you to the commissariat of police, where I shall demand the
recompense due me for such insults as yours. Choose!"

"In such weather as this," I replied, "I have no choice. To
the commissariat, by all means." And there we went.

The commissariat, only a few doors from mine, was not
unfamiliar to me. I had been there several times before, on
less quarrelsome matters, and as the driver and I entered

the bare room side by side the *commissaire*, sitting in lonely authority behind his desk, greeted me as an acquaintance. "Good afternoon, Monsieur," he said, calling me by name. "I can help you? What is it you wish?"

But the old man, to whom the *commissaire* had barely nodded, gave me no chance to speak. "It is I who wish!" he cried. "It is I who wish to complain against this foreigner! Three times he has treated me like an idiot, Monsieur! Three times he has insulted me grossly! I demand justice, Monsieur!"

The *commissaire* stared at him, his face expressionless; I felt that he, like me, was wondering in just what condition the old man was; then, turning to me, he asked me if I would have the kindness to make my deposition. He took up a pen, opened a large blank book, and as I spoke, took down my story in a flowing, plumy hand. The giving of my address to the driver, the two incorrect turns, the mutterings, the missing of my street, the rage, the ultimatum; all the *commissaire* inscribed imperishably in whatever the French call the Spencerian style; once or twice he interrupted me to reprimand the driver, who muttered beside me at various portions of my testimony. When I had finished, the *commissaire* continued to write for a moment, ended with a particularly fancy flourish, blotted his last line, and thanked me. Then he turned to the driver. "And now you," he said gruffly. "You depose, too, so that I may make up my mind on this perplexing question."

The old man, however, had no deposition to make. "Three times!" was still all he could say, in his thick, angry voice, gesticulating at the *commissaire* and glaring at me. "Three times, Monsieur! Three times treated like an idiot, and three times grossly insulted! By this foreigner! It is not to be borne, Monsieur!"

The *commissaire* looked up crossly from his notebook, where these accusations had been duly inscribed. "But the circumstances? Describe in detail what took place while you were with this gentleman. If the circumstances which he has related are not true," he said, casting me a glance of apology, "correct them."

But once again "Three times!" was all my accuser could say, and the *commissaire* laid down his pen rather briskly. "It is entirely clear," he said in a very definite voice, "that it is you, Monsieur, who are the injured party in this affair, and I shall be happy to indicate my decision by requiring this person to drive you to your door without charge. If Monsieur will now have the goodness to grant me the favor of a brief glance at his papers—a formality required by law in such cases as these—I shall dispose of the matter at once. Your *carte d'identité*, Monsieur, if you please."

Like a plummet, my heart sank. In my mind's eye I saw the desk in my study, and lying on it, forgotten, the identification card which foreign residents are required by French law to carry at all times. "Due to the penetrating rain, Monsieur," it hastily occurred to me as the only thing to say, "I have left my card at home, lest the moisture of the weather permeate it, and perhaps destroy it completely. In the morning I can easily bring it to you, Monsieur, and I hope that this will satisfy your requirements, which I realize are strict and necessary."

But I had done the unforgivable, and everything was changed and over with. "That will not satisfy the requirements," the *commissaire* said sternly, his face like stone. "It is true that you will bring your card here tomorrow morning, but in view of the present circumstance I am forced to alter my judgment in this affair. Due to the fact that it is raining, I shall request this gentleman to drive you to your door, but I shall require you to pay him not only for the entire journey from beginning to end but also for the time he has lost by coming to this bureau. I assume, Monsieur," he said to the old man, "that you have left your meter running?"

The driver nodded, and the *commissaire* rose. "Then *au revoir*, Monsieurs," he said, unsmiling. "Monsieur will not forget tomorrow morning," and side by side as we had entered, we left the commissariat. I had seen a gleam come into my accuser's eyes when the judgment had been reversed, but apart from that he had given no signs of triumph, and he continued to give none: he drove me home without a word. It was only when we arrived, and I handed him the exact fare, carefully counted out, that he spoke. "Monsieur has no doubt forgotten his promise of a good *pourboire*, that we might part in friendly fashion?" he said.

Tom Varnish

BY RICHARD STEELE

Because I have a professed aversion to long beginnings of stories, I will go into this at once, by telling you, that there dwells near the Royal Exchange as happy a couple as ever entered into wedlock. These live in that mutual confidence of each other, which renders the satisfaction of marriage even greater than those of friendship, and makes wife and husband the dearest appellations of human life. Mr. Balance is a merchant of good consideration, and understands the world, not from speculation, but practice. His wife is the daughter of an honest house, ever bred in a family-way; and has, from a natural good understanding and great innocence, a freedom which men of sense know to be the certain sign of virtue, and fools take to be an encouragement to vice.

Tom Varnish, a young gentleman of the Middle Temple, by the bounty of a good father, who was so obliging as to die, and leave him, in his twenty-fourth year, besides a good estate, a large sum which lay in the hands of Mr. Balance, had by this means an intimacy at his house; and being one of those hard students who read plays for the improvement of the law, took his rules of life from thence. Upon mature deliberation, he conceived it very proper, that he, as a man of wit and pleasure of the town, should have an intrigue with his merchant's wife. He no sooner thought of this adventure, but he began it by an amorous epistle to the lady and a faithful promise to wait upon her at a certain hour the next evening, when he knew her husband was to be absent.

The letter was no sooner received, but it was communicated to the husband, and produced no other effect in him, than that he joined with his wife to raise all the mirth they could out of this fantastical piece of gallantry. They were so little concerned at this dangerous man of mode, that they

236

plotted ways to perplex him without hurting him. Varnish comes exactly at his hour; and the lady's well-acted confusion at his entrance gave him opportunity to repeat some couplets very fit for the occasion with very much grace and spirit. His theatrical manner of making love was interrupted by an alarm of the husband's coming; and the wife, in a personated terror, beseeched him, "if he had any value for the honour of a woman that loved him, he would jump out of the window." He did so, and fell upon featherbeds placed there on purpose to receive him.

It is not to be conceived how great the joy of an amorous man is, when he has suffered for his mistress, and is never the worse for it. Varnish the next day writ a most elegant billet, wherein he said all that imagination could form upon the occasion. He violently protested, "going out of the window was no way terrible, but as it was going from her"; with several other kind expressions, which procured him a second assignation. Upon his second visit, he was conveyed by a faithful maid into her bed chamber, and left there to expect the arrival of her mistress. But the wench, according to her instructions, ran in again to him, and locked the door after her to keep out her master. She had just time enough to convey the lover into a chest before she admitted the husband and his wife into the room.

You may be sure that trunk was absolutely necessary to be opened; but upon her husband's ordering it, she assured him, "she had taken all the care imaginable in packing up the things with her own hands, and he might send the trunk abroad as soon as he thought fit." The easy husband believed his wife, and the good couple went to bed; Varnish having the happiness to pass the night in the mistress's bedchamber without molestation. The morning arose, but our lover was not well situated to observe her blushes; so all we know of his sentiments on this occasion is, that he heard Balance ask for the key, and say, "he would himself go with this chest, and have it opened before the captain of the ship, for the greater safety of so valuable a lading."

The goods were hoisted away; and Mr. Balance, marching by his chest with great care and diligency, omitting nothing that might give his passenger perplexity. But, to consummate all, he delivered the chest, with strict charge, "in case they were in danger of being taken, to throw it overboard, for there were letters in it, the matter of which might be of great service to the enemy."

Over the Hill

BY JOHN STEINBECK

🁢 🁢 🁢

Sligo and the kid took their forty-eight hour pass listlessly. The bars close in Algeria at eight o'clock, but they got pretty drunk on wine before that happened and they took a bottle with them and lay down on the beach. The night was warm, and after the two had finished the second bottle of wine they took off their clothes and waded out into the quiet water and then squatted down and sat there with only their heads out. "Pretty nice, eh, kid," said Sligo. "There's guys used to pay heavy dough for stuff like this, and we get it for nothing."

"I'd rather be home on Tenth Avnoo," said the kid. "I'd rather be there than anyplace. I'd like to see my old lady. I'd like to see the World Series this year."

"You'd like maybe a clip in the kisser," said Sligo.

"I'd like to go into the Greek's and get me a double chocolate malted with six eggs in it," said the kid. He bobbed up to keep a little wavelet out of his mouth. "This place is lonely. I like Coney."

"Too full of people," said Sligo.

"This place is lonely," said the kid.

"Talking about the Series, I'd like to do that myself," said Sligo. "It's times like this a fella gets kind of tempted to go over the hill."

"S'posen you went over the hill—where the hell would you go? There ain't no place to go."

"I'd go home," said Sligo. "I'd go to the Series. I'd be first in the bleachers, like I was in '40."

"You couldn't get home," the kid said; "there ain't no way to get home."

The wine was warming Sligo and the water was good. "I got dough says I can get home," he said carelessly.

"How much dough?"

"Twenty bucks."

238

"You can't do it," said the kid.

"You want to take the bet?"

"Sure I'll take it. When you going to pay?"

"I ain't going to pay; you're going to pay. Let's go up on the beach and knock off a little sleep. . ."

At the piers the ships lay. They had brought landing craft and tanks and troops, and now they lay taking in the scrap, the broken equipment from the North African battle-fields which would go to the blast furnaces to make more tanks and landing craft. Sligo and the kid sat on a pile of C-ration boxes and watched the ships. Down the hill came a detail with a hundred Italian prisoners to be shipped to New York. Some of the prisoners were ragged and some were dressed in American khaki because they had been too ragged in the wrong places. None of the prisoners seemed to be unhappy about going to America. They marched down to a gangplank and then stood in a crowd awaiting orders to get aboard.

"Look at them," said the kid, "they get to go home and we got to stay. What you doing, Sligo? What you rubbing oil all over your pants for?"

"Twenty bucks," said Sligo, "and I'll find you and collect, too." He stood up and took off his overseas cap and tossed it to the kid. "Here's a present, kid."

"What you going to do, Sligo?"

"Don't you come follow me, you're too dumb. Twenty bucks, and don't you forget it. So long, see you on Tenth Avnoo."

The kid watched him go, uncomprehending. Sligo, with dirty pants and a ripped shirt, moved gradually over, near to the prisoners, and then imperceptibly he edged in among them and stood bareheaded, looking back at the kid.

An order was called down to the guards, and they herded the prisoners toward the gangplank. Sligo's voice came plaintively. "I'm not supposed to be here. Hey, don't put me on dis ship."

"Shut up, wop," a guard growled at him. "I don't care if you did live sixteen years in Brooklyn. Git up that plank." He pushed the reluctant Sligo up the gangplank.

Back on the pile of boxes the kid watched with admiration. He saw Sligo get to the rail. He saw Sligo still protesting and fighting to get back to the pier. He heard him shrieking, "Hey, I'm Americano. Americano soldier. You canna poot me here."

The kid saw Sligo struggling and then he saw the final triumph. He saw Sligo take a sock at a guard and he saw the guard's club rise and come down on Sligo's head. His friend collapsed and was carried out of sight on board the ship. "The son-of-a-gun," the kid mumured to himself. "The smart son-of-a-gun. They can't do nothing at all to him and he got witnesses. Well, the smart son-of-a-gun. My God, it's worth twenty bucks."

The kid sat on the boxes for a long time. He didn't leave his place till the ship cast off and the tugs pulled her clear of the submarine nets. The kid saw the ship join the group and he saw the destroyers move up and take the convoy under protection. The kid walked dejectedly up to the town. He bought a bottle of Algerian wine and headed back toward the beach to sleep his forty-eight.

An Attempt at Reform

BY AUGUST STRINDBERG

▢ ▢ ▢

She had noticed with indignation that girls were solely brought up to be housekeepers for their future husbands. Therefore she had learned a trade which would enable her to keep herself in all circumstances of life. She made artificial flowers.

He had noticed with regret that girls simply waited for a husband who should keep them; he resolved to marry a free and independent woman who could earn her own living; such a woman would be his equal and a companion for life, not a housekeeper.

Fate ordained that they should meet. He was an artist and she made, as I already mentioned, flowers; they were both living in Paris at the time when they conceived these ideas.

There was style in their marriage. They took three rooms at Passy. In the centre was the studio, to the right of it his room, to the left hers. This did away with the common bedroom and double bed, that abomination which has no counterpart in nature and is responsible for a great deal of dissipation and immorality. It moreover did away with the inconvenience of having to dress and undress in the same room. It was far better that each of them should have a separate room and that the studio should be a neutral, common meeting-place.

They required no servant; they were going to do the cooking themselves and employ an old charwoman in the mornings and evenings. It was all very well thought out and excellent in theory.

"But supposing you had children?" asked the sceptics.

"Nonsense, there won't be any!"

It worked splendidly. He went to the market in the morning and did the catering. Then he made the coffee. She made the beds and put the rooms in order. And then they sat down and worked.

When they were tired of working they gossiped, gave one another good advice, laughed and were very jolly.

At twelve o'clock he lit the kitchen fire and she prepared the vegetables. He cooked the beef, while she ran across the street to the grocer's; then she laid the table and he dished up the dinner.

Of course, they loved one another as husbands and wives do. They said good night to each other and went into their own rooms, but there was no lock to keep him out when he knocked at her door; but the accomodation was small and the morning found them in their own quarters. Then he knocked at the wall.

"Good morning, little girlie, how are you today?"

"Very well, darling, and you?"

Their meeting at breakfast was always like a new experience which never grew stale.

They often went out together in the evening and frequently met their countrymen. She had no objection to the smell of tobacco, and was never in the way. Everybody said it was an ideal marriage; no one had ever known a happier couple.

But the young wife's parents, who lived a long way off, were always writing and asking all sorts of indelicate questions; they were longing to have a grandchild. Louisa ought to remember that the institution of marriage existed for the benefit of the children, not the parents. Louisa held that this view was an old-fashioned one. Mama asked whether she did not think that the result of the new ideas would be the complete extirpation of mankind? Louisa had never looked at it in that light, and moreover the question did not interest her. Both she and her husband were happy; at last the spectacle of a happy married couple was presented to the world, and the world was envious.

Life was very pleasant. Neither of them was master and they shared expenses. Now he earned more, now she did, but in the end their contributions to the common fund amounted to the same figure.

Then she had a birthday! She was awakened in the morning by the entrance of the charwoman with a bunch of flowers and a letter painted all over with flowers, and containing the following words:

"To the lady flower-bud from her dauber, who wishes her many happy returns of the day and begs her to honor him with her company at an excellent little breakfast—at once."

She knocked at his door—come in!

And they breakfasted, sitting on the bed—his bed; and the charwoman was kept the whole day to do all the work. It was a lovely birthday!

Their happiness never palled. It lasted two years. All the prophets had prophesied falsely.

It was a model marriage!

But when two years had passed, the young wife fell ill. She put it down to some poison contained in the wall-paper; he suggested germs of some sort. Yes, certainly, germs. But something was wrong. Something was not as it should be. She must have caught cold. Then she grew stout. Was she suffering from tumour? Yes, they were afraid that she was.

She consulted a doctor—and came home crying. It was indeed a growth, but one which would one day see daylight, grow into a flower and bear fruit.

The husband did anything but cry. He found style in it, and then the wretch went to his club and boasted about it to his friends. But the wife still wept. What would her position be now? She would soon not be able to earn money with her work and then she would have to live on him. And they would have to have a servant! Ugh! those servants!

All their care, their caution, their wariness had been wrecked on the rock of the inevitable.

But the mother-in-law wrote enthusiastic letters and repeated over and over again that marriage was instituted by God for the protection of the children; the parents' pleasure counted for very little.

Hugo implored her to forget the fact that she would not be able to earn anything in future. Didn't she do her full share of the work by mothering the baby? Wasn't that as good as money? Money was, rightly understood, nothing but work. Therefore she paid her share in full.

It took her a long time to get over the fact that he had to keep her. But when the baby came, she forgot all about it. She remained his wife and companion as before in addition to being the mother of his child, and he found that this was worth more than anything else.

The Three Hermits
AN OLD LEGEND CURRENT IN THE VOLGA DISTRICT

BY LEO TOLSTOY

"And in praying use not vain repetitions, as the Gentiles do: for they think that they shall be heard for their much speaking. Be not therefore like them: for your Father knoweth what things ye have need of, before ye ask Him."
Matthew vi:7,8.

A Bishop was sailing from Archangel to the Solovétsk Monastery, and on the same vessel were a number of pilgrims on their way to visit the shrines at that place. The voyage was a smooth one. The wind favorable and the weather fair. The pilgrims lay on deck, eating, or sat in groups talking to one another. The Bishop, too, came on deck, and as he was pacing up and down he noticed a group of men standing near the prow and listening to a fisherman, who was pointing to the sea and telling them something. The Bishop stopped, and looked in the direction in which the man was pointing. He could see nothing, however, but the sea glistening in the sunshine. He drew nearer to listen, but when the man saw him, he took off his cap and was silent. The rest of the people also took off their caps and bowed.

"Do not let me disturb you, friends," said the Bishop. "I came to hear what this good man was saying."

"The fisherman was telling us about the hermits," replied one, a tradesman, rather bolder than the rest.

"What hermits?" asked the Bishop, going to the side of the vessel and seating himself on a box. "Tell me about them. I should like to hear. What were you pointing at?"

"Why, that little island you can just see over there," answered the man, pointing to a spot ahead and a little to the right. "That is the island where the hermits live for the salvation of their souls."

"Where is the island?" asked the Bishop. "I see nothing."

"There, in the distance, if you will please look along my hand. Do you see that little cloud? Below it, and a bit to the left, there is just a faint streak. That is the island."

The Bishop looked carefully, but his unaccustomed eyes could make out nothing but the water shimmering in the sun.

"I cannot see it," he said. "But who are the hermits that live there?"

"They are holy men," answered the fisherman. "I had long heard tell of them, but never chanced to see them myself till the year before last."

And the fisherman related how once, when he was out fishing, he had been stranded at night upon that island, not knowing where he was. In the morning, as he wandered about the island, he came across an earth hut, and met an old man standing near it. Presently two others came out, and after having fed him and dried his things, they helped him mend his boat.

"And what are they like?" asked the Bishop.

"One is a small man and his back is bent. He wears a priest's cassock and is very old; he must be more than a hundred, I should say. He is so old that the white of his beard is taking a greenish tinge, but he is always smiling, and his face is as bright as an angel's from heaven. The second is taller, but he also is very old. He wears a tattered peasant coat. His beard is broad, and of a yellowish grey color. He is a strong man. Before I had time to help him, he turned my boat over as if it were only a pail. He too is kindly and cheerful. The third is tall, and has a beard as white as snow and reaching to his knees. He is stern, with overhanging eyebrows; and he wears nothing but a piece of matting tied round his waist."

"And did they speak to you?" asked the Bishop.

"For the most part they did everything in silence, and spoke but little even to one another. One of them would just give a glance, and the others would understand him. I asked the tallest whether they had lived there long. He frowned, and muttered something as if he were angry; but the oldest one took his hand and smiled, and then the tall one was quiet. The oldest one only said: 'Have mercy upon us,' and smiled."

While the fisherman was talking, the ship had drawn nearer to the island.

"There, now you can see it plainly, if your Lordship will please to look," said the tradesman, pointing with his hand.

The Bishop looked, and now he really saw a dark streak—which was the island. Having looked at it a while, he left the prow of the vessel, and going to the stern, asked the helmsman:

"What island is that?"

"That one," replied the man, "has no name. There are many such in this sea."

"Is it true that there are hermits who live there for the salvation of their souls?"

"So it is said, your Lordship, but I don't know if it's true. Fishermen say they have seen them; but of course they may only be spinning yarns."

"I should like to land on the island and see these men," said the Bishop. "How could I manage it?"

"The ship cannot get close to the island," replied the helmsman, "but you might be rowed there in a boat. You had better speak to the captain."

The captain was sent for and came.

"I should like to see these hermits," said the Bishop. "Could I not be rowed ashore?"

The captain tried to dissuade him.

"Of course it could be done," said he, "but we should lose much time. And if I might venture to say so to your Lordship, the old men are not worth your pains. I have heard say that they are foolish old fellows, who understand nothing, and never speak a word, any more than the fish in the sea."

"I wish to see them," said the Bishop, "and I will pay you for your trouble and loss of time. Please let me have a boat."

There was no help for it; so the order was given. The sailors trimmed the sails, the steersman put up the helm, and the ship's course was set for the island. A chair was placed at the prow for the Bishop, and he sat there, looking ahead. The passengers all collected at the prow, and gazed at the island. Those who had the sharpest eyes could presently make out the rocks on it, and then a mud hut was seen. At last one man saw the hermits themselves. The captain brought a telescope and, after looking through it, handed it to the Bishop.

"It's right enough. There are three men standing on the shore. There, a little to the right of that big rock."

The Bishop took the telescope, got it into position, and he saw the three men: a tall one, a shorter one, and one very small and bent, standing on the shore and holding each other by the hand.

The captain turned to the Bishop.

"The vessel can get no nearer in than this, your Lordship. If you wish to go ashore, we must ask you to go in the boat, while we anchor here."

The cable was quickly let out; the anchor cast, and the sails furled. There was a jerk, and the vessel shook. Then, a boat having been lowered, the oarsmen jumped in, and the Bishop descended the ladder and took his seat. The men pulled at their oars and the boat moved rapidly towards the island. When they came within a stone's throw, they saw three old men: a tall one with only a piece of matting tied round his waist: a shorter one in a tattered peasant coat, and a very old one bent with age and wearing an old cassock—all three standing hand in hand.

The oarsmen pulled in to the shore, and held on with the boathook while the Bishop got out.

The old men bowed to him, and he gave them his blessing, at which they bowed still lower. Then the Bishop began to speak to them.

"I have heard," he said, "that you, godly men, live here saving your own souls and praying to our Lord Christ for your fellow men. I, an unworthy servant of Christ, am called, by God's mercy, to keep and teach His flock. I wished to see you, servants of God, and to do what I can to teach you, also."

The old men looked at each other smiling, but remained silent.

"Tell me," said the Bishop, "what you are doing to save your souls, and how you serve God on this island."

The second hermit sighed, and looked at the oldest, the very ancient one. The latter smiled, and said:

"We do not know how to serve God. We only serve and support ourselves, servant of God."

"But how do you pray to God?" asked the Bishop.

"We pray in this way," replied the hermit. "Three are ye, three are we, have mercy upon us."

And when the old man said this, all three raised their eyes to heaven, and repeated:

"Three are ye, three are we, have mercy upon us!"

The Bishop smiled.

"You have evidently heard something about the Holy Trinity," said he. "But you do not pray aright. You have won my affection, godly men. I see you wish to please the Lord, but you do not know how to serve Him. That is not the way to pray; but listen to me, and I will teach you. I will teach you, not a way of my own, but the way in which God in the Holy Scriptures has commanded all men to pray to Him."

And the Bishop began explaining to the hermits how God had revealed Himself to men; telling them of God the Father, and God the Son, and God the Holy Ghost.

"God the Son came down on earth," said he, "to save men, and this is how He taught us all to pray. Listen, and repeat after me: 'Our Father.'"

And the first old man repeated after him, "Our Father," and the second said, "Our Father," and the third said, "Our Father."

"Which art in heaven," continued the Bishop.

The first hermit repeated, "Which art in heaven," but the second blundered over the words, and the tall hermit could not say them properly. His hair had grown over his mouth so that he could not speak plainly. The very old hermit, having no teeth, also mumbled indistinctly.

The Bishop repeated the words again, and the old men repeated them after him. The Bishop sat down on a stone, and the old men stood before him, watching his mouth, and repeating the words as he uttered them. And all day long the Bishop labored, saying a word twenty, thirty, a hundred times over, and the old men repeated it after him. They blundered, and he corrected them, and made them begin again.

The Bishop did not leave off till he had taught them the whole of the Lord's Prayer so that they could not only repeat it after him, but could say it by themselves. The middle one was the first to know it, and to repeat the whole of it alone. The Bishop made him say it again and again, and at last the others could say it too.

It was getting dark and the moon was appearing over

the water, before the Bishop rose to return to the vessel. When he took leave of the old men they all bowed down to the ground before him. He raised them, and kissed each of them, telling them to pray as he had taught them. Then he got into the boat and returned to the ship.

And as he sat in the boat and was rowed to the ship he could hear the three voices of the hermits loudly repeating the Lord's Prayer. As the boat drew near the vessel their voices could no longer be heard, but they could still be seen in the moonlight, standing as he had left them on the shore, the shortest in the middle, the tallest on the right, the middle one on the left. As soon as the Bishop had reached the vessel and got on board, the anchor was weighed and the sails unfurled. The wind filled them and the ship sailed away, and the Bishop took a seat in the stern and watched the island they had left. For a time he could still see the hermits, but presently they disappeared from sight, though the island was still visible. At last it too vanished, and only the sea was to be seen, rippling in the moonlight.

The pilgrims lay down to sleep, and all was quiet on deck. The Bishop did not wish to sleep, but sat alone at the stern, gazing at the sea where the island was no longer visible, and thinking of the good old men. He thought how pleased they had been to learn the Lord's Prayer; and he thanked God for having sent him to teach and help such godly men.

So the Bishop sat, thinking, and gazing at the sea where the island had disappeared. And the moonlight flickered before his eyes, sparkling, now here, now there, upon the waves. Suddenly he saw something white and shining, on the bright path which the moon cast across the sea. Was it a seagull, or the little gleaming sail of some small boat? The Bishop fixed his eyes on it, wondering.

"It must be a boat sailing after us," thought he, "but it is overtaking us very rapidly. It was far, far away a minute ago, but now it is much nearer. It cannot be a boat, for I can see no sail; but whatever it may be, it is following us and catching us up."

And he could not make out what it was. Not a boat, nor a bird, nor a fish! It was too large for a man, and besides a man could not be out there in the midst of the sea. The Bishop rose, and said to the helmsman:

"Look there, what is that, my friend? What is it?" the Bishop repeated, though he could now see plainly what it was—the three hermits running upon the water, all gleaming white, their grey beards shining, and approaching the ship as quickly as though it were not moving.

The steersman looked, and let go the helm in terror.

"Oh, Lord! The hermits are running after us on the water as though it were dry land!"

The passengers, hearing him, jumped up and crowded to the stern. They saw the hermits coming along hand in hand, and the two outer ones beckoning the ship to stop. All three were gliding along upon the water without moving their feet. Before the ship could be stopped, the hermits had reached it, and raising their heads, all three as with one voice, began to say:

"We have forgotten your teaching, servant of God. As long as we kept repeating it we remembered, but when we stopped saying it for a time, a word dropped out, and now it has all gone to pieces. We can remember nothing of it. Teach us again."

The Bishop crossed himself, and leaning over the ship's side, said:

"Your own prayer will reach the Lord, men of God. It is not for me to teach you. Pray for us sinners."

And the Bishop bowed low before the old men; and they turned and went back across the sea. And a light shone until daybreak on the spot where they were lost to sight.

The Doctor's Heroism

BY VILLIERS DE L'ISLE-ADAM

📖 📖 📖

To kill in order to cure!
—Official Motto of the Broussais Hospital

The extraordinary case of Doctor Hallidonhill is soon to be tried in London. The facts in the matter are these:

On the 20th of last May, the two great waiting rooms of the illustrious specialist were thronged with patients, holding their tickets in their hands.

At the entrance stood the cashier, wearing a long black frock coat; he took the indispensible fee of two guineas from each patient, tested the gold with a sharp tap of the hammer, and cried automatically, "All right."

In his glassed-in office, around which were ranged great tropical shrubs, each growing in a huge Japanese pot, sat the stiff little Doctor Hallidonhill. Beside him, at a little round table, his secretary kept writing out brief prescriptions. At the swinging doors, covered with red velvet studded with gold-headed nails, stood a giant valet whose duty it was to carry the feeble consumptives to the lobby whence they were lowered in a luxurious elevator as soon as the official signal, "Next!" had been given.

The patients entered with dim and glassy eyes, stripped to the waist, with their clothes thrown over their arms. As soon as they entered they received the application of the plessimeter and the tube on back and chest.

"Tick! tick! plaff! Breathe now! . . . Plaff . . . Good . . ."

Then followed a prescription dictated in a second or two; then the well-known "Next!"

Every morning for three years, between nine o'clock and noon, this procession of sufferers filed past.

On this particular day, May 20th, just at the stroke of nine, a sort of long skeleton, with wild, wandering eyes, cavernous cheeks, and nude torso that looked like a parchment-covered cage lifted occasionally by a racking cough—in short a being so wasted that it seemed impossible for him to live—came in with a blue-fox skin mantle thrown over his arm, and tried to keep himself from falling by catching at the long leaves of the shrubs.

"Tick, tick, plaff! Oh, the devil! Can't do anything for you!" grumbled Doctor Hallidonhill. "What do you think I am—a coroner? In less than a week you will spit up the last cell of this left lung—the right is already riddled like a sieve! Next!"

The valet was just about to carry out the client, when the eminent therapeutist suddenly slapped himself on the forehead, and brusquely asked, with a dubious smile:

"Are you rich?"

"I'm a millionaire—much more than a millionaire," sobbed the unhappy being whom Hallidonhill thus peremptorily had dismissed from the world of the living.

"Very well, then. Go at once to Victoria Station. Take the eleven-o'clock express for Dover! Then the steamer for Calais. Then take the train from Calais to Marseilles—secure a sleeping car with steam in it! And then to Nice. There try to live on watercress for six months—nothing but watercress—no bread, no fruit, no wine, nor meats of any kind. One teaspoonful of iodized rainwater every two days. And watercress, watercress, watercress—pounded and brayed in its own juice . . . that is your only chance—and still, let me tell you this: this supposed cure I know of only through hearsay; it is being dinned into my ears all the time; I don't believe in it the least bit. I suggest it only because yours seems to be a hopeless case, yet I think it is worse than absurd. Still, anything is possible. . . . Next!"

The consumptive Croesus was carefully deposited in the cushioned car of the elevator; and the regular procession commenced through the office.

Six months later, the 3rd of November, just at the stroke of nine o'clock, a sort of giant, with a terrifying yet jovial voice whose tones shook every pane of glass in the doctor's office and set all the leaves of all the tropical plants a-tremble, a great chubby-cheeked colossus, clothed in rich furs—burst like a human bombshell through the sorrowful ranks of Doctor Hallidonhill's clients, and rushed, without ticket, into the sanctum of the Prince of Science, who had just come to sit down before his desk. He seized him round the body, and, bathing the wan and worn cheeks of the doctor in tears, kissed him noisily again and again. Then he set him down in his green armchair in an almost suffocated state.

"Two million francs—if you want," shouted the giant. "Or three million. I owe my breath to you—the sun, resistless passions, life—everything. Ask me for anything—anything at all."

"Who is this madman? Put him out of here," feebly protested the doctor, after a moment's prostration.

"Oh, no you don't," growled the giant, with a glance at the valet that made him recoil as from a blow. "The fact is," he continued, "I understand now, that even you, you my savior, cannot recognize me. I am the watercress man, the hopeless skeleton, the helpless patient. Nice. Watercress, watercress, watercress! Well, I've done my six months of watercress diet—look at your work now! See here—listen to that!"

And he began to drum upon his chest with two huge fists solid enough to shatter the skull of an ox.

"What!" cried the doctor, leaping to his feet, "you are—my gracious, are you the dying man whom I . . ."

"Yes, yes, a thousand times yes!" yelled the giant. "I am the very man. The moment I landed yesterday evening I ordered a bronze statue of you; and I will secure you a monument in Westminster when you die."

Then dropping himself upon an immense sofa, whose springs creaked and groaned beneath his weight, he continued with a sigh of delight, and a beatific smile:

"Ah, what a good thing life is!"

The doctor said something in a whisper, and the secretary and the valet left the room. Once alone with his resuscitated patient, Hallidonhill, stiff, wan and glacial as ever, stared at the giant's face in silence for a minute or two. Then, suddenly:

"Allow me, if you please, to take that fly off your forehead!"

And rushing forward as he spoke, the doctor pulled a short "Bulldog revolver" from his pocket, and quick as a flash fired into the left temple of the visitor.

The giant fell with his skull shattered, scattering his grateful brains over the carpet of the room. His hands thrashed automatically for a few moments.

In ten cuts of the doctor's scissors, through cloak, garments, and underwear, the dead man's breast was laid bare. The grave surgeon cut open the chest lengthwise, with a single stroke of his broad scalpel.

When, about a quarter of an hour later, a policeman entered the office to request Doctor Hallidonhill to go with him, he found him sitting calmly at his bloody desk, examining with a strong magnifying glass, an enormous pair of lungs that lay spread out before him. The Genius of Science was trying to find, from the case of the deceased, some satisfactory explanation of the more than miraculous action of watercress.

"Constable," he said as he rose to his feet, "I felt it necessary to kill that man, as an immediate autopsy of his case might, I thought, reveal to me a secret of the gravest importance, regarding the now degenerating vitality of the human species. That is why I did not hesitate, let me confess, *to sacrifice my conscience to my duty.*"

Needless to add that the illustrious doctor was almost immediately released upon a nominal bond, his liberty being of far more importance than his detention. This strange case, as I have said, is shortly to come up before the British Assizes.

We believe that this sublime crime will not bring its hero to the gallows; for the English, as well as ourselves, are fully able to comprehend *that the exclusive love of the Humanity of the Future without any regard for the individual of the Present is, in our own time, the one sole motive that ought to justify the acquittal under any circumstances, of the magnanimous Extremists of Science.*

The Beggar-Woman of Locarno

BY HEINRICH VON KLEIST

     📖 📖 📖

At the foot of the Alps, near Locarno in Upper Italy, stood once a castle, the property of a marquis; of this castle, as one goes southward from the St. Gotthard, one sees now only the ashes and ruins. In one of its high and spacious rooms there once lay, on a bundle of straw which had been thrown down for her, an old, sick woman who had come begging to the door, and had been taken in and given shelter out of pity by the mistress of the castle. The Marquis, returning from the hunt, happened to enter this room, where he usually kept his guns, while the old woman lay there, and angrily ordered her to come out of the corner where the bundle of straw had been placed and to get behind the stove. In rising the old woman slipped on the polished floor and injured her spine severely; so much did she hurt herself that only with unspeakable agony could she manage to cross the room, as she was ordered, to sink moaning behind the stove and there to die.

Some years later the Marquis, owing to war and bad harvests, having lost most of his fortune, decided to sell his estates. One day a nobleman from Florence arrived at the castle which, on account of its beautiful situation, he wished to buy. The Marquis, who was very anxious to bring the business to a successful conclusion, gave instructions to his wife to prepare for their guest the above-mentioned room, which was now very beautifully furnished. But imagine their horror when, in the middle of the night, the nobleman, pale and distracted, entered their room solemnly assuring them that his room was haunted by something which

was not visible, but which sounded as if somebody lying on
straw in one corner of the room got up slowly and feebly but
with distinct steps crossed the room to lie down moaning
and groaning behind the stove.

The Marquis, horrified, he did not know himself why,
laughed with forced merriment at the nobleman and said he
would get up at once and keep him company for the rest of
the night in the haunted room, and when the morning came
the nobleman ordered his horses to be brought round, bade
farewell, and departed.

This incident, which created a great sensation, unhappily
for the Marquis frightened away several would-be buyers;
and when amongst his own servants strangely and mysteri-
ously the rumor arose that queer things happened in the
room at midnight, he determined to make a definite stand in
the matter and to investigate it himself the same night.
For that reason he had his bed moved into the room at
twilight, and watched there without sleeping until midnight.
To his horror, as the clock began to strike midnight, he became aware of the mysterious noise; it sounded as though
somebody rose from straw which rustled beneath him, crossed
the room, and sank down sighing and groaning behind the
stove. The next morning when he came downstairs his wife
inquired what he had discovered; he looked around with
nervous and troubled glances, and after fastening the door
assured her that the rumor was true. The Marquise was more
terrified than ever in her life, and begged him, before the
rumor grew, to make a cold-blooded trial in her company.
Accompanied by a loyal servant, they spent the following
night in the room and heard the same ghostly noises; and
only the pressing need to get rid of the castle at any cost
enabled the Marquise in the presence of the servant to
smother the terror which she felt it would be easy to discover. On the evening of the third day, as both of them,
with beating hearts, went up the stairs to the guest-room,
anxious to get at the cause of the disturbance, they found
that the watch-dog, who happened to have been let off his
chain, was standing at the door of the room; so that, without
giving a definite reason, both perhaps unconsciously wishing
to have another living thing in the room besides themselves,
they took him into the room with them. About eleven o'clock
the two of them, two candles on the table, the Marquise
fully dressed, the Marquis with dagger and pistol which he
had taken from the cupboard beside him, sat down one on

each bed; and while they entertained one another as well as they could by talking, the dog lay down, his head on his paws, in the middle of the room and slept. As the clock began to strike midnight the horrible sound began; somebody whom human eyes could not see raised himself on crutches in the corner of the room; the straw could be heard rustling beneath him; and at the first step the dog woke, pricked up his ears, rose from the ground growling and barking, and, just as though somebody were making straight for him, moved backwards towards the stove. At the sight the Marquise, her hair rising, rushed from the room, and while the Marquis, who had snatched up his dagger, called "Who is there?" and received no answer, she like a madwoman had ordered the coach to be got out, determined to drive away to the town immediately. But before she had packed a few things together and got them out of the door she noticed that all around her the castle was in flames. The Marquis, overcome with horror, and tired of life, had taken a candle and set fire to the wooden panelling on all sides. In vain she sent people in to rescue the wretched man; he had already found his end in the most horrible manner possible; and his white bones, gathered together by his people, still lie in that corner of the room from which he had once ordered the beggar-woman of Locarno to rise.

The Phoenix

BY SILVIA TOWNSEND WARNER

    🕮   🕮   🕮

Lord Strawberry, a nobleman, collected birds. He had the finest aviary in Europe, so large that eagles did not find it uncomfortable, so well laid out that both humming-birds and snow-buntings had a climate that suited them perfectly. But for many years the finest set of apartments remained empty, with just a label saying: "PHOENIX. *Habitat: Arabia.*"

Many authorities on bird life had assured Lord Strawberry that the phœnix is a fabulous bird, or that the breed was

long extinct. Lord Strawberry was unconvinced: his family
had always believed in phœnixes. At intervals he received
from his agents (together with statements of their expenses)
birds which they declared were the phœnix but which turned
out to be orioles, macaws, turkey buzzards dyed orange, etc.,
or stuffed cross-breeds, ingeniously assembled from various
plumages. Finally Lord Strawberry went himself to Arabia,
where, after some months, he found a phœnix, won its confidence, caught it, and brought it home in perfect condition.

It was a remarkably fine phœnix, with a charming character—affable to the other birds in the aviary and much attached
to Lord Strawberry. On its arrival in England it made a great
stir among ornithologists, journalists, poets, and milliners, and
was constantly visited. But it was not puffed by these attentions, and when it was no longer in the news, and the visits
fell off, it showed no pique or rancour. It ate well, and seemed
perfectly contented.

It costs a great deal of money to keep up an aviary. When
Lord Strawberry died he died penniless. The aviary came
on the market. In normal times the rarer birds, and certainly
the phœnix, would have been bid for by the trustees of
Europe's great zoological societies, or by private persons in
the U.S.A.; but as it happened Lord Strawberry died just
after a world war, when both money and bird-seed were hard
to come by (indeed the cost of bird-seed was one of the
things which had ruined Lord Strawberry). The London
Times urged in a leader that the phœnix be bought for the
London Zoo, saying that a nation of bird-lovers had a moral
right to own such a rarity; and a fund, called the Strawberry
Phœnix Fund, was opened. Students, naturalists, and school-
children contributed according to their means; but their
means were small, and there were no large donations. So
Lord Strawberry's executors (who had the death duties to
consider) closed with the higher offer of Mr. Tancred Poldero,
owner and proprietor of Poldero's Wizard Wonderworld.

For quite a while Mr. Poldero considered his phœnix a
bargain. It was a civil and obliging bird, and adapted itself
readily to its new surroundings. It did not cost much to feed,
it did not mind children; and though it had no tricks, Mr.
Poldero supposed it would soon pick up some. The publicity of the Strawberry Phœnix Fund was now most helpful.
Almost every contributor now saved up another half-crown
in order to see the phœnix. Others, who had not contributed

to the fund, even paid double to look at it on the five-shilling days.

But then business slackened. The phœnix was as handsome as ever, and as amiable; but, as Mr. Poldero said, it hadn't got Udge. Even at popular prices the phœnix was not really popular. It was too quiet, too classical. So people went instead to watch the antics of the baboons, or to admire the crocodile who had eaten the woman.

One day Mr. Poldero said to his manager, Mr. Ramkin:

"How long since any fool paid to look at the phœnix?"

"Matter of three weeks," replied Mr. Ramkin.

"Eating his head off," said Mr. Poldero. "Let alone the insurance. Seven shillings a week it costs me to insure that bird, and I might as well insure the Archbishop of Canterbury."

"The public don't like him. He's too quiet for them, that's the trouble. Won't mate nor nothing. And I've tried him with no end of pretty pollies, ospreys, and Cochin-Chinas, and the Lord knows what. But he won't look at them."

"Wonder if we could swap him for a livelier one," said Mr. Poldero.

"Impossible. There's only one of him at a time."

"Go on!"

"I mean it. Haven't you ever read what it says on the label?"

They went to the phœnix's cage. It flapped its wings politely, but they paid no attention. They read:

"PANSY. *Phœnix phœnixissima formosissima arabiana.* This rare and fabulous bird is UNIQUE. The World's Old Bachelor. Has no mate and doesn't want one. When old, sets fire to itself and emerges miraculously reborn. Specially imported from the East."

"I've got an idea," said Mr. Poldero. "How old do you suppose that bird is?"

"Looks in its prime to me," said Mr. Ramkin.

"Suppose," continued Mr. Poldero, "we could somehow get him alight? We'd advertise it beforehand, of course, work up interest. Then we'd have a new bird, and a bird with some romance about it, a bird with a life-story. We could sell a bird like that."

Mr. Ramkin nodded.

"I've read about it in a book," he said. "You've got to give them scented woods and what not, and they build a nest and

sit down on it and catch fire spontaneous. But they won't do
it till they're old. That's the snag."

"Leave that to me," said Mr. Poldero. "You get those
scented woods, and I'll do the ageing."

It was not easy to age the phœnix. Its allowance of food
was halved, and halved again, but though it grew thinner its
eyes were undimmed and its plumage glossy as ever. The
heating was turned off; but it puffed out its feathers against
the cold, and seemed none the worse. Other birds were put
into its cage, birds of a peevish and quarrelsome nature.
They pecked and chivied it; but the phœnix was so civil
and amiable that after a day or two they lost their animosity.
Then Mr. Poldero tried alley cats. These could not be won
by manners, but the phœnix darted above their heads and
flapped its golden wings in their faces, and daunted them.

Mr. Poldero turned to a book on Arabia, and read that
the climate was dry. "Aha!" said he. The phœnix was moved
to a small cage that had a sprinkler in the ceiling. Every
night the sprinkler was turned on. The phœnix began to
cough. Mr. Poldero had another good idea. Daily he stationed
himself in front of the cage to jeer at the bird and abuse it.

When spring was come, Mr. Poldero felt justified in beginning a publicity campaign about the ageing phœnix. The old
public favourite, he said, was nearing its end. Meanwhile he
tested the bird's reactions every few days by putting a few
tufts of foul-smelling straw and some strands of rusty barbed
wire into the cage, to see if it were interested in nesting yet.
One day the phœnix began turning over the straw. Mr.
Poldero signed a contract for the film rights. At last the hour
seemed ripe. It was a fine Saturday evening in May. For
some weeks the public interest in the ageing phœnix had
been working up, and the admission charge had risen to five
shillings. The enclosure was thronged. The lights and the
cameras were trained on the cage, and a loud-speaker pro-
claimed to the audience the rarity of what was about to
take place.

"The phœnix," said the loud-speaker, "is the aristocrat of
bird-life. Only the rarest and most expensive specimens of
oriental wood, drenched in exotic perfumes, will tempt him
to construct his strange love-nest."

Now a neat assortment of twigs and shavings, strongly
scented, was shoved into the cage.

"The phœnix," the loud-speaker continued, "is as capri-
cious as Cleopatra, as luxurious as la du Barry, as heady as a

strain of wild gypsy music. All the fantastic pomp and passion of the ancient East, its languorous magic, its subtle cruelties . . ."

"Lawks!" cried a woman in the crowd. "He's at it!"

A quiver stirred the dulled plumage. The phœnix turned its head from side to side. It descended, staggering, from its perch. Then wearily it began to pull about the twigs and shavings.

The cameras clicked, the lights blazed full on the cage. Rushing to the loud-speaker Mr. Poldero exclaimed:

"Ladies and gentlemen, this is the thrilling moment the world has breathlessly awaited. The legend of centuries is materializing before our modern eyes. The phœnix . . ."

The phœnix settled on its pyre and appeared to fall asleep.

The film director said:

"Well, if it doesn't evaluate more than this, mark it instructional."

At that moment the phœnix and the pyre burst into flames. The flames streamed upwards, leaped out on every side. In a minute or two everything was burned to ashes, and some thousand people, including Mr. Poldero, perished in the blaze.

Slipping Beauty

BY JEROME WEIDMAN

📖 📖 📖

He was a little man with an untidy beard and a prominent paunch that seemed startlingly out of place because of his emaciated appearance. Winter and summer he wore a battered cap, a leather vest, and a look of indifferent resignation, well seasoned with disgust, that gave no hint of the almost violent loquacity he could attain without even a moment of preparation. In a world of trucks and automobiles he drove a flat, open wagon behind a huge, drooping horse. And although his seltzer bottles came in neatly cased boxes of ten, he preferred to carry them by their spouts, five in each hand, like clusters of grapes, and take his chances on opening doors with shoulder shoves and kicks. His service was erratic, but adequate, and when, by his strange method of rotation, your name came up again to the top of his list, you could no more prevent him from making his delivery than you could convince him that his prices were exorbitant. He has come on Sundays and holidays, during parties and illness, and once, when a severe snowstorm had tied the city's traffic into a knot, he rang the bell after midnight and carried in his ten bottles of seltzer without a word of apology or explanation.

"Look here, Mr. Yavner," I said irritably, "you can't make deliveries as late as this. You can't come ringing bells at this—"

"I *can't?*" he asked and his eyes widened in a look of surprise that should have warned me.

I knew from experience that it wouldn't do any good. But when you're aroused after midnight from a sleep that you have attained with difficulty and need very much to admit a middle-aged man with his hands full of seltzer bottles that, considering the temperature and the season, you don't need at all, you are apt to forget the things that experience has taught you.

"I mean," I said stubbornly, "you'll just have to learn, Mr. Yavner, that when—"

"Learn?" he said, and the surprise was now in his voice. "I gotta *learn?*"

I could tell by the glint in his eyes that, from the standpoint of my much-needed sleep, I could have chosen a far more opportune time to bring order into Mr. Yavner's chaotic delivery system. I made a hasty, desperate attempt to head him off.

"Not that I *mean* anything, Mr. Yavner," I began conciliatingly.

But I was too late.

"In America," Mr. Yavner was saying, shaking his head like a tolerant master with a slow pupil, "in America there's no such thing as learn. In America *nobody* learns. In America they only *teach.*"

He set down his clusters of empty seltzer bottles and faced me squarely.

"A minute you could listen," he said bluntly. "In the old country, my father, he should rest in peace, he told me I shouldn't play with the knife, I'll cut myself; so if I didn't listen to him, and I played with the knife, so what happened, so I cut myself! He told me, maybe, I shouldn't go in street without the coat, I'll catch a cold; so I went in the street without a coat, so like he said, I caught a cold! But in America?"

He shrugged for emphasis and the habitual look of disgust on his face deepened a shade or two.

"Go try teach children something in America, go," he said. "Listen what *I* got. I got two daughters, the Above One should take care of them, they're beauties. Sucha two girls like I got, it could be—I don't care—even a *gov*ernor, he would *still* be happy to have sucha two daughters, the way mine look. The oldest, my Yettie, is already ten years she's bringing money in the house, steady, every week. She went to business school, she studied hard, she got a good job, she makes steady wage, she puts in the bank, she brings home; is good, no? Comes at night, she comes home, she eats, she helps maybe the mother a little, she reads a book, she listens a little the radio, she goes to sleep like a regular person. Is bad, maybe? In Europe, a girl like that, a girl like my Yettie, she knows to cook, to sew, to bake, to clean, she knows what a dollar is; a girl like that in Europe she could find a dozen— a dozen? A *hun*dred!—she could find a hundred fellahs they should kiss their fingers to the sky seven days a week if she would only *look* on them a little the right way! But in America? Go be smart in America!

"Then my other daughter, my Jennie, the baby. To look at?—a doll! But lazy?—the Above One should save us from sucha lazy ones. Came in the middle high school, all of a sudden she got tired! By her, it's no more school. By me, she says no school, so all right, is no school. But instead she should get a job like her older sister, Like Yettie, instead that, so a whole day she lays in bed with megazines and the tsigarettes, and the whole night she's running around with the boys, those little *rutzers*, they'n got even a *job*, not one of them in the whole bunch! A whole night long you don't see her, and comes by day, the whole day it's the megazines and the tsigarettes. A whole day long it's smook, smook, smook, smook, smok, smook smook! No job, no work, no nothing! Only like a king's daughter she lays in the bed the whole day, and you gotta bring her eat, yet, too, and the whole night she's running around the Above One alone knows where!

"But I'm a father; by me is the same thing my Yettie, she

works and brings money in house, or my Jennie, she lays
in bed there a whole day. So I talk to her. I tell her she
should make something from herself; she should get a job
and go sleep early like a regular person and get up early and
put money in bank and stop so much with the tsigarettes and
the boys! Like her sister Yettie, I tell her she should be. She
should learn to cook and sew and keep a house clean and
put a little money in bank, so'll come a nice fellah some day,
with a good steady job, he'll see what a nice girl she is, she
knows what's in a house to do, so he'll marry her, like some
day'll happen with her sister Yettie, I tell her, and she'll
make for him a good wife. So you think she listens to me?
Like I should talk to the wall!

"In Europe, a father talks to a child, so it happens she
should know the father was right. But in America?"

He leaned toward me and tapped my shoulder with his
finger as he spoke.

"In America is different," he said. "One day, she's laying
there in the bed with the megazines and the tsigarettes
and the smook; all of a sudden the blankets they catch on
fire, in a minute more it's the whole bed, then the curtains,
and in one, two, three is there the fire engines and the policemen and the firemen and there's excitement!—Above One in
heaven, don't ask! And from the firemen there comes running in one, a nice young fellah, and he picks her up and
carries her down from house, and before you can turn yourself around he falls in love with her and two weeks later,
they're in a big hurry, they run get married! And he's got
yet such a steady job by the city, there, a whole year regular
he gets wages."

Mr. Yavner paused, and the disgust in his face gave way
to a look of meditative resignation.

"How you think it makes a father feel, he sees his oldest
daughter sitting and sitting and the youngest, she gets married? Is nice, maybe? So my Yettie, she's older, she went
to business school, she's got a job, she knows to cook, and to
sew, and to everything, so she's still sitting, waiting! And my
Jennie, she's younger, from schools she got right away tired,
a job she never had, a whole day she laid in bed smoking
tsigarettes, and a whole nights she ran around; so my Jennie,
she's the one she's got now a fine husband with a steady job!"

He reached down for his clusters of bottles, swung the
door open with his foot, and held it wide for a moment with
his shoulder as he looked in at me.

"That's your America," he said with the faintest hint of
derision in his voice. "That's where you want I should
learn things," he said, as he stepped away from the door,
and it shut behind him with a crash that echoed throughout the midnight stillness of the house.

The Hour of Letdown

BY E. B. WHITE

When the man came in, carrying the machine, most of us
looked up from our drinks, because we had never seen anything like it before. The man set the thing down on top
of the bar near the beerpulls. It took up an ungodly amount
of room and you could see the bartender didn't like it any
too well, having this big, ugly-looking gadget parked right
there.

"Two rye-and-water," the man said.

The bartender went on puddling an Old-Fashioned that
he was working on, but he was obviously turning over the
request in his mind.

"You want a double?" he asked, after a bit.

"No," said the man. "Two rye-and-water, please." He
stared straight at the bartender, not exactly unfriendly but
on the other hand not affirmatively friendly.

Many years of catering to the kind of people that come
into saloons had provided the bartender with an adjustable
mind. Nevertheless, he did not adjust readily to this fellow,
and he did not like the machine—that was sure. He picked
up a live cigarette that was idling on the edge of the cash
register, took a drag out of it, and returned it thoughtfully.
Then he poured two shots of rye whiskey, drew two glasses
of water, and shoved the drinks in front of the man. People
were watching. When something a little out of the ordinary
takes place at a bar, the sense of it spreads quickly all along
the line and pulls the customers together.

The man gave no sign of being the center of attraction.
He laid a five-dollar bill down on the bar. Then he drank one

of the ryes and chased it with water. He picked up the other rye, opened a small vent in the machine (it was like an oil cup) and poured the whiskey in, and then poured the water in.

The bartender watched grimly. "Not funny," he said in an even voice. "And furthermore, your companion takes up too much room. Whyn't you put it over on that bench by the door, make more room here."

"There's plenty of room for everyone here," replied the man.

"I ain't amused," said the bartender. "Put the goddam thing over near the door like I say. Nobody will touch it."

The man smiled. "You should have seen it this afternoon," he said. "It was magnificent. Today was the third day of the tournament. Imagine it—three days of continuous brainwork. And against the top players of the country, too. Early in the game it gained an advantage; then for two hours it exploited the advantage brilliantly, ending with the opponent's king backed in a corner. The sudden capture of a knight, the neutralization of a bishop, and it was all over. You know how much money it won, all told, in three days of playing chess?"

"How much?" asked the bartender.

"Five thousand dollars," said the man. "Now it wants to let down, wants to get a little drunk."

The bartender ran his towel vaguely over some wet spots. "Take it somewheres else and get it drunk there!" he said firmly. "I got enough troubles."

The man shook his head and smiled. "No, we like it here." He pointed at the empty glasses. "Do this again, will you, please?"

The bartender slowly shook his head. He seemed dazed but dogged. "You stow the thing away," he ordered. "I'm not ladling out whiskey for jokestersmiths."

" 'Jokesmiths,' " said the machine. "The word is 'jokesmiths.' "

A few feet down the bar, a customer who was on his third highball seemed ready to participate in this conversation to which we had all been listening so attentively. He was a middle-aged man. His necktie was pulled down away from his collar, and he had eased the collar by unbuttoning it. He had pretty nearly finished his third drink, and the alcohol tended to make him throw his support in with the underprivileged and the thirsty.

"If the machine wants another drink, give it another drink," he said to the bartender. "Let's not have haggling."

The fellow with the machine turned to his new-found friend and gravely raised his hand to his temple, giving him a salute of gratitude and fellowship. He addressed his next remark to him, as though deliberately snubbing the bartender.

"You know how it is when you're all fagged out mentally, how you want a drink?"

"Certainly do," replied the friend. "Most natural thing in the world."

There was a stir all along the bar, some seeming to side with the bartender, others with the machine group. A tall, gloomy man standing next to me spoke up.

"Another whiskey sour, Bill," he said. "And go easy on the lemon juice."

"Picric acid," said the machine, sullenly. "They don't use lemon juice in these places."

"That does it!" said the bartender, smacking his hand on the bar. "Will you put that thing away or else beat it out of here. I ain't in the mood, I tell you. I got this saloon to run and I don't want lip from a mechanical brain or whatever the hell you've got there."

The man ignored this ultimatum. He addressed his friend, whose glass was now empty.

"It's not just that it's all tuckered out after three days of chess," he said amiably. "You know another reason it wants a drink?"

"No," said the friend. "Why?"

"It cheated," said the man.

At this remark, the machine chuckled. One of its arms dipped slightly, and a light glowed in a dial.

The friend frowned. He looked as though his dignity had been hurt. as though his trust had been misplaced. "Nobody can cheat at chess" he said. " 'Simpossible. In chess, everything is open and above the board. The nature of the game of chess is such that cheating is impossible."

"That's what I used to think, too," said the man. "But there *is* a way."

"Well, it doesn't surprise me any," put in the bartender. "The first time I laid my eyes on that crummy thing I spotted it for a crook."

"Two rye-and-water," said the man.

"You can't have the whiskey," said the bartender. He

glared at the mechanical brain. "How do I know it ain't drunk already?"

"That's simple. Ask it something," said the man.

The customers shifted and stared into the mirror. We were in this thing now, up to our necks. We waited. It was the bartender's move.

"Ask it what? Such as?" said the bartender.

"Makes no difference. Pick a couple big figures, ask it to multiply them together. You couldn't multiply big figures together if you were drunk, could you?"

The machine shook slightly, as though making internal preparations.

"Ten thousand eight hundred and sixty-two, multiply it by ninety-nine," said the bartender viciously. We could tell that he was throwing in the two nines to make it hard.

The machine flickered. One of its tubes spat, and a hand changed position, jerkily.

"One million seventy-five thousand three hundred and thirty-eight," said the machine.

Not a glass was raised all along the bar. People just stared gloomily into the mirror; some of us studied our own faces, others took carom shots at the man and the machine.

Finally, a youngish, mathematically minded customer got out a piece of paper and a pencil and went into retirement. "It works out," he reported, after some minutes of calculating. "You can't say the machine is drunk!"

Everyone now glared at the bartender. Reluctantly he poured two shots of rye, drew two glasses of water. The man drank his drink. Then he fed the machine its drink. The machine's light grew fainter. One of its cranky little arms wilted.

For a while the saloon simmered along like a ship at sea in calm weather. Every one of us seemed to be trying to digest the situation, with the help of liquor. Quite a few glasses were refilled. Most of us sought help in the mirror —the court of last appeal.

The fellow with the unbuttoned collar settled his score. He walked stiffly over and stood between the man and the machine. He put one arm around the man, the other around the machine. "Let's get out of here and go to a good place." he said.

The machine glowed slightly. It seemed to be a little drunk now.

"All right," said the man. "That suits me fine. I've got my car outside."

He settled for the drinks and put down a tip. Quietly and a trifle uncertainly he tucked the machine under his arm, and he and his companion of the night walked to the door and out into the street.

The bartender stared fixedly, then resumed his light housekeeping. "So he's got his car outside," he said, with heavy sarcasm. "Now isn't that nice!"

A customer at the end of the bar near the door left his drink, stepped to the window, parted the curtains, and looked out. He watched for a moment, then returned to his place and addressed the bartender. "It's even nicer than you think," he said. "It's a Cadillac. And which one of the three of them d'ya think is doing the driving?"

Moonlight Sonata

BY ALEXANDER WOOLLCOTT

If this report were to be published in its own England, I would have to cross my fingers in a little foreword explaining that all the characters were fictitious—which stern requirement of the British libel law would embarrass me slightly because none of the characters is fictitious, and the story—told to Katharine Cornell by Clemence Dane and by Katharine Cornell told to me—chronicles what, to the best of my knowledge and belief, actually befell a young English physician whom I shall call Alvan Barach, because that does not happen to be his name. It is an account of a hitherto unreported adventure he had two years ago when he went down into Kent to visit an old friend—let us call *him* Ellery Cazalet—who spent most of his days on the links and most of his nights wondering how he would ever pay the death duties on the collapsing family manor-house to which he had indignantly fallen heir.

This house was a shabby little cousin to Compton Wynyates, with roof-tiles of Tudor red making it cozy in the noon-day sun, and a hoarse bell which, from the clock tower, had been contemptuously scattering the hours like coins ever since Henry VIII was a rosy stripling. Within, Cazalet could afford only a doddering couple to fend for him, and the once sumptuous gardens did much as they pleased under the care of a single gardener. I think I must risk giving the gard-ener's real name, for none I could invent would have so appropriate a flavor. It was John Scripture, and he was as-sisted, from time to time, by an aged and lunatic father, who, in his lucid intervals, would be let out from his captivity under the eaves of the lodge to putter amid the lewd topiar-ian extravagance of the hedges.

The doctor was to come down when he could, with a prom-ise of some good golf, long nights of exquisite silence, and a ghost or two thrown in if his fancy ran that way. It was characteristic of his rather ponderous humor that, in writing to fix a day, he addressed Cazalet at "The Creeps, Seven-oaks, Kent." When he arrived, it was to find his host away from home and not due back until all hours. Barach was to dine alone with a reproachful setter for a companion, and not wait up. His bedroom on the ground floor was beauti-fully paneled from footboard to ceiling, but some misguided housekeeper under the fourth George had fallen upon the lovely woodwork with a can of black varnish. The dowry brought by a Cazalet bride of the mauve decade had been invested in a few vintage bathrooms, and one of these had replaced a prayer closet that once opened into this bedroom. There was only a candle to read by, but the light of a full moon came waveringly through the wind-stirred vines that half curtained the mullioned windows.

In this museum. Barach dropped off to sleep. He did not know how long he had slept when he found himself awake again, and conscious that something was astir in the room. It took him a moment to place the movement, but at last, in a patch of moonlight. he made out a hunched figure that seemed to be sitting with bent, engrossed head in the chair by the door. It was the hand, or rather the whole arm, that was moving tracing a recurrent if irregular course in the air. At first the gesture was teasingly half-familiar, and then Barach recognized it as the one a woman makes when em-broidering. There would be a hesitation as if the needle were being thrust through some taut, resistant material, and then, each time, the long, swift, sure pull of the thread.

To the startled guest, this seemed the least menacing activity he had ever heard ascribed to a ghost, but just the same he had only one idea, and that was to get out of that room with all possible dispatch. His mind made a hasty reconnaissance. The door into the hall was out of the question, for madness lay that way. At least he would have to pass right by that weaving arm. Nor did he relish a blind plunge into the thorny shrubbery beneath his window, and a barefoot scamper across the frosty turf. Of course, there was the bathroom, but that was small comfort if he could not get out of it by another door. In a spasm of concentration, he remembered that he *had* seen another door. Just at the moment of this realization, he heard the comfortingly actual sound of a car coming up the drive, and guessed that it was his host returning. In one magnificent movement, he leaped to the floor, bounded into the bathroom, and bolted its door behind him. The floor of the room beyond was quilted with moonlight. Wading through that, he arrived breathless, but unmolested, in the corridor. Further along he could see the lamp left burning in the entrance hall and hear the clatter of his host closing the front door.

As Barach came hurrying out of the darkness to greet him, Cazalet boomed his delight at such affability, and famished by his long, cold ride, proposed an immediate raid on the larder. The doctor, already sheepish at his recent panic, said nothing about it, and was all for food at once. With lighted candles held high, the foraging party descended on the offices, and mine host was descanting on the merits of cold roast beef, Cheddar cheese, and milk as a light midnight snack, when he stumbled over a bundle on the floor. With a cheerful curse at the old goody of the kitchen who was always leaving something about, he bent to see what it was this time, and let out a whistle of surprise. Then, by two candles held low, he and the doctor saw something they will not forget while they live. It was the body of the cook. Just the body. The head was gone. On the floor alongside lay a bloody cleaver.

"Old Scripture, by God!" Cazalet cried out, and in a flash, Barach guessed. Still clutching a candle in one hand, he dragged his companion back through the interminable house to the room from which he had fled, motioning him to be silent, tiptoeing the final steps. That precaution was wasted, for a regiment could not have disturbed the rapt contentment of the ceremony still in progress within. The old lunatic had not left his seat by the door. Between his knees he still held the head of the woman he had killed. Scrupulously, happily, crooning at his work, he was plucking out the gray hairs one by one.

God

BY EUGENE IVANOVICH ZAMIATIN

An ancient realm it was—and a rich, famed for the fertility of its womenfolk and the valour of its men. As for the whereabouts of this realm—why it was at the back of the stove in Mizumin the postman's place, and there was a certain cockroach there, named Senka, the foremost troublemaker and daredevil in all that cockroach realm. There wasn't a female woman he'd let pass by, he didn't give one good hoot in hell for his elders, and as for God, he just didn't believe in him: "There ain't none," he'd say.

"What do you mean, there ain't none, damn your shameless eyes? You just crawl out when it's light, and open your peepers. But no, you got to come out with things like 'there ain't none!'"

"Well, why not. I'll crawl out." Senka made out he wasn't afraid. And one day he did crawl out, crawled right out, and let out a gasp. There was a God, and that's a fact. There He was—right there: God, awesome, unbearably enormous, in a shirt of rose-coloured calico.

And the god, Mizumin the postman, was knitting away at a stocking: he liked keeping himself busy with that handicraft in his spare time. When Mizumin laid his eyes on Senka, he was glad to see him:

"A-ah, cockroach that I love, my friend from behind the stove—where you been keeping yourself? Greetings!"

Right then Mizumin felt like unburdening his heart, but there wasn't anybody around just at that time, except this Senka.

"Well, Senka, I'm getting married, brother. Get this through your head, you cockroach soul: she's a girl from a good family, and she's got a dowry of a hundred and fifty rubles! Oh, but it's a fine life you and me will be leading! Won't we now, Senka? Eh?"

But Senka, now, he was so moved his eyes were popping out of his head; he'd forgotten every word he ever knew.

Mizumin's wedding was set for Low Sunday, and his high-born bride had given him the strictest orders to buy himself new rubbers before the wedding, without fail. It was a downright shame, really: for years past all counting Mizumin had been wearing his father's leather canal-boats, size 14. And no sooner did Mizumin show himself in the street than all the little boys got after him:

"Hey, hey! Canal-boats! Canal-boats! Catch him! Canal-boats!"

So Mizimun finished knitting those stockings and took himself to the Trubnaya, to the flea-market, to sell them and buy himself rubbers. But what should Mizumin come across but some caged goldfinches—not mere goldfinches, mind you, but something that made you forget everything in the world, just looking at them.

"Maybe I'd better get a couple of them goldfinches with the money? Those old rubbers, now—there's a lot of wear in them yet!"

So he bought a cage with two birds, and took the whole business to his bride as a present.

"There, I knitted a pair of stockings, and sold them, and bought these young goldfinches for you. Don't look down on them—I give them to you with all my heart."

"What! Stockings? And still wearing those canal-boats? Oh, no! No, you don't! I'm at the end of my patience. The very idea—being married to a hosemaker! No, no-o—and let's have no further discussions!"

She drove Mizumin out of her sight. Mizumin got stewed to the gills in a ginmill, and came home drunk as could be, holding on to the walls.

And on one of the walls, waiting for the coming of his God, was Senka the cockroach—waiting to hear, with a touched heart (as he did every evening), what God would say.

Mizumin the postman, gulping bitter tears, was groping with his hand over the wall. And somehow, without meaning to do it, he brushed a finger over Senka; Senka, he flew head over heels into Tartarus the bottomless pit.

When he came to, he was sprawled out on his back. The

sides were smooth, slippery; the abyss was frightful. Somewhere way, way up he could barely make out the ceiling.

And Senka raised his voice in prayer to his God:

"Work Thy will, help me! Have mercy upon me!"

But no; the abyss was such that even God, most likely,
couldn't reach it; Senka would rot where he was.

Mizumin the postman gulped down, noisily, many bitter
tears; with the hem of his rose-coloured shirt he wiped his
nose.

"Senka, little Senka—you're the only one left me now.
. . . And where are you? Oh, wherever did I sent you
to, my own, my dear one?"

Mizumin found Senka at last in one of his canal-boats.
With his finger he dug Senka out of the abyss, out of his
size 14 canal-boat, and he placed him on a wall: "Creep on!"

But Senka couldn't even creep, being completely out of
his senses. How unbearably great was God, how merciful,
how mighty!

As for Mizumin the postman, Senka's God Himself, he
just kept on sniffling and wiping his nose with the tail of
his rose-coloured shirt.

How Grandpa Came into the Money

BY ELSE ZANTNEV

▯ ▯ ▯

He was a sweet soul, my grandfather, but when the brains
were passed out he must have been absent. I still marvel
how Grandmother could raise a family on his earnings.

We all lived in one little house and we were a scrawny lot.
Nobody ever had to coax any of us children to eat. In fact,
after having had lunch at my mother's, I would go upstairs
to Grandmother and have another one. And then I would
visit Aunt Bertha, who lived a few doors away, and eat some
more.

What a ripe apple tasted like I found out only when I was
well over fifteen and apprenticed to a shopkeeper in the
city. Apples did not ripen in our village—they never had a

chance. They were so sour they would have pulled the holes in our stockings together. But no apples ever tasted as good again as those little green ones!

One time in my entire childhood I felt good and full: Aunt Bertha had forgotten to lock the larder and I detected, disappeared with, and devoured twenty-two doughnuts. The rest of the family never forgot nor forgave me. Years later when I would arrive at family gatherings someone would always shout, "Watch the doughnuts!"

Perhaps you can imagine what it meant when, one fine day, fortune smiled on Grandfather. He got himself in a trainwreck!

Now, if something like that happened to you (and you survived) you had it made. The railroad would pay! So all of the lucky passengers knew exactly what to do: they commenced to groan piteously and writhe upon the ground while waiting for the doctors and stretcher bearers to arrive.

All but Grandfather!

He had a better appetite than the rest of us combined. Never in his life had he missed a meal and he was not going to start now. No sir! Not for a puny trainwreck. So he cut himself a stout walking stick and set out for home—a three-hour walk.

In the meantime, the news of the wreck had already reached the village and the telegram had said, "No fatalities."

I cannot describe the many looks that passed across my grandmother's face when she saw her husband come striding in the door, covered with dust, a bit tired from his long walk, but sound of limb and smiling broadly for he was just in time for dinner. First came relief at seeing her man unharmed. Then the relief mingled with and finally was replaced by fury.

Grandfather had passed up his one and only golden opportunity!

So she turned into a kind of tornado. Before he knew what was happening, he found himself minus his pants and in bed. His plaintive protests did him no good. Grandma slapped a wet towel on his head while Mother went to search for the only medicine we had in the house—castor oil!

Grandfather cried out in horror and tried to disappear under the blanket, but Mother clamped his nose shut and dosed him anyway. Poor man! The only thing he really needed was his dinner. But what could he or anyone else do once his wife and daughter had made up their minds.

Having accomplished this much, one of the children was dispatched to get hold of the doctor. He came, gave Grandpa a thorough examination, and was just about to congratulate him on his excellent state of health when my mother went into action.

She planted herself firmly in front of the doctor, drew herself up to her full height of four feet, ten inches, and told him in no uncertain terms, that Grandpa had suffered a severe shock and concussion of whatever brains he had. How else to explain the fact that he walked away from this chance of a lifetime! Did the doctor have another explanation? Ha?

The doctor took one look at her grimly determined face. He had dealt with her before and he knew when he was licked. He resigned himself, accepted my mother's diagnosis, and left.

And then came the time of waiting. The two women did all they could to keep Grandpa in bed and coached him carefully on what to say and what not to say when the railroad people came. Grandpa nodded wisely and promised to cooperate.

But did you ever try to keep an eel in bed? He gave them the slip as often as not. And when, in desperation, they hid his pants, he bribed one of us children to find them for him and got out of bed anyway.

And out of bed he was when we heard the long awaited commotion outside of the house. Peeking through the window we saw the railroad investigators, with the entire village gathered respectfully behind them, waiting to learn the outcome.

Pants, boots and all, Grandpa was stuffed into bed and the covers were pulled up to his chin. The shades were lowered, the bottle of castor oil was placed prominently by his bedside, and the investigators were ushered in.

From the first moment it was clear that Grandpa had forgotten all of the careful coaching. He beamed welcome at the distinguished visitors and complimented them on their good looks. He then went on to talk of the weather and then of the crops. When the railroad doctor finally managed to ask him what injuries he had sustained my mother signalled frantically by pointing to her head.

"Well," said grandfather with an angelic smile, "There's really nothing at all wrong with me that 100,000 gulden couldn't cure."

Mother promptly fainted. Grandma shrieked and ran from the room. And the claims adjustors doubled up with laughter.

After they had recovered, and revived poor Mama, they awarded Grandpa 5,000 gulden—making him the richest man in the village!

But to his dying day, he could never understand why they had given him the money.

The Three Veterans

BY LEANE ZUGSMITH

📖 📖 📖

As far back as the memory of Miss Riordan, which was three months, for she had been the attending nurse in the clinic for that long, the three old women regularly appeared twice a week. Only when they managed to sit together on the bench, with their old, high-veined legs stiff ahead of them, was she able to distinguish one from the other. Otherwise, Mrs. Farrell could be mistaken for Mrs. Gaffney, or either of the two for Mrs. Betz. Each showed gaps in her front teeth when she broke into her cackle, each had yellow-gray hair wisping from beneath a moldy hat; each wore stained, shapeless outer garments; and each had the same kind of bad leg.

Outside the dispensary, the three old women did not lay eyes on one another from one clinic day to the next, but inside they formed a sisterhood. Together, they would question newcomers and advise them on their ills, but once The Doctor was in the room, they would remain respectfully silent unless he made one of his lame jokes or scolded them. Promptly then, they would cackle. Anything The Doctor said was a signal for their ingratiating brays of laughter.

The first three to enter Room 4 this morning, they sat together on the long bench, eyes alert on the door as Miss Riordan called to the patients outside, "Number 6 and 7 for Room 4."

When the pale young woman with the fretful infant came in, relinquishing her numbered green ticket for Room

4, and sat opposite them, Mrs. Betz crooked her soiled finger. "Gutsie-goo," she said to the baby. Then she addressed the mother. "Something wrong with it?" Mrs. Farrell and Mrs. Gaffney turned professional eyes on the child.

"She had an infected arm, and now she don't eat." The young woman jogged the whimpering infant with her knee.

"Only your first?" asked Mrs. Farrell, who had borne nine.

"Yes," said the young mother.

The three old women smiled knowingly at one another. Mrs. Gaffney flapped her hand down from the wrist. "Sure, you're always worrying your poor head off about the first. Isn't it the truth?" Mrs. Farrell and Mrs. Betz vigorously nodded their heads, and their moldy hats gave off a little puff of dust.

"When it don't eat, you want to pull ten hairs from the right side of your head, and braid them and twist them around its little toe," said Mrs. Betz.

"Give it honey and tea," said Mrs. Gaffney.

"It's always that way with the first of them," said Mrs. Farrell. "You'll be wanting to—"

"Who's in attendance around here? You or me?" It was The Doctor, his voice harsh, his face red.

Mrs. Gaffney and Mrs. Betz nudged Mrs. Farrell, who left her mouth open to giggle quickly with them.

"Just let me know when you want to take my job," he said, and stalked to the end of the room to visit the patients behind the screens.

The old women held their forefingers against their simpering lips. Now they would not even look at the ailing baby.

"Anyone else for Room 4?" called Miss Riordan, out in the corridor.

The eyes of the three old women frogged at the sight of the beautiful peroxide-blonde lady in a beautiful imitation-fur jacket. Everything about her seemed sweet and ripe as she handed over her green ticket and sat on the bench beside them. The three old women watched her pull down her silk stocking; she had only a little two-inch scratch on her fine, shapely leg and her skin was whiter than milk.

But Mrs. Gaffney could no longer stare at her, for now The Doctor was pressing his finger into her highest vein and she must keep her eyes submissive on his face. He whispered to the nurse and then, without looking into Mrs. Gaffney's submissive eyes, said, "You better quit staying out dancing all night, or that'll never get right."

The three old women cackled with delight. Mrs. Betz kept a meek smile on her face as The Doctor examined her leg. When he came to Mrs. Farrell, he wrinkled up his nose. "Suppose you wash your leg off yourself," he said. "Give the poor nurse a break. Just rub it up and down with *soap* and *water*. Ever heard of it?"

This time the brays of laughter from the three old women were wilder than ever. Seeing him turn to the baby, all three of the old women tried to retard Miss Riordan's manipulations of their legs so that they could remain to watch The Doctor and the beautiful peroxide-blonde lady in the beautiful imitation-fur jacket. Mrs. Gaffney elbowed Mrs. Betz as The Doctor stood before the lady.

"What's wrong with you?" he said.

She smiled invitingly up at him. "I tripped on the stairs —my landlord doesn't know enough to have safe stairs in his house—and it's been bothering me." She pointed a tapering white finger at the abrasion.

He looked at it carefully before whispering his orders to Miss Riordan. Mrs. Gaffney started to edge out of her seat, disappointed, when the beautiful lady said, "Is it serious, Doctor?"

"It hurt you, didn't it?" he said, sarcastically.

At the familiar tone, Mrs. Gaffney, Mrs. Farrell, and Mrs. Betz chuckled, but softly for fear of being sent away, now that their legs were wrapped.

"Yes," said the beautiful lady, "but I want to know what to tell my lawyer, in case—"

"Oh, your lawyer?" said The Doctor, witheringly. "I see. You want to bring suit. Well, Madam, you can tell your lawyer that anyone who's so careless as to trip on the stairs deserves more than the little scratch you have there."

The three old women lowered their heads, their soiled fingers at their mouths to curb the explosions of laughter. The beautiful lady's eyes flashed. "I don't see why you have to use that tone of voice!" she exclaimed with resentment. "Just because it's free is no reason why we can't be treated like human beings!"

The three old women waited breathlessly, their lips ready to stretch at his sally. Their waiting ears were met by silence. Their rheumy eyes saw The Doctor turn his back and regard the table of ointments and bandages. As he stood there, whistling softly, the three old women found themselves staring at one another, and not one was smiling. With gray, tired faces, they rose together. At the door, their way was blocked by the man in white whom they called The Specialist Doctor.

"Just the old friends I may want!" he cried in his ringing tones. He turned to The Doctor. "Are they varicose?"

"All three, Chief," said The Doctor.

"Are they interesting? Good enough for my Friday-night lecture?"

"I'll show you their charts," said The Doctor.

The Specialist Doctor rubbed his hands. "How would you girls like to dance in my chorus Friday night?" he boomed cheerfully.

The three old women looked at one another. The beautiful peroxide-blonde lady clack-clacked her high heels across the floor.

"No," said Mrs. Betz, heavily.

"No," said Mrs. Farrell, without looking up.

"No," said Mrs. Gaffney, plucking at the edge of her stained wrap. "Just because it's free don't mean we aren't human beings."

Then, with lowered heads and sombre faces, the three old women trudged out.

Kong at the Seaside

BY ARNOLD ZWEIG

Kong got his first glimpse of the sea as he ran on the beach, which stretched like a white arc along the edge of the cove. He barked vociferously with extravagant enthusiasm. Again and again, the bluish-white spray came dashing up at him and he was forbidden to hurl himself into it! A tall order for an Airedale terrier with a wiry brown coat and shaggy forelegs. However, Willie, his young god, would not permit it; but at any rate he could race at top speed across the firm sand, which was still damp from the ebbing waters, Willie following with lusty shouts. Engineer Groll, strolling after, noticed that the dog and his tanned, light-haired, eight-year-old master were attracting considerable attention among the beach-chairs and gaily striped bathing-houses. At the end of the row, where the sky was pale and dipped into the infinite—whereas it was vividly blue overhead and shed relaxation, happiness, and vigor on all these city people and their games in the sand—some controversy seemed to be in progress. Willie was standing there, slim and defiant, holding his dog by the collar. Groll hurried over. People in bathing suits looked pretty much alike, social castes and classes intermingled. Heads showed more character and expression, though the bodies which supported them were still flabby and colorless, unaccustomed to exposure and pale after a long winter's imprisonment within the darkness of heavy clothing. A stoutish man was sitting in the shade of a striped orange tent stretched over a blue framework; he was bending slightly forward, holding a cigar.

"Is that your dog?" he asked quietly.

A little miss, about ten years old, was with him; she was biting her underlip, and a look of hatred for the boy and the dog flashed between her tear-filled narrow lids.

"No," said Groll with his pleasant voice, which seemed to rumble deep down in his chest, "The dog belongs to the boy, who, to be sure, is mine."

"You know dogs aren't allowed off the leash," the quiet voice continued. "He frightened my daughter a bit, has trampled her canals, and is standing on her spade."

"Pull him back, Willie," laughed Groll. "You're quite right, sir, but the dog broke away and, after all, nothing serious has happened."

Willie pushed Kong aside, picked up the spade and, bowing slightly, held it out to the group. Its third member was a slender, remarkable pretty young lady, sitting in the rear of the tent; Groll decided she was too young to be the mother of the girl and too attractive to be her governess. Well gotten up, he reflected; she looks like Irish with those auburn eyebrows.

No one took the spade from the boy, and Willie, with a frown, stuck the toy into the sand in front of the girl.

"I think that squares it, especially on such a beautiful day," Groll smiled and lay down. His legs behind him, his elbows on the sand, and his face resting on his hands, he looked over the hostile three. Willie has behaved nicely and politely; how well he looks with his Kong. The dog, evidently not as ready to make peace, growled softly, his fur bristling at the neck; then he sat down.

"I want to shoot his dog, Father," the girl suddenly remarked in a determined voice; "he frightened me so." Groll noticed a gold bracelet of antique workmanship about her wrist—three strands of pale green-gold braided into the semblance of a snake. These people need a lesson. I shall give it to them.

Groll nodded reassuringly at his boy, who was indignantly drawing his dog closer to him. Those grown-ups seemed to know that the girl had the upper hand of them, or, as Groll told himself, had the right to give orders. So he quietly waited for the sequel of this charming conversation; after all, he was still there to reprimand the brat if the gentleman with the fine cigar lacked the courage to do so because the sweet darling was not accustomed to proper discipline.

"No one is going to shoot my dog," threatened Willie, clenching his fists; but, without deigning to look at him, the girl continued:

"Buy him from the people, Father; here is my checkbook." She actually took the thin booklet and a fountain-pen with a gold clasp from a zipper-bag inside the tent.

"If you won't buy him for me, I'll throw a soup-plate right off the table at dinner; you know I will, Father." She spoke almost in a whisper and was as white as chalk under her tan; her blue eyes, over which the sea had cast a greenish glint, flashed threateningly.

The gentleman said: "Ten pounds for the dog."

"The dog is not mine; you must deal with my boy. He's trained him."

"I don't deal with boys. I offer fifteen pounds, a pretty neat sum for the cur."

Groll realized that this was an opportunity of really getting to know his eldest. "Willie," he began, "this gentleman offers you fifteen pounds for Kong so he may shoot him. For the money, you could buy the bicycle you have been wanting since last year. I won't be able to give it to you for a long time, we're not rich enough for that."

Willie looked at his father, wondering whether he could be in earnest. But the familiar face showed no sign of jesting. In answer he put an arm about Kong's neck, smiled up at Groll, and said: "I won't sell him to you, Father."

The gentleman in the bathing suit with his still untanned pale skin turned to Groll. Apparently the argument began to interest him. "Persuade him. I offer twenty pounds."

"Twenty pounds," Groll remarked to Willie; "that would buy you the bicycle and the canoe, which you admired so much this morning, Willie. A green canoe with double paddles for the water, and for the land a fine nickel-plated bicycle with a headlight, storage battery, and new tires. There might even be money left over for a watch. You only have to give up this old dog by handing the leash to the gentleman."

Willie said scornfully: "If I went ten steps away, Kong would pull him over and be with me again."

The beautiful and unusual young lady spoke for the first time. "He would hardly be able to do that," she said in a clear, sweet, mocking voice—a charming little person, thought Groll—and took a small Browning, gleaming with silver filigree work, out of her handbag. "This would prevent him from running very far."

Foolish of her, thought Groll. "You see, sir, the dog is a thorough-bred, pedigreed, and splendidly trained."

"We've noticed that."

"Offer fifty pounds, Father, and settle it."

"Fifty pounds," repeated Groll, and his voice shook slightly. That would pay for this trip, and if I handled the money for him, his mother could at last regain her strength. The sanatorium is too expensive, we can't afford it. "Fifty pounds, Willie! The bicycle, the watch, the tent—you remember the brown tent with the cords and tassels—and you would have money left to help me send mother to a sanatorium. Imagine, all that for a dog! Later on, we can go to the animal welfare society, pay three shillings, and get another Kong."

Willie said softly: "There is only one Kong. I will not sell him."

"Offer a hundred pounds, Father. I want to shoot that dog. I shouldn't have to stand such boorishness."

The stoutish gentleman hesitated a moment, then made the offer. "A hundred pounds, sir," he said huskily. "You don't look as though you could afford to reject a small fortune."

"Indeed, sir, I can't," said Groll, and turned to Willie. "My boy," he continued earnestly, "a hundred pounds safely invested will within ten years assure you of a university education. Or, if you prefer, you can buy a small car to ride to school in. What eyes the other boys would make! And you could drive mother to market; that's a great deal of money, a hundred pounds for nothing but a dog."

Willie, frightened by the earnestness of the words, puckered up his face as though to cry. After all, he was just a small boy of eight and he was being asked to give up his beloved dog. "But I love Kong, and Kong loves me," he said, fighting down the tears in his voice. "I don't want to give him up."

"A hundred pounds—do persuade him, sir! Otherwise my daughter will make life miserable for me. You have no idea," he sighed—"what a row such a little lady can kick up."

If she were mine, thought Groll, I'd leave marks of a good lesson on each of her dainty cheeks; and after glancing at his boy, who, with furrowed brow, was striving to hold back his tears, he said it aloud, quietly, clearly, looking sternly into the eyes of the girl. "And now, I think, the incident is closed."

Then a most astounding thing happened. The little girl began to laugh. Evidently the tall, brown man pleased her, and the idea that anyone could dare to slap her, the little lady, for one of her whims fascinated her by its very roughness.

"All right, Father," she cried; "he's behaved well. Now we'll put the check-book back in the bag. Of course, Father, you knew it was all in fun!"

The stoutish gentleman smiled with relief and said that, of course, he had known it and added that such a fine day was just made to have fun. Fun! Groll didn't believe it. He knew too much about people.

Willie breathed more freely and, pretending to blow his nose, wiped away two furtive tears. He threw himself down in the sand next to Kong, happily pulled the dog on top of himself, and began to wrestle with him; the shaggy brown paws of the terrier and the slim tanned arms of the boy mingled in joyful confusion.

However, Groll, while he somewhat reluctantly accepted a cigar and a light from the strange gentleman and silently looked out into the blue-green sea, which lay spread before him like shimmering folds of silk with highlights and shadows—Groll thought: Alas for the poor! If this offer had come to me two years ago when my invention was not yet completed and when we lived in a damp flat dreaming of the little house we now have, then—poor Willie!—this argument might have had a different outcome, this struggle for nothing more than a dog, the love, loyalty, courage, and generosity in the soul of an animal and a boy. Yet, speaking in terms of economics, a little financial security was necessary before one could indulge in the luxury of human decency. Without it—he reflected—no one should be asked to make a decision similar to the one which has just confronted Willie and me; everyone was entitled to that much material safety, especially in an era which was so full of glittering temptations.

The little girl with the spade put her slim bare feet into the sand outside of the tent and called to Willie: "Help me to dig new ones." But her eyes invited the man Groll, for whose approval she was striving.

She pointed to the ruined canals. Then, tossing her head, she indicated Kong, who lay panting and lazy in the warm sunshine, and called merrily: "For all I care, he can trample them again."

The whistle of an incoming steamboat sounded from the pier.

START A COLLECTION

With Bantam's fiction anthologies, you can begin almost anywhere. Choose from science fiction, classic literature, modern short stories, mythology, and more—all by both new and established writers in America and around the world.

DISCOVER
THE DRAMA OF LIFE
IN THE LIFE OF DRAMA

THE NAMES THAT SPELL GREAT LITERATURE

Choose from today's most renowned world authors—every one an important addition to your personal library.

Hermann Hesse

☐	BENEATH THE WHEEL	2509	• $1.50
☐	MAGISTER LUDI	2645	• $1.75
☐	DEMIAN	2944	• $1.75
☐	NARCISSUS AND GOLDMUND	6891	• $1.75
☐	ROSSHALDE	7370	• $1.50
☐	STEPPENWOLF	7979	• $1.50
☐	GERTRUDE	10060	• $1.95
☐	THE JOURNEY TO THE EAST	10136	• $1.75
☐	SIDDHARTHA	10266	• $1.75

Alexander Solzhenitsyn

☐	AUGUST 1914	2997	• $2.50
☐	ONE DAY IN THE LIFE OF IVAN DENISOVICH	2949	• $1.50
☐	THE LOVE-GIRL AND THE INNOCENT	6600	• $ .95
☐	STORIES AND PROSE POEMS	7409	• $1.50
☐	CANCER WARD	8271	• $1.75

Jerzy Kosinski

☐	STEPS	2597	• $1.50
☐	THE DEVIL TREE	7865	• $1.50
☐	THE PAINTED BIRD	8257	• $1.75
☐	BEING THERE	10625	• $1.75

Doris Lessing

☐	THE SUMMER BEFORE THE DARK	2640	• $1.95
☐	THE GOLDEN NOTEBOOK	7747	• $1.95
☐	THE FOUR-GATED CITY	7937	• $1.95

André Schwarz-Bart

☐	THE LAST OF THE JUST	7708	• $1.50
☐	A WOMAN NAMED SOLITUDE	7880	• $1.75

Buy them at your local bookstore or use this handy coupon for ordering:

READ TOMORROW'S LITERATURE—TODAY

The best of today's writing bound for tomorrow's classics.

☐	PORTNOY'S COMPLAINT Philip Roth	2189	• $1.95
☐	BEING THERE Jerzy Kosinski	2265	• $1.50
☐	RAGTIME E. L. Doctorow	2600	• $2.25
☐	THE SUMMER BEFORE THE DARK Doris Lessing	2640	• $1.95
☐	MEMOIRS OF HECATE COUNTY Edmund Wilson	2794	• $2.25
☐	ONE DAY IN THE LIFE OF IVAN DENISOVICH Alexander Solzhenitsyn	2949	• $1.75
☐	THE END OF THE ROAD John Barth	2995	• $1.75
☐	AUGUST 1914 Alexander Solzhenitsyn	2997	• $2.50
☐	THE GOLDEN NOTEBOOK Doris Lessing	7747	• $1.95
☐	AMERICAN REVIEW #25 Theodore Solotaroff, ed.	7925	• $2.45
☐	THE SOT-WEED FACTOR John Barth	8068	• $1.95
☐	THE PAINTED BIRD Jerzy Kosinski	8257	• $1.75
☐	GRAVITY'S RAINBOW Thomas Pynchon	10271	• $2.95
☐	V. Thomas Pynchon	10689	• $2.50

Buy them at your local bookstore or use this handy coupon for ordering:

Bantam Books, Inc., Dept. EDO, 414 East Golf Road, Des Plaines, Ill. 60016

Please send me the books I have checked above. I am enclosing $_____ (please add 35¢ to cover postage and handling). Send check or money order —no cash or C.O.D.'s please.

Mr/Mrs/Miss_____

Address_____

City_____State/Zip_____

EDO—2/77

Please allow three weeks for delivery. This offer expires 2/78.

REACH ACROSS THE GENERATIONS

With books that explore disenchantment and discovery, failure and conquest, and seek to bridge the gap between adolescence and adulthood.

☐	PHOEBE Patricia Dizenzo	2104 •	$ .95
☐	BONNIE JOE, GO HOME Jeanette Eyerly	2490 •	$1.25
☐	MY DARLING, MY HAMBURGER Paul Zindel	2662 •	$1.25
☐	NOBODY WAVED GOODBYE Elizabeth Haggard	2670 •	$1.25
☐	THE UPSTAIRS ROOM Johanna Reiss	2858 •	$1.25
☐	DAVE'S SONG Robert McKay	2893 •	$1.25
☐	I KNOW WHY THE CAGED BIRD SINGS Maya Angelou	6478 •	$1.50
☐	I NEVER LOVED YOUR MIND Paul Zindel	7993 •	$ .95
☐	RICHIE Thomas Thompson	8327 •	$1.50
☐	THE FRIENDS Rosa Guy	8541 •	$1.25
☐	OX GOES NORTH John Ney	8658 •	$1.25
☐	WHERE THE RED FERN GROWS Wilson Rawls	8676 •	$1.25
☐	RUN SOFTLY, GO FAST Barbara Wersba	8713 •	$1.25
☐	ELLEN: A SHORT LIFE, LONG REMEMBERED Rose Levit	8729 •	$1.25
☐	SUMMER OF MY GERMAN SOLDIER Bette Greene	10192 •	$1.50
☐	HATTER FOX Marilyn Harris	10320 •	$1.75
☐	THE BELL JAR Sylvia Plath	10370 •	$1.95
☐	IT'S NOT THE END OF THE WORLD Judy Blume	10559 •	$1.25
☐	THE MAN WITHOUT A FACE Isabelle Holland	10757 •	$1.25

Buy them at your local bookstore or use this handy coupon for ordering:

Bantam Books, Inc., Dept. EDN, 414 East Golf Road, Des Plaines, Ill. 60016

Please send me the books I have checked above. I am enclosing $_____ (please add 35¢ to cover postage and handling). Send check or money order —no cash or C.O.D.'s please.

Mr/Mrs/Miss_____

Address_____

City_____State/Zip_____

EDN—1/77

Please allow three weeks for delivery. This offer expires 1/78.

Bantam Book Catalog

It lists over a thousand money-saving best-sellers originally priced from $3.75 to $15.00 —bestsellers that are yours now for as little as 60¢ to $2.95!

The catalog gives you a great opportunity to build your own private library at huge savings!

So don't delay any longer—send us your name and address and 25¢ (to help defray postage and handling costs).